Helping Sophia

by Anastasia Suen
illustrated by Jeff Ebbeler

Content Consultant:
Vicki F. Panaccione, Ph.D.
Licensed Child Psychologist
Founder, Better Parenting Institute

visit us at
www.abdopublishing.com

Published by Red Wagon, a division of the ABDO Publishing Group, 8000 West 78th Street, Edina, Minnesota, 55439. Copyright © 2008 by Abdo Consulting Group, Inc. International copyrights reserved in all countries. All rights reserved. No part of this book may be reproduced in any form without written permission from the publisher. Looking Glass Library™ is a trademark and logo of Red Wagon.

Printed in the United States.

Text by Anastasia Suen
Illustrations by Jeff Ebbeler
Edited by Patricia Stockland
Interior layout and design by Becky Daum
Cover design by Becky Daum

Library of Congress Cataloging-in-Publication Data

Suen, Anastasia.
  Helping Sophia / Anastasia Suen ; illustrated by Jeffery Ebbeler.
      p. cm. -- (Main Street school)
  Summary: When Sophia's helper is absent, her fellow third-graders help out by learning how to push her wheelchair.
  ISBN 978-1-60270-030-7
  [1. People with disabilities--Fiction. 2. Wheelchairs--Fiction.
3. Schools--Fiction. 4. Friendship--Fiction.] I. Ebbeler, Jeffrey, ill.
II. Title. III. Series.

PZ7.S94343He 2007
[E]--dc22

                              2007004759

"Good morning, class,"
said Miss K. "I have some news."
She looked at Sophia. So did
everyone else in the class.

Sophia smiled knowingly
at Miss K.

4

"Sophia's helper is going to be away for a while," said Miss K.

"Is Mrs. Lopez sick?" said Latasha.

"Her daughter has a new baby," said Miss K.

"Mrs. Lopez was here yesterday," said Megan. "She didn't say anything about a baby."

"The baby was born last night," said Miss K.

"I hope she brings the baby for us to see," said Megan.

Sophia nodded her head.

"Maybe later," said Miss K. "The baby was just born. They are still taking care of him at the hospital."

"Who is going to help Sophia?" asked Rachel.

8

"We are," said Miss K. "After all, this is the third grade. Everyone is old enough to help."

"Yeah," said Sam.

"What are we going to do?" asked Rachel.

"We're going to have a wheelchair driving class," said Miss K.

Omar raised his hand. "Right now?" he asked.

"Right now," said Miss K.

"Okay, Sophia," said Miss K. "Please come up to the front of the class."

Everyone watched as Sophia pushed her wheelchair to the front of the class.

"Do we have to pull on the wheels like Sophia does?" asked Alex.

"Mrs. Lopez never did that," said Yasmin. "She pushed on the handles."

Sophia reached the front of the class
and turned around.

"How would you like them to do it?"
asked Miss K.

"The handles are better," said Sophia.

"Then that's what we'll do," said Miss K.
She looked at the class. "Can I have
a volunteer?" asked Miss K.

All of the hands in the class went up.
Miss K looked at Sophia. "You choose."

Sophia looked at the class.
She wondered how
she would choose.
She was friends with
everyone. Sophia
looked at Miss K.

"We'll give everyone
a turn," said Miss K.
"How's that?"

Sophia smiled
with relief.

Then no one will be mad at me, thought Sophia. *That's good.*

Sophia looked at the class again. Isaiah was the tallest. "Isaiah," she said.

Isaiah came up to the front of the class.

"Are you ready?" asked Miss K.

Isaiah gripped the handles. "Ready," he said.

Isaiah pushed the wheelchair but nothing happened. "It won't move."

"The brakes are still on," said Sophia.

"Brakes?" asked Isaiah.

"There's one on each wheel," said Sophia. "See?" She reached over and pulled one up.

"I get it," said Isaiah.
He pulled up the other brake.

19

"Now we can go,"
said Isaiah. He pushed the
wheelchair forward. Sophia's
feet hit the shelf.

"Sorry," said Isaiah. He
pulled the wheelchair back.
"This is harder than it looks."

"Don't worry," said Sophia.
"My brother does that all
the time."

"Let me try," said Dalton.
"Okay," said Sophia.

Dalton came up to the wheelchair. He
checked the brakes. Then he held the
handles. "Are you ready?" he asked.

"Ready," said Sophia.

Dalton spun the wheelchair around.
Sophia slid to one side.

"Was that too fast?" asked Dalton.
"A little," said Sophia.

"My turn," said Rachel. "I do this all the time."

"You do?" asked Sophia.

"Almost," said Rachel. "I have to push the stroller for Mama. The babies take too much room in the grocery cart."

"I'm not a baby!" said Sophia.

"I don't think Rachel meant to be cruel," said Miss K.

"I didn't mean you were a baby, Sophia!" said Rachel. "Babies can't talk or do math. They can't draw cool things like you can. But wheels are wheels. Here we go!"

She pushed the wheelchair forward. The chair went down the aisle. Clunk!

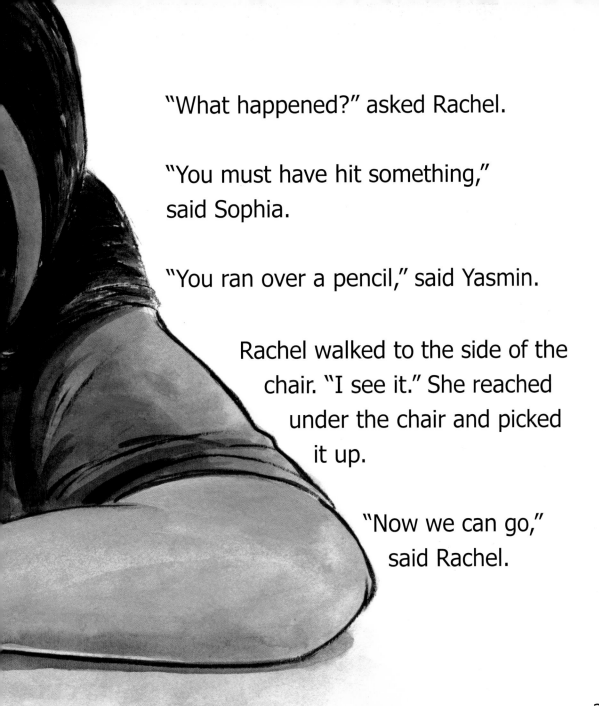

"What happened?" asked Rachel.

"You must have hit something," said Sophia.

"You ran over a pencil," said Yasmin.

Rachel walked to the side of the chair. "I see it." She reached under the chair and picked it up.

"Now we can go," said Rachel.

"That's right," said Miss K. "It's time to go to music."

Sophia turned around. "Can Rachel bring me?"

"Of course," said Miss K. "She can be your helper today."

"What about me?" asked Yasmin.

"Everyone will have a turn," said Miss K. "Would you like to help Sophia tomorrow?"

Yasmin nodded. Sophia smiled. *This was going to be great!*

What Do You Think?

1. Why does the class need to help Sophia?
2. Why is it hard for Sophia to choose a helper?
3. How does Sophia feel when the class wants to help her?

Words to Know

care—concern or attention.

cruel—causing pain to another person.

friend—someone you enjoy being with.

kind—friendly, helpful, and generous.

wheelchair—a chair on wheels for people who are too weak to walk or have trouble using their legs.

Miss K's Classroom Rules

1. Be kind.
2. Help other people.
3. Don't do or say cruel things.

Web Sites

To learn more about caring, visit ABDO Publishing Company on the World Wide Web at **www.abdopublishing.com**. Web sites about caring are featured on our Book Links page. These links are routinely monitored and updated to provide the most current information available.

CONTENTS

3 EMERGENT LITERACY
WHEN AND HOW SHOULD WE BEGIN?   34

4 PHONEMIC AWARENESS
THE SOUNDS OF OUR LANGUAGE   54

5 PHONICS INSTRUCTION

WHY AND HOW   72

6 SPELLING

DEVELOPING LETTER–SOUND CORRESPONDENCE   94

ACQUIRING WORD MEANINGS

THE BUILDING BLOCKS OF LITERACY   114

READING COMPREHENSION

MAKING SENSE OF PRINT   136

9 READING–WRITING CONNECTIONS

RECIPROCAL PATHS TO LITERACY   160

10 MEDIATED READING

CREATING A LITERATE COMMUNITY   188

11 INFORMING INSTRUCTION

12 EARLY LITERACY
....
ORCHESTRATING A BALANCED PROGRAM   240

APPENDICES
....
A CHILDREN'S LITERATURE REFERENCES   257

B TEACHER REFERENCES FOR EARLY LITERACY   260

C COMMERCIAL ASSESSMENT INSTRUMENTS   264

D INFORMAL CHECKLIST AND ASSESSMENT
   DEVICES   266

List of Activities

PREFACE

Is it possible for educators to teach young children the underlying skills necessary for literacy acquisition, while at the same time instilling a passion for the reciprocal activities of reading and writing? This is the major question *Striking a Balance: Positive Practices for Early Literacy* was expressly designed to address. My challenge in writing this text was to show preservice and practicing teachers how to teach reading and writing in a skillful, yet motivational way; how to create a classroom climate where the joy of language, literacy, and learning thrive; and most importantly, how to inspire the heterogeneous garden of learners in today's primary classrooms to want to read and write, while believing they can.

Because of the extent of recent media coverage, it is probably clear to all that literacy instruction has been undergoing major changes and shifts in emphasis. My research and recent experiences in schools have confirmed that the change is as profound as it is reported to be. As educators, we ask ourselves this question: Is this dramatic shift in practice a positive spiraling of knowledge or simply the educational pendulum swinging back yet again from the opposite extreme, as many would have us believe?

If we behave as reflective professionals, then every time the model shifts, we learn much from where we have been. The most recent shift is a case in point. Many of the resultant instructional changes I see are causes for guarded optimism; in some classrooms, there is nothing short of a literacy Renaissance occurring. This positive turnabout has been spurred by a wealth of evidence from literacy and other educational researchers suggesting that a balanced, language-based, interactive program of direct instruction in the skills of literacy combined with an abundant exposure to quality children's literature creates a comprehensive program that has an extraordinary chance of developing learners who *can* read and write, and *choose* to do so. Instead of emphasizing bits and pieces of fragmented reading and other language skills, a balanced literacy program focuses more on reading, writing, listening, speaking, and thinking as interrelated communication processes—processes that are pivotal to *all* learning.

Readers of this book will be given strategies and procedures that suggest how to implement a balanced early literacy program by teaching children the basic skills within the context of rich and varied reading and writing experiences.

There are so many programs, procedures, and strategies available for literacy instruction today that selecting among them can be confusing to the seasoned teacher and overwhelming to the beginning one. Therefore, I have chosen samples that seem to represent the most effective practices according to current research and the host of outstanding teachers who were observed and interviewed for the writing of this book.

Though today's teachers are eager to be told how to teach literacy effectively, they also are aware of the need to make sound professional decisions about their pedagogical choices based on state-of-the-art research about best practices. This book is intended to be a practical application of research on the best-known practices from the literature as well as from my observations of exemplary early childhood classrooms. This information, coupled with a caring teacher's on-going assessment of learners, is what is needed to take the first step toward developing eager young readers and writers.

SPECIAL FEATURES

Some of the special features of *Striking a Balance* aid the reader in understanding new concepts and vocabulary. Other features are designed to foster reflection and mastery of the material, and to encourage the reader to try out ideas in the field. The following features are particularly noteworthy:

- **In the Classroom**   Each chapter begins with a vignette in which readers will observe an authentic classroom setting and see how a practicing teacher deals with the subject addressed in the chapter. These small glimpses of literacy instruction build background and trigger the reader's prior knowledge about the chapter's topic. Throughout the chapter and in some of the activities I refer to the vignette so the reader can make the connection between the new concepts and classroom instruction.

- **Activities**   Several chapters include Activities, designed for use in the classroom. These specific, step-by-step procedures allow readers to put into practice the ideas and strategies they encounter in the chapter.

- **Questions for Journal Writing and Discussion**   Questions at the end of each chapter help readers to reflect on and internalize key ideas in the chapter. These questions are suitable for response in journal form or for stimulating lively discussion.

- **Suggestions for Projects and Other Activities**   This special section makes the connection from research and theory to real classroom practice. At the end of each chapter, the reader is offered several suggestions for surveying, interviewing, or observing local classroom teachers to compare strategies presented in the chapter with actual practice. Other activities ask the reader to try out a strategy or activity in the chapter with a small group of primary school children.

- **Chapter on "Orchestration"**   In the last chapter of the book I provide an intimate view of the urban classroom of an exemplary first grade teacher who demonstrates many of the procedures, strategies, and ideals presented in the rest of the book. The reader receives a rare insider perspective on how a seasoned teacher makes decisions about classroom climate, materials, room arrangement, and how to best utilize the limited available instructional time.

- **Glossary** An extensive book-end glossary is included allowing readers to review vocabulary highlighted throughout the text.

- **Appendices** Included at the end of the book are references for children's literature, teacher and parent resources for early literacy, a variety of literacy checklists for classroom use, and a list of widely used commercial evaluation instruments.

ACKNOWLEDGMENTS

Many outstanding professionals, friends, family members, and former students have helped me to bring my rudimentary vision to fruition. First of all, I would like to thank the extraordinary primary teachers who graciously allowed me to attend their classrooms and share the amazing ways they are balancing skill-based and holistic instruction to teach children to joyfully read, write, and think. The voices of many of these fine teachers permeate this book. I especially wish to thank Maria Ramon, Janet Rodgers, Rita Lehman, Linda Bernard, and Maria Oropeza, the classroom teachers who allowed me to observe how they bring to life the concept of a balanced literacy program. I also wish to extend a special thanks to the Phase I and II students in San Juan Center for reading the manuscript and providing suggestions.

Reviewers of the manuscript offered critical feedback that I welcomed and incorporated into the final book. I am grateful for their help. First, my sincere thanks to Sherron Killingsworth Roberts, University of Central Florida, for her insightful and constructive comments at various stages of the project's creation. In addition, I want to thank E. Sutton Flynt, Austin Peay State University; Dana L. Grisham, San Diego State University; Dee Holmes, Emporia State University; Timothy L. Krenzke, Concordia University; Priscilla M. Leggett, Fayetteville State University; Susan Davis Lenski, Illinois State University; and Edward T. Murray, Sacred Heart University.

The support of my publisher has been helpful beyond words. Colette Kelly, Editor, shared my vision of a literacy program that is balanced, creating readers who can read and who want to read.

Finally, I extend heartfelt gratitude to my husband, Gary, and daughter, Chrissy, who were ever patient as I took time away from them and family activities to write and edit this book. Without your unceasing love, support, and unwavering belief in me, I would have given up long ago.

Striking a Balance

POSITIVE PRACTICES FOR

EARLY LITERACY

1 A CHILD LEARNS TO READ

Process and Product

FOCUS QUESTIONS

- What are the fundamental processes of reading?

- Why is it important for teachers in the field to understand all aspects of the reading process?

- How is reading currently defined by researchers and practitioners in the field?

IN THE CLASSROOM

Although this vignette is titled "In the Classroom," in actuality the learning to read process begins long before four-year-old Lydia ever enters school. She has developed certain concepts about the function of print from the numerous signs in her urban environment and by observing the readers in her home interact with books, magazines, newspapers, and other reading material. For example, when she sees her older brother scan the fast food menu and then order a hamburger and fries, she is discovering that those black squiggles carry meaning. When she asks her mother to write her name and her mother sounds it out in front of her, she observes that words are composed of a string of letters and that those letters are composed of sounds that hold meaning.

When she snuggles in her Grandma's lap and "reads" the fairy tale she has memorized after hearing it nearly a hundred times,

Lydia demonstrates her understanding that many words together can tell a story. She asks for a second story and Grandma complies. She puts a chubby finger on the words as Grandma says them. Lydia is again revealing her understanding of the matching of spoken and written word.

Lydia knows lots about reading, but can she actually read?

WHAT IS READING?

At first glance, it would hardly seem worth the trouble to answer the basic question of what reading is because, in a sense, everybody knows perfectly well what it is: most people do it, in one form or another, every single day! But definitions underlie all intellectual endeavors. Definitions are assumptions that determine future educational activities. In other words, what teachers will do to teach beginning reading will be determined, in large part, by what they believe reading is.

To define reading we must know exactly what is involved in this activity that sets it apart from other similar activities. It is not enough, for example, to define reading as "a thought-getting process" because we can get thoughts just as easily from a lecture, conversation, or from watching a film. There are, to put it another way, many similarities between reading a page of difficult text and hearing the same text read to us by another person. The problem of comprehension is paramount for both reader and listener.

No one would deny that a major purpose of reading is "to get information or enjoyment of some sort from the printed page." But since we get information in the same way from spoken language, this purpose does not define reading in a way that distinguishes it from engaging in conversation. As soon as we understand this point, the problem of definition begins to resolve itself. If we see that meaning resides in the relationship between the language and the receiver, we might then ask how writing (which we read) is related to language (which we hear). If language, which is composed of sounds, carries the meanings, then what is writing? Writing is a device, or a code, for representing the sounds of a language in a visual form. The written words of a language are, in fact, just symbols of the spoken words, which are sounds.

So reading, then, becomes the process of turning these printed symbols back into sounds again. The moment we say this, however, some reasonable soul is bound to ask, anxiously, "But what about meaning? Can we propose to define reading as just deciphering the words without regard to the meaning?"

The answer is yes, but only partly. **Reading** is, first of all, the mechanical skill of turning the printed symbols into the sounds of our language. Of course, the reason we turn the print into sound—in other words, the reason we *read*—is to get at the meaning. We decode the printed symbols to get what the author is attempting to *say* and then, more importantly, we make some meaning connection to the world as we know it (Pearson, 1993).

But there is even more to it than that. Reading entails both reconstructing an author's message and constructing one's own meaning using the print on the page as a stimulus. We can think of it as a transaction, or an exchange, among the reader, the text, and the purposes and context of the reading situation. A reader's reconstruction of the ideas and information intended by the author is somewhat like a listener's reconstruction of ideas from the combination of sounds the speaker makes. An artist creates a masterpiece that means one thing to him and a host of different things to different admirers of his piece. Likewise, the reader, like the listener, may create meanings that are different from those intended by the author. What readers understand from the reconstructed and constructed meanings depends on the readers' prior knowledge, prior experiences, and their maturity and proficiency in using language in differing social contexts.

THEORIES OF READING ACQUISITION

Two theories regarding how we learn to read are at the heart of the current debate over how reading should be taught. Each of these theories offers us important insights about how children think about reading.

Nonstage Theory

The earlier theory is a **nonstage theory** that holds that unskilled and skilled readers essentially use the same strategies to figure out unknown words. This theory, revisited by Goodman in 1997, posits that readers use predictions based upon the context of sentences, as well as the letter–sound correspondence, to determine unknown words. They depend mostly, however, on the grammar, or syntax, and the semantics, or underlying meaning, to decipher the message. In this process, the reader uses strategies to sample and select from the information in the text, makes predictions, draws inferences, confirms or rejects, and regresses when necessary to make corrections in reading. Visual and sound features of the words, or the **graphophonic information,** are used as necessary. Such a theory suggests that certain apparent "errors" that children make while reading, such as saying the word *Dad* for the key word *father*, offer observers an actual "window into the child's brain"; such **miscues** are not errors at all, according to the theory, but merely deviations from text, occurring because the child is trying to make sense of print.

nonstage theory

graphophonic information

miscues

Stage Theory

A study by Juel (1988) indicates that unskilled and skilled readers use different strategies to unlock unknown words. Unskilled readers become "stuck"

stage theory

with strategies such as guessing or trying to memorize every new word and, therefore, are not as successful as those learners who have internalized a wide range of helpful strategies. The **stage theory** holds that children go through three stages in acquiring literacy: During the first stage, the "selective cue stage," children might use only the context of surrounding words as well as illustrations to predict what unknown words might be, or focus on limited components of words to decode them, for example, recognizing only the first and last letters in words. At the second stage, the "spelling–sound stage," they listen for known sounds and letters to determine what new words might be. When children have arrived at the final stage, called the "automatic stage," they have reached the fluent, or automatic, level of reading. At this sophisticated stage, they almost subconsciously scan every feature of a word and compare it, instantaneously, to patterns with which they are familiar. Very little mental effort needs to be directed toward decoding unknown words and most of the reader's attention can be focused on obtaining personal meaning from text.

CUEING SYSTEMS

cueing systems

Perhaps in an attempt to synthesize the above reading acquisition theories, some researchers have suggested that there are four systems that make communication possible, and skilled readers must use all four systems at once as they read, write, listen, and speak (Clay, 1991). These **cueing systems** help children create meaning by using language in a way that most English speakers accept as "standard." Effective teachers of beginning literacy are aware of these systems and model and support students' use of them in all areas of communication. The four cueing systems are described briefly below.

The Grapho-Phonological System

phonemes

graphemes

There are roughly 44 to 48 sounds, or **phonemes**, in the English language and children learn to pronounce these sounds in many different combinations as they begin to speak. Teachers support experimentation with how these sounds correspond to letters **(graphemes)** by teaching children how to use temporary or experimental spellings to sound out words; modeling how to pronounce words; calling attention to rhyming words and alliterations; and directly teaching other decoding skills, such as showing how to divide words into syllables. For example, by pointing out the rhyme scheme in "Twinkle, Twinkle, Little Star," the teacher shows children how the words *are* and *star* have similar ending sounds but different beginning sounds.

The Syntactic (Sound Stream of Language) System

The syntactic system, which includes but is not limited to grammar, governs how a language is structured or how words are combined into sentences.

Teachers support this cueing system by showing children how to combine sentences; add affixes to root words; use punctuation and inflectional endings; and write simple, compound, and complex sentences. To begin, a teacher might use the nonsensical group of words, "boy fell the down," to show children the importance of order in language. Further, a teacher might show children how to combine the two sentences, "The boy fell down" and "The boy was not watching where he was going" to become "The boy fell down because he was not watching where he was going."

The Semantic System

The major components of the semantic system are meaning-making and vocabulary. An even smaller unit of meaning-making is the **morpheme,** the smallest unit of meaning in English words, highlighted when we use the *s* to make *cats* plural, or the prefix *re* to make *do* into *redo*. Teachers support the semantic system by providing meaningful literature and relevant reading topics, focusing children's attention on the meanings of words, discussing multiple meanings of words, and introducing synonyms, antonyms, and homonyms. For example, a teacher might explain to children that, although they already know the meaning of the word *change,* it can be used very differently in math when we "make change." In the intermediate grades, teaching children dictionary skills, in context, also supports this system.

morpheme

The Pragmatic System

The final cueing system is pragmatics, which addresses the social and cultural functions of language. People use language for differing purposes, and how they speak or write is determined partly by their purposes and intended audience. Teachers can support the use of this cueing system by showing children how different forms of language are appropriate for different situations. For example, a teacher might discuss how playground language differs in form and content from that of a shared experience in class, or how we use different language for giving directions than we do for conducting a pretend dialogue with a prince.

THE READING PROCESS

The act of reading is composed of two basic parts: the global reading process and the reading product. By *process* we mean a movement toward an end that is accomplished by going through the necessary steps to crack the code and construct meaning from what the author has said. These aspects of the reading process ideally combine to produce the reading *product.*

Skills Used in the Reading Process

Clearly, the beginning reader has many available options for figuring out unknown words. Some of these—such as random guessing—are more inefficient than others. Learning to read, then, involves sorting through a cafeteria of problem-solving choices and discarding those that are ineffective for the situation, while selecting those that will allow for success. To make maximum progress, the beginning reader must acquire three closely related skills at approximately the same time (Clay, 1991):

- using letter–sound relationships
- acquiring a sight vocabulary of immediately recognized words
- gaining meaning from context

Using letter–sound relationships

phonics

Some experts believe that the most immediate goal of early reading instruction is teaching children **phonics**—how to "crack the code" by associating the printed letters with the speech sounds they represent and helping them to immediately apply this knowledge to meaningful text. Every word in spoken English can be printed using only 26 different letter symbols. This is possible because, in general, letter and letter combinations stand for the same speech sounds in thousands of different words. Although there is not a perfect one-to-one correspondence between letters seen on the printed page and the speech sounds represented, learning to decode depends on a true understanding of the sound–spelling relationship of the English language (Moats, 1995).

For children to become proficient spellers and fluent readers, they must master the helpful skills of "sounding out" words using their knowledge of the sound–spelling relationship in a real reading context. The child says to herself (very quickly and unconsciously), "I know that this word says *baby* and this word says *bed.*" Then, pointing to the *b,* she asks herself, "I wonder if it makes the /buh/ sound every time?" The child is giving herself a brief lesson in phonics; she is also using excellent inductive reasoning, but many children need to have these sound relationships pointed out to them directly. After children have learned two or three sound–spelling correspondences, such as the sounds for *b, a,* and *t,* a skilled teacher can then teach the children how to blend these sounds into words. The teacher can then demonstrate how to move sequentially from left to right through spellings so that children can sound out or say the sound for each spelling. To be most effective, it seems, phonics should be taught to children formally by teachers trained in the appropriate ordering of phonics skills and how to blend and segment sounds.

Acquiring a sight vocabulary

Many words used frequently in the English language cannot be easily sounded out, or decoded, such as the words *the, give, come, to, was, could,* and *once,* to name just a few, because they do not follow any phonics rule. Such words appear so often in English speech and writing that it would seem wasteful for a child to even try to sound out these words each time they are met. Therefore, words such as those offered above must be taught whole, using what has been called the "whole word," or "look–say" method. These words are known as **sight vocabulary words**, or words that children should recognize about as quickly as they recognize their own names. The repetition of these words many times, in many different ways, fixes them in the child's memory. With enough repetition, recognition of the words then becomes automatic and instantaneous. Coupled with burgeoning decoding skills, the child will now be able to read simple sentences and stories without undue frustration.

  For early readers, the most appropriate method of teaching sight words as well as concepts about print is through the use of *shared reading* with *big books* (see Chapter 3), especially those with predictable or familiar texts (Clay, 1991; Holdaway, 1979). Motivational big books with repeated word patterns are ideal resources for helping children to memorize sight words. Encouraging tracking using such materials is also invaluable in fostering print awareness and understanding, and familiarity with differing grammatical phrases.

sight vocabulary words

Gaining meaning from context

When a child is reading for meaning, the **context** (the surrounding information in the sentence) in which an unknown word is met can often be useful in suggesting what that word might be. At times, only a few words could possibly complete the sentence. For example:

context

> The girl went swimming at the _____ .
>
> The hungry boy walked to the _____ .
>
> The girl _____ when she won the prize.

In the first example, probably fewer than a dozen words could logically be inserted in the blank space (swimming pool, pool, pond, park, lake, river, ocean, YMCA). If the child possesses rudimentary phonics skills, and the word begins with a *p,* the child can further narrow the possibilities. Some choices would also be less logical than others, depending upon what has happened in the story prior to this sentence, allowing children to make an "educated guess" as to what the word might be. When children are shown how to use the context to aid them in narrowing the possibilities of an unknown word, they have another strategy at their command.

  A number of devices are used by authors to provide contextual clues that help readers determine the meaning of new words as well as difficult concepts. One of these is to incorporate a description–definition in the text (Heilman, 1997).

> The [swan] swam in the pond. This [bird] was bigger than any of the other birds in the water.

Other contextual techniques to decipher unknown words include comparison or contrast and the use of synonyms or antonyms.

The apple was very [small]. No one but the new boy wanted the apple because it was so little.

Solving the pronunciation of the unknown word is made easier by (1) the meaning of the total sentence in which the word occurs, and (2) the meaning in the surrounding sentences.

The above approaches to figuring out new words are probably not of equal value in learning how to read, although each is necessary to some degree. Research quite clearly shows that overemphasizing prediction from contextual clues for word recognition can be counterproductive, possibly even delaying reading acquisition if it is stressed above trying to analyze words by their sound/spelling components (Stanovich, 1992). On the other hand, too little or too much phonics instruction may contribute to the failure to learn to read (Freppon, 1991).

Additionally, it must be kept in mind that different children may benefit from and rely on one method more than others, while some approaches, such as pure memorization by the form of the word, have limited usefulness beyond the earliest stages of learning how to read. It seems clear that automatic, fluent reading would not be the result if a child had to go through a series of trial-and-error approaches in which all three approaches were tried out every time a new word was encountered! Efficient readers tend to use all three methods of word recognition instantaneously and simultaneously, lending even more support to a balanced approach to reading instruction in which all strategies are employed (Bissex, 1980; Barone, 1990; Eldredge, 1995).

Characteristics of the Reading Process

The reading process consists of several fundamental characteristics. If we explore these characteristics, a better understanding of the complex nature of the activity emerges (Hyde and Bizar, 1989).

Reading is a holistic process

Reading is not the sum total of the discrete skills that we have children practice in order to teach them to read; rather, reading is a holistic process whereby the various subskills, such as **decoding**, finding the main idea, and locating important details must be integrated to form a smooth, coherent whole. The subskills, though crucial, must be applied to the act of reading by a competent teacher.

decoding

If we want children to be thinkers, we must structure our instruction toward active participation in the search for meaning. Children must be given time every school day to read material that is on their own level and that is of interest to them. Children at all grade levels must also be read to. Teachers who read to children and give them the opportunity to discuss and wrestle with ideas and concepts are providing a sophisticated model of the kinds of thinking they must do when reading on their own.

Reading is a constructive process

We have come to think of reading as the construction of meaning from text (Spiro et al., 1980). As readers interact with the text, meaning is being constructed in their mind. The meaning does not lie on the page but in the mind of the reader. Readers use what is in their heads and what is on the page and construct a meaning based upon a fusing of the two forces.

Teachers must be aware of the constructive nature of the reading process so that they can help children develop the necessary tools to participate in this meaning-building process. This can be accomplished by providing an opportunity for children to display a wide range of thinking about text. Asking an abundance of open-ended questions—those for which there is no one "right" answer—encourages and validates children who are struggling to make their own meaning from text.

Reading is a strategic process

Good readers use different strategies depending on their purposes for reading and the difficulty of the material. The purpose of reading may be purely for entertainment, to memorize a poem, or to discover how to put together some object. Having these different purposes leads us to read in different ways, depending upon the nature of the task.

Teachers need to teach children to set their own purposes for reading and then to be able to check to see that their purposes are being met. Teachers can teach children to think about their own thinking by modeling different strategies as they read aloud to children. They can also do this by discussing how reading rate and strategies change according to the type of reading that is being done.

Reading is an interactive process

Finally, we have come to think of reading as a process in which the reader must interact with the author in order for meaning to occur. What readers bring to the activity in terms of prior knowledge of content, structure, and vocabulary determines how well they will be able to derive a rich meaning from the text. We have all had the experience of reading something about which we had little or no background knowledge. When this happens, we soon realize that although we may know most of the words, we cannot make sense of the material. We do not have the content knowledge that we need to construct a rich meaning to take with us from the reading.

As teachers, we must provide activities that will activate, access, and build on the knowledge of the children with whom we are working. One way to do this is by showing video excerpts or pictures, or reading short informative passages about the study topic. Another way would be to simply brainstorm with the group to elicit what the children know about the topic. For example, if the selection to be read is about koala bears, the teacher asks the children to raise their hands and tell the group anything they know about the animals, information the teacher writes on the board. What one child contributes often triggers a response in other children. This process helps to bring to the surface everything the children know about the topic and also provides information for those who may know little or nothing about it. The children are now able to attach new information to known information. They are ready for the active search for meaning.

THE READING PRODUCT

The reading *product* should always be meaningful because it is some form of communication—the reader's transaction with the writer's printed ideas. A wealth of knowledge is available to people today because we are able to read what others have written in the past. Americans can read of events and accomplishments that have occurred at other times in other parts of the globe. Knowledge of great discoveries does not have to be laboriously passed from person to person by word of mouth; such knowledge is freely available to all who read (Spiegel, 1992).

As well as being a means of communicating generally, reading is a means of communicating specifically with friends and acquaintances who may or may not be nearby. Reading a note can tell a child that his mother has gone shopping, or it can inform a babysitter who to call in an emergency. A memo from a person's employer can specify exactly what work is to be done.

Reading can be a way of sharing another person's insights, joys, sorrows, or creative undertakings. Being able to read can make it possible for a person to vicariously visit places she has never visited before, to take advantage of bargains and discounts, or to avoid disaster by heeding warning signs. It is difficult to imagine what life would be like without this vital means of communication!

The rich form of communication described above is dependent upon comprehension, which is affected by all aspects of the reading process. Being able to decipher the code and put sounds to the symbols is essential, but comprehension involves much more than turning the symbols into the appropriate sounds; the reader must derive meaning from these symbols, and in some way connect them to experiences or impressions from her own life. Some children may be able to read a passage and pronounce all the words beautifully and still have no idea what they have just read, or understand the words but lack the ability to relate the ideas to anything that has happened in their own lives.

Teachers who understand that all aspects of the reading process have an effect on the comprehension of written material will be better able to survey children's reading difficulties and as a result create sound instructional programs based upon their needs. Poor performance related to any aspect of the reading process may result in less than satisfactory reading ability, or an inability to learn to read at all. Three conditions that suggest a child is at risk for poor performance in reading are the following:

1. The child does not see the symbols or letters on the page; he may not be able to recognize them.

2. The child has developed confusions or incorrect associations between a number of sounds and letters; incorrect recognition of words will result and comprehension will be lessened.

3. The child has little experience with or knowledge of the topic about which she is reading; she will have less comprehension of the passage than one who has had a rich background in the topic.

The bottom line for teachers, then, is to ensure that children are given an abundance of direct instruction on the graphic symbols, or letters, that represent the sounds of our language so that they can begin to build a strong association between the letters and the sounds they make. Additionally, to achieve the greatest transaction between author and reader, any decoded message must have some connection to the child's life and experiences. Therefore, the teacher must make sure children have the necessary background information and knowledge to understand any given material; if this is not the case, he must provide the background vicariously through discussion, pictures, video excerpts, or similar means to ensure adequate processing.

SUMMARY

Learning to read is a complicated, rather miraculous process. Because few of us adults can accurately remember how we managed to accomplish this feat, we are hard-pressed to provide any earthshaking insights into how it is done. Understanding just how children learn to read is further complicated by the fact that whenever we observe a teacher instructing a child in reading, we are seeing only one tiny piece of an on-going process, and even then we cannot see what is really taking place within the reader. Moreover, if we were to watch a particular child as she reads silently, all we can do is try to guess what is going on in her brain from the behaviors she is showing us at the moment; however, if we were to be a fly on the wall in a classroom where this same first-grader was struggling with her burgeoning reading ability over several months, we might get a better overview of the child's perspective of this intricate process. We could listen to the set of strategies she uses to read aloud and how she responds to what she has read, observe how the teacher facilitates the process, and watch as literacy blossoms.

What we do know is that the act of learning to read may be arduous and time-consuming, or quick and immediately gratifying—we know that it will not be exactly the same for any two youngsters. For some children, much learning about how to read has occurred before they enter school, through supportive interactions with a literate environment, where they have been frequently read to, and where evidence of the importance of print is everywhere. But it would be wrong to assume such exposure is enough.

Although some children learn to read at home prior to direct school instruction, many children with the same exposure do not. Sometimes formal instruction is needed for a child to put together the observations they have made through their experiences with print. For those children who have had few experiences with print, exposure to a print-rich environment in school is not enough. Such children need explicit instruction in letter–sound relationships so that they can figure out unknown words; they must build a basic sight vocabulary of words they recognize immediately; and they must decide on a method of exacting meaning from unknown words through context. Equally importantly, they need to understand how to construct meaning by connecting an author's message to their own experiences. They need to be able to strategize how they will adjust their reading and thinking to the demands of the task at hand. Finally, they need to be supported in their use of the four cueing systems that make communication possible and will allow them to create meaning through socially shared situations.

Because we care about them, we give children affection, attention, exercise, and nutritious things to eat; we try to teach them to be polite, good-natured, thoughtful, and fair. We do these things because we believe it is the best way to start them on their way to healthy, happy lives. We must do as much with reading. When a child has learned how to construct his own meaning from text—and understands letter–sound relationships, has a beginning sight vocabulary, and a way to derive meaning through context—he soon enters into a considerably richer world, one where he is able to communicate with all sorts of people he may never even meet. He is able to discover a new dimension of ideas, facts, and opinions that may take him anywhere he wishes to go.

QUESTIONS

for Journal Writing and Discussion

1. What is your definition of reading? How do you think your understanding of what reading is will affect the methods you choose to teach your students to read?

2. How would you explain the difference between "reading process" and "reading product" to a parent or any person who is not in the education profession? Why might it be important to distinguish between the two concepts?

3. What are your memories of learning how to read? Write a list of everything you can recall about initial instruction, favorite books, successes, difficulties, and how you managed to "crack the code." Solicit help from parents, older siblings, and relatives to help reconstruct your early literacy experiences. Why might such memories be important to your teaching?

SUGGESTIONS

for Projects and Other Activities

1. Try to teach recognition of two words—*they* and *elephant*—to a child who has not yet learned to read and write. Record and compare the difficulties the child encounters with the two words. Which word was easier for the child to remember? Why do you think this was so? What strategies do you feel were most successful in helping children to remember the words?

2. Talk to two first-grade children. Ask the children what reading is and what kinds of things they think they must do in order to read successfully.

3. Observe a child who is in the early stages of learning to read. Ask the child to read several sentences aloud. What are some difficulties the child encounters? What do you think the child needs to know to be more successful? Make two columns on a sheet of paper, one labeled "practice" and the other "direct instruction." Try to determine what skills would best be developed through each of these modes.

A QUEST FOR BALANCE

Moving Forward

FOCUS QUESTIONS

- What is the history of reading instruction in this country?

- What are the key issues in phonics and whole language instruction?

- How can the classroom teacher combine the elements of both approaches to create a rich and balanced literacy program?

IN THE CLASSROOM

Mrs. Johnson, a first grade teacher in Illinois, uses a holistic approach to literacy instruction with her beginning readers. Her pupils spend much of the school day sharing quality children's literature and tend to remember many new words after being engaged with them numerous times through print that is displayed everywhere in the classroom. Mrs. Johnson's students leave her classroom at the end of a year with a deep appreciation for reading and writing. By contrast, Mr. Ruiz, down the hall, teaches his young learners the names and sounds of each letter of the alphabet. The children spend many hours practicing these sounds so they can immediately sound out unfamiliar words. Mr. Ruiz explains that his pupils love to read because they are empowered by their ability to figure out many words quickly. The two colleagues spend the entire year comparing notes on beginning reading and which approach is the most effective for their children; finally they agree to disagree. The same dialogue is occurring in schools across the country.

THE HISTORY OF EARLY LITERACY

Few educational issues have engendered as much dialogue as the current discussions over a *skills-based* versus a more *holistic* approach to early literacy instruction. It seems such dialogues have quite a history. As long ago as 1844, Horace Mann, considered the "father of public education," wrote a critical report of schools that implored teachers to adopt a rigid decoding approach to teaching reading. For decades afterward, the popular thinking among educators appeared to move back and forth between a **skills-based** approach, akin to phonics instruction, and a model that was more **holistic** and meaning-centered, as stressed in the whole language philosophy.

skills-based
holistic

By the 1950s, a strong skills-based, or phonics, movement again gained momentum. This was due, in part, to the publication of a widely circulated book called *Why Johnny Can't Read* (Flesch, 1955), in which Flesch took teachers to task for abandoning traditional phonics instruction in favor of the then popular **look–say model**, which was more meaning-based and required children to use the context alone to figure out words they did not know. Flesch claimed the reason children were doing so poorly in reading and writing was that they had not been taught that every letter of the alphabet had at least one corresponding sound. Once that was understood, he contended, every child could easily read and spell every word by simply sounding it out.

look–say model

In the 1960s, however, a movement came along de-emphasizing decoding as well as discouraging over-reliance on the use of the **basal readers**, the set of graded textbooks most commonly used to teach reading. Teachers had begun noticing that while children were proficient at decoding, they did not seem to be understanding what they were reading, nor did they seem to be enjoying the activity. The "new" movement, christened the **whole language philosophy** by the National Council of the Teachers of English in 1978, stressed a pedagogy that moved from a rather narrow focus on isolated subskills to one that encouraged teachers to look at reading more holistically, as a part of the total communication process (Beck and Juel, 1995).

basal readers

whole language philosophy

Adding to these dialogues regarding reading instruction was the voice of Jeanne Chall, a Harvard professor who spent many years researching the issue of a skills-based approach versus a holistic program. Her now classic book *The Great Debate* (1967) stated that, for early literacy, learning to decode by direct instruction in phonics showed better reading achievement results than any other method in use at that time. Chall revised her book in 1983; it reaffirmed her earlier findings, as did continuing research by Johnson and Bauman (1984), Williams (1985), Jacobs et al. (1990), Samuels and Farstrup (1992), Stahl (1992), and Adams and Bruck (1995).

During the 1980s and 1990s, however, advocates for a more motivational, holistic approach to literacy again gained great popularity, despite the many published reports supporting the conclusions of Chall's work. Even the federal government became involved in the continuing public discussions. The government promptly commissioned a widely respected independent reading investigator, Marilyn Adams, to restudy and once again report on what now began to be called "The Great Debate." Adams' published report, *Beginning to*

Read: Thinking and Learning about Print (1990), again lent support to Chall's perspective, but even Chall's subsequent critique, published a year later, defending her original findings, did little to resolve the controversy surrounding the issue. As we enter the new millennium, the issue remains highly politicized, as the following examples suggest:

In 1987, California, often considered the bellwether state, adopted a curriculum based upon the whole language philosophy for its schools statewide. Siegfried Engleman, a professor at the University of Oregon, whose phonics program had been previously used in California, saw his own program being eliminated as a result of the push toward the more meaning-based philosophy. Engleman sued the state of California, successfully, citing failure of the state to clarify its reasons for its actions, which was deemed a violation of federal regulations. The results of this changeover in California schools are still being contemplated today.

Publications such as *Science News*, the *National Review*, and *Atlantic Monthly* continue to present articles that appear to separate the two perspectives on reading instruction. Newspapers, too, still report on local, state, and national reading issues with inflammatory articles such as "Why Juan and Jenny Can't R–E–A–D" (Jacobs, 1995). Moreover, two groups, The National Right to Read Foundation and the Reading Reform Movement, are attracting many members, promising to "keep the debate alive" until more pervasive decoding-based modifications in reading programs occur.

Parents of children in public schools, as well as many interested citizens who read such reviews, become alarmed and often take sides on these confusing issues without really understanding what the underlying concepts are. Many are not quite sure what is meant by the terms "phonics," "holistic," or the once common "whole language." It might be helpful to further explore these concepts.

PHONICS INSTRUCTION AND THE TRANSMISSION MODEL

The term "phonics" is much used but not always entirely understood—especially by those not directly involved in literacy education. For centuries, dating back as early as the Greek and Phoenician civilizations three thousand years ago, most approaches to early literacy instruction in alphabetic languages have included letter sequences and how such sequences corresponded to speech patterns (Mathews, 1966). Such methods, focusing on sound–symbol relationships, are what educators generally refer to as "phonics." Valentin Ickelsamer, a German teacher, is credited with being the first educator in relatively modern times (the early 1500s) to introduce a phonics approach to early literacy

FIGURE 2.1 *An early workbook activity.*

Lesson 24

MAKING WORDS

1. Choose a letter from the 4 in each box that will make a real word when you put it in the square.

2. Write a common word with these.

ade   ean   ale   ote

aid   een   ail   oat

From *Your Child Can Learn to Read* by Margaret McEathron. New York: Grosset & Dunlap, 1952.

(Balmuth, 1982). Even today, phonics approaches to early literacy instruction show evidence of the influence of Ickelsamer's early ideas.

transmission model

Phonics instruction has sometimes been associated with the **transmission model** of instruction. In other words, when using this model, in its strictest sense, teachers assume the responsibility of directly "transmitting" information, such as the knowledge of letter sounds and symbols, to their students through explicit instruction and systematic teaching of the code that is the foundation of the English alphabet. Other transmission approaches include rote instruction of sight words and the memorization of lists of word families, such as those words containing "oi": voice, noise, moist, and so forth. Such instruction is also frequently called "skills-based," as its emphasis is on presenting the smallest parts of our language—the letters and sounds—in isolation, often long before showing children the whole picture of how enjoyable the reading act can be.

Over the years, phonics instruction has at times been perceived negatively due to additional unfortunate practices that included, in some cases, more drills on isolated skills than were necessary, often to those children who were already proficient readers. Such "drill and kill," as it was often called, was many times little more than drudgery that served as busy work, and was associated with endless worksheets and mindless rote activities that too often had little or nothing at all to do with real reading.

Finally, phonics instruction has been criticized when it has focused on the teaching of a litany of abstract rules; too many of these have limited application in our language and are lost on very young children who can memorize them but who have little idea what they actually mean.

The Positive Role of Phonics Instruction

Researchers and educators seeking a balance have long been interested in the positive role that the appropriate amount of phonics instruction can play in early literacy. Many studies have been conducted in an effort to determine the value of direct instruction in the sounds and letters of the English alphabet when integrated into a total, literature-rich program.

At about the same time that Jeanne Chall was publicizing the results of her studies depicted in *The Great Debate*, the U. S. Office of Education Cooperative Research Program in First Grade Reading Instruction was initiated (Adams, 1990). Funded by this office, two prominent researchers, Bond and Dykstra (1967), published the results of a landmark research study involving many first grade classrooms and the literacy methods employed by the teachers. In many ways, this early landmark study was the first of its kind to lend support to a notion that a balance between phonics and a holistic approach just might represent ideal literacy instruction. The results of the study suggested that approaches to reading that included, but were not limited to, a form of systematic phonics instruction were somewhat more effective at producing high word recognition performance in learners than other methods used in the study. But the data from the study also indicated that including an emphasis on meaning and a connection to the children's lives produced even greater gains in reading achievement. In addition, writing instruction was found to be an important factor promoting positive results in literacy acquisition, or the ability to read and write. Perhaps the most unexpected finding of the studies, however, was that the crucial factor in teaching a child to read was not the *method* that was used but that instruction was delivered by a committed and competent teacher (Readence and Barone, 1998).

Pflaum and her colleagues (1980) conducted an analysis of the current research in early literacy instruction to compare the approaches that were then being used. The findings supported a conclusion that instructional methods that taught letters and letter sounds, initially by themselves and then blended into words, showed significantly better gains in reading achievement than methods that did not use letters and blending instruction.

In *Becoming a Nation of Readers*, a report written by the Commission on Reading in the 1980s, phonics instruction was still being advocated:

> The purpose of phonics instruction is to teach children the alphabetic principle. The ultimate goal is for this to become an operating principle so that young readers consistently use information about the relation-ship between letters and sounds to assist in the identification of known words and to independently figure out unknown words.

The Commission continued by stating that children then need to immedi-ately practice reading the new words they have encountered in meaningful context (Anderson et al., 1985). The work of these researchers suggest that the transmitting of phonics could be followed by use of a transactional instruc-tional strategy, using student-centered group discussion of the reading mater-ial. This report seemed to offer an early nod toward a balanced approach in literacy instruction.

Current leading educators advocate a "less is more" approach which sug-gests that teachers should offer small doses of direct, systematically taught phonics instruction in the primary grades to only those children who need this structure to make sense of print. Many children come to school with a wide repertoire of word-unlocking skills gained from much experience with and ex-posure to print. Such educators urge teachers to directly teach a wide range of comprehension strategies, limiting the teaching of phonics generalizations to those that are the most useful and consistent. Instead of having children mem-orize phonics generalizations, teachers are encouraged to help children dis-cover the recurring spelling patterns in English words. Finally, educators recommend connecting what is learned in phonics to specifically designed **decodable texts**
books called **decodable texts** that incorporate the exact phonic elements chil-dren are learning, providing immediate reinforcement (Shefelbine, 1995). They also encourage sharing an abundance of quality children's literature with an enthusiastic teacher. With this streamlined, less is more approach to early phonics instruction, the overall effort is directed toward the goal of developing readers who can learn to figure out words quickly so that attention can soon be focused on meaning and enjoyment (Adams, 1990; Routman and Butler, 1995; Shefelbine, 1995; Stahl, 1992).

Educators today have much more knowledge about the best way to pro-vide instruction in letters and sounds without falling prey to earlier pitfalls. Past proponents of phonics instruction often misunderstood this pivotal need for children to move quickly from isolated skills to the application of those skills using decodable texts while listening to well-constructed literature. They instead offered children stilted basal reader stories with little dis-cernible structure that used a small number of words repeated over and over, **controlled vocabulary**
called a **controlled vocabulary**. The sentences were usually short and chop-

FIGURE 2.2 *An excerpt from a basal reader, 1966.*

swing

Here I go, Mark.

See me go up in the swing.

I like this swing.

I like to go up.

I like to go down.

Come on, Daddy, come on.

From *Outdoors and In* by M. O'Donnell and B.H. Van Roekel. California State Series. Sacramento: California State Dept. of Education, 1969.

py, as this was thought to make them easier for children to read. Such basals were focused on the appropriate sounds and words the authors felt were necessary, and largely ignored a child's need to construct any personal meaning from reading.

We know now that balance in the teaching of reading is possible only when the teaching of skills does not become an end in itself but, rather, a means to an end: reading for personal meaning, acquisition of information, and enjoyment.

HOLISTIC INSTRUCTION AND THE TRANSACTIONAL MODEL

There have been many terms for and definitions given to holistic approaches throughout the literature on literacy without a clear consensus about what such terms actually encompass. In reality, whole language, the most recent manifestation of a holistic, meaning-based approach, was not an approach or a practice at all, but rather a perspective or philosophical stance. Whole language teachers were not focused on transmitting knowledge to their students but, rather, negotiating with children about their individual ideas concerning what they were reading and writing; in other words, adopting a more collaborative, **transactional model** while integrating the four language modes of reading, writing, listening, and speaking across all the curricular areas. Reading was offered not in stilted basal readers, but in high-quality children's literature. Whole language teachers believed, too, that reading occurs in the brain of the child rather than on the page of the book, as proponents of skills-based instruction seem to suggest. Indeed, whole language as a transactional, child-centered model elevates children to "collaborators in the quest for knowledge" (Goodman, 1970). Proponents often referred to literacy acquisition as a natural process, much like the universal communicative process of learning to talk (Bergeron, 1990). These ideas and a belief that children need exposure to print in all its forms were the hallmarks of whole language teaching (Altwerger et al., 1987).

transactional model

Bergeron found other common defining threads of whole language to be:

- a belief that reading is the construction of meaning from text
- a focus on child-centered vs. teacher-centered instruction
- active learner participation and choice in literacy experiences
- integration of all the language arts with other curricular areas

Later, this whole language philosophy began to be recognized as a holistic way of teaching that, unlike phonics (which teaches the sounds of letters and words and then introduces stories) would first get children interested in great literature and then proceed to the parts. Goodman (1986), often considered the father of the whole language movement, argued that skilled reading involves gaining meaning from the context of whole passages rather than simply reading words as individual entities. Goodman began to refer to reading as a "psycholinguistic guessing game," where readers use cues such as grammar, underlying meaning, and the visual and sound similarities of words to predict new words, known and unknown (Goodman, 1965). Smith (1971) concurred and went on to suggest that readers use visual and sound cues only minimally; he believed that visual processing does not take place with every word, nor do readers process each word completely (Smith, 1971; Smith, 1992). Readers, according to this view, sample just enough text to get meaning from a passage. Some advocates of whole language maintained that explicit instruction in phonics was therefore unnecessary if the gaining of meaning was adequately stressed. Carbo (1988) contended that children learn to read not through direct instruction in how sounds and letters go together, but *solely* through exposure and much interaction with language-rich environments. Such a view has been widely refuted through recent research on the importance of early phonics instruction (Adams and Bruck, 1995).

Whole language was often associated with the **constructivist model of learning** (Au, 1993). This perspective encouraged children to "actively construct their own understandings of text material" through personal experimentation with print. Learning, in the constructivist model, is learner-centered, or focused on the child and his experience, background, and understandings of the world. Thus, children become motivated by immediately seeing the large picture of what reading can be and then go on to acquire discrete skills as needed. With this model, the teacher is continually observing how each child thinks about reading by listening to the child's oral reading. For example, Jose makes wild guesses about words based solely on the way they look and sound; this practice tells the teacher that José thinks reading is little more than word-calling. Lydia, on the other hand, constantly rereads sentences in a story saying, "That doesn't make sense!" revealing that she sees reading as meaningful, but she may need help in acquiring specific decoding skills.

constructivist model of learning

After years of code-oriented emphasis, accompanied by often uninspiring basal readers, whole language seemed to offer teachers a fresh and appealing approach to beginning literacy. Quality children's literature was used for instruction rather than basals. Literature often took the form of predictable books that had rhyme, rhythm, and repetition, allowing children to, allegedly, learn the words through chiming in with their guesses. The stories were often read to children using big books, or those with considerably larger-than-usual format, suitable for reading aloud to a small group of children as they sat cross-legged on the floor. This exposure to quality literature, so the philosophy went, not only increased children's motivation to read, but through its superior story structure, provided an excellent model for children's own writing. Children were encouraged to write about topics of their own choosing by using temporary writing, or **invented spelling,** a kind of sounding out of new words. This experimentation with print was supposed to be all children needed to learn to decipher the sound and letter relationships of the English language.

invented spelling

In transactional, holistic approaches to literacy such as whole language, children are helped to figure out unfamiliar words by using the words in the context of the sentence or paragraph; the strategy of sounding out is modeled as needed. In a holistic approach, phonics is often taught within the context of meaningful text, but only as children demonstrate an expressed need for it. Advocates of whole language, in particular, have been generally opposed to lengthy, abstract phonics drills and the rote memorization of phonics general-izations that have little observable connection to real reading. They encourage children to discern their own patterns in spelling and practice them through a myriad of writing activities.

Finally, free choice in reading and writing activities and on-going assess-ment are important bywords of a transactional, holistic approach to literacy. Students' freedom to choose books they wish to read and topics they choose to write about are stressed as a way to ensure that language will always be pur-poseful and meaningful to each individual. Authentic, on-going assessment in-cludes observational techniques and analysis of oral reading to determine how children are thinking about reading, what strategies they are employing, and which ones might need to be taught. Such devices are deemed superior to stan-dardized tests because they are individualized and can be interpreted by a teacher who could see the performance in light of *all* the child's strengths and needs. Authentic assessment sometimes includes a **portfolio** that would con-tain many samples of the work the child had done over time, selected in tan-dem with the student (Clay, 1990).

portfolio

The holistic approach, particularly as it was at first idealized by whole lan-guage purists, was appealing to teachers who loved quality children's literature and were eager to share literacy tasks with their students. The philosophy broke down in actual practice, it seemed, when teachers misinterpreted the in-tent and threw out all that was good about phonics and other aspects of the transmission model. When some children came to school with little or no ex-posure to print and were offered no direct instruction in phonics, they found themselves with limited access to this wonderful world of rich reading and writing because it did *not* come naturally for them. Without direct, systematic instruction in phonics many children were simply not able to figure out how sounds and letters go together; many went from one grade to the next, falling further and further behind in acquiring literacy (Fletcher et al., 1994; Stanovich and Siegel, 1994).

A QUEST FOR BALANCE: MOVING FORWARD

Is it possible to unify these two perspectives on early literacy instruction? Both of them clearly have much to offer for the beginning teacher of young children. It is this author's view that the two can be used together to create a dynamic, synergistic program that is stronger than either alone. Research provides sup-port for the notion that a committed teacher who can integrate a program of explicit, systematic phonics into a curriculum rich with quality literature, eas-ily decodable text, and many meaningful writing experiences will result in children who not only know how to read but who do so willingly, far beyond the classroom doors (Stahl, 1992). Most reading educators have long agreed that a certain amount of instruction in phonics is vital in learning how to de-code automatically, but that incorporating the basic elements of a holistic, meaning-based program with such instruction will have a much more positive effect on children's attitudes toward reading as a chosen activity (Wink, 1996).

In any case, there is considerable evidence to suggest that the two perspectives on literacy are not as far apart in actual practice as the literature and the media would have us believe. In an extensive interview with whole language teachers from New York, Walmsley and Adams (1993) found that most such advocates were definitely not purists. For example, they often used a basal as well as quality children's literature, included direct instruction in phonics and other decoding skills, used workbooks in moderation, and administered standardized tests, along with informal and observational forms of assessment. To one degree or another, it seems, most competent teachers are trying to blend the best of the two perspectives by either infusing many meaning-based strategies with a structured, skills-based program, or by supplementing a holistic, literature-rich program with a systematic phonics program.

Strong teachers tend to see any new movement in literacy, such as the most recent one, not as a pendulum swing, but as a positive spiraling in which more exciting new information about teaching children to read is acquired each time the focus shifts. Echoing this belief, Goodman (1997) muses, "When people talk to me about cycles and pendulum swings, it helps me to remember that progress is rarely in a straight line and that knowledge takes a long time to be accommodated, absorbed, and put to work" (p. 596).

More optimism is offered by a new interest group of the International Reading Association (IRA) called "The Balanced Reading Group," which advocates an approach that incorporates the best of the two perspectives. Former president of the IRA, Susan Glazer (Feb./March, 1995), adds that phonics should be considered a critical piece of any holistic, meaning-based system, and that reading has always had three discrete components, or cueing systems: syntax, or grammar; phonology, or sounds; and semantics, or meaning. Glazer maintains that it is clear that these three components cannot be covered by either a skills-based or a holistic approach alone; both are necessary for children to learn to read successfully.

Adding to the possibility of reconciliation is the fact that current thinking on phonics instruction is not as extreme as it once was perceived to be. Most phonics proponents today support **streamlined phonics,** where children are helped to become independent, automatic decoders, but are not inadvertently turned off to reading by an overabundance of boring worksheets, isolated drills, and abstract rules with little or no possibility for application. Current thinking suggests that efficient phonics instruction that is systematic and explicit gets children decoding quickly, so that they can soon turn their attention to more important and enjoyable reading tasks (Adams, 1990; Shefelbine, 1995; Wink, 1996). Indeed, it appears that current thinking has evolved such that the question is now not *whether* to teach phonics, but *how* best to teach phonics, within

streamlined phonics

a literature-rich classroom that also stresses background knowledge, comprehension strategies, and an enormous amount of reading (Shefelbine, 1997).

Stahl (1992) offers nine guidelines for what he considers to be "exemplary phonics instruction" to be used in tandem with other more holistic, meaning-based methods. He urges that such balanced instruction should:

- build on a child's rich background about how print functions;
- build on a foundation of sound awareness (phonemics);
- be clear and direct;
- be integrated into a total reading program;
- focus on reading words rather than memorizing rules;
- include the study of beginning sounds and ending sounds;
- include practice with sound/symbol relationships through spelling;
- develop word recognition strategies by focusing on the internal structure of words;
- develop automatic word recognition skills quickly so that children can devote their attention to meaning and enjoyment, not individual words.

Routman and Butler (1995) offer additional promise that balance is possible with their research-based suggestions for using phonics as a tool to help children move from shared reading to skills instruction and on to meaningful independent reading. Their recommendations include:

- Start instruction with entire texts through the use of shared reading of nursery rhymes, poems, songs, and predictable stories to ensure engagement.
- Focus teaching on sentences taken from meaningful text sources such as predictable stories, language experience dictations, journal entries, and other narratives with much rhyme and repetition.
- Direct children's attention to words in context using activities such as word games, personal dictionaries, generating sentences, and finding alliterations.
- Focus on individual letters with activities such as alphabet books, magnetic letters, and cutting up letters and making words.
- Play with syllables and sounds to help children become aware of the alphabetic principle.
- Clap, sing, and focus on beginnings and endings of words to help children hear the sequence of sounds in words.

Routman and Butler, once closely associated with whole language, now recommend a balance between the transmission of skills and a more holistic, transactional approach to reading instruction. Their suggestions indicate that while phonics instruction is fundamental to automatic decoding for many young children, early instruction should be mainly devoted to reading, exploring the sound–symbol relationship through writing, engaging in thought-provoking conversations about words, stories, and ideas, and responding to a variety of delightful literature and other environmental print.

There is even more reason to believe that current thinking on reading instruction has evolved from the philosophy first articulated by Goodman in the 1960s. Parker (1995) advocates a comprehensive program of broad, early literacy curricula that would include phonemic awareness, phonics, rich literature-based activities, and a variety of comprehension strategies. Specifically, such a comprehensive perspective would include:

- a wide range of reading materials on many developmental levels in English and the other languages of the children in the class;
- direct teaching of concepts about print;
- direct instruction in the concept that words are a series of speech sounds;
- cueing systems, including phonics, semantics, and syntax;
- direct instruction in the strategies that skilled readers use;
- critical thinking strategies;
- vocabulary development;
- fluency through encouragement of wide reading at the students' independent reading levels;
- thorough and ongoing assessment to ensure that instruction is compatible with individual needs.

Finally, a consolidated view of literacy comes from Spiegel (1995), Atwell (1992), Mills et al. (1991), and Manning and Manning (1993). Spiegel recommends that proponents on both sides of the issue need to listen very carefully to one another's claims, as neither side has all the answers. While criticizing some of the whole language assumptions, Spiegel concedes that her own teaching was greatly enriched when she considered and adopted many holistic practices. Levine (1994) supports this notion, urging educators to think about infusing many of the more motivational and innovative meaning-based, holistic activities with traditional phonics programs.

A comparison of the three stances shows how a comprehensive program might be a selection of the best elements of both educational philosophies to create Mrs. Ramon's first grade program (outlined in depth in Chapter 12). See Figure 2.3.

A surprising epilogue to this discussion of balance in literacy comes from former education superintendent Bill Honig, who was responsible for introducing whole language practices into the reading curriculum in California in 1987. He now says he regrets how his mandate was misinterpreted by the developers of the state curriculum. According to Honig (1996), the original intent was that literature would be used as the core reading material but that basic decoding skills would also be taught. He goes on to lament that more than two-thirds of fourth-graders in California were reading below grade level on state and federal tests, putting them next to last as compared with the children of other states. Honig and some other educators believe this is a direct consequence of the exclusive use of holistic practices without a requisite core of systematic phonics instruction. Many other educators refute this notion, cit-

FIGURE 2.3 *A comprehensive view of literacy instruction.*

PHONICS (Skills-Based, Transmission Model)	HOLISTIC (Meaning-Based, Transactional)	A COMPREHENSIVE APPROACH (An Interface Between the Best of Both Stances)
Emphasis on product	*Emphasis on process*	*Emphasis on process* and *product*
Language broken into bite-sized pieces (letters and words)	Language is kept whole in connected text	Whole–part–whole model
Skills in sequence taught directly	Phonics often taught incidentally	Direct phonics instruction completed by end of 2nd grade
Phonics taught up to 3rd and 4th grades	Strategies modeled in context	Skills and strategies modeled alone and in context
Word families used for memorization	Real literature used; often no basal text	Phonics based on internal structure of words
Teacher makes curricular decisions	Literature study groups	Skills based on need per assessment
Reading groups based on ability; inflexible	Predictable books and big books used for incidental phonics instruction	Decodable text used for phonics instruction; predictable text for comprehension
Traditional basal texts with controlled vocabulary	Children choose recreational reading material	Quality literature for listening comprehension
Decodable text exclusively	Shared and guided reading for instruction	Free reading time with choice
Discussion questions from teacher or basal text	Paired reading	Shared and guided reading with imbedded phonics instruction
Sight words memorized by children	Drama, poetry, and songs used for enjoyment	Emphasis on spelling as a key to phonics
Directed reading of basal text for instruction	Writing topics chosen by children	Word walls, word building, word sorting, word hunts utilized
Writing topics chosen by teacher	Writer's workshop	Writer's workshop
Worksheets for reinforcement of skills	Journals used for response to literature	Language experience approach
Workbooks used for response to basal text	Discussion questions come from children	Drama, poetry, and songs used for phonemic awareness and enjoyment
Traditional spelling programs	Children encouraged to "invent" spelling	Journals for personal writing and literature response; logs for content areas
Growth is quantitatively measured (formal assessment only)	Growth is observable (informal assessment)	Writing as experimentation with sound/letter relationships
		Invented spelling and instruction in correct spelling
		Flexible grouping systems
		Paired reading, buddy reading, and dyad reading
		Assessment based on measurement and observation (informal and formal)

ing a host of other economic and sociocultural variables, such as overcrowded classrooms, lack of parental support, rampant poverty, linguistic diversity, and massive turnover in school populations, that may be equal, if not *more* potent causes for the alleged drop in scores (Flippo, 1997).

On a personal note, the present author, through visits to hundreds of primary grade classrooms over the past few years, has observed that there are many extraordinary teachers out in the field who are now and have *always* used phonics skills instruction within a transactional framework. With certain groups of children, such teachers will stress one stance more than others, and for some children they find it is best to use one approach exclusively. It seems clear to these dedicated professionals that the only way this long-standing pedagogical dialogue will cease is when teachers are treated as knowledgeable authorities with their pupils. They must be allowed to decide, based upon the individual needs in their classroom, what instructional methods are most appropriate (Bialostok, 1997).

SUMMARY

Unlike a purely political debate or any such hypothetical argument pertaining to abstract ideas and theoretical outcomes, the ongoing dialogue about how we should teach our nation's children to read is concrete, critical, and involves the very core of our future. Educators who have taken sides on this issue have done so with candor and a good deal of questioning, observation of children in classrooms, and a heavy dose of soul-searching. Most teachers do not take their tasks lightly; the ultimate mission of teachers is, after all, to challenge, assist, and encourage each child in his or her charge to become a good reader, responding to text in meaningful ways, both for enjoyment and for gaining knowledge. With the constant spiraling of knowledge about literacy instruction, we are more than ever realizing the best ways to reach these goals. We have learned that fluent reading requires a basic understanding of the sounds and symbols of our alphabetic language. We are now heeding the substantive body of research suggesting that early, systematic phonics instruction that moves from decoding text to abundant opportunities to read, write, and share ideas, can help teachers to accomplish their goals of teaching every child to read (Ransom, 1997).

The charge of the teacher of this millennium, then, is to become a wise diagnostician and to provide excellent literacy teaching and intervention for each child. Every child can learn to read and write. The path to literacy may begin with the presence of explicit, systematic phonics instruction, but always in the context of a print-rich environment that invites children to explore the world of literature and information while enjoying the thrill of penning their own ideas to be eagerly shared with others. The real question, it seems, is not whether systematic phonics instruction should be part of the total program; research continues to strongly support the inclusion of such instruction for beginning readers. More appropriate questions appear to be how much phonics should children receive, under what conditions, and how can such instruction be integrated into a program rich with literature and meaning? This book is an attempt to answer those critical questions.

QUESTIONS

for Journal Writing and Discussion

1. Discuss in your own words the current issues involving the relative merits of phonics and a meaning-based approach to literacy instruction. How would you explain both approaches to the parents of a primary-age youngster? How might you convince them that an ideal program can contain elements from both perspectives?

2. Describe what you remember about your own early literacy experiences. Would you characterize the instruction you recall as meaning-based, phonics, or a combination of the two?

3. React to the often heard statement, "In education, the pendulum constantly swings back and forth from a meaning-based approach to a phonics approach to literacy instruction." What do you think is the impetus for such change when it occurs? Would you characterize the cyclical changes as "swings" or as "spirals" toward progressively better literacy instruction?

SUGGESTIONS

for Projects and Other Activities

1. Scan current literacy journals such as *The Reading Teacher* or *Language Arts* for articles on prevalent practices in early literacy instruction. Summarize your findings and report them to your class. How do the issues raised relate to the issues addressed in this chapter?

2. Observe three different first grade teachers instructing their students in beginning literacy. How might you characterize the methods they are using? In what ways are these educators responding to recent changes in educational methods? How do each of the educators describe the approaches they are using? What are their reasons for making the choices they did?

3. Survey several older adults in your area. Ask them how they think literacy is being taught in the local schools. From where have they obtained their information? Ask them what their recollections are about how they were taught to read. Do they believe the methods used when they were in school were superior to those used today? What conclusions can you draw from this survey?

EMERGENT LITERACY

When and How Should We Begin?

FOCUS QUESTIONS

- How is emergent literacy defined and how does this differ from reading readiness?

- What are some of the factors that help determine whether or not a child will be successful in learning to read and write?

- How can parents and teachers best foster the development of emergent literacy?

IN THE CLASSROOM

Not all plums ripen on the same day; neither are all children able to formally read and write in the same month, year, or day. Just observe three-and-a-half-year-old Sam, on an errand with his mother. "Oh, there's K–Mart!" exclaims Sam, as his mother drives into the parking lot of the local discount store. "Hey, there's a car just like ours!" he continues. "It says 'C–h–e–v–r–o–l–e–t! Does that say 'Chevy,' Mommy?" Later, at home, Sam scribbles on a sheet of paper and informs his mother that he has written a letter to his cousin in Denver. His mother smiles approvingly and admires the child's "writing." Sam's mother feels confident that her child is showing real signs of being ready to learn to read and write.

In another part of town, in the local elementary school, five-year-old Bronson squirms at her desk as the kindergarten teacher, Mrs. McNeil, points out letters in the alphabet. An active yet shy child, Bronson is busy daydreaming about climbing her favorite tree and fiddling with the plastic dinosaur she has secreted in her pocket. Her parents worry that, though her older brother and sister caught on quickly to literacy activities, Bronson has never seemed to enjoy being read to nor has she asked how to spell her name. She seldom uses a pencil or crayons, and seems to shun any activity requiring fine motor skills.

Can this skillful teacher help Bronson to become literate along with her classmates, or kindle the enthusiasm for learning of her younger contemporary, Sam? Yes. Is Bronson destined to fail at reading and writing? No. We now know that literacy is an active process that can be helped to develop at the child's own rate and not something that happens totally by maturity, like the aging of fine wine!

WHAT IS DEVELOPMENTALLY APPROPRIATE?

Reading is not only a developmental task, like learning to speak and walk, but also a learned set of strategies. Children who fall behind in reading at an early age—kindergarten and first grade—have, in the past, tended to fall further behind over time (Fletcher et al., 1994). Such a finding contradicts the once prevalent notion that children will begin to learn to read only when they are "ready." But the good news is that most children do not need to lag behind at all in literacy acquisition. There are prerequisite experiences with literacy from which all children—especially children like Bronson—can benefit.

Awareness of language patterns and how sounds go together in the English language can and should be fostered through enjoyable language activities because such awareness is not innately developed (Grossen, 1997). Virtually every early learner is ready for some positive experiences with language and print. Focusing their attention on sounds, print, words, ideas, and conversations in a playful way can help preschool and kindergarten children to develop the background they will soon need to decode, or unlock, unknown words. However, if the children who do fall behind do not begin to become aware of sounds in language and are not offered experiences with literacy through active listening and oral reproduction activities, they are likely to fall further behind as the demands of reading become more and more complex.

DEFINING EMERGENT LITERACY

In the past few decades, the most pervasive definitions of **reading readiness** have included (a) being ready to profit from reading instruction beyond the most basic level (Dechant, 1982); (b) readiness to learn to read, as distinguished from a general readiness to learn (Reutzel, 1992); or (c) having the cognitive ability to meet the specific demands of the reading tasks (Ausubel, 1959). Although the term "reading readiness" has been used for a long time, more recent research has gradually supported a conclusion that such a model is inadequate for studying just how a young child becomes literate. The term **"emergent literacy"** has been selected to represent a profound change in the way we look at early literacy. Whereas we once defined reading readiness as the prereading period that extends from birth to the time when a child begins to recognize and read words, the term "emergent literacy" proposes the view that literacy begins at birth and continues throughout life (Reutzel and Cooter, 1996).

reading readiness

emergent literacy

This new way of thinking about early literacy supports the notion that very young children, even as young as two-and-a-half-years old, come into early childhood education with a rich yet diverse background of language experiences, including recognizing certain written symbols and having a variety of prewriting efforts from their home and neighborhood environments; for example, most children just entering kindergarten can read *something,* such as their names, Coke, K–Mart, and Toyota. Ollila and Mayfield (1992) stress that emergent literacy includes a language awareness that stems from children's active participation in communicating with those around them. This new concept of literacy places every child on a continuum of readiness in all of the components of language which springs from the child as a result of environmental stimulation. This stage of emergent literacy is said to last until children begin to formally read and write, when they become "beginning" readers and writers.

Literacy, in this current model, embraces not only reading, listening, and speaking, but also writing. During the period when literacy is emerging, children learn to understand and generate words, to follow directions, to be able to interpret pictures, to perceive sight and sound differences, and to acquire a curiosity about how things work. While such behaviors are related to literacy acquisition, they tell us little about exactly when a given child will begin to formally read and write.

Educators once believed that children had to reach a certain level of intelligence—a mental age of 6.6—and develop nonreading skills such as perceptual-motor skills and large motor coordination before they could actually learn to read (Durkin, 1966). According to this view, children were not ready to begin reading until they had been instructed in the prerequisite reading abilities, also referred to as "readiness activities." Many a parent during this time period was amazed when their child was miraculously able to "read" important words such as "McDonald's" or "K–Mart" without having been formally taught them!

This concept of a formal reading readiness period was accompanied by the related belief that literacy should be taught only in formal school settings. Parents were cautioned not to try to teach their children to read at home lest the children develop bad habits which would later have to be "untaught" by teachers. It was also believed that writing instruction should occur only after children had learned to read.

These beliefs of the early 1950s resulted in the pervasive idea that early childhood was a time during which a specific set of readiness skills should be taught as a prelude to "real" reading (Teale and Sulzby, 1986). Accordingly, reading readiness tests were soon developed to assess children's readiness abilities, and reading readiness programs with workbooks full of perceptual– motor activities (e.g., "Draw a line from the dog to the bone") became popular, although they often had little or nothing to do with reading. Kindergarten and the beginning of first grade was devoted to these kinds of prerequisite skills. Writing activities were postponed until even later, often second or third grade. Such beliefs persisted—and continue to persist—in many school settings, mostly fading with the dawning of the whole language movement. At that time, teachers began to see first-hand that readiness was not a simple matter of aging. They could actually help children become ready to learn how to read and write by building on the language background their learners already possessed and by providing a print-rich environment and language-play activities (Clay, 1991).

Perhaps a more constructive way to look at emergent literacy is to examine a few of its key components, as well as some commonly held myths about what constitutes readiness for formal and informal literacy instruction. By developing a better idea about exactly what factors need to be present in children's preliterate development, we are more able to develop a program to assist children in early literacy acquisition. In the body of literature on literacy acquisition accumulated over the last seventy years, the following factors have been most frequently discussed in association with early reading and writing success; revisiting such a list sheds some light onto what factors educators once emphasized as compared with current thinking on how a child becomes literate:

- intelligence
- chronological age
- gender
- phonemic awareness
- interest in language
- concepts about print and books

Intelligence

Since learning how to read and write are such complex tasks, it would seem obvious that high intelligence would be correlated with early success in literacy.

Though some intelligence appears to facilitate progress, a very bright child may not necessarily succeed at the task earlier than a child with average intelligence. Research by Bond and Dykstra (1967) found only a small relationship between reading ability and intelligence. Spache and Spache (1977) discovered that intelligence may be a modest predictor of reading success, but only for children at the extremes; in other words, for those with very high or very low intelligence there exists a positive relationship between intelligence and later success in reading. Finally, a review of reading readiness research by Torrey (1979) indicated that although many early readers who read before kindergarten did well on intelligence tests, the intelligence of the majority of early readers fell into the average and below average range. These studies suggest that, while high intelligence may be helpful to reading readiness, it is clearly not a deciding factor in predicting which children will do well in early literacy acquisition.

Chronological Age

As far back as the 1930s researchers were attempting to determine if there was an ideal age at which to begin reading instruction for optimal success. In a classic study, Morphett and Washburne (1931) looked at the mental ages of children in first grade reading programs. These researchers found that children who had reached a mental age of approximately six-and-a-half did well in beginning reading instruction while those who had not yet reached that level generally experienced more problems. Unfortunately, many educators misinterpreted these results to mean that the *chronological age* of six-and-a-half was the ideal age to begin reading instruction; thus, educators began to look at the possibility of delaying early reading instruction for all children until they had reached the age of six-and-a-half. In fact, the study had only indicated that a child who is functioning at the cognitive, or intellectual, level of a six-and-a-half-year-old would probably succeed at learning to read—whether that child was four, seven, or even ten years old.

Later studies suggested that many children learn to read successfully whether they are taught as early as five—as occurs in Japan—or as late as seven or eight—as occurs in Denmark and Finland (Harris and Sipay, 1990). These researchers further conclude that many children appear to read successfully regardless of chronological age on entering school and that age is, by itself, an inadequate predictor of success in early reading.

Gender

There are numerous fallacies surrounding the differences in linguistic competence between boys and girls. "Girls grow up faster than boys do" chirped a once popular singing group. Educators, too, once held fast to the belief that boys tended to have a delayed start in general readiness and therefore experienced more problems learning how to read than their female counterparts. More recent research suggests that these widely held views may have been misleading (Downing and Thomson, 1977). A landmark study by Dale Johnson (1973) supports a different conclusion. This investigator studied the reading prowess of early readers in the United States, Canada, Nigeria, and England. In most respects, in Nigeria and England the boys tended to score higher in tests of initial reading achievement than the girls. On the other hand, in Canada and the United States the girls scored more highly on the very same tests. Based upon these findings, Johnson concluded that the relative superiority of the reading of girls in English-speaking countries may have more to do with how they are acculturated and taught than on their native abilities or natural proclivities toward linguistic success.

Interest in Language

Interest is perhaps as important as any other factor in determining when a child is ready to succeed at formal literacy instruction. Because it is not as objectively measurable as, for example, chronological age, it is a quality that must be assessed by someone who is around the child in many different situations and has a chance to observe the child's interaction with her environment. Questions such as, "What does that word say?" and "How do you spell my name?" or "That story reminds me of another story that I heard. Shall I tell you about it?" or "Please read me a story!" are all examples of a child with a clear interest in and curiosity for beginning the tasks of literacy (Cecil, 1993).

Besides being motivated to begin the reading and writing processes, children must have enough confidence to believe that they have a fair shot at succeeding, and they must be emotionally strong enough not to become unduly frustrated when encountering a word or concept that they cannot easily figure out. Coupled with the interest must also be an attention span that allows them to attend to literacy instruction and practice for an extended period of time (Pflaum, 1986). Finally, this interest in literacy must be carefully fanned by beginning literacy activities that challenge but do not frustrate. Such activities must reach children at their current level by using their existing knowledge to bring them one step closer to becoming literate.

Phonemic Awareness

The ability to speak clearly and express ideas articulately has long been associated with emergent literacy. Thirty years of research into the reading success of early readers indicates that phonemic awareness plays an even larger role in this relationship than was earlier believed. In order for children to succeed at reading, especially in reading programs where phonics plays a large role, phonemic awareness is *the* most crucial component of emergent literacy (Adams, 1990)—a more potent predictor than nonverbal intelligence, vocabulary, or listening comprehension. To be truly ready to learn how to read and write, children must have an awareness of sounds; an understanding that we speak in a flow of words and that those words contain a sequence of sounds that can be represented by graphic symbols called letters. Later, children must not only be able to discriminate between the sounds of letters, such as /f/ and /v/, but they must be able to segment, blend, and isolate sounds to manipulate them, or sound them out, into meaningful words.

The ability to hear, blend, and discriminate between sounds is also an important part of listening comprehension as well as a factor in helping children understand subtle meaning differences related to stress, pitch, and intonation in speech (Pearson, 1985). For example, "I wouldn't buy *that* car!" (I'd buy a different model) has a slightly different meaning than "I wouldn't *buy* that car!" (although I might lease it). Another example of the need for accurate discrimination of distinct words is the two-word slang phrase, "Jeet yet?" as compared with the four words contained in the query, "Did you eat yet?"

Finally, the ability to segment words, also called **"rubber-banding,"** is helpful as children begin to explore sound-spelling relationships (Calkins, 1994). An example of this is when six-year-old Jessica is trying to sound out the word "man" and she stretches the word to *mmmmmmaaaaaannnnnn* as she laboriously pencils the word onto her paper. Research by Roberts (1975) supports the notion that blending ability seems most necessary in readiness for sounding out words in reading, while the ability to segment sounds into words appears to facilitate early writing.

rubber-banding

Specifically, the following hierarchy of phonemic understandings appears to be necessary for children to experience a smooth transition into formal reading instruction (Juel, 1994):

- Letter knowledge
- Ability to identify words
- Ability to identify syllables within words
- Ability to identify phonemes
- Knowledge about how print works

The Importance of Print and Books

Jim Trelease, author of *The New Read Aloud Handbook* (1995), travels around the country exhorting parents to read to their child for fifteen minutes a night to ensure later academic success. The reason he preaches this important message has much to do with emergent literacy: Children who have been read to—early and often—develop important concepts about print, such as the fact that a page in a book consists of symbols that stand for words and that there is white space around those words; a book has a front and a back; we read from left to right; punctuation at the end of a word lets the reader know when to stop reading and take a small pause. Children who have print and book knowledge can also point to individual words on a page as they read, or track. Advanced understanding of print allows children to identify the first and last word on a page, capital and lower case letters, and the first and last letters of words—all excellent precursors to the reading process (Clay, 1972; 1993). In a family setting, these understandings are developed naturally through enjoyable exposure to print.

POSITIVE PRACTICES TO FOSTER EMERGENT LITERACY

In most primary classrooms of future years, teachers will necessarily encounter a heterogeneous garden of children with a multitude of abilities and language backgrounds, as well as a diverse set of literacy experiences, such as having been read to and having sung songs. Some will enter the classroom door with many such experiences; others will have had fewer activities directly related to language development in its many forms.

While individualized instruction seems a logical solution to these diversities, such a course of action is not without a host of problems: most children are, by nature, social beings who greatly enjoy interaction with other children their own age. We also know from research and past experience that teachers should take an active stance in getting children ready to learn how to read and write, rather than simply waiting for them to become, magically, ready. Three of the factors previously mentioned—interest, development of concepts about print and books, and language experiences—are ones which teachers can readily supplement in the classroom in a small or large group setting.

What is first necessary for early literacy experiences to flourish is a teacher who is both sensitive to the physical environment of the classroom and a facilitator of learning. Such a teacher will create an environment that is print-rich and offer activities to provide a rich, motivational exposure to the English language. While the next chapter offers the reader a host of activities that can be used for direct, explicit instruction in phonemic awareness, the following section will allow the teacher to build upon what the children already know to ready them for more formalized reading and writing instruction.

Developing Concepts About Print

As children get ready for formal literacy instruction, they will need to develop some basic understandings of how print works in text; most of these concepts of print should have been mastered before a child enters first grade (California Department of Education, 1998). What seems simple to many may bewilder children who may never have been exposed to it. It is unlikely, for example, that a preliterate child will spot any patterns in a page of print if that child sometimes looks at it from right to left and at other times from left to right. All of the following concepts about print can be taught directly to children during read-aloud sessions (Clay, 1993):

- text carries meaning (we read words, not pictures)
- reading of text goes from left to right, top to bottom
- text goes from the left page, then proceeds to the right
- letters are the black squiggles on the page
- a word is composed of letters and is surrounded by white space
- punctuation marks inform inflection and meaning

- a book has a front and back cover, a title page, an author, and an illustrator
- a story has a beginning, a middle, and an end

To reinforce such concepts, teachers can use big books, posters, sentence strips in a pocket chart, songs, poetry, or any text that is large enough to share with children. Then before reading the text with children, the teacher can feign forgetfulness and ask children,

Who can show me

where the cover of the book is?

which way is right side up?

where I should start to read?

where a word is?

where the end of the story is?

where a capital (or lowercase) letter is?

On a familiar text, some children may be ready to point to the words as they are read, establishing one-to-one matching of words to print.

Providing Direct and Vicarious Experiences

Providing an adequate background of experience is an integral part of emergent literacy. Because the child who is intellectually curious reaps the most from his experiences, teachers must take every opportunity to whet his curiosity about unfamiliar activities, ideas, and objects. A broad experiential background is necessary for success in reading and writing because children must be familiar with the concepts and vocabulary they will see in written form to gain meaning from them. Indeed, experiences are the foundation for building concepts, and concepts are the foundation for building new vocabulary. Through their experiences children gain an understanding of ideas and concepts and then learn words that go with them. When they later begin to read they will better comprehend because they are able to relate their experiences to the symbols on the printed page.

Teachers may help children build experiential backgrounds in a variety of ways. As they observe and talk with their pupils, they can see where there are gaps in experience and find ways to fill them. Teachers can invite resource people into the classroom or arrange field trips to places children have never visited. Children can build experience through constructing mobiles and collages, cooking, playing with puzzles, identifying hidden objects, playing language guessing games, singing nursery rhymes, and marching to a Sousa tune.

During "calendar" or "news" time, children gain useful experience observing and discussing the weather, reciting the days of the week and months of the year, and establishing what to do in a fire drill, among other experiences. Since young children love to play, a hidden coin can be a language experience for English Language Learners where they must repeatedly ask complete sentences to determine who has the coin; a box becomes a concept-building game when children try to identify the positions of an object placed on it, over it, by it, or under it. Similarly, children can increase their understanding of the subtleties of vocabulary by responding to invitations to crawl, trot, dash, or stroll.

Experiences may be either direct or vicarious. Children usually remember direct experiences with actual physical involvement best, but such experiences are not always possible; for example, the ideal way to teach about the Laplanders in Greenland would be to climb aboard a Lear jet, observe their lives, talk to them first-hand, and spend time in their homes. Since that is not feasible, vicarious experiences such as television programs about the Laplanders, exhibits, a resource person who has been to Greenland, photographs, film excerpts, or a story or article about their lives will also serve to promote concept and vocabulary development.

Interactive Story Writing

interactive story writing

Interactive story writing is a logical extension of either direct or vicarious experiences and is an ideal vehicle through which to reinforce concepts about print. Such story writing can be planned and occur as an introduction to an experience, or be the spontaneous result of an experience. If the class writes a story following a severe thunder storm, the children should first discuss the event. By asking carefully selected questions, the teacher can encourage children to formulate valid concepts and to use appropriate vocabulary words. For example, the teacher might ask:

"Who can tell me about what the weather was like this morning?"

"What kinds of things happen during a storm?"

"How did the storm make you feel?"

"Why might rain be important to us?"

In response to a discussion generated by questions, the children then dictate sentences for the teacher to transcribe onto a chart. The resultant piece of writing might look like the one shown in Figure 3.1, recently composed by a group of second-graders.

Dictated pieces such as this provide an excellent precursor to later use of the language experience approach (see Chapter 9).

Perhaps the most important reason for writing stories with children before they are able to write their own is that they begin to grasp the critical concept

FIGURE 3.1 *An interactive story.*

THE STORM

This morning we didn't have any recess because there was a big storm.

There was loud thunder and bright lightning.

It rained very hard for a long time.

Some children were afraid of the noise.

The storm was scary, but the rain can be good.

We need the rain to make the flowers grow.

that writing is a way to record speech. This awareness occurs as their teacher reads the story back to the children in the words they have just dictated. After repeated readings by the teacher, the children may be able to "read" the story too. The teacher may make copies of the story for the children to take home and share with their families. As a result of this repeated involvement with the story, children may learn to recognize some high-interest words (e.g., "storm" in the story above) and words that were used more than once ("we" and "there"). These understandings are further reinforced when seen in multiple contexts.

Many reading and writing skills are reinforced through transcriptions; essentially, children gain an exposure, or bird's eye view, of all the skills of reading and writing. Consider: Children watch as the teacher forms letters that make up the words and she demonstrates how she sounds out the beginning letters. They begin to notice, as the teacher writes, that language consists of separate words which are combined into sentences. They see the teacher begin reading at the left side of the story and move to the right, and go from top to bottom. They become aware that dictated stories have titles which tell about the most important idea in the story, and they see that each letter of the title is capitalized. They discover that sentences begin with capital letters and end with a punctuation mark. In addition to becoming familiar with the mechanical conventions of the English language, children develop their thinking skills as the teacher guides them to summarize and organize their thoughts. Finally, as the children recall the events in the order in which they occurred, they become aware of the importance of sequencing ideas.

Reading Aloud to Children

To build upon children's knowledge of what is available in print, the teacher should choose a wide variety of reading materials to read aloud to students every day. Reading to children not only builds appreciation of literature, but it also develops listening comprehension skills and understanding of various text structures.

wordless books

predictable books

For heightened enjoyment, it is best to use a variety of well-crafted picture books with large illustrations so that children can observe the action as well as hear what is happening. Big books are commercially available for this purpose. The box below offers guidelines for selecting a big book.

At times the teacher may wish to choose stories with only pictures, or **wordless books** (see Appendix A), so that very young children have a chance to use their imaginations to help tell the story from their everyday experiences and from their experiences with other stories. **Predictable books** are other excellent options for reading aloud to children. These are children's books that, through their rhyme, rhythm, and repetition, allow children to participate in the reading and, with the teacher's help, associate the spoken words with the written ones, creating an understanding of one-to-one correspondence between oral and written words.

To acquaint English language learners with language variety, the teacher should offer a variety of styles and structures, too. Remember that children do not need to understand every word that is read to them, especially when the text is supported by appropriate illustrations. As with infants acquiring a first language, hearing new words in familiar contexts helps children begin to construct new meanings.

It is helpful to select children's literature from all genres—fiction, nonfiction, from all ethnic groups, prose, and poetry—to encourage a wide range of

---

Selecting a big book

The criteria for evaluating a big book are the same as the criteria used for selecting any children's book to be read aloud, with the addition of the following features:

1. The book should not be so large that it is difficult to hold on your lap with one hand and turn the pages with the other.

2. The print should be clearly distinguishable from the illustrations. In other words, it should be easy for the children to visually discriminate the units of print from the illustrations.

3. There should be a strong connection between the print and the illustrations; the children should be able to predict what the story is about from the pictures.

4. The print should be large enough to be seen clearly from the back of the group of children.

5. The text of the book should have specific instructional qualities, such as a rhyming pattern, a particular phonic element such as an abundance of words beginning with "b," or predictability enhanced by repetition.

interests. Early in the year the teacher can survey students' interests, hobbies, special talents, and country of birth, and choose stories and nonfiction pieces based upon this information (see the interest inventory in Appendix D).

Finally, the teacher should be sure to share reading materials that he especially enjoys, because pleasure and enthusiasm for reading and books is more effectively caught than taught.

Sharing literature is the perfect experience through which to develop the concepts about books and print as they occur naturally in the book being read. Talking about literature with children can help also develop the idea that reading should make sense, that readers are to be actively involved in thinking about what might happen next, and that the learner brings his or her own knowledge, ideas, and experiences to the text. Prereading discussions about a topic and what they know about it, the author and illustrator, and a general feeling about what they predict the story might be about will set preliterate children on the road to comprehending text. The modeling of these behaviors by a proficient reader, the teacher, will encourage children to actively construct meaning as they begin to read. The following box offers a list of classic read-aloud books.

Classic read-alouds for young readers

The following picture story books are "classics" that have withstood the test of time, offering countless children—and adult readers—enjoyable associations with literature.

Corduroy by Don Freeman
> A stuffed bear is rescued from the department store shelf by a little girl who takes him home to be her friend.

Goodnight Moon by Margaret Wise Brown
> Mother Rabbit settles her little one into bed through rhyme by saying goodnight to all the things in the bedroom.

Ira Sleeps Over by Bernard Weber
> When he is asked to spend the night at his friend's house, a little boy must decide whether or not to take along his teddy bear.

Make Way for Ducklings by Robert McCloskey
> This is the story of the city adventures of Mr. and Mrs. Mallard and their eight ducklings.

Sylvester and the Magic Pebble by William Steig
> Sylvester makes a wish on a magic pebble and is unable to undo his wish and return home to his family. The story resolves when Sylvester is reunited with his parents.

The Very Hungry Caterpillar by Eric Carle
> An egg hatches into a caterpillar that eats its way through several story book pages before turning into a beautiful butterfly.

Using Drama

Informal dramatic activities create interest in language and stories, develop the imagination of children, and allow them to use language to express their ideas and feelings. It is especially appropriate for use with English language learners, because the action involved supports and reinforces the words, thereby making the meaning accessible for all learners.

Informal drama should be spontaneous and unrehearsed, with children assuming the roles of characters from real life or from stories they have heard. They are free to think, feel, move, react, and speak in accordance with their interpretation of the characters. The drama may begin with simple movements or actions in response to poems or songs the teacher reads (and the horses went clippety-clop, clippety-clop. *Show* me what the horses did, boys and girls!). Later, children may develop their interpretational skills by pantomiming stories or actions after the teacher has read, such as the making of the porridge in *Goldilocks and the Three Bears* or dancing the horrific monster dance in *Where the Wild Things Are,* when the "wild rumpus begins."

Acting out stories not only helps build interest in stories but it develops understandings of the structure of stories. Children can progress to more sophisticated drama that more nearly resembles the entire story. As the teacher reads the story the children must pay careful attention to the sequence of events, the personalities of the characters, the dialogue, and the mood of the story. Before acting out the story the teacher can help the children review the events and characters in the story by using a simple organizer such as the one shown in Figure 3.2.

As they act, the children can be encouraged to strive to use appropriate vocabulary, enunciate clearly, and speak audibly. Puppets can be useful with shy children who are reluctant to speak themselves but are often willing to talk through a puppet. Props, such as masks, costumes, scarves, empty food containers, and cardboard boxes, help to inspire dialogue. Children will often want to act out the stories multiple times, with different children playing different characters each time. Each successive rereading allows for a deeper appreciation and understanding of the original story.

Dramatic play has many benefits, all prerequisite for learning to read and write. Because children need to carry on conversations, they are practicing their language skills. By interacting with other children, they are developing

FIGURE 3.2 *A simple story frame.*

Somebody/	Wanted/	But/	So
Goldilocks	to sit	bears	she
	to eat	came	ran
	to sleep	home	away

social and emotional readiness. The teacher can encourage children to use printed words as labels, such as street signs, character names, and package labels. Ambiguous props used in their play can also be labeled—for example, a ball becomes "bowling ball"—and will later become sight words. **Play centers** such as the ones described in Figure 3.3 can also facilitate spontaneous dramatic play.

play centers

FIGURE 3.3 *Examples of play centers.*

GROCERY STORE

Empty cereal and other boxes

Pretend money and coins

Receipt book for purchasing items

Paper sacks for bagging groceries

Calculator or cash register that prints onto tape

HOUSE

Puppets

Telephone

Cardboard boxes for furniture

Clothing appropriate for different family members

Kitchen utensils

Paper and crayons for making props

POST OFFICE

Mail boxes

Stationery

Assorted writing utensils

Old stamps or stickers

Puppets

FARM

Stuffed or plastic animals

Large boxes or crates for barn

Burlap bags for pretend feed

Pails

Plastic plants

By listening attentively to each other, children begin to develop the auditory memory and discrimination necessary for phonemic awareness in an enjoyable package that only seems like play.

COMMUNICATING WITH PARENTS

Each child comes to school with a different set of experiences that foster emergent literacy. It is axiomatic that most parents wish to have their child succeed in this vital area, but all parents may not be aware of the important part they can play in causing it to happen. Therefore, it is critical for teachers to communicate with the parents of their pupils, through conferences, by phone, home visitations, and through written correspondence, about ways they can foster literacy development in their children at home. Among the most critical ideas to relate to parents are the following:

Be a reader. Parents can share the pleasure and information they gain from reading by showing their children how they read and write for a variety of purposes. What is read is far less important than the actual doing of it on a regular basis. Parents should be told that newspapers and magazines are every bit as acceptable as novels for this purpose.

Model the reading process. Parents can talk to their children about how they make sense of what they read. They can talk about how the topic relates to their life, ask questions, and make predictions. Admitting lack of understanding, at times, gives their children permission to not always understand.

Plan family literacy activities. Parents can play language games together, such as telling add-on stories, making books, telling about favorite books they have read, and keeping journals to share with other family members. Parents can also take their children with them to the grocery store, the library, or any other routine excursion and talk about where they are going, what they are doing, and what they have seen.

Acquire a wide variety of literacy materials. Parents can give books as gifts and subscribe to children's magazines. Books and magazines can also be obtained cheaply at garage and rummage sales. A home message board could be used for family members to write notes to each other, and a graffiti wall can provide a space for copying rhymes and limericks. Magnetic letters for the refrigerator also invite experimentation with print, without causing concern to a young child who is not able to actually form the letters.

Read aloud regularly. Above all, parents can offer the one practice that has been found to be most effective of all in helping children to become literate: read to them as frequently as possible. This activity not only makes children want to read but also exposes them to the joy of books. Reading aloud also strengthens reading, writing, listening, and speaking abilities. Parents for whom English is a second language should be assured that reading to their child in their home language is just as helpful for modeling reading behavior and instilling a love for reading. (Information about "parent packets" will be provided in Chapters 5 and 10.)

SUMMARY

All young children—and everyone else, for that matter—are somewhere on the continuum of becoming proficient readers and writers; therefore, the old question of exactly *when* they will be ready to learn to read becomes irrelevant. The most current understanding of emergent literacy holds that children are emerging literate persons from birth and continue on this path until death. Success in literacy, then, will depend upon a constellation of interlocking factors; it is now deemed to be predicated neither on wholly physical nor totally intellectual maturation alone, although both of these realms seem to be at least minimally involved. Nor do modern educators believe any longer that success in literacy is something to wait for passively, as educators tended to believe in the early 1950s; we now argue that literacy is a stage onto which a child can be gently guided—and even enticed—when the appropriate methods and activities are offered to that child.

Gender, home environment, and chronological age of children may not be the most critical issues in determining who will be literate when. However, it is helpful to be aware of such factors in order to understand possible tangential reasons for certain inexplicable behaviors or unexplainable lack of progress in early literacy acquisition. On the other hand, teachers must guard against preconceived expectations for children based upon gender or chronological age, home environment, or any other nonacademic facts of the child's life which are not subject to change.

Fortunately, teachers of young children can influence their later reading success through fostering the awareness of sounds in language, or phonemic awareness. They can impact other areas correlated with success in early literacy, as well, such as background experience, interest in literacy, and language development. Teachers can fill in the experiential gaps of the children in their charge with appropriate real-life experiences or well-designed vicarious ones; they can incorporate language-rich activities, such as the transcription of stories, dramatic play, and reading aloud to children into their daily routines. Most of all, teachers have a crucial responsibility to fill their classrooms with plenty of print and language opportunities so that pupils can experiment with language in all its forms. With such print-rich and language-rich experiences at the beginning of their academic lives, the path to formalized literacy instruction will no doubt be considerably smoother.

QUESTIONS
....
for Journal Writing and Discussion

1. Discuss the prevalent practice of "red shirting," or of parents holding children back a year before sending them to kindergarten. What is your opinion of this practice? How might such a practice stratify our society along socioeconomic lines?

2. What might you say to concerned parents of a kindergarten child who asks you what they can do at home to help their child become "ready to learn to read"?

3. Schools often use a teacher's judgment as well as the data derived from reading readiness assessments to decide whether or not children are ready to begin formal reading instruction. Do you think these two sources of data are equally reliable? Why or why not? What might be some advantages of each of these forms of evaluation? What might be some limitations?

SUGGESTIONS
....
for Projects and Other Activities

1. From the information in this chapter, create a checklist that you might use to help determine if a child is ready to learn to read. Include such major factors as language development, interest in reading, and orthographic understandings. For each of these main headings, create ways to evaluate each of the factors. For example, you might say for language development, "Asks many complex questions containing five or more words," or for interest in reading, "Listens attentively when read to" or "Often talks about books he has heard."

2. Spend some time observing in a kindergarten class. Ask the teacher for a list of birthdays of the children in the class. Do there appear to be noticeable differences in the children's involvement in literacy and other behaviors depending upon their earlier or later birthdays? What are these differences? Use the list created for the previous to consider some other possible factors in the emergent literacy status of this group of children.

3. Research the emergent literacy issues of a country outside of North America. Find out: (1) When do children begin formal reading instruction? (2) What methods are used for instruction? (3) Are there any noticeable differences in the achievement levels between boys and girls on standardized reading tests in later years? (4) If there *is* a discrepancy in test results between girls and boys, to what do educational practitioners attribute this difference? What do you think accounts for the difference?

PHONEMIC AWARENESS

The Sounds of Our Language

FOCUS QUESTIONS

- What is the relationship between phonemic awareness and phonics?

- How can teachers develop phonemic awareness in their learners in motivational ways?

- Why is knowledge of phonemic awareness and the alphabetic principle so important to emergent literacy?

In the Classroom

The children in Mrs. Rodgers' kindergarten class are enthusiastically involved in brainstorming about all the foods they can think of while their teacher writes their responses on the board. For every favorite food mentioned, such as "hot dog," the children try to think of a nonsense rhyme that could go with it. "Rot hog!" Aaron exclaims gleefully, and the other children burst into a fit of giggles at this hilarious rhyme, quickly offering a "thumbs up" sign to Aaron. Mrs. Rodgers grins as she writes the letters on the board with the children helping her to sound out the words. The children in Mrs. Rodgers' class enjoy this game immensely. They are oblivious to the fact that they are also engaging in phonemic awareness activities designed to help them tune in to the sounds in the English language. Such activities will help them to be better prepared to benefit from later phonics instruction.

phonemic awareness

Until the last decade, the teaching of decoding addressed mostly phonics, or the relationship between spoken sounds and individual printed letters or letter combinations. Now, much greater emphasis is being placed on the understanding and teaching of **phonemic awareness**. This term refers to the child's understanding that we speak in a stream of individual words, and that those words are composed of a sequence of sounds that exist independently of meaning (Cunningham, 1990). Phonemic awareness is actually the child's construction of the bridge between spoken and written language (Snider, 1995). A child who possesses phonemic awareness can segment and manipulate sounds in words (e.g., pronounce just the first sound heard in the word "gap"); blend strings of isolated sounds together to form recognizable word forms; and so on (IRA Board, 1998).

Phonemic awareness is really an oral language understanding; moreover, phonemic awareness is not the same as phonics. Phonics generally refers to knowing the relationship between specific, printed letters (and combinations of letters) and specific, spoken sounds. With the application of such knowledge, children can use letter sounds and other rules to figure out, or decode, unknown words. Phonemic awareness has been shown to be an important *precursor* to phonics and successful decoding skills critical in reading (Vellutino and Scanlon, 1987; Wagner and Torgeson, 1987; Stanovich and Siegel, 1994). Studies have shown that children who lack experience with phonemic awareness activities often do not profit from phonics instruction (Griffith and Olson, 1992).

The current emphasis on the underlying awareness of the sounds in a language has come about as a result of a large volume of research into the problems of numerous children in our schools who do not seem to be learning to read at grade level (Fletcher et al., 1994; Shaywitz et al., 1992; Stanovich and Siegel, 1994). While the majority of children learn to read regardless of the reading methods used by their teachers, the percentage of children for whom reading has been a problem has consistently been about 25 percent (Adams, 1990). Early facilitation in phonemic awareness might very well be the instructional component, when integrated into a program rich with language and print, that allows educators to teach every child to read—including those children who have historically fallen through the cracks.

THE IMPORTANCE OF PHONEMIC AWARENESS

To understand why phonemic awareness is important, it is first necessary to understand a bit about the nature of our language. Linguists describe four separate areas of functioning in the human language system: phonology (sounds), syntax (grammar), semantics (underlying meaning), and pragmatics (usage) (see Chapter 2). The component of phonology is critical to eventual success in phonics. **Phonology** is the study of the sound patterns of a language. As we put our ideas into words, it is the phonological part of our language system that puts together the proper sounds of those words in the appropriate sequence; in other words, our canine best friend is a *dog* and not a *god,* only because of the precise arrangement of sounds.

phonology

About 25 years ago, Isabelle Liberman and her colleagues (Lieberman et al., 1974) suggested that the primary cause for difficulty in learning to read an alphabetic written language (as compared with an ideographic language with meaning-laden characters, such as Kanji or Mandarin), is due to a lack of awareness of the phonology, or sounds, of the language. The English language employs the **alphabetic principle**. Any alphabetic writing system uses symbols to represent the sounds of a language. Readers must first understand that words can be divided into sounds and that the same basic set of letters can be combined in a great variety of ways. Only then can a child understand that *lake* and *kale,* for instance, have the same letters but represent different words because the particular sequence of the letters—and therefore the sequence of the sounds—is different.

People need not be consciously aware of the individual sounds within words to be expert speakers of a language; in oral language, words and phrases are meaningful units as wholes and it is actually distracting to focus on the individual sounds. Only when we need to understand the representations of thousands of different words—from only a small number of written symbols—must we focus on the individual sounds these symbols represent.

The ability to hear discrete speech sounds in individual words is not easy for all young children and remains difficult—even into adulthood—for a surprisingly large number of people. This is understandable when we consider that sounds are abstract, meaningless in isolation, and often influenced by context. (What does your mouth do when you say the /s/ in *see*? When you say the /s/ in *say*?) However, in the last 20 years a large body of research has supported a conclusion that the ability to segment words into individual sounds is an absolute prerequisite to learning how to read in an alphabetic symbol system such as English. Moreover, the degree to which emergent readers are aware of the individual sounds in spoken words very often predicts future reading success. In fact, it has been shown to be a better predictor of reading success than intelligence, parents' educational background, visual or auditory perception, memory, or even eyesight (Blachman, 1991; Wagner et al., 1994)! This predictive power has been demonstrated not only among English-speaking children, but also among Swedish-speaking children (Lundberg et al., 1980); Spanish-speaking children (deManrique and Gramigna, 1984); French-speaking children (Alegria et al., 1982); Italian-speaking children (Cossu et al., 1988); Portuguese-speaking children (Cardoso–Martins, 1995); and Russian-speaking children (Elkonin, 1973).

alphabetic principle

THE COMPONENTS OF PHONEMIC AWARENESS

Phonemic awareness should be viewed not as one grand skill but as a continuum of lesser understandings, ranging from simple to complex awarenesses of the sounds, or phonemes, of our language (Ball and Blachman, 1991; Byrne and Fielding–Barnsley, 1989). At the easy end of the spectrum, to be considered phonemically aware, children are able to discriminate if words are the same or different, and appreciate, recognize, or produce rhymes. Intermediate skill occurs when children can blend sounds and split syllables; for example, they are able to segment the /m/ from the word *man*. One of the most difficult tasks in phonemic awareness is to isolate speech sounds. This task requires the child to tell the beginning, middle, or ending sound in the word *soap,* or to say the word *lake* without the /k/.

The actual hierarchy, from easiest to the most difficult, for phonemic awareness competence is shown in the box below.

The hierarchy of phonemic awareness competence

1. **Awareness of words.** Child can tell which of two words is longer.
   Example: hamburger or *cat.*

2. **Ability to rhyme.** Child can rhyme simple one-syllable words.
   Example: What word rhymes with *pin*?

3. **Ability to blend.** Child can put together an onset and rime that is given by the teacher.
   Example: /bl/ and /ack/. What would these two sounds be if they were put together?

4. **Ability to segment into words and syllables.** Child can take apart compound words, put words into syllables, and break up a sentence into words.
   Example: What are the words in this sentence: "The boy went after the ball"?

5. **Ability to identify beginning sounds (onsets).** Child can listen to a series of words and identify which has a target sound.
   Example: Which of the following begins like baby—mud, lake, or ball?

6. **Ability to segment words into phonemes.** Child can tell the sounds in a word in order.
   Example: What are the three sounds in the word *got*?

7. **Ability to substitute and manipulate beginning phonemes.** Child can replace speech sounds with others.
   Example: Can you change the word *bake* by changing the first sound to an /m/?

8. **Ability to substitute middle and ending phonemes.** Child can replace middle and ending speech sounds (rimes).
   Example: Can you change the word *cot* to another word by changing the middle sound to an /a/?

Because phonemic awareness has been shown to be strongly related to success in beginning reading, it should be developed as early as possible in children—preferably in their preschool years—through a variety of stimulating language activities (Foorman et al., 1998). These activities are not intended to replace children's interaction with meaningful language and print. Rather, the activities presented here are designed to supplement and enhance such experiences by providing a means of focusing children's attention on a critical aspect of the structure of their language—its phonemic base. Reading aloud to children, developing language experience charts, using predictable books for guided and shared reading, and journal writing are also invaluable reading experiences in a balanced early literacy program. These activities will be explored in later chapters.

Research suggests that phonemic awareness activities can maximize children's potential for a successful learning-to-read experience (Adams et al., 1998; Ball and Blachman, 1991). Therefore, teachers of young children should recognize the important role they can play in contributing to their students' phonemic awareness by spending a few minutes every day engaging children in oral language activities that explicitly emphasize the sequence of sounds in language.

DEVELOPING PHONEMIC AWARENESS

A useful way for the teacher to plan phonemic awareness activities is according to the nature of the specific phonemic skill that needs to be developed. For example, an activity may require the child to merely listen to a poem or song, match words by sounds, isolate a word by sounds, blend individual sounds to make a word, substitute sounds within a word, or even break a word into its parts. Each of these tasks is a part of phonemic awareness, yet these tasks are not equally difficult, as indicated by the hierarchy indicated earlier.

The first task for the teacher, then, is to determine exactly which component(s) of phonemic awareness needs to be developed by the child based upon the results of a careful assessment, such as the Phonemic Awareness Assessment Device (see Appendix D). The teacher can then provide experiences and activities to enhance the specific need of the youngsters.

General Guidelines

Some general considerations for facilitating phonemic awareness are important to point out here. First of all, it is critical to explain the task in which the teacher wants the children to be engaged through direct instruction, adequate modeling, and demonstration. For example, if the teacher wants the children to listen for all the words that have the /m/ sound, she must first clearly say the *name* of the letter, and then model how to say the /m/ *sound,* asking children to carefully watch her mouth. It is then helpful to pass out small hand mirrors to have children experiment with saying the /m/ sound and observing for themselves what they do with *their* mouths when producing the sound. The teacher should then ask the children to share orally what their mouths do—in their own words. She should demonstrate how to tell when the /m/ sound is heard in different words by giving some examples. The children will be more likely to succeed in this task as subsequent examples are given for practice.

Second, the teacher must analyze the task to be performed and, initially, keep it as simple as possible. Is the teacher asking the children to listen for syllables or sounds, and exactly which sound should the children be looking for and where in the word will it be found? Also, beginning with very simple two- and then three-phoneme words will help reduce confusion; rather than using a lesson that asks children to listen for the speech sounds in the words *blend, green,* or *brook* (which have blended consonants and other sounds that require more sophisticated discrimination), start with continuous sounds, such as *man, sat,* or *nut.*

Finally, for teachers of English language learners, there are sounds regularly used in English that are not part of other languages. In general, the sounds listed in Figure 4.1 are not part of the other languages' regular sound system, although they may occur in certain dialects, or sometimes just in the middle positions of words. These sounds are difficult for beginning speakers of English for two reasons: first, children have not had any practice recognizing these sounds or discriminating them from others; native English-speaking children have heard the sounds and had practice discriminating them from infancy. Second, because children have not used these sounds before, they have had no practice pronouncing them. To help children in these language groups master these sounds in readiness for later phonics instruction, teachers will need to point out the discrepant sounds to the children, exaggerate their pronunciation, and help children learn to pronounce them through practice with repetition of each sound used in the beginning, middle, and end positions of words.

Specifically, teachers can help non-English-speaking children to become phonemically aware by following the guidelines shown in the box on the following page. For more information on phonemic awareness and English language learners, see Katharine Au's *Literacy Instruction in Multicultural Settings* (1997).

FIGURE 4.1 *Sounds not occurring in other languages.*

LANGUAGE	SOUNDS NOT PART OF THE LANGUAGE
Chinese	b ch d dg g oa sh s th v z
French	ch ee j ng oo th
Greek	aw ee i oo schwa
Italian	a ar dg h i ng th schwa
Japanese	dg f i th oo v schwa
Spanish	dg j sh th z
Native English-speakers	l r st

Helping non-English speakers

FOR SPANISH SPEAKERS

- Assess children's phonemic awareness in Spanish, not English
- Allow children to do many language activities in Spanish
- Continue to develop proficiency in Spanish
- Help children see similarities in the two language systems
- Use pictures that have the same sounds in both languages (e.g., gato, cat)

FOR NON-ALPHABETIC LANGUAGE SPEAKERS

- Treat as English speaker who is struggling to "hear" the sounds in English
- Speak slowly and use lip, mouth, and tongue training in an active, fun approach
- Intensify instruction three to four times a week, building on children's progress in oral English

From Research to Practice

First of all, it is important to note that not every child needs intensive training in phonemic awareness. In kindergarten, children needing guidance in this area, for example, would be those who cannot rhyme and who don't recognize that *pat* and *pick* start with the same sounds. In first and second grades, children who cannot segment initial sounds or detect different beginning, middle, and ending sounds need additional help. On the other hand, children who already manifest phonemic awareness can be exposed to the phonics and decoding activities presented in Chapter 5.

For children who do need such assistance, there are many research-supported ways to help them develop the spectrum of phonemic awareness skills (Griffith and Olson, 1992; Yopp, 1992). Initially, children should be exposed to poems and nursery rhymes, especially those in which the rhymes are the most obvious feature of the poem. First the poems should be read for enjoyment and understanding. Then, if the poems are recited with a great deal of emphasis on the words that rhyme, almost to the point of exaggeration, the children's attention will be drawn to that rhyme. Eventually the children should be able to generate their own rhyming words. Engagement in this type of activity should be accompanied by a good deal of humor and poetic license, as "hot dog" is rhymed with "rot hog," in the opening vignette of this chapter. Certain children's literature lends itself to exactly this type of language play.

Books such as *The Hungry Thing* by Jan Slepian (Scholastic, 1985), for example, engage children in rhyming while having a rollicking good time. Other examples of appropriate books are found in Appendix A.

Phonemic awareness can also be developed by having children identify pictures for which the beginning sound or the beginning consonant and vowel sound for the picture is the same. For example, given pictures of a pig, a pin, a pot, and

a sun, the child would put the pig, pin, and pot pictures together, or tell which picture doesn't fit and explain why on the basis of their perception of sound. When children can do this easily with pictures, they can often listen to just three or four words and tell which ones go together and which ones do not. This can evolve to selecting which middle sounds go together and which ones do not fit (mat, can, lap, bit), and then performing the same tasks with ending sounds (cup, map, lot, pep).

Many phonemic awareness activities can take the form of games or puzzles and can be used in an informal, relaxed setting. One such game would be looking for objects in the classroom or in magazines whose names begin with a certain sound.

Extra challenge and interest can be added by going through the alphabet, finding one thing that starts with /a/, then /b/, and so on. The teacher will need to specify the sound and, if it is a vowel, indicate whether it is long or short.

A similar game is "I Spy with My Eye," except instead of doing colors, the teacher declares, "I spy with my eye something beginning with /th/," or "I spy with my eye something ending with /k/," choosing word parts and sounds that the children can handle without too much difficulty.

Children also enjoy counting the number of syllables in words that are pronounced for them in exaggerated fashion. The names of children in the class provide personal examples for this activity. Counting with young children can be done in a variety of ways, such as tapping the table with a pencil, clapping each syllable, or noting the number of times their jaws move up and down as the word is said. It is always most difficult for children to count the syllable in a one syllable word, as they often attempt to make discrete speech sounds into syllables, so it is helpful to warn them, "Here's a tricky one!"

As children get proficient at these activities in which they are asked to recognize how the sounds in words differ, they are often ready to manipulate the sounds themselves. For example, you can give them a word to say (e.g., *bat*) and ask them to say it without the /b/. For children who have difficulty with this, you can begin with compound words, having them leave off one of the syllables, which is a phonologically easier task. For example: "Say *baseball*. Now say it without the *ball*." "Say *baseball*. Now say it without the *base*."

When the children become comfortable with manipulating the sounds in words, but before they have been taught the actual letters, the teacher can begin to use colored chips or small pieces of paper on **sound boxes** to represent the

sound boxes

sounds (see Figure 4.2). Each different sound should be represented with a different color, but the same color does not always have to match a particular sound. For example, if you have red, yellow, green, blue, and purple chips, the word *map* may be represented by blue–green–red, red–purple–yellow, or green–blue–red, as long as each sound has a different color. A word like *pop,* using the same patterning, may be represented by green–blue–green, red–yellow–red, or blue–red–blue, as long as the beginning and ending colors are the same. Using this approach, children may be given problems to solve such as the following:

> If this says /go/ make it say /so/. (Children should replace the first chip with one of another color.)

> If this says /kite/ make it say /cat/. (Children should replace the second chip with one of a different color; silent /e/ is not represented at this early stage.) (See Figure 4.2.)

Eventually you can progress to having children delete a sound:

> If this says /man/, make it say /an/. (Children should remove the first chip.)

When children have learned the sounds and graphic representations (letters) for some consonants and a vowel, they can use letter cards or tiles for these activities, and they will have progressed to reading and spelling words!

FIGURE 4.2   *Sound boxes.*

Other Phonemic Awareness Activities

The activities presented here are categorized into word beginnings, sound isolation activities, blending activities, and sound substitution activities. The list of activities in this chapter is by no means exhaustive. Teachers may easily modify any of the preceding and following activities by targeting sounds that are developmentally appropriate for their students or discovering similar ways to draw their students' attention to the particular sounds in our language that they are ready to consider.

ACTIVITY

RHYMING

THE SHIP IS LOADED WITH . . . (ADAMS ET AL., 1998)

Seat children in a circle. To begin the game, say, "The ship is loaded with *bugs.*" Then toss a ball or a beanbag to a child in the circle. That child must produce a rhyme (e.g., "The ship is loaded with *jugs*") and throw the ball back to you. Repeating the original rhyme, toss the ball to another child. Continue the game this way until children run out of rhymes. Then begin the game again with another rhyme, e.g., "The ship is loaded with *mice.*"

When the children have become good at rhyming, each child can throw the ball to another child instead of back to you. The second child must then continue rhyming with the word suggested by the first child.

The ship is loaded with bugs.   (jugs, mugs, tugs, rugs, etc.)

The ship is loaded with mice.   (rice, lice, spice, dice, etc.)

The ship is loaded with cats.   (rats, bats, mats, hats, etc.)

ACTIVITY

WORD BEGINNINGS (ONSETS)

THE SOUND SONG

The lyrics to the following song are sung to the tune of "Mary Had a Little Lamb."

Taco starts with /t/, /t/, /t/
/t/, /t/, /t/—/t/, /t/, /t/
Taco starts with /t/, /t/, /t/
Other words do too!

It has to start with /t/, /t/, /t/
/t/, /t/, /t/—/t/, /t/, /t/
It has to start with /t/, /t/, /t/
The next word comes from YOU!

The class first sings the song together with a teacher-chosen beginning sound; then the teacher asks a volunteer to contribute another word that begins with the target sound. To add enjoyment and an extra challenge, the words can be themed, such as all food words or all boys' names or all flowers, etc. Finally, when children are adept at discriminating beginning sounds, ending sounds can be targeted using the same song.

ACTION PHONICS

Create a 3 × 5 card file that contains action words (verbs) for every beginning consonant sound (e.g., bat for /b/; walk for /w/; wink for /w/, etc.). Introduce these words using charades for each action and allow children to copy the actions. When several words and their actions have been introduced, include "action phonics" as part of your reading lesson routine. Distribute the cards to the children. (If they are unable to recognize their word, help them to sound it out.) Invite each child to perform the charade indicated on the card while the remaining children try to guess what the action is by first stating the *word* being acted out, then the *beginning sound* of that word, and finally, the *name of the letter* that makes that sound. (Note: This is an especially effective phonemic awareness activity for English language learners, who will increase their speaking vocabulary at the same time.)

COMPARING AND CONTRASTING SOUNDS

ACTIVITY

WHAT'S THE SOUND?

Children can be given a word and asked to tell what sound occurs at the beginning, middle, and end of that word. The following song, sung to the tune of "Old MacDonald," asks children to think about the placement of sounds in words.

Beginning Sounds

What's the sound that starts these words:
PAPER, PEN, and POUND?
[wait for a response from children]
/P/ is the sound that starts these words:
PAPER, PEN, and POUND.
With a /p/, /p/, here, and a /p/, /p/, there,
Here a /p/, there a /p/, everywhere a /p/, /p/
/P/ is the sound that starts these words:
PAPER, PEN, and POUND.

Middle Sounds

What's the sound in the middle of these words:

RAIN, LAKE, and CANE?

[wait for a response]

/A/ is the sound in the middle of these words:

RAIN, LAKE, and CANE.

With an /a/, /a/, here, and an /a/, /a/ there,

Here an /a/, there an /a/, everywhere an /a/, /a/

/A/ is the sound in the middle of these words:

RAIN, LAKE, and CANE.

Ending Sounds

What's the sound at the end of these words:

NECK, ROCK, and SEEK?

[wait for a response]

/K/ is the sound at the end of these words:

NECK, ROCK, and SEEK.

With a /k/, /k/, here, and a /k/, /k/, there,

Here a /k/, there a /k/, everywhere a /k/, /k/

/K/ is the sound at the end of these words:

NECK, ROCK, and SEEK.

ACTIVITY

BLENDING SOUNDS

SECRET LANGUAGE

Prepare a list of about 30 one-syllable words containing middle or ending vowels. The first 10 should have only two speech sounds (e.g., *go* or *me*); the other 20 should have three phonemes, or speech sounds (e.g., *kite* or *chin*). Explain to children you are going to tell them some words in a secret language, and they must try to guess what you are saying. Then say the word in a stretched out manner (e.g., "ch—i—n"), and see if they are able to blend the word back into a whole unit. Note: It is sometimes helpful to use a rubber band to graphically illustrate how an item can be stretched out, then snapped back to its normal position, and be exactly the same thing.

Taking this activity to another level of difficulty, make another list of common one-syllable words of two or three phonemes in length. The words should sample a variety of sounds represented by different vowel and consonant combinations. Demonstrate once more how words can be segmented into their sound components and then invite pairs of children to say each word in the secret language for their partners to guess, as you observe individual success with this task (Griffin and Olson, 1992).

WHAT AM I THINKING OF?

Tell the class you are thinking of an object or an animal. Give them a sound clue: segment each of the sounds of the word, articulating each of the sounds slowly and deliberately. The children, then, must blend the sounds together to discover the animal or object you are thinking of. For higher motivation, and especially to make the game accessible to English language learners, the teacher may use picture cards, hiding them from the children; give the segmented clue and turn the picture around to allow them to check their answers. Finally, real toys or objects in a grab bag heighten suspense when the teacher looks into the bag and says, "I see a d—o—ll in here. Can anyone tell me what I am looking at?"

SUBSTITUTING SOUNDS   ACTIVITY

SPEECH SUBSTITUTION CHANT

A voice projection exercise used by drama students makes an excellent activity to practice consonant substitution while reinforcing a variety of vowel sounds. For this activity, the teacher has the children stand up at their desks. The leader (the teacher, initially) presents a consonant sound or blend such as /d/. Then the children project, at the top of their voices, but without shouting,

> Da day dee do doo! [repeated three times]

Another leader is chosen, who gives a different consonant sound. For example /ch/. The children chorus:

> Cha chay chee cho choo! [three times]

For musical variety, the chant can be sung using one note, raising the note for every succeeding consonant, or a simple tune can be created for the chant.

SEGMENTING SOUNDS   ACTIVITY

WHAT'S THE SOUND?

Start with beginning sound (onsets) that can be held for a long period of time, such as /m/, /s/, or /f/, or the parts of the syllable that follow the initial sound (rimes) that are very common such as /-at/, /-ock/, or /-an/. Introduce the game by saying "I am going to say some words. If you hear one that starts with /m/, show me a thumbs up sign. If it starts with any other sound, show me a thumbs down." Begin mostly with words that start with the target sound. Slowly introduce words with other initial or ending sounds. Have children then volunteer to contribute words that others either accept or reject.

Finish the game by showing children pictures of some objects that have the target sound, inviting children to help you make all the sounds (segment). Discuss similarities and differences in sounds. These pictures can be bound into a class book.

ACTIVITY   **MANIPULATING PHONEMES**

SOUND SWITCH *(FITZPATRICK, 1997)*

Gather together two sets of large alphabet cards and a wall *pocket chart* (see Figure 4.3). Distribute an alphabet card containing one letter to each child. Place letters in a pocket chart to form a simple one-syllable word (e.g., get). Point to each letter in the pocket chart and have children say each sound. Then ask children to blend the sounds together to form the word. Next invite volunteers to create new words by placing their letters over those in the pocket chart, such as placing the letter "b" over the "g" to form the word "bet." Have children blend the new sounds together and decide whether or not the word is one they know (nonsense words are acceptable). Place a new one-syllable word in the pocket chart and repeat the process.

RECOMMENDATIONS FOR TEACHING PHONEMIC AWARENESS

Phonemic awareness activities can be a first step toward reading and writing for many children, as such activities will enable children to become aware of the sounds that will later help them learn to decode; however, it is critical to make these activities motivational and appropriate to the developmental level of the learners. For this reason, I have included the following five suggestions to assure that initial instruction in phonemic awareness becomes a joyful entree into literacy.

1. For younger children, do not accompany sound activities with visual cues *if* it seems that this combination is confusing for them. While there is evidence to suggest that presenting sounds for words with their visual counterparts is helpful for children who already know the letters of the alphabet (Hohn and Ehri, 1984), children who have not yet reached this level of phonemic sophistication may be better served by concentrating just on the sound units alone (Yopp, 1995; McCracken and McCracken, 1996).

2. Make the lessons playful—a "treat," not a "treatment." Children will have a pleasurable feeling of playing with language if the activities are presented by an enthusiastic, fun-loving teacher, rather than a "drill sergeant" bent on completing exercises and performing rote memorization as quickly and efficiently as possible.

FIGURE 4.3   *A pocket chart.*

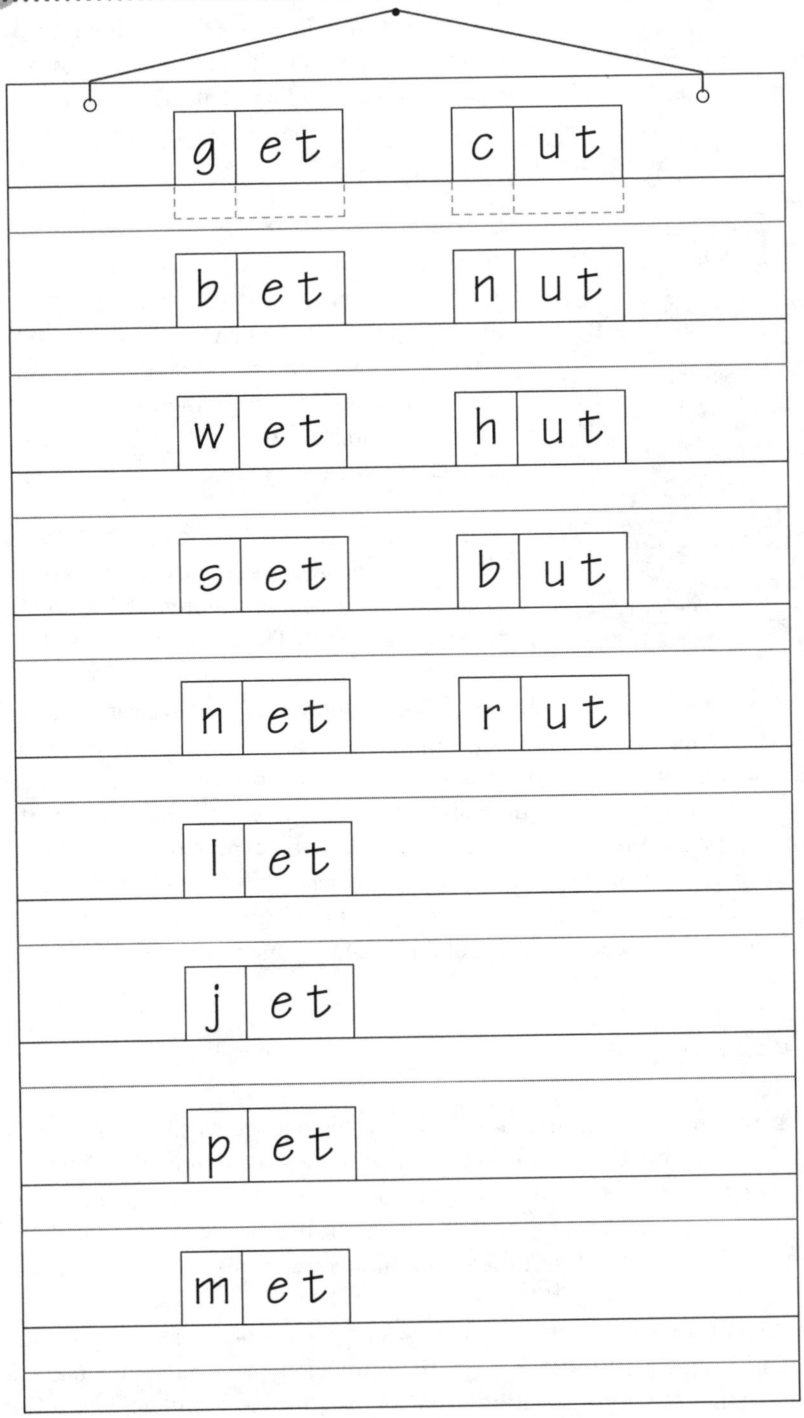

A pocket chart is a large, heavy paper, cloth, or plastic chart that has pockets into which words or sentences may be placed.

3. Encourage social interaction wherever possible. Social interactions tend to heighten language development. Therefore, invite children to learn from one another by asking them to help each other. Provide many opportunities for children to turn to a neighbor and discuss their answers, work with letters and sounds in small groups, and other team-building techniques. Make sure the environment is absolutely safe so there is never the fear of blurting out the "wrong" answer.

4. Invite children to experiment with language. When asking for rhyming words, beginning sounds, and other sound units, encourage children to manipulate the sounds and construct their own nonsensical and delightful words and humorous sounds. Demonstrate a sense of playfulness and wonder at the English language, which are infectious among children.

5. Support the self-esteem of children. If the phonemic awareness activities are conducted in group settings, some children will inevitably do better than others. Therefore, a cooperative, relaxed environment is critical—no "put-downs" from classmates are *ever* allowed! Also, children for whom hearing sounds is difficult should be given lots of support, demonstrations, and modeling to ensure they, too, have a positive language experience. Above all the teacher should allow for individual differences and realize that a tremendous amount of individual variation in hearing speech sounds is to be expected. While many children can achieve phonemic awareness by the end of first grade, not all children will do so. In time, however, with continued motivational lessons and practice, most children can become adept at this vital precursor to reading.

SUMMARY

Phonemic awareness is the bridge between spoken and written language. Some children will construct this bridge for themselves without explicit instruction, but many others will not. Lacking this bridge, written language will often remain a puzzle; children will try to figure out the puzzle only for so long before giving up on the task of learning how to read; it isn't too long before "I can't!" becomes "I won't!"

Experiences must always be provided so children can understand that reading is an activity that is undertaken for enjoyment, new understandings, and to gain desired information. But in order for that joyful activity to be accessible, learners must also be able to see how the sounds of the language are patterned into words. Extensive research over the last 30 years has supported the conclusion that phonemic awareness is the most important prerequisite to understanding the nature of the relationship between letters and sounds. Young children must therefore be exposed to experiences that invite them to blend sounds into words and to segment words into sounds before further instruction in the sound–symbol representations—phonics instruction—can take place.

Fortunately, this instruction need not be conducted through a series of repetitious workbook pages or unexciting exercises completed in isolation at the child's desk; rather, these activities can be highly motivational group activities accomplished through enjoyable language play and game-like tasks that are naturally appealing to children. While many children come to school having had much experience with language through a print- and language-rich environment in their homes, for others such activities may well bridge a gap in their language development that will ensure a bright future of success in literacy.

QUESTIONS
for Journal Writing and Discussion

1. Explain how you would describe the difference between the terms "phonemic awareness" instruction and "phonics instruction" to the parent of a child about to enter school.

2. Examine the scope and sequence of three basal readers used in area elementary schools. Determine which phonemic awareness activities are taught and when. Describe how the three series differ. Based upon your knowledge of phonemic awareness, discuss which you would prefer and why.

3. The mother of a four-year-old child asks you what she can do, besides reading aloud, to help her child become ready for kindergarten literacy instruction. What can you tell her?

SUGGESTIONS
for Projects and Other Activities

1. Look for a folk song, nursery rhyme, or camp song that would be suitable for developing a component of phonemic awareness in young children. Adapt the song as necessary. Teach the song to a small group of kindergarten children. Explain what you observed about the increased awareness of the identified sounds through this exercise.

2. Browse through some children's books in your local library without first researching which ones are recommended in the appendix of this book. With phonemic awareness in mind, identify those books that would help children develop awareness of sounds in our language. Write down the names of the books you have identified and then compare them with the ones in the appendix or other lists compiled by literacy professionals.

3. Interview two kindergarten teachers. Find out what activities they use to teach phonemic awareness to their students. If possible, observe several of these activities. Summarize your findings for your classmates.

PHONICS INSTRUCTION

Why and How

FOCUS QUESTIONS

- How does direct, systematic instruction in phonics fit into a balanced approach to literacy?

- What are the key components in a model phonics program?

- What are the most important factors to keep in mind when teaching phonics to beginning readers?

IN THE CLASSROOM

Gina has selected a book from the public library and is sitting cross-legged on the carpet, looking forward to the same enjoyment she has always experienced when she reads in class or when her grandmother reads to her. She puts a chubby finger on the cover of the book and tries to sound out the title: *The Laughing Cow.* Though she knows the beginning sound for the word *laugh* and she is able to sound out the word *cow,* the peculiar spelling of the word *laugh* makes no sense to her. Gina scratches her head and discards the book, having just received a tiny dent in self-confidence for her burgeoning reading ability.

earning to read can be a bewildering experience for children, and a confounding instructional ordeal for educators. Children become frustrated when they cannot easily figure out the words in a language that is not always "user-friendly." The task is difficult, too, because figuring out new words is an undertaking entirely different from any of a child's other previous experiences.

Literature-loving educators, on the other hand, often become disenchanted when confronted with stilted early basal readers. They are fully aware that constructing meaning from the printed page is the whole purpose of reading, and yet the material they are asked to use to teach reading, given the limited number of words young children can recognize, is not nearly as exciting as *The Laughing Cow* in the above vignette. It seems a contradiction that many children come to school knowing the meanings of most of the words to which they are exposed, yet they still cannot read because their young brains are still in the process of discovering patterns and analogies in sounds and words. They must first be provided with a compendium of decoding strategies to identify words that they do not immediately recognize; then they will be able to access the over 60,000 delightful children's books awaiting them in the public library.

The good news is there is help for both teachers and beginning readers who need to accomplish these tasks together. To learn to recognize words as quickly as possible, teachers can systematically show children the relationship between visual cues, or letters, and the speech sounds they represent. This is what the teaching of phonics is all about. After words have been identified and have been met many times, they can be recognized automatically, in much the same way as we automatically recognize an old friend or the dilapidated Honda driven by the next-door neighbor. Words that are automatically recognized are now part of a child's sight vocabulary, and further strategies for identification are no longer required for those particular words. When a child has arrived at this automatic stage with the majority of words she encounters, we can say that child has "learned to crack the code." The child can then move on to more interesting reading tasks.

WHY PHONICS INSTRUCTION?

While phonemic awareness instruction concentrates on focusing a child's attention on the way sounds are sequenced in a language, phonics instruction helps children to associate letters with those sounds. The purpose of phonics instruction is to teach beginning readers that printed letters and letter combinations represent speech sounds heard in words. In themselves the letters are meaningless squiggles. They become meaning-bearing units only when the child applies and adheres to the system of signals. In applying phonic skills, or the system of signals, to unknown words, the reader blends a series of sounds dictated by the order in which particular letters occur in the printed word. When a child is able to do that, she is able to **decode,** or unlock the code (Beck and Juel, 1995). A child needs this ability to arrive at the pronunciation of printed word symbols that are not immediately recognized. If the child does

decode

recognize the word, however, that child shouldn't need to waste time puzzling over the speech sounds represented by the individual letters.

The proper use of phonic strategies is one of a number of ways a child may figure out words he does not immediately recognize (Blevins, 1998). Phonics instruction is concerned with teaching letter-sound relationships and patterns as they relate to learning how to figure out unfamiliar written words; such careful attention to the sequence of letters in words can also contribute to spelling ability (Shefelbine, 1995). Because English spelling patterns tend to be deceptive, however, a child will sometimes arrive at only a close approximation of the needed sounds. The child may, for example, come upon the word *broad* and pronounce it so that it rhymes with *road,* or pronounce *give* so that it rhymes with *five*—both reasonable analyses of these irregular words. If the child is taught to take a flexible attitude with the sounds, however, and if the child is reading for meaning, she will frequently go back and correct these errors. After several such self-corrections, the child will not repeat the same error with these words.

Phonics instruction has long been considered a useful tool in learning how to decode automatically so that children can begin to attend to more interesting reading tasks (Adams,1990; McIntyre and Freppon, 1994; Vellutino 1991; Stanovich and Stanovich, 1995). Moreover, there exists a large body of strong and persuasive evidence to suggest that children who quickly develop efficient decoding strategies find reading enjoyable and thus read more; on the other hand, those who get off to a slow start in learning how to decode words rarely catch up to become strong readers (Stanovich, 1986). In fact, Juel (1991; 1994) asserts that children who fall behind in first grade reading have only a one-in-eight chance of ever catching up to grade level. Stanovich calls this phenomenon the "Matthew effect," where the skilled decoders get better and better through practice while poor decoders lag farther and farther behind. Though many teachers have great optimism and tend to believe

that children who fall behind will catch up in future grades, Clay (1979) concurs with Stanovich; through her own research and experience she finds that where a child is reading compared to classmates at the end of first grade is pretty much where that child will be reading compared to classmates two years later.

Phonics continues to be misunderstood by many educators. The reason for this misunderstanding becomes clear when we look closely at the language. English spelling appears to be imperfect when we look at the strange words *might, cough, should, colonel, sleigh,* and *machine;* and indeed it is challenging, for we use 26 letters to spell 44 different sounds in more than 250 different ways! This is only one side of the matter, however. If we look at all the words that are spelled regularly, and set about organizing the irregular spellings into groups and patterns suitable for beginning readers (bat, cat, pat, may; hit, bit, fit), we find that it is not so bad after all. And if we begin instruction with the most regular words, it is not overwhelming for most children to master the exceptions when they are introduced one at a time and continually reinforced. The following statistics support this belief:

Approximately 50 percent of English words are regular;

Another 37 percent have only one sound that is represented irregularly, and getting close is usually enough to connect the written letters and sounds with the actual word;

The remaining 13 percent (like the word *ocean*) must be memorized as sight words;

Even irregular words are stored in memory with the letter or letter pattern/sound correspondences (e.g., *light*).

This brings us to what may at first glance seem a startling contradiction: The "un-phonic" spelling of so many common words constitutes the strongest argument for beginning formal instruction with the regular phonics of English spelling! Why? Simply because if our spelling system is regular a good percentage of the time, it would seem logical to begin with the regular system before taking up the exceptions. When the child learns, at the beginning, one consistent pattern after another, he rapidly gains understanding of the code—and confidence. If we were to teach a dozen words only by using rote memorization, or by the sight–word method, a child may still confuse *but* and *got;* but when he has been taught all the sounds of the letters, he understands why these particular series of letters spell each word. His recognition of the two words at a glance becomes easier than it would have been if he had memorized each word using only word configuration, without the benefit of previous training in letter sounds. The sight–word method of rote memorization may be appropriate for teaching only those high-frequency words that cannot be easily sounded out, sometimes referred to as "snurks" (see p. 80).

BEGINNING PHONICS INSTRUCTION

The first few weeks of formal phonics instruction can have some rather remarkable results. Through all the previous reading experiences the child may have had, she may have met many words she did not instantly recognize, and at various times may have tried one or more of the following strategies:

- skipped the word
- asked someone
- guessed the word
- applied any phonics rules she knew
- sounded out the first letter and then guessed the rest of the word
- tried to figure out the word from the context

Clearly, the beginning reader has many available options for figuring out unknown words. Some of these—such as random guessing—are not always the most efficient choices. Learning to read, then, involves sorting through a cafeteria of choices and discarding ones that are ineffective for the situation while using others that will allow for success. To make maximum progress, the beginning reader must acquire three closely related skills at approximately the same time as discussed in Chapter 1:

- Using letter/sound relationships
- Acquiring a sight vocabulary of immediately recognized words
- Gaining meaning from context

Essential to early reading instruction is teaching children how to crack the code, learning to associate printed letters with the speech sounds they represent. Everything in spoken English can be printed using only 26 different letter symbols. This is possible because, in general, letter and letter combinations stand for the same speech sounds in thousands of different words. Although there is not always a one-to-one correspondence between letters seen and speech sounds represented, learning to read is facilitated when a child has an understanding of the sound/spelling relationship in English.

Beginning readers read words in four ways: by sight (memorization), by sounding out each letter, by **analog** (comparing patterns to ones already known), and by guessing from the context (Gaskins et al., 1997). To illustrate how this word learning works, let's focus on what the child gains by learning one spelling/sound relationship. Assume that the child has already been taught through phonemic awareness exercises to:

analog

- visually recognize the letter "m"
- associate /m/ with the sound it represents at the beginning of the words *mat, man,* and *mud*
- differentiate the /m/ sound in *man* from the /p/ in *pan* and the /c/ in *can*

Phonics instruction then invites the child to become a "word detective," or to think to himself in the following way when encountering the unfamiliar word *marker:*

> When I see the letter *m* I think of the /m/ sound because this is the same sound that begins the words *mat* and *mud.* It ends with an *er* just like in *mother* and *father.* The middle of the word has an *ark,* just like the middle of the word *bark.* The word must be *marker,* a word I have heard before. Yes, it must be, because it's talking about art and drawing, so that makes sense.

Though this process may seem unreasonably slow and tedious, remember that such thoughts go through a child's mind much more quickly than we can read about the phenomenon! As subsequent instruction focuses on other sounds represented by medial vowels and vowel combinations, the child gains new skills that enable her to decode other unfamiliar words, each skill mastered providing a greater degree of independence and automaticity, or fluency, in reading. The critical point to keep in mind is the eventual goal—to make the decoding process almost second nature so that children can expend much more of their time and energy thinking about and enjoying the material they are reading.

Every new gain the child makes in learning to read will, with sufficient practice, transfer to future authentic reading situations. For instance, after several weeks of early instruction, a child will have encountered some words so frequently that she will recognize them instantly. Once this happens, she will never again have to puzzle over the speech sounds represented by those words. Similarly, with much exposure to reading words that incorporate new phonics patterns to which she has been introduced, she will now be capable of detecting and using the pattern for other, similar words (Heilman, 1997).

APPROACHES TO SOUNDING OUT WORDS

Research has shown that direct, systematic teaching of phonics elements is more effective than the "hit-or-miss" variety that was once taught only incidentally, when phonics elements happened to be encountered in reading and writing situations (Shefelbine, 1995). With much modeling of the following process, children can be taught how to sound out unfamiliar words using phonics. The teacher of emergent readers should start with one and two regular words (never snurks) that contain the sound and use this approach several times every day, using this or a similar script:

> Listen. When I say a letter, I'll say its sound. I'll keep saying its sound until I touch the next letter. I won't stop between sounds.
> [Example: Saaaaat or Mmmmmaaaaaannnnnnn.]
>
> My turn to sound out this word.
> [Put a finger under continuous sounds for 1¹/₂ seconds and under stops (words that are *not* continuous, such as /b/, /c/, /d/) for just an instant.]
>
> Now you sound out this word with me. Get ready.
> [Touch each sound and say with children.]
>
> Your turn. Sound out this word by yourselves. Get ready.
> [Touch the word and let children make the sound.]
>
> [Encourage individual children to try it with new words.]

As children are able to blend together two and three sounds to make a word, they are ready to tackle more difficult blending tasks through phonics and analog. Although such strategies should be continually modeled incidentally whenever new words are written on the board, they should also be taught directly by explaining the use of the following approaches:

- Make the first sound. Add the second sound. Put them together before adding the third sound.
  Example: "p," "pa," *pan.*

- Make the first sound and add the **rime.**

  Example: "b," "oat," *boat.*

- Look at the rime first and put it together backwards.

  Example: "eam," "dr," *dream.*

- Identify the word parts you know.

  Example: "re," "turn," "ing" equals *returning.*

- Ask yourself: What do I know about this word?

- Ask yourself: Do I know any word that looks like this word or any part of it? Does this word make sense?

rime

A SEQUENCE FOR TEACHING PHONICS

A phonics program consists of many specific concepts. In any systematic program, the necessary compendium of skills have to be arranged in a teaching sequence that allows the young reader to build confidently on what he already knows. Figure 5.1 presents one possible sequence for teaching phonic skills (Rinsky, 1993).

TEACHING HIGH-FREQUENCY WORDS

As children begin learning how to read, they must be taught some common sight vocabulary words known as **"high-frequency words"** at the same time they are learning how to decode. High-frequency words include *both* very widespread "snurk" words, such as "the," that are easily confused (see Figure 5.2) and that children should not attempt to decode while reading, nor try to "invent" while writing, and easily decodable words such as "but." It is estimated that 50 percent of the words children see are from the 100 to 150 words in the "high-frequency word" group (see Appendix F).

Become very familiar with a list of high-frequency words, such as the Fry's 600 Instant Word List (see Appendix F) so that you can select meaningful words for classroom activities. Plan activities that focus directly on the words repeatedly, introducing one or two new words each day and reinforce through games, daily stories, and "words of the week." Incorporate new words into reading and writing activities on successive days for review. Each week, the cumulative words should be reviewed.

Abstract words are usually more difficult for children to learn than concrete words, especially for English language learners. It is important, therefore, to help children associate these words with something meaningful. For example, when teaching the word *of,* one might provide pictures of a piece *of* pie, a box *of* cookies, and label the pictures. The children would then be asked to

- Find or draw their own pictures and label them.
- Chant or cheer the word (e.g., *of! of! of!*).
- Write the word.

FIGURE 5.1 *A phonics sequence.*

. . . .

KINDERGARTEN

Begin phonemic awareness training during kindergarten and include sounds with and without letters, beginning with consonant sounds; introduce blending and segmentation skills; introduce a few high frequency sight words; introduce onsets and rimes with a few short vowels. Start with the letters that are dissimilar, the most useful, and introduce the lowercase letters first. An acceptable sequence is:

m, t, a, s, i, f, d, r, o, g, l, h, u, c, b, n, k, v, e, w, j, p, y,

T, L, M, F, D, I, N, A, R, H, G, B, x, q, z, J, E

FIRST GRADE

Review consonants and vowels and letter combinations and introduce useful rules: endings (ing, er, s), consonant digraphs (two letters that cannot be separated): sh, ch, th, wh, ph; blending and segmentation skills reinforced, frequently used sight words, the final "e" rule, consonant blends (two consonants that can be separated): fl, fr, sl, sm, sn, sw, sc, sk, sp, sq, st; then bl, br, cl, cr, dr, gl, gr, pl, pr, tr, tw; then scr, spl, spr, str; the "ed" ending; then vowel digraphs (*ai, ay, ee, ea, igh, oa, ow, ew, oo, ow, ou, oi, oy, au,* and *aw*), r-controlled vowels (*ar, er, ir, ur,* and *or*), transformations of open and closed syllables (*me* becomes *met; go* becomes *got*) and generalizations for "y" at the end of a word.

SECOND GRADE

Complete highest frequency words; review and complete single-syllable phonics patterns, then generalizations for *c* and *g* at ends of words; silent consonant clusters: *kn, wr, gn, mb, ght, ng, nk, tch;* continue word parts (prefixes and suffixes; root words) and dividing words into word parts or syllables.

THIRD GRADE

Reinforce syllabication, word parts, and introduce word derivatives (e.g., *interrogative* comes from the word *interrogate*).

. . . .

Source: Lee Ann Rinsky. *Teaching Word Recognition Skills.* Scottsdale, AZ: Gorsuch Scarisbrick, 1993. Used with permission of the author.

word wall

Finally, four or five words would be selected from the reading each week and added to a **word wall** or bulletin board in the classroom (see the box below and Figure 5.3). These words can be connected by meaning, patterns, sounds, or simply can be words that children hear and want to know how to spell. The words should be placed alphabetically by the first letter. Easily confusable

FIGURE 5.2 *Common snurks (sight words) for early readers.*

give	woman	word
the	saw	there
what	love	work
of	any	laugh
walk	some	great
to	was	choose
because	does	pear

Word walls

A word wall or word chart is a listing of high-frequency words that are of particular interest to children or are currently being studied in a reading lesson. Such words usually follow a specific pattern in their beginning sounds (onsets), vowel sounds, or endings (rimes); other times they are words related to the same topic under study. This collection of words can be alphabetized or placed under the corresponding letter of the alphabet. The words should be prominently displayed on the wall or on a bulletin board so that the children may add to the list whenever they think of an appropriate word, and they can also be used for reference during writing activities. These words should be practiced a few minutes each day at the beginning of a word lesson by having the children (1) stretch them out and read them together; (2) chant or cheer them three times; and/or (3) write them in isolation and in context. Also, all words having the same spelling patterns should be starred (Cunningham and Cunningham, 1997).

There is no one way to set up a word wall, but it should contain these features:

- The wall used should be the wall the children can see most easily when they write.
- The word wall should be dynamic. New words should go up and old ones should come down on a regular basis.
- Children should be encouraged to use the word wall as a resource when they are trying to sound out a word.

FIGURE 5.3 *A word wall inspired by discussion of five senses.*

Taste	Look	Smell	Feel	Sound
sweet	dirty	flowery	smooth	squeaky
yummy	round	nasty	rough	loud
sour	pretty	stinky	slimy	soft
yucky	red		dry	
	nice		bumpy	

words (e.g., *that, what*) can be placed on different colored paper. The following is a list of activities to use with these word walls (Cunningham, 1991):

- Ask children to use the word wall to find a word that rhymes with the word you say.
- Write the first letter you are thinking of on the board. Say a sentence, leaving out a word that begins with that letter. Have them find the word on the word wall and then chant the answer together.
- Dictate a simple sentence using word wall words.
- Play "Be a Mind Reader." Give several clues to the word you are thinking of. Clues should be based on the meaning or function of the word, or on the phonic elements. The first clue is always, "It's one of the words on the word wall." Each clue should narrow down the possibilities until the last clue has been given and every child can guess the word.

A MODEL PHONICS PROGRAM

Direct phonics instruction with decodable text is a critical component of a reading and writing program during the early grades, but it is also important that children are involved in authentic reading, writing, speaking, and listening activities as they are acquiring the tools for cracking the code. Without this rich glimpse of literacy, phonics instruction is often ineffective (Freppon and Dahl, 1991). Good teachers use direct, systematic (explicit) but also indirect (embedded or implicit) methods to impart knowledge about decoding words. For example, teachers may use short **minilessons** (5–8 minutes) to introduce specific concepts, skills, and phonic generalizations in a systematic way. These lessons also take advantage of **"teachable moments"** that can occur in any print-rich classroom as they crop up during the day, providing indirect instruction in decoding through vehicles such as language play, story writing, the language experience approach (see Chapter 9), or word walls. In general, an effective phonics program consists of all the following components (Stahl, 1992; Trachtenburg, 1990):

minilessons

teachable moments

Phonemic awareness

Teachers reinforce children's understanding of the way sounds form words in our language by having those children who need this reinforcement segment, or break words into their component sounds, and having them blend sounds into words through activities where they can try to discover how to sound out new words.

Useful phonics generalizations

Teachers teach the phonics concepts, patterns, and generalizations that have the most consistency and utility in helping children decode and spell unfamiliar words. It is best to teach these rules by showing children the pattern and having them tell what is analogous about the words through word sorting activities (Ehri and Robbins, 1992). The 18 phonics generalizations that have been shown to be most useful to children are presented in Figure 5.4 (Clymer, 1963; Baer, 1999).

Whole-part-whole instructional sequence

To make sure children get the phonics support they need but also understand how these skills are useful to them, teachers use the reading of quality literature (the whole) teach phonic concepts in isolation (the part) and then have children apply these elements immediately into decodable text, or text that incorporates all the elements with which children are familiar (the second whole).

FIGURE 5.4 *Eighteen useful phonics generalizations.*

1. An *r* gives the preceding vowel a sound that is neither long nor short.
2. Words having double *e* usually have the long *e* sound.
3. In *ay* the *y* is silent and gives *a* its long sound.
4. When *y* is the final letter in a word, it usually has a vowel sound.
5. When *c* and *h* are next to each other, they make only one sound.
6. *Ch* is usually pronounced as it is in *kitchen*, *catch*, and *chair*, not like *sh*.
7. When *c* is followed by *e* or *i*, the sound of *s* is likely to be heard.
8. When the letter *c* is followed by *o* or *a*, the sound of *k* is likely to be heard.
9. When *ght* is seen in a word, the *gh* is silent.
10. When two of the same consonants are side by side, only one is heard.
11. When a word ends in *ck*, it has the same last sound as in *look.*
12. In most two-syllable words, the first syllable is accented.
13. If *a, in, re, ex, de,* or *be* is in the first syllable in a word, it is usually unaccented.
14. In most two-syllable words that end in a consonant followed by a *y*, the first syllable is accented and the last syllable is unaccented.
15. If the last syllable of a word ends in *le*, the consonant preceding the *le* usually begins the last syllable.
16. When the first vowel element in a word is followed by *ch, th,* or *sh*, these symbols are not broken when the word is divided into syllables and may go with either the first or second syllable.
17. When there is one *e* in a word that ends in a consonant, that *e* usually has a short sound.
18. When the last syllable is the sound *r*, it is unaccented.

Minilessons

Teachers can use short, directed lessons to clearly present concepts about phonics generalizations and skills to those children who, through observation and other forms of assessment, appear to require it. They can then offer opportunities for children to apply these new skills in reading and writing situations.

Application of phonics skills

Through a variety of enjoyable activities such as word play, journal writing (see Chapter 9), word sorts (Chapter 6), the building of word walls, rhyming books (see Appendix A), and sound matching exercises (Chapter 4), children reinforce what they are learning about phonics concepts and generalizations.

Use of different types of literature

Three types of literature are necessary for an effective early literacy program:

predictable texts

Predictable texts. **Predictable texts** contain much rhyme, rhythm, and repetition and are used to teach concepts of print, English grammar, and to provide an enjoyable language experience when read to young children. While they have a critical role in a balanced reading program, they should not be used for direct phonics instruction. With such texts, children delight in trying to predict, or "guess" words, thus delaying the acquisition of important phonic skills. (See Appendix A for a list of predictable books suitable for beginning readers.)

trade books

High quality trade books. High quality **trade books** are used to build academic knowledge K–12, vocabulary, and enjoyment. There should be a variety of both fiction and nonfiction trade books available. For early literacy instruction, teachers should always read such literature aloud to children and discuss it to encourage listening comprehension and enjoyment.

decodable texts

Decodable texts. **Decodable texts** are small, beginner-oriented books used to immediately apply phonics elements just taught and needing practice. They provide struggling novices with easy textual experiences because they contain plenty of repetition and fewer complex patterns than trade books (Cole, 1998). Good decodable texts also use many high frequency words that become sight words (see Appendix A).

Teachable moments. Teachers often give spontaneous phonics lessons as they engage children in literacy lessons prompted by questions children ask about strange words or alliterative sounds, and as they model how to spell the words that come up in brainstorming sessions leading to writing activities.

Teaching a phonics lesson

While the sequence shown earlier in Figure 5.1 tells *what* to teach *when,* it gives very little information about *how* to structure a phonics lesson. It might therefore be useful to explain how to orchestrate a phonics lesson by describing how one first grade teacher, Mrs. Rodgers, designs a typical reading lesson that includes an exemplary phonics component.

1. REREAD YESTERDAY'S STORY FROM A CHART OR FROM A DECODABLE BOOK (1–2 MINUTES)

Children read chorally or in pairs the short story that was introduced on the preceding day. That story allows children to apply a new letter–sound combination immediately in a real reading situation. This **repeated reading** of the story affords deeper comprehension for the child and a chance for the teacher to revisit the story for differing purposes.

2. LEARN A NEW LETTER–SOUND COMBINATION (1 MINUTE EVERY OTHER DAY)

Mrs. Rodgers writes the new letter–sound combination /sp/ on the board with a directional arrow underneath. She points under the letters and pauses. Then she moves her finger under the letters and says the sound. Then she says, "I'll say it again" and repeats the sequence. Next she says, "Now say it with me." She points under the letters and pauses. She says, "Ready?" as she quickly moves her finger under the letters. The children say the blend with her. Then she says, "Your turn." She repeats the process while children look at the letter–sound combination and say the sound.

3. REVIEW ACTIVITY (2 MINUTES)

These first-graders have finished learning about each of the short vowel sounds; they can now identify and write each one. Mrs. Rodgers shows the children pictures of the following five items to remind them of the short vowel sounds: half an apple, yellow jello, an inch of licorice, a lollipop, and bubble gum. (Each child was given one of each of these food items to eat when they were originally introduced.) The children cheerfully chant the names of each of these food items, exaggerating the vowel sounds in each case. As the food items are shown and the names called out, the teacher asks the children to help her sound out the words as she writes them on the board. For each sound, the children then brainstorm some other words that contain these sounds.

4. ORAL BLENDING AND SEGMENTATION (2–3 MINUTES)

Mrs. Rodgers leads this activity in a very direct yet playful way. The activities in this part of the lesson are carefully sequenced with a great deal of support for the children. Using a cake mixing analogy, Mrs. Rodgers introduces the consonant blend *sp.* She has written each of the two letters on small squares of white construction paper. She takes the *s* paper and drops it into a bowl, as the children watch and make the /s/ sound; she does the same for the *p* paper. She then pretends to "stir" these two consonants telling the children to "stir and say" the sounds. Then she dramatically plucks a third paper from the bowl that contains both the letters *sp.* The children say /sp/. The teacher has graphically demonstrated that a blend is two consonant sounds blended together. Children then practice the blending by holding their arms

(continued)

FIGURE 5.5 *Stirring the blend.*

in a bowl shape on their desks. With their writing finger, they then trace each consonant inside their "bowl." They then pull their finger across the letters combining, or blending, the sounds. Mrs. Rodgers then invites them to "stir and say," and they make the /sp/ sound several times (see Figure 5.5).

5. INSTRUCTION IN BLENDING (2–3 MINUTES)

This component is considered the "heart and soul" of any phonics instruction. Children must be taught how to blend sounds together by seeing and hearing the blending process modeled explicitly. Mrs. Rodgers has several words written on her pocket chart in the reading corner of her classroom. These words, for encoding and decoding, include: *spot, spin, sped, spill,* and *spam.* She says the words aloud, slowly and deliberately, while showing them to the children. Then she writes the onsets on the board and asks for the children's help in providing the last few letters, or the rime. Individual children are asked to come up to the board and sound out the last letters of the word while blending it orally.

6. HIGH-FREQUENCY SPELLING (2–4 MINUTES)

Mrs. Rodgers follows this sequence to help children learn and remember high-frequency sight words:

- The children spell the word orally: w–a–s
- The children read the word: *was*
- The children spell the word on their boards: w–a–s
- The children do a "word cheer": Was! Was! Was!

Mrs. Rodgers also conducts a review of some other high frequency sight words that have been already been taught—*the,* and *eat.* These words are then written on a word wall or laminated and put on a word ring so the words can be practiced and reviewed in enjoyable games.

7. WRITING AND SPELLING (3–5 MINUTES A DAY)

The children in Mrs. Rodgers' class each write on their individual chalkboards (see Figure 5.6), and they also have their own chalk and a worn-out sock to be used as an eraser. They sit on the floor or at tables for the dictation activity. The children love the chalkboards. Writing with chalk is very tactile; children can actually feel the letters as they write and can correct mistakes or poor letter formations with the help of an old sock. Mrs. Rodgers asks the children to make four panels on their chalkboards and then shows them how to draw three lines in each panel.

She chooses a spelling pattern from the decodable text the children are reading and orally stretches out the blended sounds for the word *mmmmmmeeeeennnnnnnn.* She asks the children to help her stretch out the word. Next she asks them, "What is the first sound you hear?" and the children reply, "/m/." She tells them to write that sound on the first line on their chalkboards. Mrs. Rodgers and the class stretch out

(continued)

FIGURE 5.6 *Individual chalkboard with four panels.*

the word again *mmmmmmmeeeennnn*. She then asks, "What sound do you hear in the middle of the word?" The children chant, "/e/." Mrs. Rodgers repeats this process with the ending sound of the word, and soon the children have written the entire word on their chalkboards. She follows this same procedure with three more words.

8. READING (10–15 MINUTES)

The children in Mrs. Rodgers' class love to read, and the classroom is stocked with plenty of books that contain lots of words containing the sounds they are learning, as well as the high frequency words with which they are already familiar. Now the teacher does a guided reading of their current decodable basal text, enthusiastically discussing pictures with children, who follow along or track, in their books, predicting what might happen next. Tomorrow the children will read the same book with their

"reading buddies," with one child summarizing the key points of the page that the other child has just read, and then changing roles after every page. When the children are finished reading, they return to the carpet. One child in each pair summarizes the story they have read for the other children in the class.

Mrs. Rodgers listens to each child read every day, jotting down brief notes about the observed difficulties and successes of her learners. She also spends time during the day reading high quality literature which the children love to listen to and discuss.

9. JOURNALS AND EXTRA HELP (10–15 MINUTES)

At this time of the school year (March) most children are working independently in their writing journals. Mrs. Rodgers has written a sentence stem on the board:

I like to _____. But I don't like to _____.

(continued)

This is an excellent time for the children to experiment with the way print works by freely writing their thoughts and feelings. (See Chapter 9 for more information about journals.) They are invited to use temporary spelling, or "invented" spelling, to sound out words they do not know. Mrs. Rodgers goes around to each child, encouraging their attempts and praising their efforts. She often shows them the next step in their own emerging literacy odyssey; for example, Hector, a very advanced reader and writer, asks her, "Mrs. Rodgers, is this right?" Hector has written "I like to go to the post ofis." Mrs. Rodgers replies, "That is exactly the way the word *sounds,* Hector; you did a terrific job sounding it out. This is the way it *looks* in print." Then the teacher proceeds to write the word correctly in pencil for Hector to copy. Because children are working independently, Mrs. Rodgers also takes this time to give some learners extra help they need.

TALK-TO-YOURSELF CHART (REINFORCED DAILY)

A large chart is prominently displayed in Mrs. Rodger's classroom (see Figure 5.7). This chart helps children self-assess their ability to read and spell new words. This procedure has six steps which are read and reviewed with children on a daily basis (adapted from Gaskins et al., 1997):

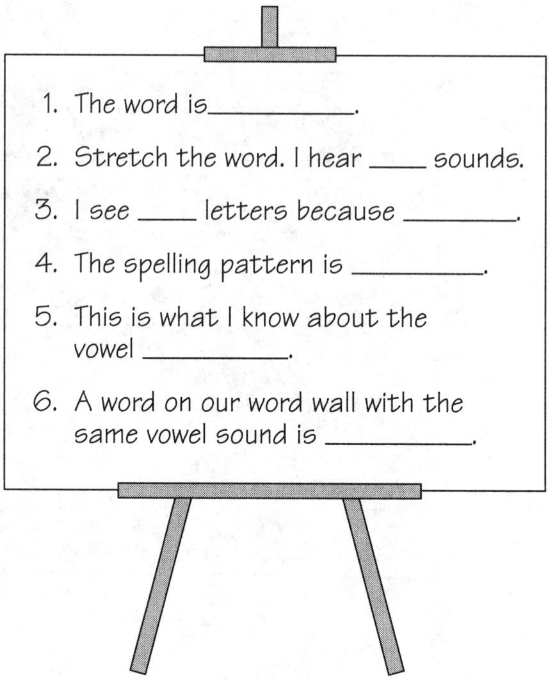

USE OF TECHNOLOGY

Small groups of the children in Mrs. Rodgers' class read **interactive electronic books** on CD–ROM independently while she is working with other groups; the groups rotate until all have had an opportunity to read the book on the computer. With these programs, available from Scholastic, Tom Snyder Productions, Computer

FIGURE 5.7 *A talk-to-yourself chart.*

1. The word is_____.
2. Stretch the word. I hear _____ sounds.
3. I see _____ letters because _____.
4. The spelling pattern is _____.
5. This is what I know about the vowel _____.
6. A word on our word wall with the same vowel sound is _____.

Curriculum Corporation, Broderbund, and others, the text and illustrations are displayed page by page on the computer screen and appropriate music accompanies each program. Children who are capable of doing so read the book themselves while the computer identifies unfamiliar words or reinforces specific sounds. The children can also choose to track along while the computer reads, making it ideal for every ability level.

Guidelines for selecting interactive books

1. Make sure the software is compatible with your computer.

2. Choose quality literature in the same way you would choose exemplary books to read aloud to children.

(continued)

3. Look for helpful accompanying activities, such as journal questions and opportunities for children to write their own books.

4. Always preview software before buying it.

HOME CONNECTION (AFTER SCHOOL)

Mrs. Rodgers makes up **parent packets** containing cards of any new, high frequency words that have been introduced during the day; today's words are *sp* words. She also sends home a decodable book for children to reread containing words the child can easily decode with the skills that have been introduced and mastered thus far in class. Again, the repeated reading for parents deepens comprehension while reinforcing high frequency words and phonic elements that have been introduced. Children will be expected to read the materials in the packet to a parent or caretaker at home, or even an older brother or sister, to receive the additional practice that will help them on the road to becoming a fluent reader. When this has been accomplished, the child asks the adult or older sibling to sign a form saying the reading has been completed. Then the child returns the packet to the teacher.

Mrs. Rodgers finds this communication with parents to be a boost to the growth of her students and a way to let parents know what is happening in class and to assist in a positive way. (See Chapter 12 for a sample parent packet.)

INSTRUCTIONAL STRATEGIES TO KEEP IN MIND

There are a few important constraints that should always be considered when a teacher is planning a phonics lesson. Such behaviors and practices are compatible with exemplary phonics instruction. Though some have been mentioned briefly earlier in the chapter, they are worth discussing here.

- *Make sure children possess the necessary prerequisites in phonemic awareness for the letter–sound correspondence being introduced.* If children are not able to hear the sequence of sounds in words, training in phonics will be a frustrating and futile experience for them. Therefore, a careful assessment of the phonemic awareness abilities of each of your learners is vital to any successful phonics program (see phonemic awareness assessment devices in Appendix D). If certain children are deficient in this area, they may be regrouped and should receive special phonemic awareness training.

- *Always base phonics lessons on the prior knowledge children already have about print.* Children come to us with a variety of language and literacy backgrounds. Some children may have a wide repertoire of rap songs they can chant; others have heard the entire collection of Dr. Seuss books. Being aware of the particular background knowledge of your learners can be a great place to connect, create discussions, and begin instruction (Stahl, 1992).

- *Focus children's attention on detecting patterns, not memorizing rules.* The human brain is a detector of patterns, not an applier of rules (Cunningham, 1995). Therefore, any phonics lesson should direct children's attention to the letter sequences and particular letter combinations that are similar to ones they already know and to the ones in the words being introduced. By contrast, phonics rules are abstract, and though children may memorize them, true application requires a stage of development at which most young children have not arrived.

- *Provide plenty of opportunities for children to experiment with print through use of invented spelling.* Experimenting freely with the way sounds and letters go together in our language is an excellent way for children to reinforce their understanding of and familiarity with the alphabetic principle and how it works (Stahl, 1992).

- *Be sure that teaching of new letter–sound correspondences is done explicitly and clearly.* Phonics instruction that is direct and clear is characterized by the teacher isolating a particular sound or combination of sounds and showing the child how the sound(s) is associated with a particular letter or combination of letters. Such instruction also includes showing the child exactly how to blend those sounds together through teacher modeling and then with guided practice by the child.

- *Provide immediate practice with newly taught letter–sound correspondences with decodable text that contains the new letter patterns.* Like any other skill that is being learned, automatic application of phonics skills will not flourish without consistent practice. Therefore, children should be given immediate practice reading materials containing words with the new phonics elements to which they have been introduced; however, avoid stilted, contrived decodable material that is limited in motivational appeal (e.g., The fat cat sat on the mat.) Also, be sure quality children's literature is used for reading aloud to children and for building listening comprehension at many times throughout the day.

- *Focus on achieving automatic word recognition skills so children can soon concentrate more on comprehension and enjoyment.* Teach the strategies for children to use when encountering an unknown word that were delineated on pages 78–79. Also, show children what *you* do when encountering a new word by modeling chunking, use of affixes, and comparing patterns in the unknown word to patterns in known words.

- *Integrate phonics instruction into a total, joyful reading program.* Phonics instruction is only a small part of reading instruction, and the least exciting part at that. Phonics should never be considered a goal in and of itself, but rather a functional *means* to a goal. The ultimate goal of reading instruction should always be to allow children to easily decode the words that they encounter so they can not only begin to read for academic purposes, but also experience the joy of a most worthwhile pastime (Adams, 1991). An exemplary reading program will include not only phonics instruction, to help children to learn to read, but also a variety of highly motivational reading and writing strategies and activities associated with outstanding examples of children's literature, so that children will want to pursue reading far beyond the classroom doors.

SUMMARY

Phonics instruction can be a vital component of an effective literacy program for early readers. Without any direct instruction in this component of a comprehensive reading program, children's strategies are limited to guessing at words by their general shape and using clues from illustrations and surrounding words to assist them. Knowing the sounds that letters and letter-combinations make is a useful addition to these strategies. Although the specious nature of the English language makes learning the alphabetic code seem confusing at times, there are sufficient words with regular patterns to make instruction in sound–letter correspondence useful for most learners.

Phonics mastery should not be considered an end in itself but rather, the means to an end. The ultimate goal of teaching a child strategies to figure out new words is always to create an enthusiastic learner who loves to read, and does so joyfully, in and outside of school. Because this is true, phonics instruction should always be as brief as possible and be immediately followed by easily decodable text that shows children the reason for such instruction. Above all, phonics instruction must take place within the framework of a total reading program that also includes numerous opportunities to experiment with written language and to share appealing children's literature with the teacher and classmates. The following chapters will contain strategies to help teachers instill a love of reading in their learners.

QUESTIONS
for Journal Writing and Discussion

1. Many words in the English language are not spelled regularly. Present a case for beginning formal reading instruction with the regular phonics of English spelling. Why is this not the contradiction it appears to be?

2. Create a list of ten decodable words that could ideally be taught using a phonics method. Make another list of ten irregular words that might be introduced by asking children to pay careful attention to their visual pecu-

liarities. What would you tell children about the differences between these two types of words?

3. Why might a beginning reader naturally confuse the letters "p," "b," "q," and "d"? Before undertaking the task of reading, what other activities, if any, might have demanded the same attention to directionality? How would you explain this letter confusion to parents who are convinced their child has a severe letter orientation problem, such as dyslexia?

SUGGESTIONS
for Projects and Other Activities

1. Imagine having to learn to read the following printed message:

   3#^ *##^ %#^#* ^%+^##^ %^^%^# *^^*##.

   Prepare a list of information and skills that would make this task possible. Prioritize your list so that a teacher might know which skills to teach first, next, and so forth. Share your list with your college class and defend the order of the introduction of skills.

2. Show a beginning reader at least ten food labels and ask the child to read them. Record each answer. Ask the child to explain how he arrived at the answer. Discuss each word with respect to how the child responded and why.

3. Create a minilesson for first grade children encouraging them to think of key words. You may want to use themes such as scary words, funny words, exciting words, or sad words. Teach this lesson to a small group of first-graders, having them help you sound out every word they contribute. When a word is not spelled exactly as it sounds, demonstrate to the children that a word can *sound* one way but *look* another. Put the words on a word wall and see which ones they remember in future visits.

SPELLING

Developing Letter–Sound Correspondence

FOCUS QUESTIONS

- Why is it important for classroom teachers to be able to identify in their pupils the stages of spelling development?

- What are the important components of an effective spelling program?

- How can temporary, or "invented," spelling be used to help children understand the alphabetic principle?

IN THE CLASSROOM

Chrissy, a child in the third month of first grade, has just drawn an elaborate picture of a princess in an especially ornate ball gown surrounded by a swarthy prince, an adoring fairy godmother, and a lake full of swans. Ms. Sullivan, after offering profuse praise for the effort Chrissy has put into her creation, asks the child if she would like to label the characters in her picture. Chrissy shakes her head vehemently, sighing, "I don't know how to write. Can you write it for me?" Ms. Sullivan smiles and urges, "Just have a go. What is the first sound you hear in *Cinderella?*" Chrissy scratches her head and hisses *S,s,s* and then laboriously pens an *s* and, later, an *n*. Chrissy is well on her way toward making the discovery that English writing is an alphabetic system in which letters are used to indicate speech sounds and, subsequently, meaning. She is just beginning to learn how to spell—and read and write.

Chrissy and very young children like her are engaged in temporary, or invented, spelling that, when carefully analyzed, can tell teachers much about the developmental stages of writing and how beginning readers and writers develop important aspects of the English sound system.

THE STAGES OF SPELLING DEVELOPMENT

There is a synchrony in learning to read, write, and spell. Development in one area generally coincides with advances in the other two areas. All three evolve in stage-like progressions that share important conceptual dimensions (Bear, 1991). Children give evidence of learning to spell by advancing through a sequence of increasingly complex understandings about the organizational patterns of words. Although memory is involved, children learn by progressively inferring the principles by which English words are spelled (Schlagel and Schlagel, 1992). A growing body of research has revealed that knowledge of letter patterns, or orthographic knowledge, develops as a process in children and that this development is reflected in their errors, or in their invented spelling (Gill and Scharer, 1996).

developmental spelling stages

In learning to communicate in written form, a child generally goes through five basic **developmental spelling stages** (discussed below) in roughly the same sequence, despite differences in educational background, although it is not uncommon for a child to evidence elements of two or more of these stages in her writing at any one time. It should be noted, however, that rate of progress through the stages varies from child to child.

The Precommunicative Stage

precommunicative stage

The initial stage of spelling development is called the **precommunicative stage** and occurs about the time the child learns the alphabet and makes the discovery that words are composed of letters, although the child may have little or no concept at this time of exactly which letter stands for which sound. In this stage, the young child strings scribbles, letters, and letter-like forms together without any particular knowledge of associated phonemes, and the writing may proceed from top to bottom and right to left, or even randomly across the page. A child at this stage might compose a story about an elephant and, to our eyes, the story will be virtually unintelligible and look something like the writing shown in Figure 6.1(a).

The Prephonetic, or Preliterate, Stage

The second stage of spelling development is called the **prephonetic stage** and evolves when the child begins to understand the alphabetic principle, or that letters have certain sounds which form words. About this time, too, the child becomes aware of the left-to-right orientation of the English language. This particular stage is somewhat like the stage in very young children's language acquisition when they use one word to symbolize a whole idea or concept, such as "Up!" to mean "I would like you to pick me up, Daddy." Similarly in this stage, one letter, which is usually the most dominant sound, will be used to represent the entire word. In the previously addressed story about an elephant, a child in this more advanced stage might represent the word elephant with an "L," because the name of the letter "L" sounds most like the beginning of the word "elephant." The story might look like the writing in Figure 6.1(b).

prephonetic stage

The Phonetic, or Letter Name, Stage

The third stage, the **phonetic stage,** is in many ways a refinement of the earlier alphabetic principle stage. Children continue to use letter names to represent sounds but they also use consonant and vowel sounds for each spoken

phonetic stage

FIGURE 6.1

(a) Precommunicative stage.

(b) Prephonetic, or preliterate, stage.

(c) Phonetic, or letter name, stage.

(d) Transitional, or within word, stage.

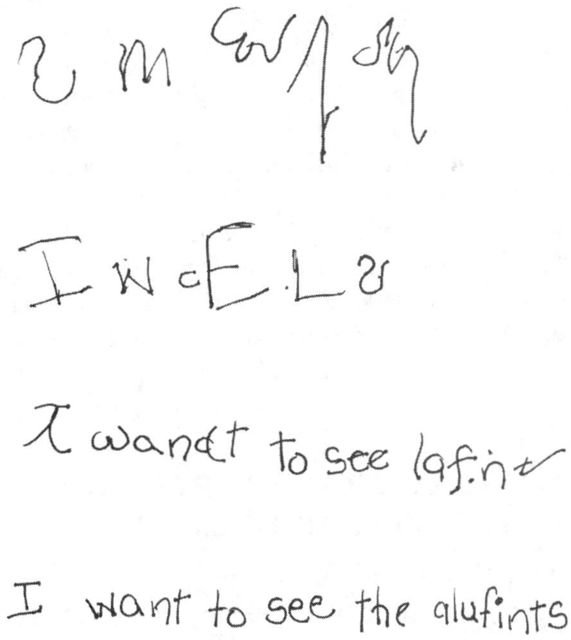

syllable at this more sophisticated stage. Although certain vowels and silent letters may be omitted, the child seems to have become aware of some of the more basic spelling patterns and families in the English language through visual attention afforded by reading. They may also have some memorized sight words. Now the story about the elephant could look like the writing in Figure 6.1(c).

The Transitional, or Within Word, Stage

transitional stage

The fourth developmental spelling stage, or **transitional stage,** occurs when the child can come close to the spelling of various English words, usually about third grade. Many words are spelled correctly, but irregular words that have not been directly taught still cause confusion. At this stage, too, children are exposed to wide reading and they are aware of more visual aspects of words that are not detectable to the ear. Vowels are correctly placed in each syllable, and common English letter sequences, such as the *ai* in *pain* and *rain* begin to emerge correctly in the child's writing. At this stage the elephant story would look something like the writing in Figure 6.1(d).

The Conventional Spelling, or Syllable Juncture, Stage

conventional spelling stage

spelling "conscience"
spelling "consciousness"

When children have mastered the basic principles of English orthography, we say they have arrived at the **conventional spelling stage,** meaning that most words are spelled correctly, as the name implies. Children in this stage are aware of syllables, but may still incorrectly spell vowels in the schwa position (e.g., *elavate* for *elevate).* At this stage, children are developing a **spelling "conscience,"** or a concern for spelling all words correctly, as well as a **spelling "consciousness,"** which means they can generally tell if a word they are trying to spell "looks right." Additionally, children learn how to spell homonyms, contractions, and become adept at doubling consonants and adding affixes to words; at this time, they also learn that there are alternative spellings to certain words.

A quick assessment device called "The Monster Test" can help teachers determine the approximate developmental spelling stage of their learners (see Appendix D for this and other spelling assessment materials).

OBSERVING TEMPORARY, OR "INVENTED," SPELLING

When children are first beginning to write it is best to encourage them to do temporary spelling, also referred to as invented, or experimental spelling—to invite them to sound out words they don't know without asking them to necessarily spell them correctly. At this early phase in emergent literacy, teachers need to be resolute about *not* showing children how to spell each word or they will not develop the strategy of making a first attempt, thus losing important opportunities to experiment with sound–spelling relationships. As learning how to spell involves problem-solving, all children should be encouraged to attempt to spell a word first, perhaps trying it several ways, and then to check its correctness with a resource (Bolton and Snowball, 1993).

Observations of the invented spellings of early writers can show teachers much about children's knowledge of the sound–spelling relationships. They can also demonstrate how knowing the names of letters can sometimes be a slight hindrance as well as a help, which we shall see in a later discussion. Additionally, we begin to understand how coupling this experimentation with systematic instruction in the visual patterns of our language, starting in the first grade, will help children become adept at using the structural patterns of the English language to learn to spell words correctly.

Children's spellings in the following examples illustrate six important concepts about how children attempt to sound out words they wish to spell.

We see from observing children's invented spelling that knowing letter names helps children spell when the word contains a long vowel sound. For example, a child will spell words with long vowels in the following ways:

> *mak* for *make*
>
> *kit* for *kite*
>
> *tigr* for *tiger*

The vowels are spelled correctly because they are spelled the way the name of the letter sounds. On the other hand, short vowels, such as those in the words *bad, hot,* and *win* are more problematic for children if they are trying to spell them based solely upon their knowledge of the names of the letters in the alphabet. A beginner's spelling of these words is often *bed, hit,* and *wen* respectively, because inventive spellers use the vowel name that is closest to the sound in the word when spoken.

When children attempt to sound out words with certain consonant blends, such as *dr* and *tr,* they often will represent these sounds with the letters *jr* or *ch* because the sounds are somewhat similar. The way words such as *dress* and *try* are pronounced sheds some light onto why this may be so: a sophisticated speller is aware of how such blends *look* in relation to their sound; beginning writers are concentrating on what their mouths and tongues are doing as they sound out a word slowly, and these sounds tend to cause a slight friction at the front of their mouths as they articulate the words. Children generate their own rules for these sounds based upon their pronunciation; later, with instruction, their focus will change to the similarity of the phonetic features of the beginning sounds to other words they know, which sophisticated writers learn through instruction in English spelling patterns and how words are supposed to *look.*

Especially at the very earliest stages of temporary spelling, children tend to represent /t/ in the middle of words with a *d*. Again, such temporary spelling underscores how children are paying attention to what they *hear* in the word as they articulate it slowly: *butter (budder)*, therefore, is often spelled *budr* by early writers, while *matter (madder)* would be sounded out *madr*, because American English does not clearly articulate these middle sounds. As soon as the child sees and understands the difference between the way we say such a word and the way it is represented, she then consistently incorporates this knowledge into subsequent spellings of words with the consonant *t* in the middle of the word.

Early spellers also tend to exclude the first letters of certain consonant pairs that are blended together in their mouths. The words *can't* and *won't*, for example, are generally spelled *cat* and *wot* in invented spelling, because the nasal sound produced when we say the /nt/ sound in these words causes their tongues to stay in only one place—in the front of their mouths. Since they do not need to *move* their tongues when they say each of these sounds, they tend to believe they need only one letter to represent both sounds. Again, they are focusing on what they *hear* and experience and are usually not yet aware of how such words *look*.

The ways in which early writers represent the final letters that signify past tense and plurals, as well as third person singular vowels, are very consistent. Proficient readers and writers understand that we add *ed* to the ending of a word to indicate that the action happened in the past, whether the *ed* is pronounced as a discrete syllable or not. Young children have no such knowledge until this visual reality is specifically pointed out. We know, for example, that *wanted* contains a final *ed* to indicate that the *wanting* occurred in the past, but we realize that *hoped* also terminates with an *ed* even though it sounds like a /t/ at the end of a one syllable word. Children using invented spelling will therefore sound out such words as *hopt, laft,* and *stopt*. Similarly, words with plurals commonly represented by the letter *s* would be spelled with the sound that is more prominently heard: *sez, stayz,* and *criz*.

In general, children are remarkably consistent in their use of the patterns they have devised in their invented spellings. This is similar to the over-generalization that occurs when children are learning their first language. They unconsciously detect the pattern that they must use to change the original word when forming a past tense, noticing that *pat* becomes *patted* and *want* becomes *wanted*. However, they overgeneralize this pattern, which results in *runned* for *ran* and *goed* for *went*. Likewise, the overall concept that becomes clear when observing children's initial attempts at spelling is that when children devise rules to govern how they will construct words according to their sounds, they tend to do so routinely.

Children move beyond invented spelling and into predicting spellings on the basis of extensive knowledge—knowledge gained through experience with and instruction on how language works, and by noticing the similar patterns, or analogs, of the words they meet. Figure 6.2 offers one child's perspective on invented spelling and how it helps in the writing process.

FIGURE 6.2 *One child's perspective on invented spelling.*

Our school's parent survey indicated that several parents remained unconvinced about the benefits of invented spelling in their children's writing. So I set out to survey students and gather information to support the necessity for invented spelling. I purposefully interviewed students at all performance levels, but my conversation with a second-grader, Tommy, held the essence of all the answers.

"Tommy, what strategies do you use when you want to write a word, but you're not sure how to spell it?" I asked.

"I sound it out or ask the kid next to me," answered Tommy confidently.

"Good. But what if all the words you wrote had to be spelled correctly—you couldn't sound them out and the kid next to you didn't know how to spell them either?"

"Oh, I know what you mean," said Tommy. "Then I use different words, like in my journal. I can't spell 'because,' so I write 'it is' instead. Like I write 'My favorite sport is baseball. It is fun' instead of 'because it is fun.' Get it?"

"Yes, I do—that's a good strategy. So baseball is your favorite sport, huh?" I asked, making conversation while I jotted down Tommy's response.

"No, it's soccer, but the kid next to me can't spell soccer."

Undaunted, I pressed on. "So, what if you were all alone in the room with no one to ask how to spell a word?"

"You mean like if I had to stay in for recess because I had messed around all morning and didn't finish my work?" asked an obviously experienced Tommy.

"Yes, like that."

"And there was no one to ask, right?" He wanted to be sure.

"Right," I answered, "no one. And you can't sound it out. What would you do?"

Tommy thought for just a moment and then said, " Then I would write, 'I do not like sports.' I can spell all that."

From Romeo, Marna Green. "On Spelling." *The Reading Teacher*, Vol. 48, No. 7, April 1995.

UNDERSTANDING OUR ALPHABETIC SYSTEM

Good spelling is more than a literary nicety, or the icing on the editorial cake. Poorly developed spelling knowledge has been shown to hinder children's writing, to disrupt their reading fluency, and even to interfere with their vocabulary development (Adams et al., 1996; Read, 1986). Although it is appropriate to encourage beginning readers, such as Chrissy in the opening vignette, to use invented spellings to express their written ideas, programmatic instruction in correct spellings should begin in first grade and continue across the school years (California State Board of Education, 1996). In addition, children—as well as many adults!—need to be guided into developing a robust conscience about and consciousness of the correctness of the spelling in all their written work.

Children can learn to spell fairly easily if they are initially encouraged to experiment freely with the way print works. With guidance, children will soon discover that all of the 44 or so phonemes in the English language can be represented by letters or groups of letters. With this understanding and further teaching in the common patterns found in English spellings, children eventu-

ally become literate (Tangel and Blachman, 1992; Tangel and Blachman, 1995). The word "discover" is used advisedly, however, because children do not learn how print works by simply learning the alphabet, then the letter sounds, and then being told that English is an alphabetic system. Although early educators believed there was little more to spelling than that for many years, current spelling research suggests that in order to become good spellers, children must understand the phonemic nature of speech by being shown that (1) we speak in a flow of individual words, (2) each word is composed of a number of sounds, and (3) the sounds of speech are expressed graphically in a specific left-to-right sequence (McCracken and McCracken, 1996).

Because an initial challenge of teachers is to develop children's phonemic awareness and knowledge of basic letter–sound correspondences, activities designed to meet these goals should begin with short, regular words, such as *man, but,* and *can.* Because the major goal of these early sessions is to develop the kind of strategizing upon which good spelling depends, these lessons should be enjoyable and exploratory. They should also model the processes literate people use to generate the spelling of words and to make logical guesses when they are stumped by unknown spelling patterns. Gradually, the focus of these spelling lessons should be expanded to more complex spelling patterns and words, moving systematically from pattern to pattern, and from two and three letter words through consonant blends, long vowel spellings, and so on (Gentry, 1982). The real challenge is to instill in children an understanding of the underlying logic and regularities of a system that, in many cases, can be highly illogical and irregular, as illustrated by the following piece (Figure 6.3) written by a child in early second grade.

FIGURE 6.3 *A second-grader's experimentation with print.*

The inportin think abowt alisoris is alisoris evin ate bad dinysawrs. Alisoris ate met. Alisoris wuz 35 fet long. He live a long long tim ago. I thing I wold like him for a pet. Woldnt you?

An effective spelling program, then, is one in which teachers help children begin to explore and understand the patterns and useful generalizations about the complex relationships within and between words, and help them apply these concepts to each new spelling encounter (Henderson, 1995; Zutell, 1996). Moreover, an informed, developmental analysis of children's efforts as they begin to write will show teachers how to match the features of words to be taught to the students' readiness for discovering them.

A program with the above components would be similar to the one described in the following section.

AN EFFECTIVE SPELLING PROGRAM

For children in early phonetic/early letter name stages, formal instructional strategies should include activities that draw children's attention to the beginning, end, and middle of words, in that order. Whenever possible, children should be involved in spelling the same words they are learning to read.

Early Phonetic/Early Letter Name
(Kindergarten–Early First Grade)

The following strategy from Moats (1995) is especially good for introducing new words to children needing help discerning individual sounds.

1. The teacher pronounces the word: "Bat."
2. The children repeat the word, hearing their own voice and feeling the articulation: b–a–t.
3. The children say the word, sound by sound; after identifying each sound, they say the name of the letter that represents the sound, and write the letter as it is being named on individual chalkboards: b /b/; a /a/; t /t/.
4. The children read back, orally, the word they have written: *bat.*

Sound–symbol correspondence can be reinforced on subsequent days using the following activities:

Word hunts. Using the beginning, ending, or middle sound being studied, the children go around the room searching for other words or objects that begin with the same sound. For example, for the /b/ sound they might find the words *Bill, boat,* and *by.* The teacher writes these words on the board as the children contribute them and help to sound them out.

Picture sorts. The teacher places picture cards among the children and sets up one or two pictures as examples of the beginning, middle, or ending sound being studied. The children take turns coming up and placing their cards with the appropriate example, saying the word as they do so. The teacher makes a list of the words, with the children helping to sound them out.

Word building activities (Cunningham and Cunningham, 1997). Children use paper or tile letters to form words. The teacher reads a word slowly (e.g., *in*), stretching out each sound. The teacher asks the children to stretch the word out using their imaginary rubber bands. Children are required to listen for beginning, middle, and ending sounds, to notice letter patterns, and to discover how capitalization is used in words as they manipulate letters and sounds through the following example sequence:

in	tin
is	tins
it	Tim
hit	this
sit	thin
nit	things

A pocket chart can be used to highlight words for all children to see. As children work through several lessons, each using a different combination of letters, they begin to internalize common word patterns, letter blends, and digraphs.

Cut, paste, and label.   The teacher creates a large poster headed with one or more pictures of things with the same beginning, ending, or middle sound being studied. Children are given magazines, catalogs, scissors, and paste. The children, in small groups, find pictures of items with the same target sound, cut them out, and paste them on the poster. As the words are said, the teacher writes them on the board asking the children to help sound them out.

Phonetic/Late Letter Name and Within-Word

(Late First–Third Grades)

As children advance to the phonetic/late letter name and within-word phases, generally in late first grade through third grade, more systematic spelling is conducted throughout the week and includes differing activities for each day, based upon a teacher-selected spelling list. An excellent resource for such grade-level-appropriate lists is *Teaching Spelling* (Henderson, 1995). However, many teachers question the use of commercial lists to teach spelling, as research on invented spelling suggests that spelling is ideally learned through copious reading and writing, especially when the words chosen from lists are unrelated to the words children are seeing in their reading and using in their writing (Gentry and Gillet, 1993; Wilde, 1992). Words chosen should always be those that children can already read, and particularly those that children use in written form, but misspell. Initially, sorting by sight and sound is the most helpful. Other ideas for more appropriate spelling lists include those listed in the box below.

A typical week's study plan might look like the one on the following pages.

Ideas for meaningful spelling lists

- A series of words containing a specific phoneme.
- Any of the dozens of common spelling patterns: "oo" words, words that end with "y" or "ey," compound words, words with double consonants, words that contain the pattern "ough," and so on
- Words from the decodable text that is being used for reading instruction
- Words with similar meanings: paper, newspaper, wallpaper, papered
- Words that have related roots: photo, photographer, telephoto
- Words from units of study: whale, ocean, tadpole, waves
- Common words we use all the time: it, the, when, my, little
- Place names: Sacramento, California, Ohio, Canada
- Any other grouping that will provide related words for sorting

Monday: Pretest

The teacher selects a spelling sound, pattern, or rule that she feels children are ready for, based upon the spelling assessment. The pattern might be as simple as the short /a/, or as complex as words that have the /k/ sound. All the words the teacher chooses will contain this pattern. The teacher selects 15 or 20 words that have this pattern or sound for the pretest, such as the following list containing variations of the /k/ sound:

like	think	king
car	call	back
bike	kitten	lock
cake	pack	talk
kind	book	walk

She administers a pretest created from these words and children proofread and correct their own attempts. The teacher then displays another slightly more difficult list of 15 to 20 words containing the sound or pattern:

ticket	camp	nickel
ache	cabin	kingdom
Canada	camel	Kansas
cape	school	market
kangaroo	cattle	camera

Children choose words from this list to study in place of any words spelled correctly in the pretest or, if they are exceptionally skilled spellers, create their own lists based upon the spelling concept in the lists (Hong and Stafford, 1998). Alternatively, some children who consistently score above 80 percent on the pretest may develop their own contracts with the teacher containing specific words they wish to learn to spell, or those words that they have recently needed for writing stories, reports, letters, or other written pieces (see the next section, "Contract Spelling").

The children then copy their individual word lists three times. One list is sent home to be shared with parents, a second is stapled to the child's writing folder for future reference, and the third is cut up into individual word cards for later sorting activities.

Tuesday: Word Sort

Children are asked to use their ears, eyes, and brains to sort out their word cards, either individually or in small groups. Such focused, small-group work on word patterns will enhance spelling and aid in reading development (Invernizzi et al., 1994; Schlagel and Schlagel, 1992). Initially, the children use their ears to listen to the sounds in their words, and sort the words by the sounds they have in common, if different sounds are included in the list. Then, they use their eyes to detect other patterns, with the help of the teacher, who is moving from group to group offering assistance. Next, they are told to under-line the letters that make the /k/ sound in each word. Finally, they are asked to use their brains to draw some conclusions, either orally with preliterate chil-dren, or in written form, about what they have discovered. One pair of students came up with the following list and set of generalizations from their list:

k	**c**	**ch**	**ck**
kingdom	cape	ache	ticket
Kansas	Canada	school	nickel
kangaroo	camera		
market	camel		
	camp		
	cattle		
	cabin		

"There are four different ways to make the /k/ sound. You can spell it *k*, *c*, *ch*, and *ck*. The most common way seems to be *c*, followed by *k*. The least common seems to be *ch*; *c* never seems to come at the end of a word; *ck* never seems to come at the beginning of a word; *ck* is never spelled *kc*."

At this juncture, the whole class comes together to share their findings. The teacher sorts the words using a pocket chart or overhead. She models how she would sort the words, thinking through her decisions aloud. The children add their insights and generalizations to hers, explaining the bases for their conclusions. All generalizations are written on chart paper, posted in the room for future reference and for periodic review.

Wednesday: Word Hunt

To allow children to apply the generalizations or rules they have just encountered, the pairs or small groups of children are given 10 or 15 minutes to search through any printed material they have available to come up with other words that con-form to the generalizations. Later, the children reconvene as a whole group to share their lists and create a new word wall that is kept visible and updated by children throughout the day as they come upon other words that fit the pattern.

Thursday: Using the Words in Context

The ability to remember how to read and write a specific word comes from un-derstanding its meaning in context. Therefore, children with rudimentary writing skills are now asked to create brief sentences—and as they grow in literacy, even stories, poems, riddles, or other text—using their individual word lists. Children are then asked to highlight all the spelling words in the piece. The post-test words will be read directly from this written material.

In order to write their words in context, children must be taught a set of strategies for figuring out what to do when they can't spell a word. Some will be more efficient when they are composing their text; others will be more useful when they are editing. While they are writing they should learn to take a guess by sounding it out, and the following strategies should be taught and then posted for them to reference during any writing activity:

- Say the word to yourself very slowly; really stretch it out so you can *listen* for the different sounds.
- Think of the beginning sound and write down the letters that make that sound; for help with the beginning sound, think of a word you know that begins with that sound.
- Think of the middle sound and write down the letters that make that sound.
- Think of the ending sound and write down the letters that make that sound.
- Look at the word carefully and see if it looks right. Read it back to yourself out loud and make sure you are able to read it even if it isn't correct.
- Always write *something,* even if it's just one letter, so you can remember the word you wanted.

After they have completed a rough draft, children even at the earliest stages need to get into the habit of editing their writing for spelling. Therefore, the following strategies should also be taught and posted for reference before finishing any piece of writing:

- Circle or underline the words you are unsure of.
- Check the spelling of the word using your personal dictionary, a word wall, a class list, or a proofreading buddy.
- If you still can't find the word, ask your teacher.
- Make the corrections you need.
- Recopy the piece and read it again.

Friday: Paired Post-Tests

Children give a final, or post-test, to each other in pairs by reading the highlighted words from the contextual material written on Thursday. Pairs may correct each other's post-tests or request that the teacher do so. Children scoring below 80 percent are targeted for future minilessons (see Chapter 5) with the week's spelling patterns. The teacher can retain the lists, writings, and post-tests to provide valuable assessment information about each child's spelling growth.

CONTRACT SPELLING

An alternative approach to spelling instruction for more advanced spellers is **contract spelling** (Hoskisson and Tompkins, 1997), whereby children have a written agreement with the teacher each week to learn specific words. Children who have the opportunity to select the words for their spelling program have a special engagement in their own learning. If they are encouraged to select words from their own writing needs, they are able to see the purpose for their spelling list; the motivation to succeed is thus heightened.

contract spelling

For this approach, the teacher has children keep a list of their own spelling mistakes and challenges from each week's writing. This becomes the master list from which the child selects a certain number of words, depending upon the child's age and ability, to study for the next week. The teacher and each participating child negotiate as to the appropriate number of words to select. Then the child takes a pretest on the words (these can be administered by the teacher or a spelling partner), fills out a spelling contract on the words, studies the words during the week, and takes a final test to see how well the contract has been met. This information provides the foundation for the new contract the following week (see Figure 6.4).

ENGLISH LANGUAGE LEARNER ISSUES AND STRATEGIES

English language learners may participate successfully in spelling instruction if they are developmentally ready, are learning to read in English, and if they understand the meanings of the words they are being asked to spell. English

FIGURE 6.4 *A sample spelling contract.*

Name: _____Carmen R._____   Grade: ___5___

Week: _____Sept. 9–13_____

Spelling Contract

Number of words spelled correctly on the pretest: ___8___

Number of words to be learned: ___2___

Total number of words contracted: ___10___

1. personal	6. popular
2. beautiful	7. women
3. curious	8. beginning
4. obvious	9. sincerely
5. mascara	10. receive

language learners who are learning to read in a language other than English may most comfortably participate by doing so orally, if they wish. The primary focus should be on comprehending spelling vocabulary and developing awareness of English sound patterns and specific spelling patterns.

English language learners who are only participating orally should not be required to take formal spelling pre- and post-tests; however, they may be asked to demonstrate knowledge of the meaning of spelling words by drawing pictures of the word or providing brief explanations of the word's meaning.

The strategy described in the activity below, called "Think, Pair, and Share," is one that can be helpful in the spelling acquisition of all children, but particularly for English language learners.

ACTIVITY

THINK, PAIR, AND SHARE

THINK

Children look at the spelling list (or, for younger children, listen as someone reads the words) and consider what they know about each word. They may write down their ideas, draw pictures, use gestures, or use any means to show what they are thinking.

PAIR

Children sit in pairs facing one another. One child chooses a word to share with the partner and completes the following sentence: "Something I know about [the spelling word] is that. . . ." Children may share drawings, and if their partner speaks the same home language, that language may be used.

SHARE

Children regroup into linguistically heterogeneous small groups and, in English, share and build on the knowledge they acquired in the pairs. They may repeat the pair activity by changing their sentences to: "Something I learned from my partner about [the spelling word] was . . . " or they may do a different activity such as a word sort or a word hunt and discuss their findings in the group. They may also choose to enter the words that reflect the concepts they have been studying for the week into a word study notebook, in columns.

PRACTICES TO AVOID

There are certain questionable practices in the instruction of spelling that have been around since before the turn of the century. In spite of volumes of research disclaiming some of these practices, many teachers still use the same unsubstantiated teaching formulas used generations ago. Because these dubious practices are widespread and continue to thrive, most books on spelling feel the need to mention those activities teachers should avoid. The following practices are not recommended because they yield nothing of value and may hinder normal spelling development (Gentry, 1981).

AVOID:

- **requiring children to write out their spelling words repeatedly.** Writing the words three times appears to be the optimal number for retention; all else is counterproductive and would be better spent on other applied writing activities. Moreover, practice doesn't always make perfect; if the word is misspelled ten times, practice has most likely been made permanent.

- **correcting spelling mistakes for children.** Children learn much more by paying careful attention to the exact sequence of letters they have confused so they can write it over correctly. A small check in the margin of the line where there is a misspelled word should be enough to call children's attention to a spelling mistake.

- **having children unscramble strings of letters to find words.** This is an unusually poor practice because it frustrates the visual recognition that is the single most important skill children can develop for spelling. Word searches are also poor exercises, as the diagonal and right-to-left placement of words reinforce poor orientation skills, especially in beginning readers.

- **lowering grades on written work solely because of poor spelling.** When children are writing drafts and getting their ideas down, they are in the creating stages of writing. At this stage, the teacher should always respond only to what the writer has to say. Later, when children have had a chance to edit their work, the spelling can be addressed.

- **giving weekly spelling bees.** Spelling bees are enjoyable for those children who are naturally good spellers, but provide limited practice for those who are experiencing problems in spelling. Moreover, the "good" spellers tend to get most of the spelling reinforcement, whereas the poorer spellers, who could use the practice, get little but a bruised ego.

- **spending more than 10 to 15 minutes a day on spelling instruction.** Good spelling is an important convention of writing, but it is only a small part of what makes a child literate. As such, teachers should actively engage children in analyzing and categorizing words and identifying generalizations for a few minutes every day; much more time should be spent applying that information into meaningful writing experiences.

SUMMARY

The purpose of spelling is to allow writers to communicate more effectively, so writing is the best way for children to learn how to spell. To become good spellers, then, children are going to have to write a lot, and that means they are going to have to begin by using invented spelling. During the primary years, children's abilities to spell lag so far behind their abilities to communicate that if they could not initially invent new spellings, they simply could not write at all. But it isn't enough to tell children to use invented spelling, however; teachers need to show them how to use strategies to sound

out new words, thus helping them to discover important concepts about sound–spelling relationships in the English language. By observing and analyzing their invented spellings, teachers can then determine what new concepts about print their students are ready to incorporate into their spelling.

Learning how to spell is not about merely memorizing words anymore; a more sensible approach to the teaching of spelling is now based upon several premises: Children must be taught about print and how it works, and they must be shown strategies that are used by competent spellers. They must be taught directly about the symbols used to represent each sound. They must also be guided to discover common spelling patterns and the generalizations that apply to many words. Most importantly, they must be given numerous opportunities to use their spelling in meaningful and varied writing activities. With a burgeoning spelling consciousness that alerts them when a word is not spelled correctly, and a spelling conscience that makes them *want* to spell correctly, young children will be well on the road to effective written communication.

QUESTIONS
for Journal Writing and Discussion

1. Describe in your own words the stages of spelling development in young children. Explain how being aware of these stages might help a teacher plan an appropriate spelling program for each learner.

2. List, in your own words, the six concepts that can be derived from observing children's invented spelling. Discuss how knowing letter names can be both a help and a hindrance to young children at the initial phases of writing.

3. The mother of a first-grader asks you why the teacher allows her child to misspell so many words in draft writing. What explanation do you offer her?

SUGGESTIONS

for Projects and Other Activities

1. Administer the "Monster Test" (see Appendix D) to three first grade children. From their responses, what stage of spelling development would you say each child is in? List what each child already knows about how print works. What do you think each child needs in order to progress toward the next stage?

2. Develop a list of 15 spelling words based upon similar or contrasting visual or sound aspects. Invite a small group of second grade children to sort the words and then make statements about their findings, as demonstrated in this chapter. Present your findings to your classmates.

3. Observe a spelling lesson taught to primary age youngsters. Through discussion with the teacher and your direct observation, answer the following questions:

   • What strategies are children being taught about how to spell new words?

   • How are children being taught about common patterns that occur in words?

   • How is spelling applied in real writing situations in this classroom?

ACQUIRING WORD MEANINGS

The Building Blocks of Literacy

FOCUS QUESTIONS

- What is the most important way children acquire new words? How should this information guide classroom practice?

- What factors comprise an effective meaning vocabulary acquisition program?

- What are the two types of meaning vocabulary instruction and when should each be used?

In the Classroom

Since words are the building blocks of sentences and thus *all* reading and writing activities, a classroom in which both teacher and children enjoy playing with and discussing new words is the sort most conducive to literacy acquisition. In one such classroom, when seven-year-old Maria chirps, "That story was so *um—memorable,* Ms. Komar!" the teacher and the students are visibly enchanted with this sophisticated new word. They immediately stop what they are doing to comment on the meaning of the word after Ms. Komar profusely congratulates Maria on using such a fine word. The teacher then enlists the students to help her sound the word out as she pens it with a black marker on a large word wall chart toward the front of the room. This prominent chart has been created for just such a purpose: to provide a tangible reminder of the group's love of words and to reinforce new words as they are discovered either through class discussion, as in this example, or through content reading, recreational reading, or other media.

Most children, like those in the classroom just mentioned, come to school with well-developed oral language. They know the meanings of thousands of words and they are able to use most of the major linguistic constructs in their home language. In fact, human beings in every culture are born with an amazing genetic language device that allows them to acquire language in the most natural of ways. Most children will become fairly proficient in their home language unless they are deprived from hearing or using it. They effortlessly pick up new words and grammar through everyday interaction with their social environment. Parents and other caregivers unknowingly scaffold, or provide support for, conversations with their children to make the language understandable and easily learned.

WHY ACQUIRING A MEANING VOCABULARY IS IMPORTANT

meaning vocabulary

Meaning vocabulary is just what the term implies—a child's understanding of the meanings of words. It is first acquired through the child's total oral language experiences and therefore begins to form many years before the child ever enters school. In kindergarten, before children know how to read, they gain their meaning vocabulary primarily through listening to and retelling stories, songs, and poems, and by having adults or older children help them focus on the meaning of new words. As children become literate, their vocabularies are also enhanced through direct instruction and independent reading. By the end of third grade, if all goes according to plan, children are able to decode any word in their meaning vocabulary.

The meaning vocabulary of children grows at an astonishing rate—by some estimates about 3,000 words a year, or approximately seven to ten new words per day (Nagy and Herman, 1985). In order to master such a large number of words, it would seem reasonable to assume that children acquire this new vocabulary both inside and outside of school. While many teachers often suppose that their students learn most new words through their direct instruction, children actually learn more new words through recreational reading and writing projects; television has also been known to have a positive effect on vocabulary acquisition (Tompkins, 1997). The number of new words children can acquire from reading, of course, depends upon exactly how much they read, and that amount can vary tremendously. As documented by research, a fifth-grader achieving at the 90th percentile in reading on standardized tests reads about 200 times more than does the 10th percentile fifth grade reader! (Nagy et al., 1985). Moreover, capable readers have larger vocabularies and a wider repertoire of strategies for figuring out new words than children who read less often (McKeown, 1985).

Written language places greater demands on children's vocabulary knowledge than does everyday spoken language. If children do not continue to develop vocabulary at a rapid rate, they will be ill-equipped to handle the extensive vocabulary demands presented in fourth grade content-area subjects, such as science and social studies. This problem is compounded for children for whom English is not the home language. Therefore, a swiftly growing vocabulary is critical to growth in every area of reading. Although the proportion of difficult words in text is the single most powerful predictor of text difficulty, a reader's general vocabulary knowledge is the best predictor of how well that reader will be able to understand text (California Department of Education, 1996). This is undoubtedly why Nagy (1988) asserts that increasing the volume of children's reading in both expository and narrative text is the single most important thing a teacher can do to promote large-scale vocabulary growth.

PRINCIPLES OF EFFECTIVE VOCABULARY DEVELOPMENT

The extensive vocabulary children need for complex tasks can be acquired if children have access to a bounty of good literature, as well as a variety of well-crafted expository texts on many topics. Moreover, they must be actively engaged with the reading material, and must be allowed a myriad of opportunities to transfer and apply newly acquired words in a variety of meaningful ways. Especially in the early grades, children need to have countless opportunities to gain meaning vocabulary through oral language development. This can take place through mediated reading (see Chapter 10), teacher-directed group reading activities, and through read-alouds, as well as by applying new vocabulary through motivational writing activities shared with classmates. Also helpful for acquiring meaning vocabulary are extensive discussions, listening and thinking activities, and orally asking and answering open-ended questions. The box below provides additional suggestions for vocabulary learning.

Teacher behaviors that enhance vocabulary learning

Link	Relate children's past experiences with present ones
Elaborate	Add more information about familiar content, or suggest a rewording of the content
Input	Introduce new vocabulary and reinforce through constant use
Connect	Tie new words to the activity or the activity to the new words
Clarify	Add examples, illustrations, or descriptions
Question	Stimulate thinking about terms through questioning
Relate	Show how new words compare to those children know
Categorize	Group new words, ideas, concepts
Label	Provide names for concepts, ideas, objects

Additionally, children need to be encouraged to read widely at home and at school, and to be given plenty of opportunities to do so.

Motivating Children to Read Independently

Independent reading is one of the most critical factors in acquiring new meaning vocabulary. Moreover, research informs us that those children who read the most, read the best and score the highest on formal and informal assessments (California Reading Association, 1996). Because this component of a comprehensive reading program is so pivotal to the reading success of all children, a plan for motivating children to read should be undertaken in every classroom, in every school.

To encourage reading at home, there should be communication with parents. Inform them that for 10 to 15 minutes every evening, their child will be expected to read, with the help of a caretaker for those at the preliterate level,

and independently as soon as they are able. (*Note:* for children whose home language is not English, reading in the home language with parents should be encouraged.) A classroom library with a variety of books on many topics and across many reading levels is a priority; the children should be able to check out these books and take them home.

During school, a time should be set aside for recreational reading—from 10 minutes in first grade to 20 minutes in third grade—so that children can practice their skills on self-chosen material. Teachers and other school personnel should also stop what they are doing during this important time and model the enjoyable activity of reading. Personal progress charts can be kept by each child so that the teacher can check reading interests and growth; incentives can be offered for specified numbers of books read.

Other Factors in Vocabulary Development

Besides extensive reading, other activities are conducive to vocabulary acquisition. The most successful vocabulary-enhancing activities are those that are highly significant to all children and involve active engagement with words taken directly from their reading. Activities that teach children how to determine the meaning of unknown words themselves (Blachowicz and Lee, 1991) are preferred over traditional methods that have, in the past, demanded that children memorize dictionary definitions of commercial lists of arbitrarily chosen words that children are then asked to use in sentences (Blachowicz, 1987).

A number of other key strands must be present in a reading program that seeks to increase meaning vocabulary. Above all, to foster vocabulary development, children should be read to as much as possible from a wide variety of quality narrative and expository material; there is much evidence to suggest that children learn vocabulary incidentally by hearing text read aloud to them (Elley, 1989). Teachers must also attempt to build upon the vocabulary children already have whenever introducing new reading material. For example, if children already know the word *knife,* it is then easy to build upon that knowledge to teach them the word *saber.* Children in such a program should be systematically shown strategies for figuring out the meanings of words they encounter in text and encouraged to apply such strategies independently. Finally, studies by Stahl (1983) and Stahl and Fairbanks (1986) suggest that building background knowledge prior to reading is simply not enough to help children to overcome limited vocabulary knowledge; these researchers encourage teachers to teach new words directly by showing children exactly how to use context and other strategies to understand complex concepts.

TYPES OF VOCABULARY INSTRUCTION

Formal meaning vocabulary instruction for young children is of two main types with two different purposes. The first type is that in which the teacher provides direct instruction that helps children acquire new vocabulary words. The second type of meaning vocabulary instruction is that in which teachers help children develop vocabulary-building strategies that they can use on their own during non-instructional, independent reading times. Both of these types of meaning vocabulary instruction will be explored in the following sections.

Direct Instruction in Meaning Vocabulary

Through formal meaning vocabulary instruction, teachers will not only add new words to children's vocabulary, but they can also lessen the load of new words and concepts that children encounter in instructional reading material. By reducing the number of unfamiliar words with which children must struggle, the teacher thus increases the chance of creating a positive literacy experience. This section will explore ways teachers can provide direct study in meaning vocabulary for five different instructional situations (Graves et al., 1994).

1. Learning new words that represent new concepts
   (e.g., children come to grips with the new concept/word *culture*)

2. Clarifying and enriching the meanings of known words
   (e.g., children learn how *shed* differs from *cabin*)

3. Learning new words for known concepts
   (e.g., children know what *rain* is, and now learn the word *precipitation*)

4. Moving words into children's speaking vocabulary
   (e.g., children know the meaning of *selfish* but have never used the word)

5. Learning new meanings for known words
   (e.g., children know the word *change,* but not *to make change* in math)

Learning new words for new concepts

Learning both a new word and a new concept at the same time is a complex task but can best be accomplished by comparing both the concept and the word with those that are already familiar. The steps in the following activity, "A **Word Map**" (Duffelmeyer and Banwart, 1993), will be useful in this regard.

word map

ACTIVITY

A WORD MAP

1. Define the new word and concept by pointing out its special characteristics. For example, "Spring is a season of the year when it begins to get warm and flowers begin to bloom."

2. Describe what the new word is like and what it is unlike: "In spring, it is getting warm and it is often breezy and everything seems new. It is not snowy or freezing cold; it is not like winter."

3. Give examples of the concept and explain why they are examples: "Spring is March, April, and May. These are the months when it begins to warm up and buds come on the trees."

4. Give "non-examples" of the concept and explain why they would be poor examples: "December, January, and February are not examples of spring because it is usually very cold in those months and all the flowers have died."

5. Show examples and non-examples of the concept and ask them to explain why each was chosen: Show a picture of a warm spring day with light green everywhere; show another picture of the middle of winter with snow and trees devoid of leaves.

6. Ask children to find examples and non-examples and explain their choices.

Use words and brief descriptions from your discussions with the children to create a word map (also called a word web) similar to the one shown in Figure 7.1.

FIGURE 7.1   *A word map (also called a word web).*

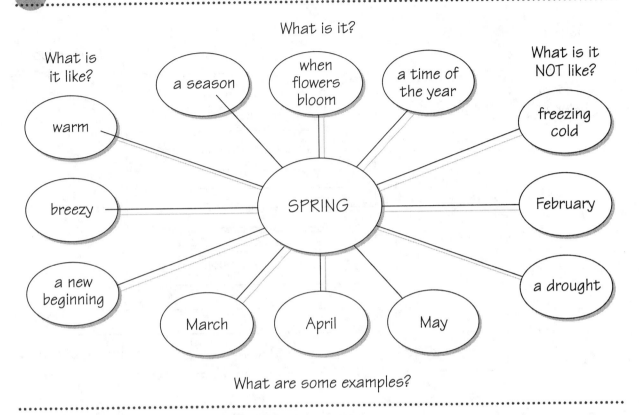

What is it?

What is it like?

What is it NOT like?

a season

when flowers bloom

a time of the year

warm

freezing cold

breezy

SPRING

February

a new beginning

a drought

March

April

May

What are some examples?

Clarifying and enriching the meaning of known words

Semantic maps (Johnson and Pearson, 1984) are important vehicles for helping children put together related information and develop additional words for the same concepts (see Figure 7.2). The steps outlined in the following activity are a guide that can be adapted for individual purposes.

semantic maps

A SEMANTIC MAP

ACTIVITY

1. Choose a key word from a book, story, or passage children will soon be reading.

2. Write the word on a large sheet of chart paper, an overhead transparency, or on the board.

3. Ask children to think of as many words as they can that are related to the word as you list them in broad categories. (*Note:* You may want to add any important words to the categories that have been overlooked.)

FIGURE 7.2 *A semantic map.*

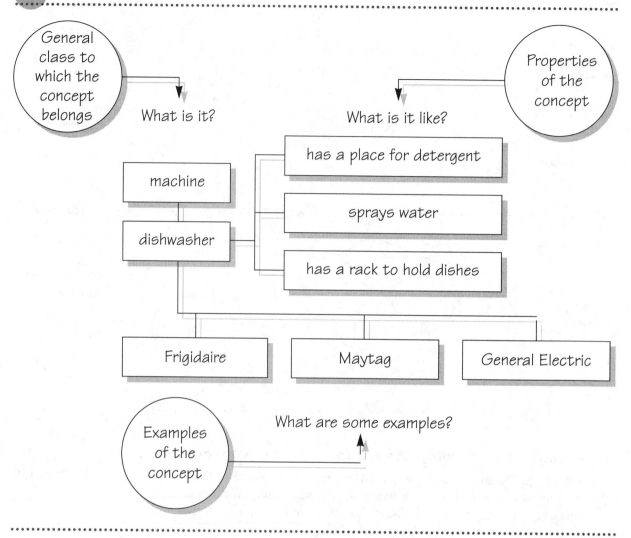

4. Lead children in a discussion of the broad categories and invite them to help you label them. Some words may fit into more than one category.

5. When the map is completed, discuss the categories and focus attention on those that will be highlighted in the passage to be read, such as the one about dishwashers in Figure 7.2.

6. After the reading of the passage, revisit the map and augment it with new words that were not mentioned in the original map-making.

Learning new words for known concepts

When children are already familiar with a concept but are acquiring a new word to go with their existing meaning base, a method called the **context–relationship procedure** (Aulls and Graves, 1985) can be used to help chil-

context-relationship procedure

dren integrate the new word into their meaning vocabularies. The steps of this procedure are outlined in the following activity.

CONTEXT–RELATIONSHIP PROCEDURE

1. Write the word on the board for children and pronounce it for them. Have the children look at the word as they say it several times.

2. Present a paragraph on the board, overhead, or individual copies, in which the word is used three or four times. Read it with the children.

   EXAMPLE: The newspaper said there was a chance of *precipitation*. Everybody got out their umbrellas to prepare for the rain. *Precipitation* can mean more than just rain. It could be snow or sleet or hail. *Precipitation* means that there will be something wet coming down from the sky.

3. Ask children a question such as the following:

   Precipitation means:

   A. wet weather

   B. an earthquake

   C. sunshine

4. Read the possible definitions and ask children to choose the best one. Discuss the answers given.

5. Read the word and its definition once again.

Moving words into children's speaking vocabularies

Children can be encouraged to expand their speaking vocabularies, or the words they use in oral language, when appropriate word usage is recognized and praised in the classroom, and when plenty of time and encouragement for word play prompts children to experiment with words of their own choosing. The following two activities foster the development of expanded speaking vocabularies.

SEMANTIC GRADIENT

1. Allow small groups of children to choose two known words with opposite meanings, such as *good/bad, hot/cold,* or *run/walk.*

2. Have the children put one of the words toward the top of a sheet of paper and the other toward the bottom.

3. Through small group discussion about word meanings, have children think of words that would fit, meaning-wise, between the two words, and other words that might fit above and below the words. Stress that there are no right or wrong answers.

EXAMPLE (2nd grade):   perfect

   excellent

   good

   okay

   naughty

   mischievous

   bad

   terrible

   evil

4. Ask children to share their lists and explain why they placed the words where they did by giving examples of how they would use the words in sentences.

ACTIVITY

CAMOUFLAGE (CECIL, 1994)

1. Pass out 3 × 5 word cards, each of which has a word written on it that is in the children's meaning vocabulary but not in their speaking vocabulary. Tell children they may look at their own card but not each other's.

2. Children take turns answering questions generated by other members of the class. For example, a class member might ask an easy personal question such as, "What is your favorite subject?"

3. The child whose turn it is must answer the question while attempting to hide, or camouflage, the word written on the card into the answer.

   EXAMPLE (2nd grade, hiding the word *fond*): "My favorite subject is math. But I also like spelling because my big sister helps me with it. I am *fond* of her even though we often have huge arguments. But I guess I like math best."

4. When the child is finished responding, the other children raise their hands and try to guess which word they think the child has hidden. If the number of incorrect guesses is greater than the number of correct guesses, the original child wins. (*Hint:* Tell children the best strategy is to use the most "grown-up" words they can think of to throw the other children off.)

Learning new meanings for known words

Many words in the English language are **polysemantic,** or have multiple mean-ings. The word *fast,* for example, has many different meanings, ranging from *se-cure,* when used as a verb, to *rapid* when used as an adjective, and many more meanings when used as a noun or adverb. If a new meaning for a word does not represent a difficult concept, it can be taught simply by discussing with children their current understanding of the word's meaning, presenting the word's new meaning, and then noting the similarities and differences when the word is used in this new way. However, if the new meaning is more complex, then the method outlined in the following activity, ideal for expository text, may be more helpful.

polysemantic

POSSIBLE SENTENCES
(STAHL AND KAPINUS, 1991)

ACTIVITY

1. From an upcoming reading assignment, choose several key words that might be difficult because they are used in an unfamiliar context.

   EXAMPLE: *change, spend, left*

   Choose a few additional words with which the children are already familiar.

   EXAMPLE: *boys, ball, bat, buying*

   Write these words on the board or overhead.

2. Provide short definitions for the difficult words or encourage any children who know the words to define them.

3. Ask children to make up sentences using the words in *possible sentences* that might be in the passage they are about to read.

4. Write the sentences the children suggest on the board. Read them together.

5. After the reading of the passage, revisit the sentences the children have written and decide if they could or could not be true based upon new in-formation from the passage.

6. If the sentences could *not* be true, have children help you to revise them to make them true.

   EXAMPLE: The boy has left his ball and bat. (Could *not* be true)
   The boy has change left after buying a ball. (Revised)

Strategies to Enhance Independent Meaning-Vocabulary Growth

Since, as we noted earlier, children by some estimates learn as many as 3,000 words a year, it would seem obvious that each new vocabulary word cannot possibly be taught individually by the teacher. Therefore, teachers must also be armed with strategies that help their pupils become independent word learners through avenues such as the following, which will be explored below:

- Using the context
- Utilizing word structure
- Using the dictionary
- Figuring out unknown words
- Developing an appreciation for words

Using the context

Arguably the best independent vocabulary-enriching strategy children can be taught is how to use the surrounding information in a sentence to predict the meaning of an unknown word, or how to use the *context* (see also Chapter 1). Context clues, however, take a variety of forms. Sometimes the word is defined in the sentence (e.g., "When someone *exchanges* something, they trade it for something else") or it may be defined later in the paragraph. At other times synonyms or antonyms are used, or examples give the reader an idea of the meaning of the word (e.g., "The boy *exchanged,* or traded, the ball for a bat"). Teachers may find a *think-aloud* strategy (see Chapter 8) helpful for modeling how to use context clues. The steps in the following activity provide a guideline.

ACTIVITY   **USING THE CONTEXT THINK-ALOUD**

Sentence: Carla wants to keep her candy, but José wants to exchange his for a new toy.

1. Write the above sentence on the board or overhead.

2. Read the sentence aloud, sharing how you think through the problem as in this example:

   "I wonder what *exchange* means? Let's see; the sentence says that Carla wants to keep her candy, but José wants to exchange his. It also says José wants a toy instead. The *but* must mean that José wants to do something different from keeping the candy. When I get something I don't like, I take it back to the store and trade it for something I do like. Maybe that is what José is going to do. I guess *exchange* must mean trade."

3. Provide other unknown words in context and ask student volunteers to verbalize their context usage strategies for the rest of the class or in small groups.

When texts do not provide enough context for children to determine the meaning of an unknown word, the following activity will help teach them to make informed guesses about a word's meaning when they are reading independently.

CONTEXTUAL REDEFINITION (TIERNEY, READENCE, AND DISHNER, 1995)

ACTIVITY

1. Select two or three unknown words to be pretaught.

2. Write several sentences for each word with enough clues provided for children to guess the meaning of the word. Try to use different strategies such as definitions, synonyms, and antonyms. If the actual text has enough clues to expose the meaning, use that.

   EXAMPLE (1st grade): The boy had played baseball all day long. His arms and legs were very tired. He went to bed early. The boy was *exhausted.*

3. First present the words in isolation. Pronounce the words for the children and have them repeat. Then ask the children to guess what they think the words might mean.

4. Then present the words in context using the sentences you have created. Read them aloud for the children and have them discuss what the meanings might be from the words around them.

5. Finally, to help the children see the value of contextual information, guide them in a discussion of the difference between trying to guess the meanings of words in context and in isolation.

Utilizing word structure

Knowing the meanings of common **prefixes** and **suffixes** and combining them with meanings of familiar base words can help children discover the meanings of many new words. For example, if children know the meaning of *heat* and also know that the prefix *pre* means *before,* they can conclude that the word *preheat* means to heat the oven *ahead of time.* Likewise, children can often determine the meaning of **compound words** by combining the meanings of the component parts together: *dollhouse* means a house for dolls. Even the earliest readers can be taught to use word parts as they discover that the simplest, most basic structure of a word, the **morpheme,** can change the meaning of a word: *dog* with the addition of an *s* becomes more than one dog.

Children can be made aware of the value of word structure through the following activities.

prefixes
suffixes

compound words

morpheme

ACTIVITY   **WORD HUNTS (BEAR ET AL., 1996)**

1. As you introduce a new prefix or suffix, prepare several flip strips. To create a flip strip, print root words on the front left-hand side of colored strips of construction paper. On the back, print the suffix so that when the paper is folded, a new word appears (see Figure 7.3). Give the flip strips to the children to practice making words using the particular affixes.

2. Using magazines, books, and newspapers, invite children to search for words that have the same structural feature, such as the prefix or suffix that was introduced. For example, children will search for all the words they can find with the suffix *ful*. Provide a time limit.

3. Children write their words in a special word study notebook.

4. Following the word hunt, bring the children back together and record on the board or on chart paper all the words that were discovered.

5. Discuss the meaning of each word with the children. Have them verify that it contains the focus structural element, in this case *ful*.

6. Words that did not contain the element should be put in a "miscellaneous" column, studied closely, and discussed to discover other patterns and word features.

FIGURE 7.3 *Flip strips for suffixes.*

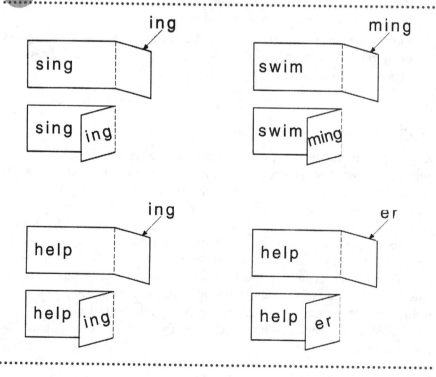

TABLE 7.1 *Common word parts.*

PREFIXES	ROOTS	SUFFIXES
1. auto (self)	graph (writing)	mania (madness for)
2. anti (against)	phon (sound)	phobia (fear of)
3. tele (far)	hydr (water)	itis (inflammation)
4. bi (two)	therm (heat)	ist (one who)
5. dia (through)	meter (measure)	ic (pertaining to)
6. con (together)	dic (say)	ism (condition of)
7. trans (across)	vit (life)	able (able to)
8. re (again)	port (carry)	ment (state of)
9. in, im, un (not, in)	pen, pun (punish)	er (one who)
10. pre (before)	vert (turn)	ion, tion (act of)

Using the dictionary

The use of the dictionary must be taught in a way that will leave children with a positive attitude toward this important tool. Teaching of dictionary skills should begin in kindergarten and proceed through the primary grades until children know and understand the components of a dictionary and can use them effectively. In kindergarten and first grade, the basic concept of a dictionary can be taught using a picture dictionary. Children can begin to learn how to locate words or pictures based upon beginning sounds as soon as they have some knowledge of the alphabet; they can then make picture dictionaries of their own. Older children, or more advanced readers, with rudimentary dictionary skills and the ability to alphabetize, can be engaged in coining their own words with some initial direct teaching of the common word parts shown in Table 7.1. The "Class Dictionary" activity that follows allows them to coin words in a creative way.

CLASS DICTIONARY   ACTIVITY

1. Over several weeks, introduce each of the word parts in Table 7.1 with example words for each.

2. Conduct a word hunt as each new part is introduced.

3. Put children in small groups and ask them to form three new words by combining a prefix, a root, and a suffix in new ways.

4. Instruct each group to define each of their new words by considering the meanings of each element. (*Note:* Tell the children the definitions can be humorous or serious.)

Autohydrable—a child's illustration.

5. Encourage a spokesperson for each group to share each of their new words with the other class members, encouraging them to guess the meanings of the new words from their own knowledge of the components.

6. Have each group make an illustration to accompany each of their new words. For example, see the sketch above illustrating autohydrable: adj. capable of bathing oneself.

7. As a whole class, help children to alphabetize all the words and put them into a class dictionary.

Figuring out unknown words

When children are reading independently, they will need a general strategy they can consistently use to unlock the meaning of unfamiliar words as they are encountered. Getting children into the habit of using such a strategy is not easy, but with a careful introduction and much guided practice, it can be accomplished. The following strategy is based upon the work of Graves (1986) and has been adapted for beginning readers.

ACTIVITY   **LEARNING NEW WORDS**

Teach the following procedure by first explaining the process, modeling the steps using a think-aloud (see Chapter 8), and then offering constant guided practice as children attempt the procedure themselves.

1. When you come to a word you don't know, read to the end of the sentence or paragraph to decide if the word is important to your understanding. If the word is unimportant, just keep reading.

2. If the word *is* important, reread that sentence or paragraph. Try to use the other words around it to figure out what the word means.

3. If the other words are not helpful, look for roots, prefixes, or suffixes that you know.

4. Try to sound out the word. Is it a word you have heard before?

5. If you still don't know the word, ask someone to tell you what it means, or ask an older person to look it up for you in the dictionary.

6. Once you think you know the meaning of the word, reread the text and see if it makes sense.

Another activity illustrates the kind of child-centered instruction that encourages independence as well as vocabulary development. Watson (1987) suggests allowing children to select the words that are the focus of instruction. In addition, his technique provides the teacher with an informal assessment of how well the children are reading.

READER-SELECTED VOCABULARY PROCEDURES (RSVP)

ACTIVITY

1. Children are given several strips of paper to use as bookmarks. The strips are cut from typing paper or notebook paper and are two to three inches wide and three to five inches long.

2. The children are instructed to read as usual, but when they come to a word they do not know, and it interferes with their comprehension, they are to place the bookmark there and continue to read. Children are encouraged to continue reading until they reach the end or come to a logical stopping point.

3. At the end of the independent reading time, children are asked to go back to the place where they have placed their markers. They choose the one or two words that *most* affected their comprehension.

4. On their bookmarks, children write down the words and the sentences in which they came across the word and hand these to the teacher.

5. The teacher can use the bookmarks to organize future instruction around the vocabulary problems the children have identified. Children who are having similar problems can be grouped together for small group instruction planned by the teacher.

Developing an appreciation for words

Teachers who truly find the study of language fascinating can pass this excitement on to their students by constantly directing their attention to words or phrases that they find particularly effective in literature, media, discussion, or informal conversation.

For example, while reading a poem to her class, one teacher stopped when she came to "a plethora of pink poppies," and had the children say it with her. She pointed out the alliteration of the sounds, allowing children to observe how the beginning letters "exploded" on their tongues. Then she eagerly explained the meaning of the words *plethora* and *poppies* to her pupils, who were thrilled to acquire such exciting new vocabulary.

A more direct way of imparting an appreciation for words is to have children collect words and then write them on cards to be stored in their personal word banks or shared on word walls (see Chapter 5). As a precursor to reading a Halloween story, for example, children can participate in a brainstorming session to generate "scary" words. Similarly, children can be encouraged to accumulate "pretty words," "animal words," "summer words," "Arabic words," or words specific to any topic they are studying in a content area.

Even modern technology can help with vocabulary appreciation through the use of captioned television programs. The captions can be seen on ordinary television sets that are equipped with TeleCaption decoders. On captioned television programs, sentences corresponding to the words spoken on the video are printed onto the screen, allowing children to actually see the words contextualized by the action. The captioned television broadcast can be an excellent prereading activity to introduce new vocabulary and build background in an enjoyable way. Many captioned videos, such as Reading Rainbow programs, can be obtained from area video stores or educational publishers (Tompkins, 1997).

Another way to foster children's appreciation for words is to use the following activity, orally for preliterate children and in written form for beginning writers. This activity is especially suitable for classrooms with many linguistically diverse children.

ACTIVITY

WORD AEROBICS

1. Write a simple sentence on the board or overhead. This sentence should contain only a subject and a simple verb or predicate.

2. Read the sentence to the children and then ask them to repeat the sentence.

   EXAMPLE: The man ran.

3. Ask the children to think about how they could make the sentence more vivid by answering questions such as, "Where was the man going?" "What does he look like?" "Why was the man running?"

4. Invite children to think of a revised sentence that would give more information about the sentence.

    EXAMPLE (2nd grade): The tall, thin man ran after the gray cat.

5. Encourage children to share their revised sentences. Discuss how adding
descriptive words and phrases helps to create a richer sentence.

MODIFYING TRADITIONAL APPROACHES

Many activities purporting to develop students' vocabulary accompany most
basal readers, but they are not always effective or appropriate. With a few adjustments, however, these approaches can often be made more constructive.
Here are some ideas to keep in mind when following basal manual instructions
for introducing new meaning vocabulary:

1. Begin instruction with what the children already know.
Instead of telling children the meaning of words they may not know, first ask
them, "What do you know about these words?" It is never too early to begin to
encourage children to take risks by guessing and hypothesizing about new
words based upon what they do know.

**2. Use as many senses as possible when introducing new
words.** Instead of always *telling* children the meanings of new words, action
words can be acted out by the class ("*Show* me exhausted!"), other words can
be sung, drawn, or demonstrated ("This is how you pirouette!"), and don't forget the old saying, also true in vocabulary acquisition, that a picture is worth a
thousand words.

**3. Give children meaningful opportunities to use their new
words.** Using only the strategy of providing definitions before reading a
story or reinforcing new words with workbook pages does not markedly increase meaning vocabulary unless children actually use the words introduced.
The words must be used in daily conversations and writing to become part of
the children's permanent knowledge.

4. Encourage children to teach each other. Sometimes children
are better able to explain new words and concepts to each other than a teacher
or a glossary provided at the back of a basal. Because young children think
concretely, they can often present examples of the word that will help others
who are not relating the word to anything they already know. This strategy is
particularly helpful with children for whom English is a second language.

5. Model curiosity about words and good dictionary habits. An
excellent preliminary introduction to the dictionary habit for children not yet
ready to use one is to observe a respected adult musing, "I wonder what that
word means?" and then looking it up and sharing the meaning with the class.

SUMMARY

Children learn to identify words in order to develop reading fluency and to understand the meanings of words as they add approximately 3000 words to their vocabularies every year. This chapter has focused specifically on meaning vocabulary and what we know about how it is acquired and how it grows in beginning readers.

Effective meaning vocabulary development strategies include helping children appreciate words, encouraging wide reading and application of new words, presenting strategies for independently figuring out new words, and direct teaching of vocabulary and vocabulary-related skills. The ultimate goal of all vocabulary instruction should be to inspire children to become independent word collectors who enjoy acquiring new words. Such learners become the students who comprehend best and, thus, read the most, entering into a self-perpetuating cycle of success.

Learning the meanings of many new words is unquestionably an integral part of a balanced comprehensive literacy program for early readers. The more numerous the reading, writing, listening, and speaking experiences young children have, the more they will come into contact with intriguing new words. And it is through just such experiences that the meaning vocabularies of children grow, just as it is through the excitement of reading and writing that they actually blossom into readers and writers.

QUESTIONS

for Journal Writing and Discussion

1. Think back to your own early schooling. Do you remember having to look up definitions for vocabulary words? Do you feel you benefited from that experience? How will you teach vocabulary differently?

2. Design and discuss an ideal classroom environment in which meaning vocabulary acquisition could flourish. What, if anything, would you change in your design if you had many English language learners in your classroom? Why?

3. How will you explain your approach to vocabulary instruction to parents of your students? Pair up with another member of the class and role-play, presenting your explanation to a parent. Change roles and attempt to make a similar explanation to a teacher who believes only in having children memorize definitions.

SUGGESTIONS

for Projects and Other Activities

1. Construct a board game that requires players to respond with synonyms or antonyms when they land on certain spaces or draw certain cards. Demonstrate the game to your classmates, asking them to role-play primary-age children, or use the game with second- or third-graders in a regular classroom setting.

2. Ask three 5-year-old children, three 6-year-old children, three 7-year-old children, and three 8-year-old children to tell you the meanings of the following words: *ask, tell, sister,* and *girl.* Record their responses. Were there differences in the children's abilities to give precise definitions for the words? Discuss your findings with your classmates.

3. Select several difficult new terms contained in this chapter. Decide which ones could be defined, or partially defined, using the context or word parts. Teach these words to a small group of your classmates using one of the vocabulary development activities in this chapter.

READING COMPREHENSION

Making Sense of Print

FOCUS QUESTIONS

- How is reading comprehension currently defined by reading researchers and practitioners? How does such a definition inform instruction?

- What are some strategies that skilled readers employ to help them construct meaning from text?

- What are some components of an effective program for teaching reading comprehension?

IN THE CLASSROOM

Seven-year-old Tiffani reads the words slowly and deliberately to the teacher: "Bobby will go to the party if his sister cleans her room." Tiffani is able to pronounce each of the twelve words in the sentence perfectly. Moreover, since English is her first language, she has likely known the meaning of each of the individual words in the sentence for several years. But Tiffani reports, after reading this sentence, "I get it! The sister went to the party while Bobby cleaned his room!" Mr. Nguyen is rather surprised at this misinformed interpretation of the sentence, but he probably shouldn't be. Simply being able to read the words on a page does not ensure that Tiffani or other beginning readers like her will necessarily understand what they are reading.

Early readers like Tiffani need to be taught directly how language works within the context of a sentence, paragraph, and book. They also need support in acquiring specific strategies that skilled readers use in order to fully comprehend what they are reading. Then they need plenty of opportunity to use these strategies freely under the watchful eye of a competent and caring teacher.

WHAT IS COMPREHENSION?

Perhaps the most dramatic changes in reading instruction in the last 20 years have occurred in the area of comprehension. Once thought of as simply the natural result of decoding plus oral language, comprehension is now viewed as a much more complex process involving an interface among background knowledge, experience, critical thinking, and direct instruction. The acquisition of comprehension skills by beginning readers depends heavily on awareness about the world at large and the domains of language and print. Successful comprehension necessarily demands a high level of critical thinking, not simply a literal echoing of an author's words.

comprehension
Comprehension is currently thought of as the construction of meaning and is the ultimate goal of exemplary, balanced reading instruction. Proficient readers and beginning readers, too, construct meaning by making connections—by integrating what they already know about a topic to what they are currently encountering in print. As they establish meaning, skilled readers also use their knowledge about the structure of the text they are reading—*expository* or *narrative,* folk tales or historical fiction—to make predictions about what they expect to discover. They also use problem-solving strategies to monitor their thinking and expand on the text (Barrantine, 1996).

In a balanced literacy program, comprehension is now seen as an interactive process. There *is* meaning and content embedded in the text, but every reader also brings particular knowledge and personal ideas to the reading task; comprehension occurs when the reader thinks critically, making meaning by collaborating and negotiating with the author's meaning and then coming to grips both with the text and the writer of the text (Finn, 1990; Vogt, 1997). The discerning teacher, then, assumes the role of coach, encouraging the trial and error that accompanies fledgling meaning-making, and moderating unsuccessful attempts without in any way discouraging the child.

AN IDEAL CLIMATE FOR CRITICAL THINKING

An ideal classroom climate for thinking and comprehending in a balanced literacy program is one in which children's faces are alive with excitement and every hand is up because every child's imagination is churning and producing ideas about the reading material at hand. Young minds are being stimulated and challenged, and many questions are asked for which there are no right or wrong answers. The moment an observer enters such a classroom, that person notices how questions and answers proliferate, many of them initiated by the children themselves. Classrooms that embody this kind of enthusiastic interchange strengthen the spirit of children and spark the flames of curiosity. In such classrooms, children respect their own thoughts and ideas and the thoughts and ideas of others, and are open to new experiences and ways to figure things out. Such a classroom climate is most conducive to producing children who feel up to the task of negotiating meaning with texts.

One way to foster the willingness and the ability to think critically and to comprehend is for the teacher to remove any factors that block—in herself or in her students—the willingness to accept new ideas. To do this the teacher must in some cases eradicate ingrained patterns of behavior, such as the tendency to evaluate all answers children give to thought questions. In other cases the teacher may need to take more of a direct role than usual and provide children with a rudimentary background-knowledge base from which they can begin to think about what they are reading (Cecil, 1995). Specifically, the teacher–coach in a classroom conducive to thinking and comprehending must consider the following issues: knowledge, think time, and praise.

Knowledge

For children to think about what they are reading, they must have some basis of factual awareness, or background knowledge, of the topic being considered. This is sometimes called a **"schema,"** or the background of expectations, knowledge, attitudes, feelings, and predictions that an individual may hold about a topic. Clearly, children cannot critically examine a topic if they know nothing at all about the subject. For example, a teacher may wish to introduce an expository piece about snakes with a critical question such as, "Why are snakes important to us?" Although it seems to be an excellent open-ended question, it may be a poor first question to introduce the piece, for it is possible that many children do not have enough background knowledge about snakes to formulate an answer to the question. By contrast, after reading children an article about snakes, showing excerpts of videos about snakes, showing pictures of different species of snakes, and discussing them with children—all excellent prereading strategies—children are more able and eager to respond to the original question, backing up their ideas, thoughts, and opinions with facts gleaned from the information they have just received. These activities have either helped to create a schema for children or in some cases merely recalled background they already had. Helping children to acquire a knowledge base is often a first step in the total process of comprehending text.

schema

Think Time

Thinking through comprehension strategies takes time. Unfortunately, it is often the children who are quick thinkers or vociferous who respond in class to critical thinking questions, thus getting most of the practice in such skills. Moreover, children from various cultural groups, such as some Southeast Asians, are often taught at home to be unfailingly polite and even self-effacing, and may often be overshadowed by more assertive students. These students quickly establish a pattern in the classroom: The teacher demonstrates a comprehension strategy and follows up with a critical thinking question. Six "eager beavers" have their hands in the air or are shouting out the answer before the others have even had a chance to consider the question. The other children begin to realize if they delay raising their hands, the quicker, more assertive children will answer and the slower thinkers, or less forthcoming youngsters, will not be held accountable for thinking. To avoid this pitfall, it is advisable for the teacher to provide as much "think time" as is necessary for *all* children to think through an answer to a critical thinking question.

Praise

A strong (perhaps overly strong) praise response is exemplified by a teacher who responds to a child's answer with, "That's exactly the right answer! Excellent job!" On the other hand, a more tempered response, such as, "Yes, Kay, that is one way to think about the boy's problem," acknowledges the child's thinking rather than the response, and also keeps the window open for different responses by other members in the class.

The use of profusive praise is sometimes appropriate—as when working with very young children, second-language learners who are just emerging from their **silent period** (the period during which they are faced with a new language and are not speaking, but are developing receptive language skills), children with special needs, or when asking a question of factual or low-level recall, such as, "Raúl, what was the name of the little boy's dog?" On the other hand, when the goal is to have the children think critically or creatively about text, the teacher should temper strong praise to student responses, as teacher's praise often becomes the reason children are answering rather than for the mere sharing of their ideas. The goal should be to help children discover intrinsic sources for their motivation. Strong praise tends to encourage conformity, causing children to depend on the praise-giver for the worth of their ideas, rather than on themselves and their own satisfaction with their thinking.

silent period

STRATEGIES NECESSARY FOR COMPREHENDING

A *reading comprehension strategy* is one of a compendium of skills proficient readers use to connect to and gain personal meaning from literature. Good readers and writers are *always* in the process of creating meaning. They select and use from among a constellation of appropriate strategies, monitoring their understanding as they read, and refining that meaning as they encounter new information in the text. Some of the most critical comprehension strategies, discussed below, are as follows (Tompkins, 1997):

- making predictions
- tuning in to prior knowledge
- visualizing
- making connections
- monitoring understanding
- generalizing
- evaluating
- asking and answering questions

Making Predictions

Proficient readers make mental predictions, or calculated hunches, about what might happen next in the text they are reading. Their hunches are based upon what they already know about the topic, what they know about the literary structure the author is using—e.g., is it narrative or expository text? a fairy tale or an autobiographical incident?—and what they have learned thus far in the text. As skilled readers continue, they tend to confirm or deny their previous hunches, according to new understandings that occur. With expository text, they often preview the text to get an overview of what information will be covered and look through the text to see if it matches their expectations. Skilled readers also ask themselves questions for which they hope to find answers as they read, thus setting their own purposes for reading the text.

Tuning in to Prior Knowledge

Good readers think about what they already know about a topic before they begin reading and then assimilate the new information with their prior knowledge during the reading process. Such background knowledge may include, but is not limited to, knowledge of the text structure the author is using, familiarity with the literary genre, vocabulary, and information about the topic. This prior knowledge constitutes a schema for the topic, with which further learning will need to be reconciled.

Visualizing

Proficient readers tend to create pictures in their minds' eye as they read text, especially text containing elaborate imagery or well-developed story characters. Placing themselves in the story as the main character, facing the same trials and tribulations as that character, helps them appreciate, remember, and internalize the story that is unfolding before them. Because the experience of mental vision is so personal and intense, readers skilled in this strategy are often disappointed when they see the film version of a story they have read, as it frequently pales in comparison to what occurs in their rich imaginations.

Making Connections

Proficient readers tend to personalize whatever they are reading by relating it directly to their own lives. They categorize events according to their own sets of experiences and compare story characters to people they know. Experienced readers also compare what they are reading to other literature they have read. Making connections can extend even further when the skilled reader compares books written by the same author, or various versions of the same tale or event.

Monitoring Understanding

Proficient readers are continually checking their own understanding as they read, making sure what they are confronting conforms to what they already know and assuring themselves that they haven't missed something. It is, therefore, quite normal for skilled readers to make frequent regressions, or to go back and reread a sentence or passage, to check that they initially "got it right." Such monitoring of understanding can best be described as that encounter that takes place when a skilled reader is reading an unstimulating text late at night and suddenly realizes that not a word has been understood—a phenomenon to which most readers of this text can relate!

Generalizing

Proficient readers tend to remember important ideas and information they discover throughout a text and bring them together to draw conclusions. Such conclusions then form the "big picture" of the reading material; such a strategy is the basis upon which skilled readers are able to summarize what they have read, or to articulate the main idea in expository text and separate it from the supporting details. Generalization is also the basis upon which readers are able to identify particular underlying themes in literature.

Evaluating

Proficient readers reflect upon and form personal opinions about the texts they read; they internalize the meanings certain works have held for them, review ideas frequently, and evaluate what they have read compared with other texts and what they had hoped to gain from the text. Such opinions and reflections about text are not transmitted to the child by a teacher but emanate directly from the reader's own thinking about the personal transaction with the material.

Asking and Answering Questions

One of the most valuable ways proficient readers construct text meanings is by asking and answering important questions about text as they read. They are aware of the difference between "thinking-type" questions and "locating information-type" questions, and they are able to later reflect on the caliber of the questions they have asked themselves.

INSTRUCTIONAL ACTIVITIES FOR TEACHING COMPREHENSION

The activities offered in the next section incorporate the comprehension strategies discussed in the preceding section. Specific activities have been designated for use during prereading, reading, or postreading, as appropriate. The activities can begin with children as early as kindergarten when no written response is requested. Written responses can be included as soon as children have the writing proficiency to answer the questions, but oral responses should always be an option. Oral discussions during the activities, accompanied by pictures, objects, or other visuals, have the added benefit of allowing English language learners to listen to the way others are thinking and participate as they feel comfortable.

DIRECTED READING THINKING ACTIVITY (DRTA)

ACTIVITY

The objective of the Directed Reading Thinking Activity, developed by Stauffer (1969), is to improve comprehension by having children focus on a particular passage and to make predictions about it based on those textual features. The DRTA is one of the most commonly used approaches to a reading lesson; most basal readers more or less follow this format. Though it can be conducted in various ways, the steps include the following:

Prereading

1. Direct the children's attention to the title of the passage and ask them to predict its content. After the children have volunteered their predictions and the reasons for their responses, ask a preselected group whether they agree or disagree and why.

During Reading

2. Read or have a child read several sentences, and ask the children what they think the story is about based on this new information.

3. Direct the children's attention to particular vocabulary or phrases that are prominent to the meaning of the text. Ask them to use these words to hypothesize what the piece will be about.

4. Ask them to look at pictures, graphs, and figures and make more predictions based upon this new information.

Postreading

5. Ask the children to read the text to confirm or negate their predictions and hypotheses. Discuss findings.

STRUCTURED LISTENING ACTIVITY (SLA)

ACTIVITY

structured listening

For preliterate children, comprehension can be enhanced in an enjoyable way through a **structured listening** activity which establishes the story line with visuals, allowing even non-English-speaking children to participate in the telling and retelling of a story. Here are the steps to be followed:

1. Draw or trace, color, and cut out felt visuals of each of the main characters and props to set the story you have chosen to read to the children, for example, *The Gingerbread Boy*. Use these visuals on a flannel board. (See Figure 8.1.)

FIGURE 8.1 *Flannel board depicting the ending of the story, "The Gingerbread Boy."*

OTHER PROPS:

Grandmother
oven
bird
rabbit
cat
rabbit
cat
horse
happy gingerbread boy
house

FIGURE 8.2 *Story frame for retelling.*

Somebody	Wanted	But	So
Gingerbread Boy	to run & play	a fox came	he got eaten

Prereading

2. Introduce the key concepts in the story, e.g., "Have you ever run away from anyone? Why?"

During Reading

3. Read the story once without the visuals. Reread the story, focusing children's attention on the visuals that support the events in the story.

Postreading

4. Ask the children to retell the story with the help of a chart such as the one shown in Figure 8.2.

5. Help them fill in this chart, as they filled in the chart in Figure 8.1 for *The Gingerbread Boy.*

6. Ask for volunteers to retell the story while other children manipulate the visuals. *Note:* Non-English speakers may be encouraged to retell the story in their home language.

DYAD READING

ACTIVITY

dyad reading

Dyad reading is a form of paired oral reading (also called "buddy reading" or "say something") that has the added dimension of reinforcing the important comprehension strategies of summarizing and questioning (Cecil, 1995). The activity consists of the following format:

1. Select two children to demonstrate the activity. Have one read a paragraph aloud. (With younger children, this can be reduced to one sentence.)

2. As that child reads, have the other child listen carefully and then summarize (orally or in writing) what was in the paragraph. For variation, the second child may simply draw what was read, then describe the picture.

Postreading

3. Have the reader ask the listener critical comprehension questions.

4. Encourage the children to discuss the answers and, where there is disagreement, have them refer to the paragraph to support their answers.

5. Have children change roles with succeeding paragraphs.

When children appear ready to practice this activity independently, divide the class into pairs or threesomes. (*Note:* By using a threesome, a child who is an English language learner or a nonreader can get the gist of the passage simply by listening to it being read and then summarized.)

ACTIVITY

STORY PREDICTION

Story prediction can be used as a written adaptation of the DRTA to help children develop elaborate predictions about the basal reader or trade book stories they will read (Buckley, 1986). For this activity, pair students or divide the class into small groups. Then follow the sequence below:

Prereading

1. Have the partners or members of the group leaf through the illustrations in the story in order. Then have each partner or group member take turns carefully describing what is happening in each illustration. After each illustration is described, have the next child in rotation predict aloud what will happen in that part of the story.

2. After all the illustrations in the story have been discussed in this way, ask each child to write a story predicting what will happen in the story according to what was described in the illustrations. (Younger children can record their predictions into a tape recorder.)

3. Have partners or group members share their stories with the rest of the class and discuss their opinions about the accuracy of each of the predictions.

During Reading

4. Have the partners or group members take turns reading the story aloud (or silently) to check their predictions. (For younger children, the teacher may read the story.)

Postreading

5. Have the partners or group members then compare the actual story with their predictive stories and discuss, as a group, who they think came closest to the actual events in the story.

ACTIVITY

THINK ALOUD

think aloud

Think aloud is one of the most effective ways a teacher can model all the effective comprehension strategies a fluent reader uses to gain meaning from the printed page. The teacher can utilize this activity in the following way:

1. Beforehand, the teacher makes copies of the text passage that will be demonstrated or prepares it for an overhead projector.

Prereading

2. After looking at the cover or the title and the illustrations in the passage, the teacher ruminates aloud as to what the passage might be about.

During Reading

3. The teacher reads the passage aloud as the children track. The teacher continually organizes images by explaining the passage after every sentence or paragraph.

4. The teacher answers aloud such questions as,

   "What am I reminded of here that I already know?" (tapping prior knowledge)

   "What are some ways I can get help in understanding unfamiliar words and/or ideas?" (monitoring understanding)

   "What does this remind me of in my own life?" (making connections)

5. After modeling the reading of several paragraphs in this fashion, the teacher invites children to add their own problem-solving tactics and personal impressions by reading succeeding passages in pairs.

RECIPROCAL TEACHING

ACTIVITY

The **reciprocal teaching** activity has been found to foster comprehension by helping children to actively monitor their thinking (Rosenshine, 1996). During this question-generating activity, the teacher demonstrates how to monitor reading comprehension, how to observe the thinking process while reading, and determine when they are succeeding and when they are not (Palinscar, 1987). The teacher then asks the children to attempt the same activity on their own, offering them feedback on their performance. The procedure contains five subcomponents—reading, summarizing, questioning, predicting, and clarifying—and is conducted as follows:

reciprocal teaching

Prereading

1. As the children listen, read a paragraph from a passage of text aloud.

Postreading

2. Model how the paragraph might be summarized. Focus on the main ideas in the paragraph, include the topic sentence, and point out that a summary should be no more than one-third of the original paragraph.

3. Ask the group an important question about the paragraph, one that focuses on the key issues. Solicit other questions from the group.

4. Predict aloud what might be expected to be in the remainder of the passage. Solicit other predictions from the group.

5. Think aloud about any clarifying information that might be helpful to have in order to understand the paragraph more completely. (*Note:* This step is not always necessary in well-written paragraphs that are appropriate for the reader's skill.) Solicit other ideas about what information might be needed.

ACTIVITY

THE KNOWLEDGE CHART (ALSO CALLED K-W-L)

knowledge chart

Teachers can use this activity to show children how to access their background knowledge, or schema, for a topic through guided questions; they can then help children identify their new knowledge gained by reading and place it on a chart. Modeled after a procedure developed by Ogle (1986), the **knowledge chart** is intended to be used before and after reading or listening to a selection containing factual material. The procedure, in outline form, goes as follows:

Prereading

1. *Knowledge.* Ask the children: "What do you know about [the topic]?" Record all responses in the first column of a large sheet of chart paper under the heading "What We Know" or "Knowledge."

2. *Questions.* Ask: "What would you *like* to know about [the topic]?" Record the children's responses in the second column of the chart paper under the heading "Questions We Have."

Postreading

3. *New Knowledge.* After the reading of the selection, ask: "What have you learned about [the topic]?" Help the children to revise the knowledge from the first column, answer the questions from the second column, and list new facts not considered prior to the reading. Place it in a third column labeled "What We Learned."

4. *Research.* Distribute student-initiated questions that have not yet been answered from the second column to children interested in researching the answers. Help them find more information on the topic. This information may be added to the chart in a new column, as in Figure 8.3.

5. *Evaluation.* Ask a provocative question that will lead children to a personal evaluation of the topic, such as "How did this selection change your feelings about [the topic]?" Place new appreciations in a new column labeled "How We Feel Now" or "Evaluation."

FIGURE 8.3 *Knowledge chart on lemmings.*

LEMMINGS

What we know	Questions we have	What we learned from reading	What we learned from research	How we feel now
little animals live far away	what do they eat? good pets? how big? in zoos? where do you get one?	eat leaves and bugs too wild 4 or 5 inches not in zoos found in Norway	Lemmings drown themselves. No one knows why. Scientists think to keep population down or instinct.	We think it's an interesting mystery!

EXPERIENCE–TEXT RELATIONSHIP (ETR)

ACTIVITY

Children are not always able to relate their own experiences to a topic before reading about it, even though research confirms such a skill is critical to adequate comprehension—background must be brought to bear at all phases of the reading process (Cecil, 1995). An effective activity to help a wide range of learners achieve enhanced comprehension by making their past experiences an integral part of reading is through **experience–text relationship** (Au, 1979). Using Au's method, the teacher asks questions about passages that are difficult for the children due to inadequate background, attempting to fill in the experiential gaps. Through the teacher's questioning, cueing, and prompting, the children are better able to integrate features of the text with their existing experiences. The activity is composed of three phases: (1) an *experience* phase for eliciting existing background; (2) a *text* phase, for determining what children are deriving from the text; and (3) a *relationship* phase, in which children compare their own experiences with what they have just read. The activity proceeds as follows:

experience–text relationship

Prereading

1. *Experience.* Ask the children questions about experiences they have had, or ask them to share certain knowledge they have that is in any way related to the selection they are about to read or hear.

During reading

2. *Text.* After all the children have had an opportunity to share their knowledge or experiences, have them read or listen to short passages of the selection (usually a paragraph or a page at a time), asking them critical-thinking questions about the content after each section is read. Listen for responses that reveal lack of understanding due to differing world views or lack of experience with the topic. Add necessary background to correct misunderstandings. This can be in the form of personal anecdotes, pictures, questions, and/or discussion.

Postreading

3. *Relationship.* Attempt to make connections for the children between the content of the selection, as discussed in the *text* phase, and the children's own experiences and knowledge, as shared in the *experience* phase.

ACTIVITY

QUESTION–ANSWER RELATIONSHIPS (QARs)

Question–answer relationships, or QARs (Raphael, 1982), help children to enhance their comprehension by learning to answer a range of questions and understand each question's relationship to the text, the author, and to themselves. With this strategy, children ask themselves, "Where would I find an answer to this question in the text?" and use the following hierarchy of questions and answers to help them decide:

Literal Question (type 1)

The answer is "right there." This tells the child that the answer to the question is easy to find in the text. In fact, the exact words in the question are contained within the text.

Inferential Question (type 2)

The answer can be found if you "think and search." This tells the child that the answer is in the text, but two ideas will have to be brought together; that is, the words used in the question may be a bit different from the words used in the text, so the answer will be a bit harder to find.

Critical Question (type 3)

The answer is in the mind of "the author and you." The answer is not directly stated in the story, but if readers bring their own ideas to the text and combine them with the opinion the author seems to hold, they will be able to answer the question.

Creative Question (type 4)

The answer has to be determined "on your own." The child won't find a direct answer to the question in the text. There is no right or wrong answer to the question; it must emanate from the child's imagination or from information he already has about the topic.

See Figure 8.4.

FIGURE 8.4 *Question–answer relationships (QARs).*

IN THE BOOK QARs

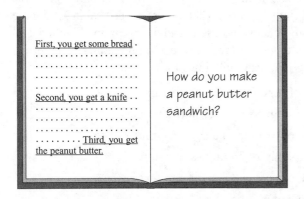

IN MY HEAD QARs

RIGHT THERE

The answer is in the text, usually easy to find. The words used to make up the question and words used to answer the question are Right There in the same sentence.

AUTHOR AND YOU

The answer is *not* in the story. You need to think about what you already know, what the author tells you in the text, and how it fits together.

THINK AND SEARCH (PUTTING IT TOGETHER)

The answer is in the story, but you need to put together different story parts to find it. Words for the question and words for the answer are not found in the same sentence. They come from different parts of the text.

ON MY OWN

The answer is not in the story. You can even answer the question without reading the story. You need to use your own experience.

From "Teaching question answer relationships, revisited," by Taffy E. Raphael. *The Reading Teacher, 39(6),* 516–522. Used with permission.

Following is an outline of how children can be guided to incorporate the use of these questions to boost their own comprehension:

Prereading

1. Give children four passages with questions for which the question types have already been determined.
2. Using the first passage, model how the answers to each question might be found in the text by identifying the appropriate QAR.

During Reading

3. Read the second passage aloud to children. Ask the questions aloud and have volunteers explain which kind of question is being asked and how they would find the answer in the text.

During/Postreading

4. Divide the class into small cooperative groups. Ask them to read the third passage, and answer the questions identifying the appropriate QARs.
5. Have children follow the same procedure individually, as the teacher goes around the classroom offering assistance as needed.

COMPONENTS FOR A SUCCESSFUL COMPREHENSION PROGRAM

A review of the important research in the last few years offers classroom teachers surprisingly consistent findings about what factors are critical in setting the stage for a successful comprehension-based reading program. Fielding and Pearson (1994), synthesizing the findings of research on reading comprehension, suggest the following practical guidelines for teachers:

- Provide a large block of time for actual text reading
- Provide direct instruction in comprehension strategies
- Provide opportunities for reading in a social setting
- Provide children with plenty of children's literature
- Provide opportunities for personal response to text
- Consider the language and culture of all learners

Provide a Large Block of Time for Actual Text Reading

As a rule of thumb, children should have more time during the school day to actually practice reading than the combined total allocated for learning about, talking about, or writing about what they are reading. In a truly balanced reading program for primary grades, this is true even for the most fledgling of beginning readers. Such time can be built into the curriculum through programs such as "Drop Everything and Read" (DEAR) described in the box below.

To ensure that such practice actually translates into enhanced comprehension, however, children should be given some choice about what they read. They should also be provided with reasons to reread some materials to increase fluency, and the material offered should be appropriate in difficulty; that is, not so difficult as to be frustrating, but not so easy that nothing challenging is encountered (Fielding and Pearson, 1994).

How to implement "Drop Everything and Read" (DEAR)

In order for children to increase their reading comprehension, they must be given plenty of opportunities to practice the strategies they have been learning. A block of time set aside just for enjoyable application of these skills is time well spent. One such program is DEAR. This is what you do:

1. Put together a classroom library that includes a wide variety of topics and reading levels. Include fiction and nonfiction, paperbacks as well as hardcover books, magazines, newspapers, comic books, catalogs, manuals, books and stories written by students, as well as an assortment of multicultural literature.

2. To introduce children to silent reading time, explain that they will all be reading something for a few minutes at the same time each day. "Talk up" a few of the selections from the classroom library. Help children make one or two selections ahead of time that they will be browsing or reading during the first DEAR session. Do not coerce children to read certain books you think are appropriate for them; any selection they make is valid.

3. Explain the rules for DEAR:
   Everyone is silent.
   Everyone is reading or looking at a book.
   Children stay in their seats or in the reading area.

4. The role of the teacher, as an actively reading role model, is *essential.*

5. Start with a brief exposure, perhaps three minutes in kindergarten, to allow children to get used to the procedure. Gradually build up to ten minutes (kindergarten) to twenty minutes (third grade). To be most effective, DEAR must be done every day at the same time. After lunch, when children need to be settled down, is an ideal time.

In the past, the most able readers, because of their ability, were given far less specific, isolated comprehension strategy instruction and were, therefore, allotted more time to read than other, less able readers. Today researchers are speculating on whether that very discrepancy might have caused an even wider gap between the able and less able readers (Anderson et al., 1988).

From this research, it seems clear that children should be provided with plenty of time during the day to practice reading. Reading material should include texts that are easily decodable so that children can apply recently learned decoding strategies to text. Free time to select from a wide variety of trade books appealing to differing interests and encompassing all independent reading levels in the class should also be a prominent part of the reading program. Finally, teachers should demonstrate the use of the compendium of strategies through the reading aloud of quality children's literature that, while above the decoding level of many of the children in the class, can still be used effectively to spur interest and enhance comprehension.

Provide Direct Instruction in Comprehension Strategies

A landmark study by Durkin (1979) found that although teachers were spending an inordinate amount of time assessing comprehension through a wide variety of basal workbook pages, only a fraction of instructional time was spent actually showing children how to read strategically in order to optimally comprehend.

Researchers have now attested that children must be taught, directly, what each comprehension strategy is, how and when to use such a strategy, and under what circumstances. Each strategy should first be modeled by the teacher, then the children should receive guided practice in applying the strategy, and finally they should use it independently while obtaining feedback from the teacher (Duffy, 1988). The strategies offered in this chapter are prototypes of those that, when introduced in this manner, will serve to develop the reading comprehension of students.

Provide Opportunities for Reading in a Social Setting

Children, especially English language learners, learn best when they are able to talk about what they are doing and learn from each other. Besides enhancing their learning by adding sensory input and vocabulary development provided by oral discussion, reading, when social, is more enjoyable for most children.

A continuum of reading configurations should therefore be used in a classroom. Shared and guided reading (see Chapter 10), where the teacher is prominent and working with small groups, are ideal formats for direct instruction. Other more collaborative approaches include dyad reading, discussed earlier, simple partner reading, and echo reading, with the children repeating the lines the teacher reads. When children begin to possess a modicum of fluency and independence, they can immediately move toward small, independent reading discussion groups, where they are in charge of sharing their personal reactions to text.

Provide Children with Plenty of Children's Literature

Quality children's literature is a necessity in beginning literacy instruction. Literature does much more than merely teach children how to read; it also contributes to language development, stimulates the senses, provokes emotional response, and exposes children to a variety of thoughts and ideas (Jalongo, 1988). While decodable texts are critical for use in reinforcing phonic elements and decoding skills, children's literature is the ideal vehicle through which to model comprehension strategies for children. The primary classroom should be stocked with picture books, or books that use both pictures and text to tell the story; award winners, such as the Children's Choice and Newbery medal winners and runners up; predictable books that contain phrases that can easily be anticipated by children, such as rhyming patterns, repeating verses, or cumulative verses; and big books, which are oversized versions of favorite children's books suitable for sharing in small groups. Besides being used for modeling by teachers, such literature can be used for browsing during free reading time and can be tape-recorded for individual read-alongs.

Provide Opportunities for Personal Response to Text

Not so long ago it seemed that teachers often became so concerned with assessing comprehension and completing the lists of comprehension questions provided at the end of each basal reader story, that little time was left for rich, personal discussion of text—the kind of voluntary conversation that is the most significant to children. Eeds (1989) calls these two contrasting types of discourses the difference between a "gentle inquisition," a barrage of mainly factual, assessment-oriented questions about text, versus "grand conversations," where the children are asked to reflect upon the personal relevance of the text, much as adults are invited to do in the intimate setting of a book club. Such conversations are vital to developing a genuine love for reading and have the added value of elevating the classroom climate to one of a "community of readers" (Hansen, 1987).

To act upon this suggestion, teachers must ensure that they do not limit themselves to only factual-type questions, but allow plenty of time for critical and creative questions for which there is no one "correct" answer, and for which every child has an opportunity to voice an opinion. It is also helpful for teachers to sometimes create provocative questions about text for which they themselves do not have an answer, thereby assuring that they will not be "fishing" for the response they have in mind, or for that provided by the basal instructor's manual. Moreover, adequate time should be set aside for sharing journal reactions to literature in small interest groups where the atmosphere is safe and conducive to personal conversations about text.

Children can also share responses about books they are reading using electronic dialoguing. Using a computer, children write their thoughts and feelings about their books and send them to students in other classrooms, older students, or preservice students at a university. The "computer pal," if wisely chosen, can encourage children to elaborate on their entries, make personal connections, and reflect more deeply on their reading (Moore, 1991).

Consider the Language and Culture of All Learners

There are great differences in how rapidly and how well children learn to speak English. When children who are struggling with English are asked to comprehend printed material in their second language too soon, it can lead to frustration and confusion. Such children can be encouraged in a supportive classroom where instruction not only provides for but celebrates differences. Teachers may find it helpful to use a variety of predictable texts, multisensory teaching, and repetition to improve comprehension strategies. Most important, they need to also create a language-rich environment and to provide many opportunities for cooperative interaction with English-speaking children (see the box below).

Suggestions to improve comprehension for English language learners

1. Use multisensory materials, such as videos, CD–ROM, pictures, recordings, and other supports.
2. Use gestures and body language.
3. Speak slowly and enunciate clearly.
4. Use longer pauses between phrases and sentences.
5. Use much repetition and review.
6. Use short sentences and simpler syntax.
7. Use fewer pronouns.
8. Exaggerate intonation, especially when introducing phonemic elements.
9. Use high frequency vocabulary.
10. Use fewer idioms and slang terms.
11. Maintain a low anxiety level.
12. Emphasize cooperative learning.

Teachers can also improve comprehension in all learners by offering a variety of multicultural reading material that reflects the prior knowledge and background of the diverse learners in the classroom (Wiseman, 1992). For example, classrooms should be supplied with literature that represents a wide range of values, lifestyles, customs, and historical traditions. An example of an effective comprehension activity that encourages multicultural awareness for all children is to compare folk tales, such as *Cinderella* with its African counterpart, *Mufaro's Beautiful Daughters* (Steptoe, 1987) or the Chinese *Lon Po Po* (Young, 1989) with its European counterpart, *Little Red Ridinghood.*

SUMMARY

Learning to sound out words through phonics and other word-unlocking strategies is certainly critical, but if this component of literacy has been accomplished, can we then say a child has "learned to read"? No. For real reading to occur, the child has to be simultaneously constructing meaning from the words that have been decoded; that meaning, then, must be assimilated into the child's world view. This meaning-making is a complex and arduous process best consummated through a program that offers guidance in specific comprehension strategies and many opportunities to apply them with quality literature as well as with decodable text. The teacher in such a program becomes a kind of coach who is there to model, guide, and provide feedback to learners.

Proficient readers possess a constellation of strategies from which they choose to interact with text and construct meaning. These strategies must be directly taught to burgeoning readers through modeling, guided instruction, and plenty of independent application with actual text. Additionally, they must be given the opportunity to share their personal responses to text with each other in a variety of social settings.

A literacy program so myopically focused on meaning-making to the exclusion of instruction in decoding skills may create a rich literacy environment that is, inadvertently, inaccessible to many learners; on the other hand, a program lacking in ways to derive personal meaning from text may well create learners who can read but who choose not to do so. For a literacy program to be truly balanced, it must enable learners to decode text but it must also offer them guidance in strategic reading and ample opportunity to read for meaning and enjoyment.

QUESTIONS

for Journal Writing and Discussion

1. What is your definition of reading? How do you think your definition will determine the importance of comprehension instruction to your total reading program?

2. Think about what you do when you read. What comprehension strategies did you use as you read the beginning of this chapter? Make a list of the strategies you can identify. Then spend several minutes reading a novel or other narrative text. Make a second list of the strategies you used with the narrative text. Compare the two lists. Are there major differences? Why?

3. The parent of one of your students visits your classroom. She expects to see lots of silent workbook activities. Prepare an argument that you might give to this parent who wonders why you are spending so much time allowing children to read self-selected material and discussing it in small share groups.

SUGGESTIONS

for Projects and Other Activities

1. Select one of the comprehension activities outlined in this chapter. Find a selection from a primary basal reader that would be appropriate content for such a strategy. Teach the strategy to a small group of your classmates. Discuss their reactions.

2. Conduct the above activity, or another of your choice, with a small group of third-grade children. What problems did they have with the lesson? What did they like about using the strategy? Discuss your findings with your class.

3. Observe a primary classroom as the teacher conducts a reading lesson for an entire week. Make a list of all activities in which the teacher and the students are engaged during the week and the time spent on each. How much time was spent on the direct teaching of comprehension strategies? What percentage of the total teaching time was actually spent on teaching comprehension? How much time was spent on the application of these strategies or in actual reading by the students?

9 READING– WRITING CONNECTIONS

Reciprocal Paths to Literacy

FOCUS QUESTIONS

- What are appropriate writing goals for primary grade children? How can these goals be achieved for every child?

- How can "writer's workshop" be used to help young children learn about print and see themselves as authors?

- In what ways can teachers use modeling and writing structures to encourage emergent writers to acquire the conventions of written language?

In the Classroom

Seven-year-old Maria turns to her trusted friend, Josh, to get some objective feedback about her current writing ideas.

"I'm thinking of writing a story about three frogs, or maybe about when my dog ran away," Maria declares, showing Josh a paper full of half-formed ideas. "Which one do *you* think I should write about?"

Josh looks up from his own writing and asks Maria what exactly she has to say about the frogs. Maria ponders this for a moment. Then she replies that she really doesn't know much about frogs, but that she's read lots of stories that contain three animals, although not necessarily about frogs. Abruptly, Josh poses an insightful question.

"Well, what about your dog running away? Was that a big deal?" "Oh, yes!" replies Maria, her face clouding over with the memory.

Maria begins to tell Josh a woeful tale about a recent time when her dog, Puppy, jumped the fence; the family had thought the dog was gone for good.

Josh listens intently and then shrugs; Maria has answered her own question and both children suddenly realize it.

Talking about her writing before she puts pen to paper has provided Maria with a kind of mental rehearsal for her writing and a clearer picture of what she really wants to talk about.

Like the children in the above vignette, most children in the primary grades come to school with excitement and enthusiasm for learning. They tend to be highly motivated and interested in engaging in the reciprocal communicative skills of reading and writing. Their image of being "grown-up" and attending school includes involvement in authentic literacy activities such as those they have seen all around them. Most of these young children have probably picked up the idea that they would be learning to write as soon as they entered school.

Farnan et al. (1992) suggest that early attempts at writing are perfect opportunities for children to experiment with print and extend their understanding of text; Richgels (1995) claims that early writing provides children with invaluable practice with phonic skills, such as blending sounds into words and segmenting words into parts. It is not surprising, therefore, that a major research finding in emergent literacy is that writing—if much experimentation is encouraged—can play a pivotal role in children's learning to read. Rather than developing *after* reading, as educators once assumed, we now know that writing accompanies young children's growing interest in naming letters and reading print. Early-grade teachers would therefore benefit from putting research into practice by accommodating young children's wishes to quickly read and write, providing them with immediate opportunities to participate in real writing along with their initial reading instruction.

WRITING GOALS FOR EARLY READERS

Emergent literacy depends on much more than providing a print-rich environment and then allowing children to "go to it naturally," although such a background is enormously helpful. But there must also be literate models—teachers, parents, siblings, or caretakers—to demonstrate the "how-to's" of writing. As in reading, it is important to directly point out the conventions of written language and to answer children's burgeoning questions about print.

With these ideas in mind, the following is a list of suggested literacy goals that are appropriate for fostering the reading–writing connection in kindergarten through third-grade children.

1. Development of oral-language fluency for native English speakers as well as English language learners.

2. Development of an awareness that writing is constructing meaning with thoughts and speech in written form.

3. Development of a positive, confident, and conscientious attitude toward writing and its conventions (i.e., spelling, punctuation, etc.).

4. Development of an awareness and appreciation of self as writer.

5. Development of awareness and appreciation of self as collaborator and evaluator in the writing process.

6. Development of an interest in personal, meaningful writing and experimentation within a widening variety of formats.

The remainder of this chapter will be devoted to program attributes and positive practices designed to help a teacher reach these early literacy goals.

THE WRITING PROCESS AND WRITER'S WORKSHOP

The **writing process** is a set of stages in which a writer engages in activities designed to solve certain problems unique to a particular stage. It is exactly this problem-solving approach that makes the writing process more effective than traditional approaches that tend to focus merely on the completed product. A final product in traditional writing programs is often simply a second draft consisting of a mindless recopying of a teacher's red pen corrections.

writing process

The writing process and methods of teaching writing have evolved considerably over the years, but two beliefs have remained consistent: (1) the creation of a piece of writing is a developmental process that takes place over a period of time; and (2) writers engage in different activities depending upon their stage of development.

The writing process can be introduced to emergent writers as early as kindergarten or first grade. The process, modified for young children, often takes place in a *writer's workshop,* which is a popular way of organizing a writing class in the same way professional writers do. It is based on the premise that writers write best when they write frequently, for extended periods of time, and on topics of their own choosing. A writer's workshop for the primary grades should roughly follow the format shown in Figure 9.1.

During writer's workshop, children work through the following stages over a period of several days, or sometimes weeks (Peha, 1996):

- prewriting
- drafting
- sharing

- revising
- editing
- publishing

FIGURE 9.1   *Components of writer's workshop.*

Minilesson **(5–10 minutes)**	This is a short lesson focused on a single, narrow topic that the children need based upon the teacher's observation of the children's daily writing. The teacher may see a need in only certain students and invite just them to meet for the lesson.
Status of the class **(2–3 minutes)**	This is a brief survey by the teacher to find out what each child is working on as well as what stage of the writing process each is in.
Writing time **(15–20 minutes)**	The children write, choosing topics from their writing folder. The teacher conferences with individual children.
Sharing **(5–10 minutes)**	Children read what they have written and seek specific feedback from an audience (whole class, small groups, or partners).

Prewriting (Exploring the Topic)

In this initial stage, children think, plan, talk, and take rudimentary notes about something they want to write about. Children are urged to write about topics they know well. Many things qualify as prewriting activities. Some of the most helpful activities for young children are conversations with a friend about the topic, reflecting, drawing, brainstorming, visualizing personal experiences, and jotting down notes.

writing prompts

To ignite the thinking process, it is sometimes helpful for the teacher to offer creative or reflective **writing prompts,** or motivational ideas, to inspire the children and get their imaginations churning. For example, the teacher might offer a sentence, such as "When I opened my front door, I saw a cute puppy just sitting on my doorstep," and ask children, orally, to add some ideas to turn the sentence into a story. Another prompt might be to brainstorm a "What if?" question with the children; for example, "What if everyone looked exactly alike?" or "What if we could talk to animals?" or "What if we were invisible?" Such prompts, followed by much oral discussion and subsequent brainstorming, make most children eager to write.

Drafting (Putting Ideas Down on Paper)

Drafting is where formal writing begins. Young children usually write single draft compositions, adding words to accompany drawings they have made. (See Figure 9.2.)

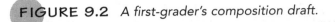

FIGURE 9.2 *A first-grader's composition draft.*

The emphasis here is on expressing ideas, never on spelling or handwriting. It is absolutely vital at this stage to respond to what the children have to say with positive oral comments or, with older children, written ones. As in the prewriting stage, in the drafting stage it is important that emergent writers are given sufficient time and encouragement to engage in risk-free exploration of their subject matter.

It may be helpful to introduce the chart shown in Figure 9.3 to the children and then have it prominently displayed in the room.

Sharing (Getting Feedback)

The writer of a draft is looking for reactions and suggestions and may ask the responder, sometimes called the peer editor, to consider one or more questions. For example: Is the piece interesting? Is there something missing? Should the ideas be organized differently? These questions can be answered through a conference with another child, through a teacher–student conference, by sharing it with the class or a small group of students, or through discussion with friends, parents, or others.

The sharing phase can occur after each draft or as often as the child desires. Children need to be taught to respond to each other's writing in a way that is constructive, helpful, and tactful. The guidelines for responding shown

FIGURE 9.3 *Writing steps.*

1. Choose a topic. (Planning)

2. Discuss your writing with a partner in a comfortable place. (Planning)

3. Write down all your ideas for your piece. (Composing)

4. Share your writing with a partner, with the class, or with your teacher. Ask your partners questions about your writing. (Sharing)

5. Use what your partner says to help you add information, get rid of information, or change words or ideas. (Revising)

6. Reread your piece. Correct mistakes you find. (Proofreading)

7. Read your piece to the class, a share group, or a partner. (Presenting)

8. Store your writing in your folder. Later you may decide to publish it.

9. Choose a new topic and begin again.

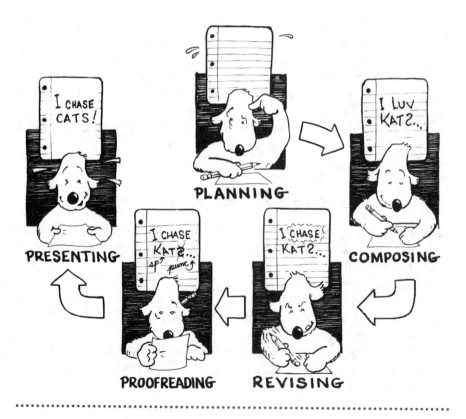

in Figure 9.4 should be introduced to children and used several times with anonymous writing (from other classes or previous years) so children can see which messages are helpful and which ones are not.

Listed in Figure 9.5 are a few examples of questions a teacher might ask during an author/teacher conference.

FIGURE 9.4 *Guidelines for sharing writing with a peer editor.*

1. Ask a partner to listen to your writing.
2. Move quietly to a comfortable place where you can talk in 6" (tiny, inside) voices.
3. Ask your partner questions such as the following:
   - Do you think the opening "grabs" you?
   - Is there any part I should throw away?
   - Did I use any "tired" words?
   - What is the best part of my writing?
   - Is there any part you didn't understand?
   - Do I need a different ending?
   - Are there any sentences I should combine or separate?
   - What do you like best? Why? Least? Why?
4. Return to your seat and decide which, if any, of the suggestions you will use.

FIGURE 9.5 *Guidelines for conferencing (teacher).*

What can I help you with?

How do you think you are doing?

What is the most exciting part of your piece?

How do you want the reader to feel after reading this?

Does your opening sentence get the reader's attention?

What is the most important part of your piece?

Can you tell me more about . . . ?

What makes a good ending?

Does this sound like you talking?

What is happening in this picture?

What were you thinking about when this happened?

What else do you know about this topic/happening?

Revising (Taking Another Look)

Teachers do not introduce this stage until children have learned the importance of changing their piece to meet the needs of their audience. At first, emergent writers simply reread their writing to see that they have included everything they wanted to say; and make very few changes. As they gain more experience, they begin to make changes to clarify their writing and add more information to make it complete.

Editing (Making Corrections)

This stage is also played down until emergent writers have learned conventional spellings for many words and have acquired a rudimentary understanding of punctuation and capitalization rules (approximately 2nd grade). To introduce editing, the teacher helps children make a couple of corrections by putting a line through the error and writing the correction in pencil above the child's writing, eventually progressing to just a check in the margin of the sentence. As children become more fluent, the teacher encourages them to make more of their own corrections. Eventually the teacher allows children to read each other's compositions and check for errors in order to begin developing a spelling consciousness (see Chapter 6).

Publishing (Polishing for Presentation)

Kindergartners and first-graders usually do not recopy their writings, but sometimes the teacher types the final copy for the child, editing it and putting it into conventional form (Forseth and Avery, 1993). Children get their piece polished and ready to read to others. They then share their writing and show their drawings, often in a special chair labeled and set aside for writers, commonly called the *author's chair* (Graves and Hansen, 1983). Children and the teacher sit in the chair to share books they have read and other books they have written and this is the only time anyone sits in the chair. Specifically, children can be taught the steps shown in Figure 9.6 for publishing and sharing.

WRITING STRUCTURES

Most teachers expect children to begin school with some awareness of narrative, or story structure, as a result of being read to and seeing hundreds of stories on television and on videos. However, many primary-grade youngsters have been found to have only a partially developed sense of story. Teaching children about narrative structure using *story frames* has been found to directly improve their reading comprehension as well as their writing ability (Spiegel and Fitzgerald, 1986). Moreover, providing a structure, or template, allows English language speakers and struggling writers to reach a higher level of achievement than that possible *without* the structure (Peregoy and Boyle, 1996).

FIGURE 9.6 *Publishing steps.*

1. Decide which of your writings you would like to publish.

2. Share your writing with a partner, with the class, or with your teacher. Begin by telling what your piece is about, where you are in the process, and what help you need from the listener.

3. Change your writing if you need to by adding something, getting rid of something, or changing something.

4. Edit your writing for spelling, capitals, punctuation, and correct words.

5. Prepare the paper for your final copy.

6. Add pictures. Rewrite it in your best handwriting.

Story Frames

Story frames, also called story grammars, are structured templates that can be used orally as early as kindergarten to help children understand what comprises story structure. The following steps can be used to encourage story writing and improved comprehension through the use of the prepared structure:

story frames

1. Read children a well-formed story, pointing out the elements that are usually found in a story, i.e., setting, main characters, problem, solution, and ending.

2. Write a story with the children, using the board or overhead. Provide the structure for them, but have them fill in the blanks with what they remember from the story, using a story frame such as the one illustrated in Figure 9.7.

3. When the story is completed, read it to the children and then ask for volunteers to read sentences.

4. Give the children a blank story grammar and invite them to write their own original stories. The teacher may want to initially brainstorm with the whole class to help get them started, and do an original story as a class (see Figure 9.8).

Expository Frames

Primary-grade children's knowledge of **expository structures,** content organized around a main idea and supporting details, is usually far behind their knowledge of narrative structures. This is because they have typically had less exposure to expository passages, and because the structure of expository texts

expository structures

FIGURE 9.7 *A basic story frame.*

(Story Title)

Once upon a time in __(setting)__ there lived a __(main character)__. (S)he was very __(description)__ and always liked to __(character's favorite activity)__. One day __(when)__ __(character)__ wanted very much to __(goal)__. But there was a problem. The problem was __(problem)__. So __(character)__ tried and tried and finally __(how the character resolved the problem)__. The story ends when __(resolution and ending)__.

FIGURE 9.8 *Example of a story written by a second-grade class using the story frame above.*

Petey the Lion

Once upon a time in a tiny village in Texas there lived a very strange lion named Petey. He was very shy and quiet and always liked to run and hide when the other lions roared. One day Petey wanted very much to play with the other lions. But there was a problem. The problem was that they didn't like Petey because they thought he was a coward. So Petey tried and tried and finally showed them he wasn't a coward. He saved the life of a baby lion cub who was drowning. The story ends when Petey is playing with the other lions. Now they like him because he is no longer shy but mighty.

tends to be more complex (Englert and Hiebert, 1984). Using expository frames can help children understand expository structure by providing a systematic way to write about content material they have read. These frames can also be used to review and reinforce specific content and to familiarize children with the different ways in which authors can organize informational material. In effect, the frames serve as bridges that help to ease the often difficult transition from narrative to expository reading and writing.

By the second semester of first grade, most children can begin working with content area expository frames that are organized sequentially. The sequential pattern appears to be one of the easiest structures for children to recognize and use in their own writing and is a skill taught and reinforced regularly in basals.

Therefore, children are already familiar with **signal words,** such as first, next, then, and last, that are used as transitional devices within sequential paragraphs.

To ensure success in completing expository frames, the teacher begins instruction with a prewritten expository paragraph rather than a blank frame, as in the following activity (Cudd, 1990).

USING EXPOSITORY FRAMES   ACTIVITY

1. Write a simple paragraph about a topic that lends itself to sequential ordering, using the signal words first, next, then, and last.

2. Copy the sentences on sentence strips.

3. With the class, review the topic and logical sequence of events.

4. In a pocket chart, have the children arrange the sentences in correct order.

5. Read the completed paragraph together.

6. Have the children re-order the paragraph on their own and paste it on construction paper in paragraph form.

7. Invite the children to illustrate the details or some important part of the paragraph.

Gradually introduce a sequentially ordered expository frame for the children to complete independently, as in Figure 9.9.

FIGURE 9.9   *A child's expository frame for sequence.*

Setting the Table

In order to set the table, you need to go step by step. First, you must ___(get knives, forks, and spoons)___. Next, you need to ___(put napkins under the forks)___. After this, you ___(get glasses of milk for everyone)___. Last of all, ___(you give everybody a plate of food)___. When you are finished, ___(you eat dinner!)___

FIGURE 9.10 *A child's expository frame for comparison/contrast.*

(Title)

Comparing Insects with Spiders

Insects differ from spiders in many ways. First, insects __(fly while spiders don't)__ . Second, insects __(don't spin webs but spiders do)__ . I think the easiest way to tell an insect from a spider is __(to count the legs. A spider has eight legs. An insect only has six)__ .

organizational models
cause/effect patterns
problem/solution patterns
comparison/contrast pattern

Other frames using different **organizational models,** such as **cause/effect patterns, problem/solution patterns,** and **comparison/contrast patterns** are also helpful for assisting children in writing expository text. Figure 9.10 is a comparison/contrast example.

Literacy Scaffolds

literacy scaffolds

For children, especially those for whom English is a second language, writing prose and poetry can be overwhelming, even frightening. This fear can be alleviated with additional structural support. **Literacy scaffolds,** which are temporary frameworks for narrative or expository writing and somewhat looser in structure than story frames, enable all children to achieve success with writing prose and poetry. With a structure provided, children can formulate their ideas in ways that might be difficult, if not impossible, without the framework. Literacy scaffolds offer easy-to-follow patterns, or "formulas," for writing so children can focus on their ideas rather than the mechanics like capitalization and spelling. These scaffolds can be offered as an option so children with greater ability and more proficiency with the English language are not restricted by their use.

Many repetitive patterns, such as those found in published poems or songs, can be turned into literacy scaffolds. The activity below is an example of a simple literacy scaffold and the steps for employing it (Cecil, 1994).

ACTIVITY   **A SIMPLE LITERACY SCAFFOLD**

1. Have the children listen to "These Are a Few of My Favorite Things" from *The Sound of Music.*
2. Have them recall the singer's favorite things as they are listed on the board.
3. Invite them to brainstorm their favorite things and add them to the list.

4. For each of the favorite things, ask the children if they can think of a "downside" to it; for example, gentle rain is nice, but thunderstorms can be scary.

5. Provide each child with a photocopied sheet containing the following scaffold:

I Like

I like ___ice cream___.

But I don't like ___to eat ice cream in the wintertime___.

(Repeat as often as desired.)

6. As a class, write a group piece soliciting a response from each child. Read the group effort chorally.

7. Have the children write their own "I Like" pieces.

Children also enjoy writing **patterned stories** based on books such as *Fortunately* by Remy Charlip. Cumulative stories like John Burningham's *Mr. Grumpy's Outing* and *Mr. Grumpy's Motorcar* and Ed Emberley's *Drummer Hoff* create writing models for children. Additionally, folk tales such as *Chicken Little* and *The Little Red Hen* provide repetitive phrases that can be emulated (Tompkins, 1997).

patterned stories

JOURNAL WRITING

There has always been a time for children to engage in some amount of intimate oral communication in the early grades. But until rather recently, there was no place in the literacy curriculum of primary grades for personal writing, leaving a large void in this mode of communication. Journal writing provides the opportunity for personal expression as well as valuable writing practice. Of the variety of journal writing techniques used in elementary schools, three seem to be well-suited for emergent writers and will be explored here.

Dialogue Journals

In a **dialogue journal,** the teacher and student can carry on a written conversation about any topic of interest to the child. By making written comments in the margins of a notebook in direct response to the child's words, asking questions, and providing positive written feedback in response to what the child has written, the teacher helps the student grow as a writer. The frequent writing that occurs in dialogue journals helps promote students' writing fluency, and the reading of the teacher's comments provides valuable reading experience, and an intimate relationship between teacher and student.

For preliterate students, the dialogue journal can be used with pictures, interspersed with letters and, eventually, words, as the child learns them. The

dialogue journal

teacher can initially ask the child to tell about the pictures. The teacher then transcribes exactly what the child composes above the picture, carefully modeling the sounding out of the words until, gradually, the child begins to use invented spelling to write down ideas (Cunningham and Allington, 1993).

Reading Response Journals

reading response journal

Young children become interested in literature, for the most part, to the degree that it affects them. Teachers can begin to solicit personal responses to reading by asking children to write in a **reading response journal** a first reaction to something they have read, saying whatever they like, without penalty (with the exception of simply "I liked it" or "I didn't like it"). Alternatives to traditional book reports in journal format can include responding to a quotation from the book, questioning the author, continuing the story, or writing another version of the story from another character's point of view (Sweeney and Peterson, 1996).

expressive writing

This type of journal is an ideal vehicle for personal expression, often called **expressive writing.** Children can write fluently without fear of criticism because they are not burdened with the task of polishing their writing for another reader. Journal writers are free to answer the question, "What did I really think of that?" as they read, think, and write.

sentence stems

Teachers may adapt reading journals for use with early writers by providing **sentence stems** that ask questions designed to connect what they have read with their own experiences. For example, the following questions can be used after reading a story to prompt journal writing:

1. This character is like me because _____.

2. I like/dislike this character because _____.

3. This story reminds me of _____.

4. If I were _____, I would have _____.

5. I would like the story to have ended this way _____.

Learning Logs

learning log

For content area material, children can begin to crystallize their understandings via the **learning log.** This activity requires that children write in their journals immediately after a content area subject lesson such as social studies. Their journal entry would then include:

1. A summary or examples of what they understand has been presented or read.

2. A summary or examples of what they do *not* understand about what has been presented or read.

3. Questions they have about what has been presented or read.

4. A personal reaction to what has been presented or read.

These logs can be interactive, where the teacher responds to them regularly, answering their questions and directing their attention to important concepts. Figure 9.11 shows examples taken from the mathematics learning logs of a third grade class. The teacher answered their thoughtful questions in the margins of the log.

THE LANGUAGE EXPERIENCE APPROACH

The **language experience approach** (LEA) is well-suited for modeling beginning reading and writing because it uses children's own language as writing material. Later it can be transcribed by the teacher and read by the children—thus graphically illustrating the connection between the two communication processes (Ashton–Warner, 1965; Lee and Allen, 1963; Stauffer, 1980). Because the language patterns utilized are determined by children's own speech and the content is determined by their own experiences, it is relatively easy for children to remember the text of these stories, and they are eager to read them again and again.

This approach, which stems back to the story and sentence methods of reading instruction popular around the turn of the twentieth century, is an ideal way for teachers to demonstrate the interrelatedness of reading, writing, listening, and speaking—the language arts. Children watch the teacher *write* down

language experience approach

FIGURE 9.11 *Examples from a third-grader's learning log.*

How is multiplication like addition?

You are adding, but you're doing it much more quickly.

How do I know when to divide?

Look for the word "each."

What problems should I watch out for when I am borrowing?

Be sure to cross out the old number and put in the new one so you're not confused.

Why do I need to know the times tables when I have a calculator?

You may not always have one with you!

their story as they *speak.* They *listen* as the teacher reads the story, and finally they *read* the story themselves. This helps children realize that (1) what they experience can be talked about; (2) what they talk about can be written down; and (3) what they write can be read. It also helps children to grasp the idea that written language often has the same purpose as oral language: the communication of meaning (Allen, 1976; Hall, 1981). As teachers take dictation, they also have an excellent opportunity to demonstrate the conventions of written language: that it proceeds from left to right and from top to bottom, that words have spaces between them, that the first word in a sentence is capitalized, and so forth.

Language experience compositions can be composed using a chart and chart paper (see Figure 9.12) by groups of children or individuals and are ideal for English language learners because of the many senses being used simultaneously. The format is the same in either case and includes the steps listed on the following page (Cecil, 1993).

FIGURE 9.12 *Making a language experience chart.*

1. Use regular 24" × 16" (or larger) ruled chart paper, oak tag, or posterboard.

2. Keep a 2" margin on both right and left sides, and a 3" margin from top of paper.

3. Use short one-line sentences for beginners.

4. Do not divide a word or phrase at the end of a line.

5. Invite children to illustrate the piece—at the top, bottom, or even the sides of papers—but do not let pictures break up a sentence.

6. Use manuscript writing, crayon, lettering pen, or felt-tip marker.

7. "Pack" together the letters of each word, leaving the space of an "o" between words.

The Snake

Robert brought a snake to school. The snake was green and skinny. Robert let us hold him but some children were scared. We thought he would be slimy but he wasn't. He was dry! We hope the snake enjoyed being in school!

- provide a stimulus for discussion and writing
- conduct an oral discussion about the stimulus
- brainstorm about the stimulus
- help children compose the passage
- read the passage aloud; reread several times
- recruit children to read individual sentences
- have the children follow directions and highlight patterns
- have the children name the passage
- conduct a phonics mini-lesson
- duplicate the passage

Provide a stimulus for discussion and writing

The stimulus for writing or discussion is usually a concrete object or a current event, but it has been broadened to encompass anything that has recently been experienced by all members of the group. For example, a language experience story could be written about a snowman made at recess, a seasonal thunderstorm, a television program that everyone happened to see, a story the class just enjoyed listening to, chocolate pudding all have enjoyed eating, or a garter snake brought in by one of the class members. The single most important criterion is that the subject has captured the interest of the children and they would now like to talk, write, and read about it.

Conduct an oral discussion about the stimulus

Oral discussion is a natural bridge between the sensory stimulus and reading and writing about it. After the stimulus has been experienced, the teacher can encourage the sharing of thoughts and ideas about it. The teacher's task is that of interested facilitator, positively, and nonjudgmentally responding to comments by discussants, paraphrasing what may be unclear.

Brainstorm about the stimulus

This step provides an opportunity for children to think critically and creatively about the stimulus and provides words and phrases for the word bank that will be helpful in writing the passage. The teacher guides the children into categorizing the responses. If, for example, the class were writing a language experience story about a garter snake that a child had brought to class, the brainstorming might proceed as follows:

Associations. "What kinds of things do you think of when you think of a snake?" (*poison, rattles, grass*) "Why?" (*after each response*)

Description (adjectives). "What words could we use to tell about a snake? How does it look, smell, sound, feel?" (*skinny, slimy, scary*)

Actions (verbs). "What do snakes do?" *(slither, crawl, bite)*

Reactions. "How do snakes make you feel? Why?" *(scared, like running away, curious)*

Similarities. "What are some other things that are kind of like snakes? How?" *(worms, spaghetti, sticks)*

Differences. "What are some things that are very different from snakes? How?" *(Elephants, because they are big and snakes are small. Note: Almost any answer is acceptable here if children can offer a reasonable explanation for their choice.)*

Phonics element. "What are some words that rhyme with snake?" *(bake, make, take)* or "What words begin like <u>snake</u>?"

The responses to the group brainstorming are written prominently on the board or chart paper, as the children help the teacher sound out the phonemes according to their current knowledge.

Help children compose the passage

Referring to the words on the board, the teacher suggests the children write a passage about the stimulus. (*Note:* The word "story" is studiously avoided so that the piece can be written in either expository or narrative format.) The teacher asks for a beginning for the piece and solicits suggestions and continues until children run out of ideas. The teacher then requests an ending. A typical second grade piece might look like the one shown earlier in Figure 9.12.

During the dictation phase, the teacher should accept the children's ideas verbatim; however, if an unclear thought or incorrect thought are offered, the teacher should paraphrase the sentence correctly, keeping the meaning intact by asking a question, "Do you mean . . . ?" This approach, diplomatically employed, can assist an English language learner's transition to standard English in a positive way.

Read the passage aloud

Follow the dictation with several readings of the passage for different purposes. First the teacher reads the passage aloud to the children while they follow along, phrase by phrase, to avoid stilted word-by-word reading. The teacher may then "echo read," or have children repeat every line after she models it. Then the teacher points at each word and deliberately exaggerates the left to right progression and the return sweep to the next line while children read the passage chorally with the teacher. English language learners and less able readers are thereby participating in the reading experience by being "fed" the words they hear around them but avoiding the usual embarrassment that can occur with oral reading when every word is not known. Plus, they are able to hear the syntax, rhythm, and cadence of the new language repeatedly.

Recruit children to read individual sentences

All children have read the entire story; now the teacher recruits children to read each individual sentence and, thus, the children's attention is focused on the sentence unit as part of the passage. Also, more reinforcement is being provided for high frequency words, as well as new ones.

Have children follow directions and highlight patterns

To further bolster new vocabulary and to provide practice listening and looking for particular phonic elements and patterns, the next step is essential. The teacher gives an oral riddle, incorporating words that contain phonic elements or patterns that the children have previously studied. For example the teacher might say:

> "Can someone come up to the chart and put a circle around the word that has the same ending sound as the word cry?"

> Or:

> "Can someone come up to the chart and put two stars over the word that has an 'ake' in it, as in 'make'? The word is in the first and the last sentence."

Have children name the passage

Determining the main idea of a paragraph is one of the most difficult comprehension skills. However, with much daily practice selecting the titles for language experience passages, children can soon grasp the idea of honing in on one general thought that conveys the central idea in the passage. Several nominations of titles for the passage should be solicited followed by a short discussion of why one title does a slightly better job of summarizing the main idea. For example, the teacher might want the children to see, through another rereading, why "The Snake" is a more appropriate title for the second-grader's story than "Our Pets," which was also offered.

Conduct a phonics minilesson

After the language experience passage has been written, read, and reread for different purposes, the teacher selects six to ten new vocabulary words (depending upon the difficulty and the children's grade and ability level) from the passage and/or word bank that incorporate some phonic element that needs reinforcement, for the class as a whole or in small groups. The minilesson proceeds as described in the activity that follows.

ACTIVITY

A PHONICS MINILESSON BASED ON A LANGUAGE EXPERIENCE

1. Put the words on the board and have the children copy them onto 3 × 5 cards. (This is done for the children if they are preliterate.) Point out specific sounds to be emphasized by underlining those letters, or make them a contrasting color and ask the children to do the same:

   bake   take

   lake   snake

   shake   rake

2. Pronounce each word for the children (or ask for volunteers to say them) and stress the sounds being considered, in this case, a review of the *ake* rime, or the word ending. Ask children what they notice about the ending part (or beginning, or middle) of the words.

3. Ask the children to look closely at the words as they say them and come up and point out the part that is the same for all the words.

4. Invite them to verbalize in their own words what the similarities are.

5. When you feel all the children have made the deduction, ask them to listen as you say more words, with or without the pattern. Have them determine which words fit the pattern. Encourage them to think of more words that fit the pattern.

Duplicate the passage

Each passage written by the children in this manner could be carefully duplicated, with space for a personal illustration, so that each child has a copy to reread at home and a copy to compile into a collaborative class book. Passages should be reviewed often with children to reinforce phonic elements, high frequency words, and new vocabulary. Children will also be proud and eager to read their books to other classes, or to create taped read-alongs for children needing more reinforcement. Every so often the passage can be revisited to allow for further rereadings and review.

Variations on the Basic LEA (Salinger, 1993)

The following group writing activities can be used to vary the standard language experience lesson just presented.

interactive writing

Interactive writing.   **Interactive writing** is a collaborative strategy in which both the teacher and the students work together to create a piece of writing. With help from the teacher, the children dictate sentences about a shared experience, such as a story, a video, or an event (see Chapter 3). The teacher verbally "stretches" each word so children can distinguish its sounds and letters, as children use chart paper to write the letter while repeating the sound to themselves. After each word is completed, the teacher and children reread it. The children take turns writing letters to complete the words and sentences. The completed charts are put up on the wall so they can reread them or rely on them for standard spelling.

Morning message.   Each day, the teacher writes a brief **morning message** about the day's weather and upcoming events and records it on a chart (which may be specially made to allow enough space). Sometimes the children dictate the message. This chart provides a model for the children's own daily writing in their journals.

morning message

Individual dictation.   The teacher may take **individual dictation** from each child and record her work in small notebooks. Transcribing a caption for artwork falls into this category.

individual dictation

Sentence strips.   The teacher records transcriptions on long strips of paper or index cards and cuts the **sentence strips** into word cards. Children use these word cards to create sentences at their desks or in pocket charts. Children are encouraged to copy their sentences into a notebook.

sentence strips

Word bank.   Children request individual words from the teacher and keep them in a **word bank** to study on their own, play with, swap with friends, and so forth. Frequently the teacher and students review the words and discard the ones the children cannot read. This strategy complements the sentence strip strategy.

word bank

Content area use.   The teacher keeps records through LEA strategies of the children's work in content areas, such as science and social studies. Observations of experiments, field trips, and even math activities lend themselves to this approach.

OTHER MOTIVATORS FOR EMERGENT WRITERS

Even the most reluctant writers can be motivated to write if they are given an initial boost, through fixed writing structures, as discussed earlier, a provocative writing prompt, or an outright gimmick (Sweeney and Peterson, 1996). The following teacher-tested ideas contain one or more of these elements and have been used often with emergent writers who have a difficult time getting started (Cecil, 1994).

Book Making

One of the most motivational ways for children to publish their individual or group writing is by putting their work into a book. Simple booklets can be constructed by folding a sheet of paper into quarters, like a greeting card. Children write the title on the front cover and use the three remaining sides for their com-

position and accompanying drawings. Children can also make booklets by stapling sheets of writing paper together and adding covers from construction paper or wallpaper from old sample books. Figure 9.13 shows a sample of an early first grade class's literature-response book.

Computer Composing

For early writers, especially those for whom the physical act of producing a neat composition is an onerous chore, using a word processing program can be an added incentive to writing (DeGroff, 1990). Not requiring the substantial fine motor coordination needed to write words, word processing allows children to focus on their ideas. As a result, they tend to write more and enjoy seeing the professional-looking results. Using programs designed for early writers, such as *First Writer* (Houghton Mifflin) or *Bank Street Prewriter* (Scholastic), children can more easily revise and edit rough drafts, and receive the added bonus of a

FIGURE 9.13 *Sample of a class literature-response book.*

I like cats.

folded tape

staples

I like cats by Chrissy

clean copy every time. Most programs include tutorial lessons ideal for independent small group work after an initial introduction by the teacher.

ANIMAL CRACKERS

Place an animal cracker on the desk of each child with instructions to look at it and think about it, but not to eat it. Make a list of all the animals represented, sounding them out with children, and brainstorm words that describe each animal. Then, returning attention to each child's animal, discuss the following questions:

Are these animals alive?

How do you think your animal felt about being in the box?

How does it feel to be out of the box?

What language does your animal speak?

What does your animal eat?

Does your animal know it will soon be eaten?

How does it feel about that?

Finally, have the children write several sentences about their animal, using ideas from the discussion and descriptive words on the board. For less able writers, provide a sentence stem to help them, e.g., "My *(animal)* feels _____." When they are finished, invite them to eat their cracker.

IMAGINE WHAT HAPPENS!

Select a picture book such as *The King, The Cheese, and the Mice* by Nancy and Eric Gurney. Read the story aloud and stop at the most exciting point. Ask children to predict what might happen next, using a "predictive web" such as the one shown in Figure 9.14.

Invite children to use one of the brainstormed ideas or one of their own and write (or draw for preliterate children) their version of the ending of the story. Allow children to read or tell about their original endings. Finally, read the author's ending and compare it to the children's predictions.

BALLOON SENSITIVITY

Beginning writers are inspired by concrete items they can see, hear, and touch. Help each child to blow up and tie a balloon. Divide children into groups of

FIGURE 9.14 *Predictive web.*

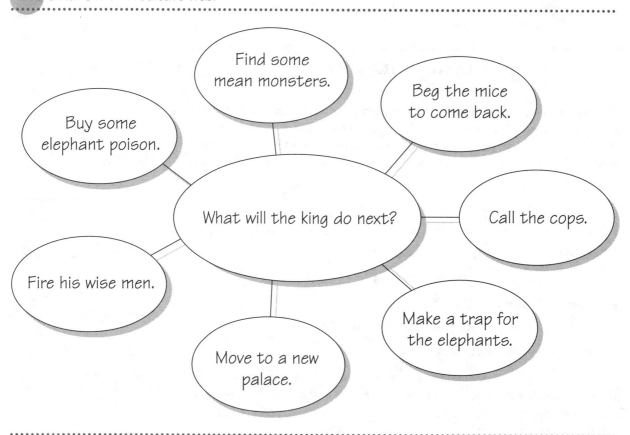

five. Give them time to experiment with the balloons using their five senses: how do their balloons look, sound, feel, taste, smell? Give each child a sheet upon which is written one of the five sentence stems:

My balloon looks _____.

My balloon sounds _____.

My balloon feels _____.

My balloon tastes _____.

My balloon smells _____.

ACTIVITY

WISHING ON A STAR

With children's input, write on the board a number of things that can be wished on, such as a wishbone, an eyelash, a penny thrown into a well, etc. Write the following poem on the board and ask children to recite it chorally with you:

Star light, star bright, first star I see tonight,

I wish I may, I wish I might, have the wish I wish tonight.

Encourage children to share some things they have wished for. Hand out lined paper in the shape of a star and ask children to write about some things they wish for, with every line beginning with "I wish . . ."

SUMMARY

Before they began school, most children scribbled on sidewalks, newspapers, and even wallpaper with chalk, crayons, lipstick, pencils, pens—*anything* that would make a mark. The child's mark said, "I am." Whereas, in reading, children create their meaning from a given text, in writing, children create their own texts in order to make meaning—at first for themselves, and then for other readers. Children *want* to write. They want to write the first day they enter school.

School is merely where the beginning of children's formal literacy instruction takes place. The formal writing program for emergent writers has already begun with the child drawing pictures and continues with scribble writing, precursors to the developmental spelling stages that lead to conventional writing. Guided by teacher modeling, inspired by provocative ideas, a fertile imagination, and the freedom to experiment with print, children soon learn to express their own thoughts and feelings in their own language. They gradually evolve to become conventional writers, and quickly realize the power of the written word to make their thoughts visible to others, graphically illustrated by one little boy's intercepted note to his little classmate that proclaims, "I luv yuw!"

QUESTIONS

for Journal Writing and Discussion

1. How many ways can you think of in which spoken language can be structured in a primary classroom to provide a foundation for writing activities? Make a list and share it with your class.

2. Consider the importance of providing emergent writers with appropriate feedback and encouragement during the process of drafting a piece of writing. Do you or your classmates remember receiving this kind of encouragement? Discuss.

3. Discuss the individual writing processes of a small group of your class-mates as they prepare to write an essay. How do they generate and record their ideas? How do they write a first draft? How do they revise and edit their writing?

SUGGESTIONS

for Projects and Other Activities

1. Interview two children at different primary grade levels to determine how much writing they say they do in class and how they feel about the writing and themselves as writers.

2. Obtain permission to teach a language experience lesson to a small group of primary-grade youngsters. Bring in a toy or another object to use as a stimulus for discussion, brainstorming, and writing. Follow the steps in this chapter to teach the lesson. Share with your classmates what worked well, what you would do differently next time, and what you learned about the children's ability to compose.

3. Observe a writer's workshop over the period of one week. Ask the children to show you their favorite pieces. Ask them to tell you what they are learn-ing about writing. Finally, ask the teacher what he or she has learned about each of the writing skills of the children in the class through this process. Share your insights with your college class.

MEDIATED READING

Creating a Literate Community

FOCUS QUESTIONS

- How can shared reading be used to model effective reading strategies?

- How can teachers use guided reading to help children construct personal meanings from text?

- How can the practices of shared and guided reading be kept exciting for both the students and the teacher?

In the Classroom

The children are sitting cross-legged on their carpet squares in the back of Mr. Kohl's first grade classroom, eagerly awaiting the second reading of *The Three Billy Goats Gruff.* Prior to the first reading of this story, children scanned the colorful illustrations of the oversized book and made predictions about what they thought was happening on each page. Several children made comments about similar stories they were reminded of, and one little girl shared that her uncle owned a pygmy goat—much to the delight of the other learners. Mr. Kohl took the opportunity afforded by the story to introduce the children to the /tr/ blend and pointed it out each time it was encountered, as the goats went "trip, trap, trip, trap" across the bridge three times. By the third time the goats reached the bridge, the children were rhythmically and enthusiastically chanting the words "trip, trap, trip, trap" with Mr. Kohl as he pointed to them in the story.

On this day, which is the second reading of the story, the children brainstorm some ways they might talk to the troll and convince him they really should be allowed to cross the bridge. As the story is read aloud this time, the children turn to each other after every page and take turns summarizing in their own words what has happened on that page. Occasionally, the teacher stops the reading, points to a word, and asks "What is this word? Can anyone raise a quiet hand and tell me?" Eighteen small hands shoot up and one child is called upon to tell Mr. Kohl that the word is *bridge;* they have seen the word over thirty times now, and they can all recognize it. Mr. Kohl then asks the children to think of some other words that begin with the same blend, or the /br/ sound. He writes their answers carefully on the small writing board (*brag, broken, broccoli, brick*) as the children help him to sound out the words.

Mr. Kohl is using *shared reading* with his students, a technique useful in modeling reading for children by reading a book aloud and ultimately inviting the children to join with him. In this chapter we will explore how this strategy, and a similar one requiring more student independence, called *guided reading,* can be used to blend phonemic awareness and beginning phonics instruction with strategies that engage the reader in the printed word. Both activities are forms of mediated reading instruction through which the teacher, through modeling and direct instruction, demonstrates how sophisticated readers decode and gain meaning from text.

SHARED READING

shared reading

The mediated reading activity known as **shared reading,** or the *shared book experience,* was developed by Holdaway (1986) as a means of introducing early readers to the use of favorite books, raps, chants, rhymes, and poems in a highly motivational way. In shared reading, children participate in reading, learn critical concepts of how print works, and get the feel of the fluency and smoothness of reading without the possibility of error, because the teacher is doing the decoding for them. The teacher reads with fluency and expression and eventually invites the learners to read along. Each reading situation is a relaxed, social one, with emphasis on appreciation of the text. Shared reading is also an excellent technique for allowing children to identify sight words because it stresses the external features and sounds of individual words while maintaining a focus on meaning. Integrated with a direct and explicit phonics program (see Chapter 5), such a technique can ensure that children not only know *how* to read but also thoroughly enjoy doing so.

The use of the mediated strategy of shared reading is ideal for a teacher wishing to balance meaning-based and skills-based instruction. Through shared reading, the teacher models for children how proficient readers "get" the message the author is trying to communicate and then shows how it can be related to one's own life experiences. Such mediated reading instruction also uses modeling to show how proficient readers sound out words. It is based on the extensive body of research that suggests that young children become accomplished at language through the synergistic processes of talking, listening, experimenting with written language, and interacting with the various language models in their environments (Clay, 1991). These studies found that young children who have learned to read at home before coming to school generally accomplished this task by having their favorite books read aloud to them over and over in a relaxed, joyful atmosphere (Baghban, 1984; Bissex, 1980). Holdaway's (1979) procedure capitalizes on the natural learning processes of young children and builds on their innate curiosity to help them grow into literacy. Numerous teachers and researchers have used this procedure to successfully teach children of various ability levels and background to become engaged in reading (Bridge et al., 1983; Harlin, 1990).

Purposes for Shared Reading

Shared reading builds on children's natural desire to read and reread favorite books, imitating and recreating the intimacy of sitting on a parent's lap listening to a story. Au (1991) suggests that such reading doesn't have to be simply random rereading, however. Rather, each time a book is reread with the teacher, it can be for an entirely different purpose: to extend, refine, and deepen a child's abilities to decode text and construct meaning. Following are six major purposes for shared reading and rereading text (Cooper, 1993):

- to develop print concepts
- to reinforce decoding skills in context of authentic text
- to explore language
- to think creatively
- to improve comprehension skills through listening
- to foster an appreciation of reading

Developing print concepts

First of all, children at the emergent literacy stage are developing crucial concepts about print through shared reading. Children learn about the conventions of our language—words, letters, sentences, punctuation, etc.—as they are discussed in the context of the story being read. For example, in the introduction of *The Three Billy Goats Gruff* story (Simpson, 1993), the teacher might have pointed out how quotation marks were used whenever one character talked to another, or how a capital letter always began a sentence (see Figure 10.1).

Reinforcing decoding skills

Another advantage of using this strategy is that children's decoding skills are reinforced in the context of authentic text. With teacher guidance, children learn to figure out unfamiliar words using the various cues provided in the language of the text—context, structure (prefixes, suffixes, inflectional endings), and recurring patterns or phonic elements. Part of learning to decode is rereading texts with numerous examples of the exact element to which the children

FIGURE 10.1   *Excerpt from* The Three Billy Goats Gruff.

Suddenly, *up* popped the ugly troll! "Who's that trip-trapping over *my* bridge?" he roared.

"It's only me… the littlest billy goat Gruff," said the frightened goat in a tiny voice. "I'm off to the meadow to eat the green grass."

"Then I'm coming to gobble you up!" roared the troll.

Source: Joan Stimson, *The Three Billy Goats Gruff.* Illustrated by Chris Russell. Loughborough, UK: Ladybird Books, 1993. Used with permission.

have recently been introduced through direct instruction. For example, through the reading of the fairy tale, the children were ready to learn the *tr* blend. The teacher pointed out this phonic element in the story, exaggerated it, and asked the children to think of other words beginning with the same sound.

Exploring language

Additionally, through shared reading, children are continually engaged in exploring language. By examining unusual or repetitive language patterns, the teacher guides the children in developing a greater appreciation for language while learning about structure and cues that will help them to construct meaning. Often the language pattern can serve as a basis for having children then write a new story. For example, in *The Three Billy Goats Gruff,* children explored the language pattern created by the goats tramping across the bridge. They were invited to use the blends they had been studying to make new sounds the goats might have made, using a similar language pattern: The goats went "hip, hop, hip, hop" or the goats went "clip, clop, clip, clop."

Thinking creatively

A fourth by-product of shared reading is that children are developing the ability to think creatively. At times the teacher urges listeners and readers to jump far beyond what an author is saying to formulate original ideas. When this happens, the author's words serve as a trigger that often ignites a new train of thought; children may even stop listening momentarily to what an author is saying to ruminate on their own exploding ideas. They may ask themselves, "What can I do with this information? What does this mean in my life? Where can I go with this? What would I do if I were in this character's shoes?" The result of thinking about such questions is often a unique personal invention or a totally original idea.

Improving comprehension skills

Another benefit of shared reading is that children's comprehension skills are constantly evolving through intent listening. The teacher begins by reading the book to the group, inviting the children to chime in if they know words or phrases, asking them to make predictions, or to listen for a specific purpose. Sometimes children are encouraged to summarize sections of text by recounting them to another classmate, as occurred in Mr. Kohl's second reading of *The Three Billy Goats Gruff.* Children may at other times be asked to think about the motivation of characters, to enumerate episodes in the story, to guess outcomes, or to share what the text reminds them of in their own lives.

Appreciating reading

Above all, through shared reading children are developing an appreciation for reading. The primary reason for a young child to read a book is, after all, to construct personal meaning; if the child acquires the skill of reading but doesn't care for reading, that child will soon fall into the category of alliterate, or one who *can* read but chooses *not* to. Therefore, teachers reading aloud should use methods that will encourage children to enjoy books and to become excited about them. During shared reading, the teacher can talk about the illustrations, the characters, things that happened in the story, things the children liked, didn't like, and how certain events or characters made them feel. All these activities help children to form an appreciation for the characters and events in the story. Books may be reread many times for this purpose alone. In fact, this appears to be the primary reason that most children choose to reread any book.

Procedures for Shared Reading

Carefully-chosen stories in big book format (see Chapter 3) are perfect for engaging very young children in thinking critically and creatively. Stories from quality children's literature (try Newbery Award winners or Children's Choice selections) or literature-based basal readers, usually have an easily discernible structure that teaches children what to look for when they encounter narrative structure in their independent reading. Such stories should grab the imagination of young children and stimulate a range of feelings. Moreover, if wisely chosen, they provide an enjoyable association with reading.

Many educators break the shared reading activity into several related parts: (1) A "warm-up" activity where familiar nursery rhymes, chants, and songs are read and sung, using large print as a guide, (2) introducing the book ("into" the text, or *before* reading), (3) reading and responding to the book ("through" the text, or *during* reading), (4) rereading the book one or more times for various purposes, and (5) extending the book ("beyond" the text, or *post-reading*). The time frames for each of these elements is flexible and can be adapted, shortened, or lengthened, as the teacher sees fit or as time allows (Peetom, 1986).

"Into" the book: Introducing the text

The introduction of a book in a shared reading activity, conducted successfully, usually meets with a joyous sense of anticipation that begins with focused attention to the cover. The teacher may read the title and ask the children what they think the book might be about. The teacher discusses the author and illustrator, and tells the children about any other familiar books the author and illustrator may have created.

picture walk

predictive questions

Next the teacher gets the children excited about reading the book by showing a few selected pictures to "whet the children's appetite," or doing a **"picture walk,"** in which each of the pictures is shown and the children tell what they think is happening in each one. The teacher asks **predictive questions,** questions that encourage children to think about what is going to happen, thus constructing text. Examples of predictive questions are:

> "Who do you think are going to be the main characters in this story? What do you think is going to happen to them?" (anticipating; predicting)

"Where do you think the goats are going?"   (inferring from cover clues)

"What do goats usually eat? Where do they usually live?"   (activating prior knowledge)

"Does anyone know what goat's feet are called?"   (assessing prior knowledge)

"What kind of sound do you think their hooves make?"   (inferring, to prepare students to hear the words *trip*, *trap*)

The teacher records the children's predictions on the chalkboard to refer to later. This introduction can take anywhere from 3 to 20 minutes (see Chapter 8 for more information on developing appropriate questions). *Note:* When the teacher is reading the shared reading text for the first time, it can be recorded. Children could then work at a listening center to listen to the story again while tracking along.

"Through" the book: Reading and responding to the text

In the next phase, the teacher reads the book aloud to the children as they are gathered around her, holding the text so they can see each page clearly. The teacher runs her hand or a pointer along each line of print so that the children develop a sense of the left-to-right orientation of English text and also match speech to print. The teacher invites the children to join in but, for the initial reading, many will just listen.

The first reading is often rather quick to allow children to get an overview of the story. The teacher reads with enthusiasm, modeling the fluency of a proficient reader, yet stopping often to ask predictive questions and to field children's comments and reactions about the text.

At the conclusion of the text, the teacher asks open-ended, prompting questions designed to get children engaged in discussion about the story, such as:

"How did your predictions match what actually happened in the story?"

"What was your favorite part of the story?"

"What did the story remind you of in your own life?"

"Who was your favorite character? Why?"

"Which billy goat do you think you are most like? Why?"

"How did the story make you feel?"

"What would you have done if you were a billy goat trying to get across the bridge?"

"How would the story have been different if it had been told from the point of view of the troll?"

Rereading and revisiting the text for various purposes

The teacher then returns to the story and does a second reading, this time encouraging the children to join in, especially with rhyming and repetitious parts. Many times children will, after the second reading, spontaneously exclaim, "Let's read it again!" which certainly means they have enjoyed the story and having been participants in it. If time permits, it is quite appropriate to do another reading, because when children are excited about reading, a lifelong love is being kindled.

The teacher may wish to select a variety of purposes for revisiting the story. Children may now be ready to reflect on it in a more individualistic way. The method the teacher uses to encourage responses may vary according to the nature of the story or the wishes of individual children. Some reflective responses (but by no means an exhaustive list) are as follows (Hennings, 1992):

- Tell a classmate about a favorite part.
- Retell the story to a partner.
- Write a sentence about the story in your journal.
- Draw a picture about the story with a caption.
- Draw and/or write about a favorite character.
- Explain why you didn't like a certain character.
- Prepare a skit of your favorite scene in the story.

literary sociogram

The story can also be revisited to help children visualize the relationships among the story's characters. A **literary sociogram** (Butler and Turbil, 1986; see Figure 10.2) can be used to have children better understand the relationships between story characters and helps them see the differences in feelings that one character may have from another. This device may be employed by asking children parallel questions about characters. For example, when reading the story "Little Red Ridinghood," the teacher might ask: "How did Mother feel about Red Ridinghood? What evidence do you have?" and "How does Red Ridinghood feel about Mother? What evidence do you have?" After writing down children's responses on arrows, discuss why the feelings pairs of characters have toward each other may differ.

In another session, *The Three Billy Goats Gruff* might be revisited to help children make contact with their feelings through those of the characters. For example, the teacher might ask the children:

"How do you think the last billy goat felt when he was left all alone? Have you ever felt that way?"

"Why was the troll so upset that the goats were going over the bridge?"

"What are some other things the billy goats might have done to keep the troll from being angry?"

"How would you have felt if it had been your bridge?"

FIGURE 10.2   *A literary sociogram.*

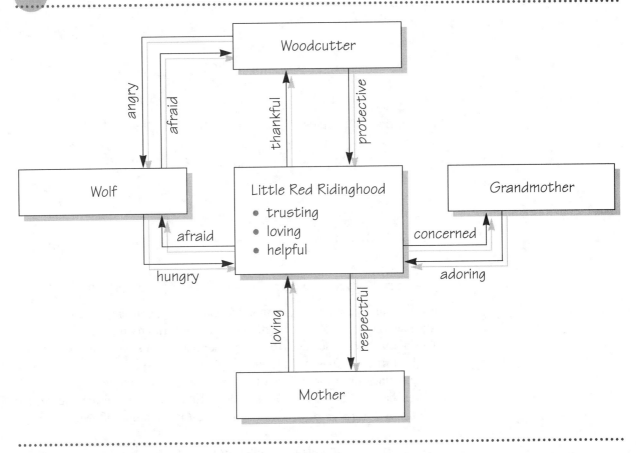

In yet another session, *masking devices* (described later in this chapter) could be used to isolate individual words and focus children's attention on the details of print. For example, the teacher might mask off several words, starting with the blend *tr,* and help the children discover that these words all start with the same sound. **Oral cloze** activities, in which the teacher deliberately omits words in the story and pauses for the children to supply the missing words, can be used to promote prediction and contextual analysis skills:

oral cloze

EXAMPLE: Now, there was a _____ over the river, and under this bridge lived a very fierce and ugly _____.

Yet another revisiting of the text might be to encourage children to compare and contrast the present story with another one the children have read in the past; for example, the teacher might use a **Venn diagram** (see Figure 10.3) to have children compare and contrast the story of the Billy Goats Gruff with the story of the Three Little Pigs. This device of two overlapping circles allows children to graphically view the similarities and differences of two stories or ideas.

Venn diagram

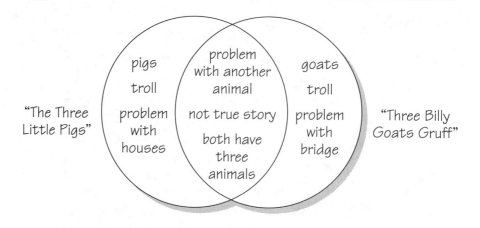

FIGURE 10.3 *Venn diagram.*

"Beyond" the book: Extending the text

The extending phase is really another chance for children to respond to the text; however, with extension activities, oral or written creative expression is the primary focus. Such activities may take place in a small group or be individual efforts, and may include such experiences as skits, puppet shows, murals, painting, or the creation of a class book from individual statements children have written about the story. Extended activities following several readings of *The Three Billy Goats Gruff* might include the following:

- Singing a song about goats that includes hand actions

- A dramatization of the story using student-created props

- A flannel board retelling of the story with felt cut-outs

- A group-written poem using the rime from goat—*oat*

- A tempera paint mural showing the events in order

- A retelling using three sizes of masks for the goats and three different voices

- An activity where one child plays the part of the troll and fields questions from other classmates about his motivation

- Creating another adventure with the same characters

- Asking a story character some questions

- Explaining what they would have done at a particular point in the story if they were the character

GUIDED READING

Guided reading is a mediated group reading activity in many ways similar to shared reading, but with guided reading the children are usually decoding the text independently, often silently but sometimes orally, and a major emphasis is on asking children questions, asking for predictions, and helping them formulate their own questions about the text (Fountas and Pinnell, 1996). Children try to answer these questions after they have read a designated section of the text.

guided reading

This type of reading is usually initially teacher-led (later done independently) and usually conducted in small groups, giving children the opportunity to develop as individual readers while participating in a socially supported activity. At the early stages of reading development, children use their fingers to finger-point read. Finger-pointing involves children in **tracking,** or indicating an understanding of the one-to-one correspondence of spoken and written words (Reutzel, 1995). At the conclusion of each section, the children stop and discuss with the teacher the answer to their questions or predictions. At each stopping point, the teacher allows and encourages children to respond to what they have read. The teacher is then able to observe each child's processing of new text. By taking notes on each learner, the teacher becomes aware of what further instruction each child requires in specific phonics elements or other decoding strategies.

tracking

Purposes for Guided Reading

Guided reading is an ideal strategy when small groups of children need additional support in constructing meaning from the text, either because of the text difficulty or because of the children's limited experience or ability. This approach also allows the teacher to adjust the level of modeling needed for understanding, or to **scaffold,** according to the children's needs (see Chapter 9). For example, children are reading a story about a boy going into a cave. After a brief survey, the teacher realizes the children have limited backgrounds for this story; most have never been in a cave. Using a scaffolding technique, the teacher would "walk" the group of children through the story, offering helpful information about caves along the way, (e.g., "Caves have pieces of limestone hanging down that look kind of like icicles. They are called stalactites.") checking their understanding at every point with probing questions (e.g., But *why* do you think the boy's hands were trembling as he entered the cave?"), and clarifying concepts as needed.

scaffold

Guided reading is ideal for use in *literature-based units.* Using this alternative to the basal, group-selected literature is read by the children in small groups, and the teacher demonstrates comprehension strategies, clarifies misconceptions, introduces new vocabulary, and takes advantage of "teachable moments" to discuss any other instructional issue that may arise. The small group arrangement also gives the teacher a chance to observe individual children reading orally, providing an opportunity for informal diagnosis of decoding skills and monitoring comprehension (Tompkins, 1997).

Because of its flexibility, guided reading is a very powerful tool; it should not be overused, however. The teacher can relinquish some of the control by providing more support at the beginning of the reading and gradually releasing the responsibility to the children as they become more confident with the reading of the story. With guided reading, the teacher can control the amount of scaffolding given through

1. the types of questions asked before reading and during the discussion;
2. the amount of text children read at any one time;
3. the type of discussion held between reading sessions;
4. the number of comprehension strategies modeled by the teacher via think-alouds (see Chapter 9).

When maximum support is needed, for example, the teacher can direct the discussion to underscore a specific fact or idea; then, as children have grasped the idea, the teacher decreases the direction and the children take more responsibility by carrying out and directing their own discussion with a partner.

Questions play a vital role in guided reading and should always go beyond simply asking children to restate what they have just read. By asking provocative questions that help them get an overall mental picture, children will begin to understand how to construct meaning from text (Beck, 1984; Durkin, 1990). Many of the questions asked should be open-ended—or those that cannot be answered with a simple "yes" or "no"—should require critical thinking by the child, and the teacher should allow plenty of time for all children to formulate a response. During guided reading, questions should meet the specific criteria discussed next. See Figure 10.4 for examples of each.

Before reading.   Questions posed to children *before* the reading of the text should guide children's attention to the key concepts, or the most important ideas, in the piece to be read. In narrative text, these ideas may include the plot, the theme, the main character, the problem, or the main events. In expository text, children's attention should be focused on the major concept to be presented.

During reading.   Questions asked *between* sections of the text, on the other hand, should bring together ideas brought out in the reading and are designed to build relationships among facts and ideas.

After reading.   Questions asked *after* the reading of the text should be designed to help children internalize narrative text by helping them to identify with the main characters or events in the story and, thus, grow in appreciation of the reading experience; for expository text, the final questions should be created to help children apply the new information to their own lives.

FIGURE 10.4 *Typical questions for guided reading.*

BEFORE READING

Narrative text:	Why might [the main character] want to run away from home?
	Have you ever wanted to run away from home? Why or why not?
Expository text:	Why are trees important to us?
	What would the world be like without trees?

DURING READING

Narrative text:	What made the boy realize that he cared about his family?
	Why do you think they welcomed him home and were not angry?
Expository text:	From what you have read, what are some other ways trees are important to us?
	Why are loggers cutting down the trees?

AFTER READING

Narrative text:	What would you now say to a friend who says he wants to run away?
	What are some other ways you can solve a family problem?
Expository text:	Why are there fewer trees in our cities?
	How can we take better care of our trees?

Procedures for Guided Reading

The guided reading lesson can be broken into three main parts: (1) the new book or story orientation, (2) the oral or silent reading of the text, and (3) a *"grand conversation"* between teacher and class members and/or the explicit phonics instruction component, as needed. As with shared reading, guided reading should be considered flexible and can be expanded, condensed, or modified to meet the group needs and the time constraints of the teacher.

New book orientation

Before the new book or story is introduced, the teacher will want to link any new ideas or difficult concepts to the children's prior experience through the use of a discussion, a visualization of what they are about to read, a video excerpt, or any other technique that will help children, especially English language learners, relate to the text.

The teacher then holds up the book and shows the cover, reads the title, and briefly talks about the main idea in the book. Covering the text, the teacher "walks through" the text, discussing the pictures and providing an opportunity for children to make predictions about the text, asking key questions, as discussed earlier, and using some of the vocabulary and language structures found in the text so children will not find them troublesome when they are reading the book independently.

Depending upon the children's developmental levels, the first reading is initially done by the teacher while the children track with their fingers. Later, the teacher gradually relinquishes responsibility for the first reading to the children by sharing the reading role and then fading into the role of supporter.

Oral/silent reading of the book

When children are ready to read independently, the teacher gives each child a copy of the book. In some cases, the teacher has a large edition of the book, or a big book (see Chapter 3), and the children have smaller versions of the same text. The teacher and children discuss the title, author, and illustrator. Until one-to-one correspondence is established, children should be allowed to point to the words as they read. Repeating the key concept they are to look for, the teacher directs them to read individually at their own pace. While the children are reading, the teacher works with them on an individual basis in the following ways:

1. At the very early reading level, the teacher checks for evidence of, and/or prompts for, directionality and one-to-one matching of spoken to printed word. *Example:* "Who can find the word *is* on this page?"

2. When children have mastered the above skills, the teacher checks for evidence of, and/or prompts for, self-monitoring of understanding ("No, that doesn't make sense"), the ability to search through the repertoire of decoding skills, accuracy, and self-correcting behavior.

Retelling of the story

Children then retell what they have read to their teacher, to their peers, or to a partner. Typically, a teacher will say, "Can you tell me (or a partner) about what you have just read?" Sometimes the teacher will probe, or further explore children's answers, by asking specific questions to prompt recall. The teacher often takes notes during this phase to check language facility and comprehension of individual children.

Grand conversation and/or explicit phonics instruction

The teacher helps the children to internalize and appreciate what they have just read through a **grand conversation.** As in any book club in which adult readers have participated, appreciation of a book is best created by asking open-ended questions and allowing each of the children to voice their opinions about what they liked, disliked, what they found humorous, what "grabbed" them, and so forth. A conversational tone is set when the teacher starts with an open-ended question (e.g., "Would you have chosen Leslie for a friend? Why or why not?") and encourages children to ask questions of and respond to each other for the sheer joy of discussing their feelings about the book. The teacher's role, then, becomes that of facilitator, ensuring that all who want to respond get an opportunity and not just the most vociferous.

grand conversation

When appropriate, the teacher may do an additional minilesson (5 to 7 minutes) on some aspect of phonics or structural analysis development that she deems necessary. Such a lesson may be conducted before the piece is read to increase reading independence, or after, to reinforce patterns that have been introduced previously. This lesson may include (1) letter/sound association, or focusing children's attention on certain beginning or ending sounds found in the story; (2) word chunks or word patterns, or briefly drawing children's attention to a word chunk used in the story, such as a specific blend, ending, or rime; or (3) reinforcement of high frequency words, or picking several repeated words from the story and asking children to find, frame, and say them.

Follow-up

The most appropriate follow-up activity to a guided reading lesson is to invite the children to take the finished book home to demonstrate their reading ability to parents, caretakers, or siblings. Such a follow-up not only provides needed practice, but also promotes increased confidence and fluency for beginning readers.

GROUPING FOR INSTRUCTION

Children can be placed in temporary, small, homogeneous groups for guided reading instruction based upon their knowledge, skills, interest, and experience. While there should be many times during the day when children come together for whole group reading, there are also times when it is helpful to group small numbers of children together who can read at about the same level, meeting with them three to five days a week. With ongoing assessment of their abilities, these groups should be fluid and frequently changed. Finally, to avoid the stigma of low ability groups, the teacher should maintain other heterogeneous groups during the day for reading aloud, shared reading, discussion groups, writing, and other activities.

The following flexible grouping systems each have a place in a balanced literacy program:

- Skill groups
- Interest groups
- Pairs
- Peer editing groups
- Cooperative groups

Skill, or ability, groups

Teachers often conduct a guided reading lesson to a homogeneous group of five or six children who are reading at about the same grade level. This practice helps to avoid frustrating a struggling reader and helps ensure that more capable readers are not held back from appropriately challenging material. Similarly, small skill groups are often formed when a child is having a problem with a specific skill or strategy and needs reinforcement in that area. For example, several children seem to be having problems with the *ain* word chunk or pattern that was introduced in the day's guided reading lesson. The teacher will form a temporary skill group from those children and provide a brief minilesson on words containing *ain*. The group will last only until the skill is mastered.

Interest groups

As children grow in independence, there can be time set aside during the day when children with the same reading interest—for example, those interested in mysteries, horse stories, or the books of R. L. Stine—come together to read and discuss those books. Such reading groups can evolve into writing groups as children decide to write letters to the author or add an epilogue to the text. Children in the groups can often decide to do *reader's theatre* (explained later in this chapter), puppet shows, or murals using the text as inspiration. Interest groups can be temporary or permanent, often lasting as long as the children's interest.

Pairs

Since children are social beings, they often enjoy reading aloud to one another. Such partnerships can be cross-age "reading buddies," pairing a sixth-grader from another class with a first-grader, or just friends getting together to take turns reading. Also pairs of children can participate in dyad reading (see Chapter 8) for the purpose of improving listening and summarizing skills.

Peer-editing groups

When children are writing during writer's workshop or in response to a piece they have read during guided reading, peer editors can offer helpful advice (see

Chapter 9). In groups containing no more than two or three children, each child is both writer and editor and obtains feedback on parts of the writing that may not make sense, offers suggestions for improvement in the style and word choice, and calls attention to mechanics errors that the author may have overlooked in self-editing. The children in these groups are rotated so they obtain different feedback from many editors during the school year.

Cooperative groups

To foster a collaborative atmosphere in the classroom and to avoid the stigma of low ability groups, cooperative groups are ideal; they also foster language acquisition for English language learners. Typically, teachers assign children to four- or five-member groups mixed in ability (there may be one high achiever, one low achiever, and two average achievers per group), gender, and primary language. The teacher presents a lesson to the entire class, and then asks the children to work on follow-up material (workbook pages, spelling words, word sorts, posters) in groups. The children help one another because each is invested in the achievement of the other members since everyone gets credit for the work done by the group.

OTHER PRACTICES FOR MEDIATED READING

To keep mediated approaches for early reading instruction fresh and exciting for both the teacher and the students, the following six techniques and tools can be integrated with either approach:

1. masking
2. music
3. pocket charts
4. word walls
5. reader's theatre
6. cloze activities

Masking

When the teacher wants children to focus on a particular word or word part, an ideal way to do this is by **masking,** using a sliding frame or post-it notes to call attention to just that part of the word (see Figure 10.5). Usually masking and framing take place during repeated readings and not during the initial reading of a book. For example, if the teacher is reading a story to focus on decoding a specific phonic element such as the *br* blend, he can use the masking frame to call attention to that particular letter–sound relationship. The teacher may then ask the children to think of other words that begin with that sound.

masking

FIGURE 10.5 *Masking device.*

DEMONSTRATION SIZE:

1. Starting from the folded edge of a file folder, cut an 8.5 by 6 inch rectangle.
2. Using the remnants of the file folder, start at the fold and cut a one-inch wide strip that runs from the fold all the way across the folder.
3. Remove a 2 by 7 inch rectangle from the center of #1. Start cutting at the open edge so the fold remains completely intact.
4. Slide the one-inch strip over the open ends of the "U" shaped section and staple as indicated.
5. Slide the thin strip back and forth to adjust the frame to the size of the word or letter you are working on.

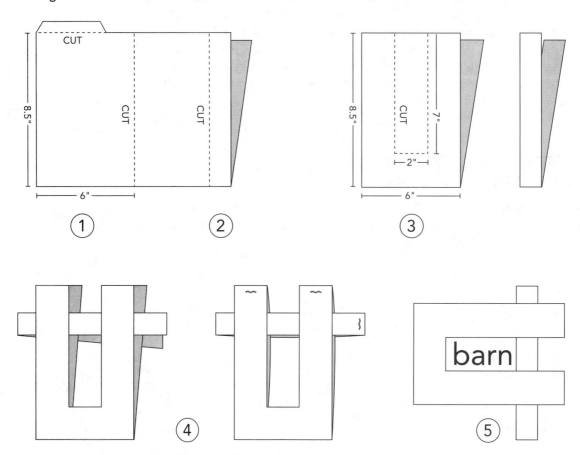

INDIVIDUAL STUDENT SIZE:

1. Follow the directions above with the following changes in dimension:

    The original rectangle cut from the fold should be 5 x 2 inches.

    Remove a .75 x 4 inch rectangle from the center of the 5 x 2 segment.

    Cut a strip .5 x 3, beginning at the fold.

    Staple or tape open edges.

Music

Carefully selected lyrics can be placed on chart paper in large black letters, with repeated or high-frequency words in color or highlighted. The lyrics can be sung (to the original tune or one with which all are familiar) or chanted. When songs, poems, chants, and raps are chosen for their rhyme, rhythm, repetition, or cumulative sequence, music brings the reading and rereading of text to new heights of motivation (Cecil and Lauritzen, 1994). Young children never seem to tire of singing a catchy tune; thus, songs selected for their patterns can familiarize children with high-frequency sight vocabulary. Songs can also be used to reinforce phonic elements in an enjoyable way, as in the "Old MacDonald" adaptation mentioned in Chapter 3. See the box below for more information on linking literacy and lyrics.

Linking literacy and lyrics

Music can be used to reinforce print in many ways:

1. Teach children a song by singing the song once (with or without accompaniment) and then inviting the children to sing along with you. Discuss the meaning of the song, and any special words that may be unfamiliar to the children. Add motions or drama as appropriate.

2. Link the song to print. Write the lyrics to the song on chart paper. Read the lyrics, inviting the children to join in. Reread the lyrics, with the children reading each word as you point to it.

3. Build phonics skills and reinforce sight vocabulary. Point out words that appear more than once. Select one or two phonic elements or patterns to work with. Have the children find all words with the same pattern, beginning sound, ending sound, vowel sound, and so forth. Use sentence strips and word cards for matching and sequencing activities.

4. Create new activities based on the song lyrics. Cover words on the song chart and encourage children to brainstorm some new words to fill in the blanks, for example:

   "Mary had a little cat, her fur was black as night."

   Change the pattern of the song, the main character, the outcome, and so on.

Reprinted with permission of the publisher, *Teaching K–8,* Norwalk, CT. From K. Barclay and T. Coffman (1990). "I Know an Old Lady: Linking Literacy and Lyrics." *Teaching K–8,* May, 47–51.

Pocket Charts

The use of pocket charts (as discussed in Chapter 4) can help develop children's ability to construct meaning and they also aid in building children's sight vocabulary. Selected words from a story can be printed on cards, or sentences from the story can be printed on sentence strips. The teacher then has the children "rebuild" the story using the words or sentence strips (McCracken and McCracken, 1986).

Word Walls

As discussed in Chapter 5, a word wall or word chart is a listing of high-frequency words that are of particular interest to children or are currently being studied in a reading lesson. The words should be prominently displayed on the wall or on a bulletin board so that the children may add to the list whenever they think of an appropriate word, and they can be used for reference during writing activities. These words should be practiced a few minutes each day at the beginning of a word lesson by having the children: (1) stretch them out and read them together; (2) chant or cheer three times; and/or (3) write in isolation and in context. Additionally, all words having the same spelling patterns should be starred (Cunningham and Cunningham, 1997).

Reader's Theatre

reader's theatre

Reader's theatre is a simple and enjoyable way to turn a favorite story into an impromptu play by using dialogue of the characters in a story. No costumes or props are required. A narrator can be used to guide the action of the characters and give clues as to gestures and other actions. If the children wish to create scripts directly from the text, a real purpose for rereading the text has been generated. (See the boxes on pages 210 and 211.) Additionally, such an activity makes the story immediately accessible to English language learners.

Cloze Activities

In the instructional cloze procedure, words or parts of words are blocked out and the reader uses clues within the text to predict what might complete the blocked portion. This technique can be used, orally or on tape, during a repeated reading to help children develop sight vocabulary, their use of prediction for decoding unfamiliar words, and to help them construct meaning using all the cueing systems (Cecil,1994). For example:

I had a cat

And I named him Buffy.

His eyes were coal black

And his fur was so _____ . (fluffy)

MAKING TEXT ACCESSIBLE FOR ALL LEARNERS

Although enabling children to become independent, silent readers is the desired goal of reading instruction, many less able children and those for whom English is a second language may need extra support, or scaffolding, to actually read a book by themselves. Mediated reading methods, with their provision for reading to children and repeated readings, are ideal ways to provide this support; the following are additional ways to make difficult books more accessible to less able readers (Guillaume, 1998; Tompkins, 1997).

Selective Pairing

Pairing an able with a less able reader is a strategy that makes the task more sociable but also more accessible for the less able reader. If low comprehension is also a problem, the teacher can use dyad reading (see Chapter 7), asking children to summarize sentences or paragraphs and make predictions.

Record Books on Tape

Many of our primary classrooms use cassette tapes to accompany favorite books. At listening posts, children follow along by tracking with their fingers to commercially-made or teacher-made recordings. While the focus is on reading for enjoyment, repeated listenings and rereadings of favorite stories aid fluency, develop sight vocabulary, deepen comprehension (Routman, 1995), and help ELL children to become familiar with the cadence of English. Reading that children cannot accomplish silently on their own may often be achieved with the support of a tape. With this nonthreatening approach, children can be encouraged to repeatedly follow along a short, troublesome section and then be prepared to read the section orally the next day in the small guided reading group.

Echo Reading

For text with a limited number of words, children can "echo" the text as the teacher reads, pointing to the words while the children repeat them. Such a strategy helps reinforce one-to-one correspondence and is especially appropriate for big books, where all children can see and follow along.

Adapting a story to a reader's theatre script

1. Select a story that has sufficient interesting dialogue between characters. If an episode of a book or a story is used, make sure the episode is self-contained; that is, knowledge of events before and after the episode is not necessary to understand and enjoy the script.

2. Make a photocopy to mark.

3. Add narrator parts to identify time, place, scene, or characters, as needed. One narrator can be added for the whole story, or more than one can be used to add variety. A narrator should introduce the script in storylike fashion.

4. Delete lines that are not critical to the further development of the plot, are peripheral to the main actions of the story, represent complex imagery, or figurative language that is difficult to express.

5. Label character and narrator parts. Most dialogue requires no rewriting for the reader's theatre scripts. Just add the reader's name in the left-hand margin, followed by a colon. It is permissible to give a character advice regarding the speaking of a particular line. These voice directions are placed within parentheses and follow the character's name.

6. Change any lines that are descriptive but could be spoken by a character or would move the story along more easily.

7. When the script seems finished, ask others to read it aloud. Sometimes listening to the script makes it easier to add voice directions, revice narration, etc.

8. Type the completed script. Make sure the lines are easy to read. On the first page type the name of the book, story, or chapter. Then type the author's name followed by "adapted for reader's theatre by (your name)." On succeeding pages, type the title and page number in the upper right-hand corner of the page.

Build Background

Often a book is difficult for some children simply because they have limited background knowledge or prior experience with the topic. If an informal survey of readers suggests this may be the case, a teacher can build background by reading a simpler text, providing hands-on experiences, showing a short video excerpt, discussing the topic, brainstorming ideas about the topic, or bringing in objects that relate to the topic before the text is read.

Partial reader's theatre script for
The Boy Who Cried Wolf (traditional)
Developed by second-graders and their teacher

The Boy Who Cried Wolf (in children's manuscript)

Narrator: Once upon a time there was a little shepherd boy who lived in a village with his mother and father. Every morning he went to the hillside to herd his sheep. One day he got bored and decided to play a little joke.

Shepherd boy: I am tired of looking after these silly sheep. I think I will play a joke. I will get the village people to come and join me. They will keep me company.

Narrator: So the boy stood up and yelled as loudly as he could:

Shepherd boy: Wolf! Wolf!

Narrator: Soon all the village people came running up the hillside to see what was wrong.

Village Person #1:   So where is the wolf, young man? I don't see any wolf.

Village Person #2:   *Yes!* We were very busy and you disturbed us. There is no wolf here!

Village Person #3:   I don't see any wolf either. Let's go back down the hill. This was a waste of our time.

Narrator: So the village people went back down the hill. The next day the shepherd boy went to the hillside again. He got bored again. He wondered if his joke would work again.

Delay Independent Reading

If many activities related to the text have occurred before the initial reading of the text, or if the text has been read aloud first, children will be much more familiar with new words and concepts before they are expected to actually decode them. Therefore, if the teacher believes the material may be excessively difficult, the independent reading should be the last activity in which the children engage.

Encourage a Variety of Responses

Although school life primarily centers on thoughts and ideas, expression of emotions and feelings should be part of the responses teachers encourage in reading. For difficult material such as science or social studies, for example, a teacher who elicits expression of feelings may notice resultant changes in attitudes, curiosity in science, or the ability to look at historical events from another's point of view—all of which would encourage a deeper engagement with the text.

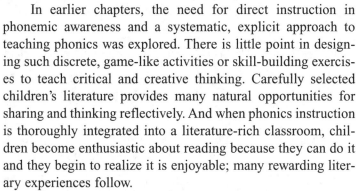

SUMMARY

The goal of a truly balanced approach to reading instruction should always be to create young learners who are able to decode fluently, interact meaningfully with text, and who read willingly for the sheer enjoyment of the activity. Listening to stories and conversing about them pave the way for the later reading of stories with insight and appreciation. By reflecting before, during, and after listening, children are learning the ways of processing text used by sophisticated readers.

In earlier chapters, the need for direct instruction in phonemic awareness and a systematic, explicit approach to teaching phonics was explored. There is little point in designing such discrete, game-like activities or skill-building exercises to teach critical and creative thinking. Carefully selected children's literature provides many natural opportunities for sharing and thinking reflectively. And when phonics instruction is thoroughly integrated into a literature-rich classroom, children become enthusiastic about reading because they can do it and they begin to realize it is enjoyable; many rewarding literary experiences follow.

Shared reading and guided reading, two mediated reading practices combining appreciation for literature with teaching children to decode and construct meaning from text, are ideal vehicles through which to help balance an effective reading program for early readers. The skills that have been introduced through direct instruction in phonics can be reinforced through literature by a skilled and enthusiastic practitioner who enjoys sharing a stimulating story with young learners—learners who are taking giant steps toward becoming literate human beings.

QUESTIONS

for Journal Writing and Discussion

1. How can shared reading and/or guided reading be used to expand each of the following:

   a. oral language

   b. phonemic awareness

   c. phonics acquisition

   d. literature appreciation

2. Making predictions about what will happen in a story has been found to ensure more engagement with the story and increased comprehension on the part of the learners. Why do you think this is so?

3. How do the similar conversational approaches of shared and guided reading compare to methods of reading instruction of which you are currently aware? How do they differ from instruction you received when you were learning to read?

SUGGESTIONS

for Projects and Other Activities

1. Plan a shared or guided reading lesson for a small group of early readers. Record their responses to this lesson. Write a short reflection statement sharing your feelings about student involvement with the lesson.

2. Using the same group of children in Question 1, read them a story "straight," without using predictive strategies, picture sharing, or any thought-provoking questions. Instead, ask only literal questions requiring factual recall, such as "What was the name of the main character?" What differences in student engagement with the story do you notice between the two lessons?

3. Observe a primary teacher who is conducting two readings of the same story with the same group of learners on successive days. What differences do you notice in the questions the teacher asks during the second reading? In what other ways is the instruction different? Do the children appear to be bored during their second encounter with the text? Why or why not?

INFORMING INSTRUCTION

Assessment of Early Literacy Development

FOCUS QUESTIONS

- What are the types of assessment possible for early literacy?

- How can literacy assessment inform instruction?

- How does a balance of formal and informal assessment offer a more accurate picture of progress in literacy?

IN THE CLASSROOM

Emilio and his first-grade teacher, Mr. Steel, are discussing which version
of his illustrated report to put in his showcase portfolio—his "favorite," or
the one he proudly considers his "best." During this conference, the child's
teacher takes *anecdotal notes*, or written observations, to guide Emilio in
the self-assessment and reflection he will be expected to attach to his report. In an upcoming end-of-the-year parent–teacher conference, Mr. Steel
and Emilio will show the boy's parents his *showcase portfolio*, filled with
samples of Emilio's written work, as well as Emilio's personal reflections
about it. Mr. Steel will also share with the parents the teacher *observational portfolio* he has compiled over the last few months, to show Emilio's literacy progress. By explaining some informal assessment data he has
collected, Mr. Steel can inform Emilio's parents of his current reading
level, how he is comprehending, and exactly which phonics elements he
has mastered and which he still needs help with; Mr. Steel suggests that

they can also help to reinforce these at home. Finally, Mr. Steel gathers together data from a standardized reading test that compares Emilio's reading with others his own age. The assessment device, administered in the fall and the spring, also shows, numerically, how much Emilio has grown as a reader over the school year. Mr. Steel ends the conference by offering to loan several books at Emilio's independent reading level, based upon a *reading interest inventory* he recently administered to discover the child's reading preferences.

Ongoing assessment of literacy development refers to the use of multiple instruments, daily observation, and many work samples to measure progress. It also refers to the ongoing analysis of the data from these instruments and observations concerning individuals, small groups, and the entire class so that the teacher can customize instruction and, when necessary, plan appropriate interventions. The assessment in Mr. Steel's classroom is ongoing and dynamic; it is the basis upon which he makes all of his instructional decisions. In an effective primary classroom such as his, all instruction is based on information acquired through valid assessment procedures. Moreover, children in the class, like Emilio, are able to recognize their own strengths and limitations and are encouraged to use strategies designed to increase their literacy competence. Finally, in a strong primary classroom like the one discussed above, the teacher is able to use and interpret the results from a variety of informal and formal assessment tools and effectively communicate those results to children, their parents or caretakers, and relevant school personnel. Emilio knows how well he is doing, and so does everyone who cares about him.

WHY ASSESS?

Assessment is more than merely gathering various information about a child's literacy progress; it must be data collection with a distinct instructional purpose (Salvia and Yesseldyke, 1998). The major reason to spend precious classroom time on administering assessment tools to children is to determine how well they are progressing at a given time with respect to a specific aspect of learning; for example: What blends is this child able to recognize? How well is she able to retell a story? What is her attitude toward writing (Sulzby, 1990)? Other information that can be gained from literacy-related assessments includes the following (Cheek et al., 1997):

- Determining a child's overall reading ability
- Examining a child's ability to use graphophonic, semantic, and syntactic cues in reading
- Analyzing a child's ability to construct meaning from the printed page
- Determining a child's experiential background for content-area material
- Determining a child's overall literacy strengths and needs

This basic information can then be used for classroom program planning and decision-making, to ensure that classroom instruction and activities are responsive to and appropriate for the current class level. Assessment information documents who might benefit from special help or need more academic challenge (Hills, 1992).

A second major reason for assessment is to help children take ownership of their learning by allowing them to see how they are doing and to establish equal partnership in fostering literacy growth. By keeping individual progress charts and writing samples over time, for example, children can actually observe their own growth. This leads to a feeling of self-pride that has been found to be surprisingly potent to a child. When young children are taught to think about and reflect on their own learning, they become more active partners in the whole endeavor.

Finally, it is important to keep careful progress records for the class as well as each individual child to demonstrate to other school personnel, parents, and to the outside community that teachers are doing an effective job teaching children to read and write. The education of children has always been on the local, statewide, and national political agenda, perhaps because every community member has been through the school system and is, therefore, a self-proclaimed "expert" on all subjects related to schools. Hence, it is of utmost importance to be able to inform others and to document progress, especially when new programs and ideas are being initiated.

PRINCIPLES OF ASSESSMENT

In order for teaching to be effective, there must be a reciprocal, synergistic relationship between assessment and teaching. In other words, teaching and assessing should be continually informing one another. It is on the basis of lesson observation that the teacher finds out what needs to be assessed, while the assessment tells the teacher what to teach, or in some cases, reteach. For example, a first grade class has been discussing the difference between "telling" and "asking," or a statement and a question. An observer, examining the teacher's lesson plans on the sentence activities, should be able to expect that the ending assessment for the lessons will be very closely aligned with the teacher's learning objectives for those lessons.

Following is a discussion of other assessment principles that can help teachers determine if their assessment plan will be complementary to instruction (adapted from Cooper, 1997).

The core of assessment should be daily observation

Teachers, who frequently observe and take notes on each aspect of literacy development, know much more about the status of their students than can be obtained from any formal testing, no matter how reliable the testing is purported to be. It is imperative that assessment be a daily event, occurring every time the student reads and writes. Through observing patterns of growth over time, the teacher is in the ideal position to get a clear picture of how the child is progressing.

Children should be actively engaged in the assessment process

Though young children cannot be involved in every aspect of literacy assessment, sometimes asking for input when evaluating their work can be a key factor in encouraging children to take charge of their own learning and inviting ownership of their successes. Since teaching and learning are ideally collaborative processes, we do not want children to view assessment as an uncomfortable practice that the teacher "does" to them. On the other hand, when children and teachers work and think together, assessment becomes a shared responsibility with children participating enthusiastically as team players in their own learning.

Assessment should take many different forms

Different types of assessment tools should be used for different purposes to ensure that a measure of each child's literacy progress is obtained. For example, writing samples, checklists about retellings of stories, and anecdotal notes give insights that are not scientific but based solely upon the teacher's judgment. Although these data are critical to effective planning and decision-making, the teacher also needs **standardized test** results that have accepted statistical **reliability** and **validity**; in other words, the tests consistently measure what they claim to be measuring. To get a truly multidimensional overview of a child's performance in any dimension of literacy, teachers need to look at the data from both sources.

standardized test
reliability
validity

Assessment must avoid cultural bias

Children from different cultures, linguistic groups, and backgrounds may have different language issues as well as varied experiences and styles of learning. When planning assessment procedures, and particularly when interpreting and reporting them to others, these factors should be judiciously considered.

An example of the importance of considering cultural bias is the little girl in a second grade class in the Virgin Islands who was diagnosed with a severe reading disability. Upon examining the test, her perceptive teacher realized that the child was certainly *not* reading disabled. She had scored poorly because she had not known many vocabulary words, such as *chimney* and *caboose*—words that have little meaning for residents of a tiny tropical island!

Assessment should mainly attempt to determine what children *can* do—not what they *cannot* do. When teachers really understand the reading and writing abilities of their learners, it becomes much easier to decide which new literacy experiences should be offered to help them develop further. Not only is this a more constructive way of looking at learning, but children benefit in other crucial ways. Children are simply able to progress more readily when the atmosphere is one where mistakes are viewed as ways to learn rather than failures to be avoided at all cost (Cousin et al., 1993).

TYPES OF ASSESSMENT

Teachers have at their disposal an almost overwhelming array of instruments to use as part of the assessment process. Many of these instruments blend naturally into instruction; others provide a separate means to assess literacy progress, either formally or informally. Because so many assessment tools are available, it is impossible to discuss each one in this chapter. Therefore, a sampling of some of the most pervasive assessment devices that are compatible with a balanced early literacy program will be explored here. An example of a comprehensive framework for guiding the assessment process is presented in Figure 11.1.

Most of the techniques discussed in the remaining portions of this chapter can be used easily on the basis of the information given; others require reviewing an examiner's handbook. Appropriate references are given for those that require more detailed study, and samples of others are presented in Appendices C and D.

Three basic types of assessments are used in primary classrooms and each offers a unique perspective for a balanced early literacy program: skills-based assessment, curriculum-based assessment, and process-oriented assessment.

Skills-Based Assessment

Skills-based assessment focuses on the use of tests to measure reading and spelling skills as well as the subskills of these areas. These tests are administered by the teacher or reading specialist and usually provide numerical scores that represent a child's rank compared to the performance of other children at the same age or grade. The data obtained from these tests can be, but are not always, related to the content of instruction. Examples of skills-based assessment would be a systematic appraisal of a child's ability to name letters, the child's knowledge of concepts of print, or the number of vocabulary words the child knows compared with others his age.

skills-based assessment

FIGURE 11.1 *A framework for guiding the assessment process.*

What do I want to know?   How am I going to find out?

	INFORMAL	ONGOING	FORMAL
Concepts about print	Observations of book handling & tracking	Checklist of orthographic knowledge	M. Clay's "Concept about Print"
Phonemic awareness	Observation of songs, rhymes, repetitions Word games	Checklist of phonemic awareness skills	Standardized tests (Torgesen's "Test of Phonemic Awareness")
Phonics	Observation of ability to generate/ identify sounds	Running records Mediated reading	IRI Miscue analysis Phonics survey
Oral reading (fluency)	One-to-one observation Paired reading	Mediated reading Anecdotal notes Running records	Tape recordings IRI Miscue analysis
Spelling	Free writing Pretests	Writing samples Journals	Weekly tests Dictations
Reading comprehension	Retellings QARs Discussions	Paraphrasing Summarizing Class contributions Cloze tests	Standardized tests (Stanford Achievement Test, Metropolitan Achievement Test)
Writing	Free writing Journals Quickwrites	Writing samples Daily work	Rubrics (scaled scores) Editing checklist
Reading/writing attitudes	Questionnaire Number books read/written	Conferences Interest inventories Reading response journals	Reading logs Surveys
Student views of own literacy	Books chosen Attitude survey Reading survey	Portfolio choices Reflection log Dialogue journals	Self-evaluations Response journals Questionnaires

Curriculum-Based Assessment

Curriculum-based assessment ties evaluation directly to the teacher's literacy curriculum to identify instructional needs and to determine what is needed for a child to "master" a concept. Such assessment may include criterion-based assessment, in which the child's performance is compared against standards deemed appropriate for mastery in a particular area. Scores from such a tool typically offer a number, or percentage, for the amount of material each child has mastered. These tools are usually administered in the classroom using items and materials derived from the curriculum. Examples of curriculum-based assessment would include asking a child to read a passage aloud from the child's basal and counting the number of words read correctly per minute, or culminating a thematic unit on dinosaurs by asking children to quickly write down (or tell, for preliterate children) everything they know about dinosaurs.

curriculum-based assessment

Process-Oriented Assessment

Process-oriented assessment refers to a teacher's observations of the child's actual reading and writing abilities. Measures used for such assessment are informal and subjective and are, therefore, usually supplemented by norm-referenced testing that objectively compares a child to others of the same age or grade. In process-oriented assessment, the literacy behavior being examined is documented in the learning context in which it normally occurs. For example, a process-oriented assessment would be an informal checklist designed by the teacher to answer such questions as, "Are the child's letters in the proper sequence?" or "Is the child able to spell words correctly in isolation but not in context?" The assessment would be taking place at the same time as the child was doing a self-selected writing task, such as writing in a journal (see Chapter 9). An *informal reading inventory* (to be discussed later in this chapter) with miscue analyses also falls under this category.

process-oriented assessment

FORMAL ASSESSMENT PROCEDURES

There are advantages and disadvantages to using **formalized assessment** devices in the classroom. While formal group tests can be used, in a very broad way, to compare student performance to a cross-section of students in other areas of the country, such tests provide little or no usable information about the specific diagnostic needs of individual students. As with any assessment device, teachers must first determine what information they are seeking and then decide if the instrument is appropriate to those goals.

formalized assessment

Achievement Tests

Norm-referenced achievement tests, often called surveys, are formal tests, usually administered in a group, and offer the teacher a "ballpark" estimate of

norm-referenced achievement tests

An assessment program

Mr. Steel, the teacher we met at the beginning of this chapter, has created an assessment program which incorporates data from a wide variety of assessment tools to evaluate the literacy growth of Emilio and the other children in his class. Those tools will be listed here and discussed at length later in this chapter.

- Twice a year the children take a norm-referenced achievement test called *"The Stanford Achievement Test"* (The Psychological Corporation) to allow Mr. Steel to obtain general literacy information about his class and an indication of how well the students in his school are doing in comparison with other children of the same age and grade across the nation (skills-based).

- At the beginning of the year children are given an *informal reading inventory* to evaluate each student's reading progress, determine at which level they are reading, and identify specific strengths and needs in comprehension and decoding (skills-based).

- Once a week Mr. Steel listens to each child read from basals and takes *running records* to check their reading fluency (curriculum-based).

- Every day Mr. Steel observes each student and takes *anecdotal notes* monitoring anything he considers significant in their struggles, their successes, and their attitudes; he sometimes uses checklists to make his observations more formal when determining their knowledge of sight words, their ability to answer a range of comprehension questions, or other skills (process-oriented).

- At the end of each basal reader unit, children are given an oral or written *cloze test* to determine their comprehension and understanding of grammar.

- Once a week Mr. Steel listens as children *retell stories* to evaluate their English language fluency, knowledge of story structure, and comprehension skills (process-oriented).

- Once or twice a week the teacher and students examine together and briefly discuss the work in their *writing portfolios* (process-oriented).

- Every six to eight weeks Mr. Steel administers a *phonics survey test* to those children who need it to measure growth in phonics elements; he also gives a quick survey of *sight words* to determine which words children still need to master (skills-based).

their students' reading performance. The results are more helpful for comparing groups than for making judgments about individual children. They provide the teacher with a **grade-level equivalency score**, e.g., 3.7, which supposedly indicates that the child is performing as well as a child in the seventh month of the third grade on the subskills tested, although such a figure should be considered only a rough estimate of the child's true ability.

grade-level equivalency score

Most of these tests, such as the *Gates–MacGinitie Reading Tests* (Riverside Publishing), are general in nature and sample the child's overall literacy achievement. They provide little specific information on a child's literacy strengths and needs, and can be culturally and linguistically biased. Most reading achievement tests for older children include subscores on vocabulary and comprehension, as well as a total reading score. Readiness tests, such as those normally administered at the end of kindergarten and/or at the beginning of first grade, frequently measure phonemic awareness skills, letter recognition, visual–motor coordination, listening comprehension, and auditory and visual discrimination. *The Test of Early Reading Ability* (PRO–ED), for example, measures knowledge of alphabet, comprehension, and reading conventions. Clay (1979) offers a more process-oriented tool to assess the emergent literacy development of a young child with her *Concepts about Print Test: Stones* (Heinemann). A list of other formal reading and reading readiness tests can be found in Appendix C.

Norm-referenced tests compare a child's performance with that of a sample group of children, called the **norming group**. This sample group has taken the test under controlled conditions and their average performance determines the norms, or average performance, for other children who take the test. As mentioned earlier, from a norm-referenced test, teachers receive a numerical grade-level equivalent score for every child. Thus, a score of 2.3 suggests that the child's score was equivalent to that of the average child in the norming group in the third month of second grade. The tests also allow for a percentile rank, enabling the teacher to quickly see how each student's score compares with that of the norming group. Finally, these tests show the range of classroom scores through the use of **stanines**, which distribute all scores into nine sections, the first three being "below average," the middle three being "average," and the top three "above average." Teachers usually find these types of scores more usable for assessment because they represent a wider range of achievement and are better suited to fluctuations that may occur in children's scores.

norming group

stanines

Scores on norm-referenced tests should be interpreted cautiously, however. Though such tests may compare groups adequately and give a fair sketch of how a class of students is doing, they can be problematic for making major instructional decisions for individual children. Since these tests are administered in groups, and because they are timed, a child who is a powerful but plodding reader may appear to be less able than she actually is; similarly, an impulsive guesser may do well on a multiple choice exam, and appear to be more skilled than is actually the case. Children from diverse cultural and/or linguistic groups may not have the background to answer the questions at all, though they may be highly literate in their own languages or do well when the context of the question items matches their own experiences.

Standardized norm-referenced tests are administered in a highly proscribed manner. A teacher's manual, or technical manual, accompanies such tests and describes in detail the procedures for giving and interpreting the test. Included in the manual are the following (adapted from Rupley and Blair, 1988):

1. *Overview and purpose.* This information details the purpose and levels of the test, tells how to select the appropriate level for the child's grade placement, and provides specific information on the literacy areas that are included.

2. *Administration.* This section tells the teacher about time limits for each subtest, and exactly what to say to students about how to complete each portion of the test. It also provides sample questions to do with children to get them familiar with the test's format.

3. *Directions for scoring.* Specific scoring information varies, but most norm-referenced tests now offer an option of either hand-scored or machine-scored. The procedures for both are usually provided.

4. *Interpreting the results.* Most norm-referenced literacy tests provide general information for planning literacy instruction based upon students' strengths and needs, and suggest specific activities to enhance specific literacy areas. There is often information on how to report classroom scores for administrative purposes.

5. *Technical data.* Selection and characteristics of the norming group, information on how reliable and valid the test is, scaled scores, and test item difficulty are usually described in this section.

Criterion-Referenced Tests (CRTs)

criterion-referenced tests

Other standardized tests frequently used to assess children's literacy development are **criterion-referenced tests.** While a norm-referenced test compares a child's performance in relation to other children's performance, a commercial criterion-referenced test, such as *Woodcock Reading Mastery Tests* (American Guidance Services), measures specific literacy skills in terms of mastery of those skills—performance standards are identified as *mastery, review,* and *reteach,* or *lack of mastery.* Many states, and sometimes districts, develop their own CRTs, which are *not* standardized. These tests are created to determine "minimum competency," or the lowest acceptable performance level, and are considered "mastery tests" designed to test specific district or state standards.

A large number of *behavioral objectives* are often found in commercially published, standardized CRTs; for example, phonics analysis may result in as many as 20 to 25 specific behavioral objectives. Such objectives often focus on reading subskill behaviors such as the following:

- Recognizes sound represented by letter *b*
- Recognizes sound represented by the letter *a* in the medial position in a word
- Knows sound represented by the letter *o* in the initial position of a one-syllable word

The major benefit of CRTs is that they are instruction-specific; that is, they reflect children's capabilities with regard to stated objectives, allow teachers to assess the varying levels of performance in their class, and then tailor programs to meet those needs. For example, a CRT might suggest that all but four children in the class can identify all the consonants when they are found in the beginning of words. Two of the remaining children need further help identifying the beginning consonants *p, d,* and *b;* the other two children need help identifying only the initial *r.*

Diagnostic Reading Tests

Many school districts use group **diagnostic reading tests.** They are popular not only because they are easy to administer and interpret but also because, unlike norm-referenced tests, they provide valuable diagnostic information about the strengths and needs of each of the children in the class. Since more diagnostic information is gained from these tools than with norm-referenced tests, some school districts prefer these formal tests, even though they generally cost more and take longer to administer. Districts appreciate the fact that such tests often have subtest scores in areas other than vocabulary and comprehension. *The Stanford Diagnostic Reading Test* (The Psychological Corporation), or SDRT, is one of the most widely used group diagnostic reading tests currently available.

When the teacher needs more detailed information, individual diagnostic tests are often given. These are typically administered by reading specialists trained to provide a more thorough assessment and analysis of a variety of severe reading disorders. Two individual diagnostic reading tests currently being used in school districts are the *Diagnostic Reading Scales* (CTB McGraw–Hill) and the *Durrell Analysis of Reading Difficulties* (The Psychological Corporation).

diagnostic reading

INFORMAL ASSESSMENT PROCEDURES

The ability to provide meaningful instruction based on the needs of children in a classroom can best be achieved by combining standardized assessment with various informal assessment measures. Informal assessment demands greater teacher knowledge in terms of test administration and interpretation, but the specificity of the information gained makes the assessment well worth the effort.

Informal assessment devices are numerous and include informal reading inventories, interest and attitude inventories, reading, spelling and writing placement tests, story retelling tasks, phonemic awareness and phonics survey tests, and written teacher observation procedures such as checklists and other anecdotal notes.

Informal Reading Inventory

informal reading inventory (IRI)

An **informal reading inventory (IRI)** is one of the most valuable tools for evaluating the reading progress of each child in the class as well as diagnosing specific reading strengths and needs. Because they actually hear the child reading aloud, observant teachers are offered a kind of window into the child's brain to see the child's strategies for decoding and constructing meaning. The IRI is an individual diagnostic reading test composed of lists of leveled sight words and a set of graded reading passages from preprimer through grade 8 or even 12, with accompanying comprehension questions for each passage. Most basal reading series include their own IRI (sometimes called a student placement test) as part of their evaluation program, but such devices as the *Basic Reading Inventory* (BRI) (Kendall/Hunt) and the *Flynt–Cooter Reading Inventory for the Classroom* (Merrill/Prentice Hall) are also commercially available. Teachers can design their own informal reading inventory by compiling a series of graded passages by using readability formulas and taxonomies for developing appropriate questions.

The IRI is an invaluable tool because it enables the teacher to:

1. identify each child's instructional, frustration, and independent and listening comprehension levels.
2. determine strengths and needs in decoding and comprehension abilities.
3. understand how children are using syntactic (structure), graphophonic (visual–sound), and semantic (meaning) cues to make sense of reading.
4. compare how a child decodes words in isolation with how that child decodes words in the context of meaningful sentences.

The IRI takes about 20 to 30 minutes to administer and is often taped; the child reads orally while the teacher records the child's miscues, or deviations from the actual text, by using a kind of shorthand. After the oral reading, the teacher asks a series of comprehension questions. When the child falls below about 90 percent in word recognition, achieves less than 50 percent in comprehension, or appears frustrated, the test is terminated; the passage level at which **frustration level** this occurs is called the **frustration level.** After the child reaches the frustration level, the teacher reads aloud passages at successively higher grade levels until the child is unable to answer 75 percent of the comprehension questions (this percentage may vary depending upon the IRI being used). The purpose of **reading capacity level** this last step is to determine the child's **reading capacity level,** also called *listening comprehension level.* A reading capacity level is the highest level of material the child can understand when the passage is read to him or her.

FIGURE 11.2 *Summary of informal reading inventory percentages.**

	WORD RECOGNITION	COMPREHENSION
Independent level	99% or above	90% or above
Instructional level	90% or above	75% or above
Frustration level	below 90%	below 50%
Listening comprehension level		75% or above

*Percentages may vary among inventories.

Material is at the child's **independent level,** appropriate for recreational reading, when that child can read the passage without stress and correctly pronounce 99 percent, or most of the words, and at least 90 percent of the comprehension questions. The passage at which the child can correctly pronounce approximately 90% of the words and answer at least 75 percent of the comprehension questions is the child's **instructional level,** the appropriate level of difficulty for classroom instruction in reading (see Figure 11.2).

After analyzing decoding and comprehension miscues to establish what instruction is needed in these skill areas, the teacher also does a **miscue analysis** to determine how the child is using clues to think about reading. The teacher looks for patterns of miscues, such as those that retain the meaning (e.g., *Dad* for *father*), miscues that retain the syntactic pattern (e.g., *being* for *beginning*), or those that simply retain the visual/sound similarities (e.g., *father* for *feather*). Miscues such as repetitions of words or phrases usually do not signify errors, but indicate the child may be rereading to try to rework a word or passage that didn't seem to make sense.

Teachers should choose a commercial IRI that corresponds as closely as possible to the instructional materials used in the classroom, and should agree with what the inventory considers a text deviation (e.g., a *repetition* is usually considered a positive second search for meaning). Also, by noting the types of comprehension questions, the number asked, and how scoring is handled, teachers can examine how the inventory evaluates comprehension. Teachers should also look at the clarity of instructions for administration, scoring, and interpretation and select the one with which they feel most comfortable.

Running Record

Another method for analyzing a child's miscues is the **running record** (Clay, 1985), which is comparable to the miscue analysis that often accompanies the IRI, but is easier to administer and much more expedient. The IRI, however, is a more thorough evaluation, as it generally requires the child to read more than one passage and makes a comparison of the child's reading of words in isola-

independent level

instructional level

miscue analysis

running record

tion compared with the reading of words in context. It is important to keep in mind that multiple samples will always offer a clearer picture of the child's "true" reading ability, but at times the expediency of the running record makes it more appealing.

With the running record, children orally read a passage of text ranging from easy to difficult. Although comprehension is not formally measured, teachers often ask children to do a retelling after the passage is read to check for understanding. Teachers are able to examine children's strengths and limitations in the use of various decoding strategies by making a check mark on a piece of paper as a child reads each word correctly and writing the word diacritically to denote substitutions, repetitions, mispronunciations, or unknown words. Alternatively, teachers can duplicate a copy of the pages the child will read and record errors next to or on top of the text copy (see Figure 11.3).

After identifying the words that the child read incorrectly, the teacher calculates the percentage of the words the child read correctly. Teachers use the percentage of words read correctly to determine whether or not the material is too easy, difficult, or at the appropriate instructional level for the child at that time using the same percentages discussed for the IRI determination of reading levels.

As with the IRI, the teacher can then do a miscue analysis, categorizing the child's miscues according to the graphophonic, semantic, and syntactic cueing systems (see Chapter 1), in order to examine what word identification strategies are being used. Errors can then be classified, charted, and instructional decisions made accordingly.

OTHER INFORMAL ASSESSMENT PROCEDURES

Many other tools are used for the informal assessment of literacy behaviors, ranging from structured, skills-based tools, such as phonics surveys, to less structured observational procedures based on the teacher's daily interaction with the class, and her professional judgment about what she observes. It is not possible to mention all the assessment devices available, nor is it necessary or possible for a teacher to use every device contained in this chapter. Because a teacher has limited instructional time, choosing which tools to use should be based upon the specific literacy needs of her class.

Anecdotal Notes

Many teachers incorrectly assume that their own observations about a child's literacy status are not as important as the results of formalized tests. Researchers strongly dispute this belief (Cambourne and Turbill, 1990). One of the most powerful and reliable parts of any teacher's assessment and evaluation process, researchers claim, is teachers' daily, systematic observation of the children, using either a clipboard or a tape recorder. Ideally, some obser-

FIGURE 11.3 *Example of a running record.*

The first thing you must do when you	✓ ✓ ✓ ✓ ✓ ✓ $\frac{what}{when}$ ✓
wash your dog is to find him. Some	✓ ✓ ✓ ✓ ✓ ✓ ✓ ✓
dogs do not like to take baths. Use a	✓ ✓ ✓ ✓ ✓ ✓ $\frac{bats}{baths}$ ✓ ✓
hose. Get the dog very wet. Then put	$\frac{horse}{hose}$ ✓ ✓ ✓ ✓ ✓ ✓ ✓
some doggy shampoo on him. Rinse	✓ ✓ $\frac{shan-}{shampoo}$ ✓ ✓ $\frac{Ring}{Rinse}$
him really well. Then dry him off. That	✓ ✓ $\frac{will}{well}$ ✓ ✓ ✓ ✓ ✓
is the part your dog will like the best!	✓ ✓ ✓ ✓ ✓ ✓ ✓ ✓ ✓
Give him a reward for letting you give	✓ ✓ ✓ $\frac{roar}{reward}$ ✓ $\frac{let}{letting}$ ✓ ✓
him the bath.	✓ ✓ ✓

ANALYSIS

Total words: _____ 67 _____

Deviations from text: _____ 8 _____

Accuracy level: _____ 84% _____

(frustration level)

_____ Chelsea H. _____
Name of student

This child read the text in a halting, word by word manner. After reading, the child was able to give the main idea of the text, but was unable to recall details due to the errors in decoding of key words. Her errors were:

Substitutions: what/when   roar/reward   ring/rinse   let/letting
horse/hose   will/well   bats/baths

Mispronunciations: shan-/shampoo

Most of her errors affected comprehension because they made no sense, semantically or syntactically, in the sentences. A series of minilessons on using the context to help decode unfamiliar words is recommended.

anecdotal notes

vation time should be scheduled every day to focus on particular children and take brief logs, or **anecdotal notes,** about the children's involvement in literacy events (Rhodes and Nathenson–Mejia, 1992). Teachers should observe children in every possible language context: one-to-one interactions, small group discussions, and large class settings. The focus should always be on what children *do* as they read and write; the most useful notes describe specific events, report rather than evaluate, and relate the events to other information about the student. Teachers can make observations about a preliterate learner's concepts about print, older children's reading and writing activities, the questions they ask, the books they are reading, what they seem to like and dislike in reading, and whether they use strategies and skills fluently or indicate some confusion. Specific notes can be organized around the literacy areas shown in the box on the following page.

These records are truly dynamic documentations of children's growth over time while also directing teachers' attention to problem areas needing direct instruction for individuals, and possible minilesson topics for small groups.

Sight Words

sight words

Teachers may wish to informally assess their students' recognition of **sight words,** or sight vocabulary, periodically and keep a running tally for each child. To accomplish this, 3 × 5 index cards can be numbered and arranged in the same order as the words on a list of sight words or high-frequency words, such as Fry's list of "instant words," appropriate for the child (see Appendix F). While holding up the cards for the child to respond to, the teacher uses the list to note which words the child recognizes and reads successfully. The child must say the word immediately, with no hesitation or sounding out. For each correct response, the teacher makes a check next to the corresponding word on the word list. The teacher should write above the word any mispronunciations or substitutions for later analysis. The child's score is the number of words checked.

Cloze Tests

Cloze is an easy-to-use device that uses a short passage from the basal reader, or other reading material, with certain words deleted (and replaced with blanks) to determine a child's ability to comprehend the ideas in the sentences and in the entire passage. Besides establishing whether or not the basal reader or other text is at the appropriate instructional level for a child, the procedure may be used to diagnose the child's ability to use context clues in reading. By listing each incorrect response made by the child, the teacher can determine if the response makes sense syntactically or semantically. Often, a response may be semantically and syntactically correct without being the exact keyed response (e.g., for "The boy *stroked* the dog" the child substitutes "The boy *petted* the dog"), which would be considered acceptable. The cloze can be designed in written form or orally, on tape, for preliterate learners.

Observable behaviors for anecdotal notes

PHONEMIC AWARENESS

Observable Behaviors

1. Can hear and pronounce the sounds of English correctly
2. Can "stretch" a word out to hear the sounds
3. Can hear the distinctions between words in continuous speech

PHONICS: LETTER AND SOUND RELATIONSHIPS

Observable Behaviors

1. Can recognize the visual form and name the letters of the alphabet
2. Can identify initial consonants in context
3. Can identify rhyming words
4. Can recognize spelling patterns and use more conventional spelling in writing
5. Can recognize some high-frequency words (list)

BOOK HANDLING SKILLS

Observable Behaviors

1. Holds the book appropriately
2. "Reads" from front to back
3. Knows the difference between the pictures and the words
4. Understands the terms "beginning of" and "end of" the book
5. Understands the term "cover of the book"

CONCEPTS ABOUT PRINT

Observable Behaviors

1. Points to the words and not the pictures while being read to
2. Is able to touch each word as it is read (one-to-one correspondence)
3. Knows that we read from left to right and top to bottom
4. Knows that we read a book from front to back
5. Knows the difference between a letter, a word, and a sentence

COMPREHENSION

Observable Behaviors

1. Answers literal questions about text
2. Paraphrases text when asked what it was about
3. Can give the main idea of a story
4. Can answer critical questions about text
5. Asks questions when meaning is not clear

Writing Folders

The writing folder is the place where children keep all their rough drafts in various stages of the writing process and other daily compositions, topics for future pieces they might like to write, and with older children, notes from minilessons (see Chapter 9). Children also include their own assessments and reflections about any piece they have completed. Material from their writing folders is the basis for teacher/student conferences on individual instructional needs, and minilesson topics are chosen from observations during these sessions.

For special displays, publications, or for parent/teacher meetings, the teacher and child often meet together and make collaborative decisions on what piece(s) should be selected to put in a special "showcase portfolio" that will be shown to parents. Writing folders are often proudly decorated and personalized by children and kept in a special place in the classroom where they are easily accessible. Anecdotal notes regarding this folder can be important assessment data on the child's writing progress.

Interest and Attitude Inventory

interest and attitude inventory

The interests and attitudes of children about reading, writing, and school in general have been found to be highly correlated with success in literacy. The **interest and attitude inventory** assesses these factors and should therefore be included in any comprehensive assessment program. Given the importance of these factors, they should be assessed and monitored incidentally, using anecdotal notes, and deliberately through an informal questionnaire, administered orally or in writing, to the whole class or to individuals. A sample *reading interest inventory* and an *attitude survey* are found in Appendix D. Teachers can design their own inventories appropriate to the age and developmental level of their learners, but the questions should be designed to solicit at least the following critical information.

- The subject areas that are motivating to the child

- The child's favorite story or book

- What the child does in his or her spare time

- What sports or hobbies the child enjoys

- The child's favorite television program

- The child's preferred instructional arrangements; for example, teacher-directed, working alone, with a small group, or with one other child

- The child's attitudes toward reading and writing

- What reading materials and experiences the child has been exposed to

Story Retelling

By listening to the **retelling** of a story or expository piece, a teacher can gain diagnostic information about the child's use of language, the child's knowledge of narrative or expository structure, and how that child comprehends or constructs meaning from text. Therefore, a series of retellings over time determines progress in this area and provides important information about each child.

To use this strategy, have the child read a passage aloud or silently (or read the text to a preliterate child). After the reading, ask the child to retell the passage. If needed, provide gentle prompts, such as "Tell me more," or "Keep going; you're doing great." If the child requires further prompting, the teacher asks questions about specific parts of the passage that the child did not mention. If retellings are tape recorded, the teacher can examine the tape to observe the child's oral language and determine how well the child comprehends the passage and can organize ideas. This sample can later be compared with past or subsequent retellings. The teacher can also review and discuss the retelling with the child, using the procedure to develop the same skills that were assessed.

Phonemic Awareness

While several norm-referenced phonemic awareness tests are available, such as the *Test of Phonological Awareness* (PRO–ED, Austin, Texas), teachers can informally measure phonemic awareness abilities at frequent intervals to determine growth and what sounds need to be taught or reinforced. Informal assessment of this important skill includes providing several examples of what the child is expected to do as the teacher goes through the hierarchy of phonemic awareness skills one at a time (see Chapter 4). These phonemic awareness skills appear in order in the box on the following page (adapted from *Phonemic Awareness Assessment,* Peddy, 1995). Examples are provided for each skill, although teachers often need to create additional examples to ensure that the child completely understands the task.

Phonics

The phonic analysis abilities of individual children in the class can be assessed formally using norm-referenced instruments, such as *The Botel Phonics Survey,* but progress in these skills can also be determined by using an informal inventory of phonics skills (see Chapter 5). Similar to the administration of the phonemic awareness assessment in the box below, this procedure also requires that the teacher offer as many examples as are necessary for the child to understand what is being asked. The inventory on page 235 can be given to the whole class at one time as a pretest and post-test to discover what skills need to be taught, or individually by having a child read each word orally so

Assessing phonemic awareness

Rhyming: "I'll say two words and you tell me if they rhyme."

> EXAMPLES: *boy, toy; go, help; we, me*

Word to Word Match: "I'll say two words and you tell me if they begin with the same sound."

> EXAMPLES: *bat, boy; day, can; run, hop*

Odd Word Out: "I'll say four words and you tell me which word ends with a different sound."

> EXAMPLES: *bat, hit, make, wet*

(Do the same with beginning sounds).

Blending: "Tell me what word we would make if we put these sounds together."

> EXAMPLES: */a/ /t/; /g/ /o/; /w//i/ /n/; /r/ /a/ /n/*

Phoneme Segmentation: "Tell me what sounds you hear in the words I tell you."

> EXAMPLES: *be, pat, got, fish*

Phoneme Counting: "Tell me how many sounds you hear in the words I tell you."

> EXAMPLES: *in, cat, ship, lake*

Sound to Word Matching: "Answer these questions about what sounds you hear."

> EXAMPLES: Is there a /p/ in *pat*? Is there a /n/ in *sun*? Is there a /sh/ in *wash*?

Sound Isolation: "See if you can hear these sounds."

> EXAMPLES: What is the first sound in *tug*? What is the ending sound in *bat*? What is the middle sound in *cane*?

Phoneme Deletion: "Tell me what word would be left if I take away these sounds."

> EXAMPLES: Say *cat* without the /c/. Say *hit* without the /h/. Say *bean* without the /n/.

the teacher can check knowledge of letter–sound correspondence. Children should be given an answer form with categories and numbers on it to use in recording their responses. Phonics elements mastered, as well as those yet to be learned, can be recorded and analyzed for each child for the purpose of future instructional planning.

Phonics Assessment Inventory

Consonant Sounds (beginning): "Write the beginning letter of each word I say."

> EXAMPLES: *hit, bat, name, just, game, pond*

Consonant Sounds (final): "Write the last letter of each word I say."

> EXAMPLES: *man, soft, jam, rub, grass, talk*

Consonant Blends (initial): "Write the first two letters of each word I say."

> EXAMPLES: *truck, crab, star, grin, drown, blame*

Consonant Blends (final): Write the last two letters of each word I say."

> EXAMPLES: *back, first, cart, jump, hand, perk*

Consonant Digraphs (initial): " Write the first two letters of each word I say."

> EXAMPLES: *shout, child, that, photo, those, chin*

Consonant Digraphs (final): "Write the last two letters of each word I say."

> EXAMPLES: *much, ring, cash, moth, sang, luck*

Long and Short Vowels: "If the vowel in the word I say is short, write *short* and the vowel. If the vowel in the word I say is long, write *long* and the vowel."

> EXAMPLES: *sat, hike, same, bone, bless, cot, rug, feet, tin, cube*

Vowel Digraphs and Diphthongs: "Write the two vowels that go together to form a team—such as /ow/, /oi/, /oy/ and /oo/—in the words I say."

> EXAMPLES: *how, look, oil, ought, boy, mood*

COMPILING AND SUMMARIZING ASSESSMENT INFORMATION

The acts of compiling and summarizing the variety of assessment data help teachers integrate, organize, manage, and keep this information accessible for whenever it is needed. In literacy assessment, information about children is gathered from multiple formal, informal, and observational sources, with many of the same behaviors appearing in several different appraisals. For example, Mr. Steel has information from writing folders, journal entries, phonics tests, story retellings, IRIs, reading achievement tests, cloze tests, and many anecdotal observations, to name just a few sources. These primary data must be put together to get the big picture of each student's capabilities. Moreover, as the year progresses, the amount of information proliferates, resulting in far more data than anyone could possibly commit to memory. Two ways to compile and summarize information is through the use of *teacher observational portfolios* for each child and *group profiles* for the entire class.

Portfolios

Artists use portfolios to demonstrate their skills and achievements; teachers can use portfolios in a similar manner to portray the literacy work and progress of each of the students in their class over an extended period of time (Valencia, 1990; Porter and Cleland, 1995).

teacher observational portfolio

There are many options for the contents of portfolios; they can be organized in any way that is helpful to teacher, children, parents, and families. Typically, the teacher will select appropriate data based on observations and informal assessments of children's reading and writing behaviors and accomplishments, and put these data into a progress file, or a **"teacher observational portfolio,"** while some of the choice materials assembled will represent a collaborative decision between the teacher and the child and go into a showcase portfolio.

video portfolio

An alternative vehicle for showcasing children's work via technology is by creating a **video portfolio,** a taped representation of a child's ongoing reading prowess, through the use of a camcorder. Children can be recorded reading aloud during various intervals during the year; they can be filmed during reading discussion groups; and writer's workshop, and special projects such as reader's theatre, can be videotaped to record progress.

Group Profiles

group profiles

Group profiles are a compilation of individual performances of all the children in the class on one or more assessments. They focus on the range of class literacy behavior and identify clusters, or subgroups, of children with similar strengths and needs. They also condense information about the whole class's performance on several sheets of paper. Unlike individual teacher observational portfolios, group profiles do not cut across different areas, but summarize one literacy area for the entire class (see Appendix D).

Group profiles are primarily planning tools to convey strengths and needs of the entire class so that appropriate activities can be planned to meet them. Instead of generalizing about what the class knows and can do, the group profile graphically shows, for example, that only two children need more direct instruction in phonemic awareness while the majority of the class is ready for formal phonics instruction; furthermore, four children need no phonics instruction but could use specific comprehension strategies (see Chapter 7) to enrich their advanced reading abilities.

SUMMARY

The major goal for literacy assessment in a primary classroom is to find out how each child is progressing in a particular area at a given time and to make instructional adjustments more closely attuned to the children's changing needs. The best way to achieve this assessment goal is by using a balance of formal, informal, and observational assessment tools.

The use of formalized reading achievement tests provides important comparative data that has been designed to be valid and reliable, but results do not always provide accurate and specific information for individual children. Data from such tests should, therefore, be interpreted with caution, especially when the test-takers are culturally diverse learners.

Informal assessments and anecdotal information derived from careful observation, though nonscientific, can support or question standardized test results. Informal assessment, if resulting data is compiled frequently and interpreted wisely, can be an excellent method of continually informing instruction.

The value of the assessment devices discussed in this chapter depends largely on reflective analysis and how the devices are used for communicating literacy progress and resultant instructional plans with the child, his parents, and others. By recognizing the strengths and limitations of different types of assessment devices, a teacher can maximize their value for creating a balanced literacy program.

QUESTIONS

for Journal Writing and Discussion

1. Interview a local primary grade teacher to determine what assessment strategies he uses or, if you are already teaching, interview a teacher from another school. What and how does the teacher assess? How does the teacher balance formal and informal assessment? Discuss your findings

with others in your class to see if there are similarities, differences, and/or conclusions that can be drawn.

2. It is no longer enough to simply give children the opportunity to learn; schools must now provide proof that learning has actually taken place, say newspapers and current education journals. Discuss this pervasive feeling in terms of its implications for literacy assessment.

3. Imagine that at a parent–teacher meeting a parent confronts you about your assessment program, complaining that you spend too much time assessing and too little time teaching, considering the brief school day. Role play the confrontation, defending your position.

SUGGESTIONS

for Projects and Other Activities

1. Select one of the informal assessment instruments discussed in this chapter and prepare to use it with first or second grade children to measure a literacy-related area or skill. Summarize the results and share them with your class.

2. Observe a classroom teacher or reading specialist as he administers an IRI or running records to a young child. Discuss the interpretation of results with the teacher. Why was the assessment given? What was learned? How will the teacher adapt instruction as a result of the information gained?

3. Examine a standardized reading achievement test that is routinely administered to beginning readers in your area. Review the teacher's manual and technical manual for information about administering and scoring the test. Evaluate the instructions and test items for clarity, and compare the norming population with the children in your area. Interview school authorities to determine how the information is reported and used to make classroom, school, and district decisions about reading instruction. Finally, peruse Buros' *Mental Measurements Yearbook* in the reference section of the library for more information on this test and how it compares with others of its kind.

12 EARLY LITERACY

Orchestrating a Balanced Program

FOCUS QUESTIONS

- What are the most important considerations when planning a balanced early literacy program?

- What is the best classroom climate for a balanced literacy program?

- How can the schedule be arranged so that time for literacy instruction is maximized?

In the Classroom

It is the first week of September and Mrs. Ramon is just getting to know her new class. The 22 children are from four diverse language groups and have entered her first grade class with an overwhelming array of linguistic, cultural, and socioeconomic backgrounds and emotional needs. For example, Hoa comes from a Vietnamese-speaking home, having arrived in California with his family when he was thirteen months old. His father is deceased and his mother is currently unemployed and speaks very little English, though she has recently begun attending English classes. Hoa's personal linguistic and cultural data pool is Vietnamese—totally different from most of the class. Responsible for two younger siblings, Hoa has grown up quickly. While he interacts verbally to a small extent with his mother, his invalid grandmother, and his church community in Vietnamese, the time he spends engaging in language activities in his home language is limited.

On the other hand, Lisa comes from an English-speaking home and her parents are both professionals in the field of education. She attended a neighborhood preschool for two years before entering public school. Lisa has had a wealth of encounters with English, listening and interacting with her parents and older brother, singing nursery rhymes at preschool, learning to spell her name, listening to a variety of stories read to her every night, and having all her questions patiently answered and elaborated upon by the many indulgent adults around her.

* * * * *

It is three weeks later and we re-enter Mrs. Ramon's class. During math and science, where hands-on activities are taking place, Hoa sits in the middle of a small group of English-speaking children who chatter to him about the task at hand—observing air pressure in a balloon. Hoa still knows very little English, but there are three other Vietnamese-speaking children in the class and, during journal writing time, they sit together, conversing in Vietnamese as they draw pictures.

Stone Soup was the focus of the classroom last week. The teacher read the story several times with much miming and dramatization, once using a flannel board to demonstrate the key events in the story. Even Hoa shyly chimed in on the repetitive refrain, "Soup from a stone? Fancy *that!*" Hoa has picked up the words *stone, soup,* and the names of an assortment of common vegetables from the repetition afforded by this engaging tale, and these words are showing up in the pictures in his journal, as evidenced when he colors a large purple turnip. When Mrs. Ramon asks Hoa about his pictures, he names some items in English as well as Vietnamese. The entire class stops what they are doing to celebrate Hoa's initial spoken words in English. Mrs. Ramon smiles warmly at the little boy and writes some abbreviated anecdotal notes about his amazing progress on her clipboard.

Lisa, in another corner of the room, prefers to labor alone, following her unique writing agenda. She pens the words *cat, mat,* and *hat* very neatly in her journal. When asked if she can write a story using some new words on the word wall, she does not answer but begins a second column, chirping to no one in particular, "I'll do *et* words now," as she begins to write the words *wet, get, met,* and *set.* Then she begins to write a story about a man who met a cat, spelling these words correctly, and using the sounding-out strategies she knows to spell mostly the surface sounds of others. When the teacher comes around, Lisa is able to read all of the words of her story on request. Mrs. Ramon grins as she jots anecdotal notes on her clipboard about Lisa's current successes, but she also notes that Lisa seems overly concerned that everything she writes must be neat and spelled correctly, thus reducing the growth that occurs when children explore and feel free to take risks.

The two children above are developing literacy skills at very different yet desirable rates because Mrs. Ramon is supporting their individual growth patterns with self-selection of literacy activities, wise grouping, and careful attention to their unique needs. This teacher knows that Hoa is busy developing his oral language in English by listening to a group of fluent English-speakers discuss what they are doing with concrete objects. Also, she recognizes that drawing instead of writing allows Hoa to talk about what he knows in two languages. By seeing him participate in the refrain of a story, Mrs. Ramon understands the child is also learning that writing can tell a story—one that he can access because of the entertaining visuals. On the other hand, the teacher is trying to encourage young Lisa to move beyond what she can do perfectly and grow as a writer by taking some risks.

The remainder of this final chapter will explore how Mrs. Ramon provides a balanced literacy program for *all* of her students by creating a climate conducive to learning, by using literacy materials appropriate for her learners, and by maximizing the limited instructional time available.

A CLASSROOM CLIMATE CONDUCIVE TO LITERACY

Mrs. Ramon is the most requested teacher at the elementary school at which she teaches, partly because the children all seem to love her, but mostly because parents are certain their children will learn to read and write by the end of the year. Though education never comes with a guarantee, Mrs. Ramon stops just short of a promise to teach every child in her class to read and write by June. How does she do it?

The answer to that question lies, at least in part, in the way this teacher makes decisions about classroom instruction. Mrs. Ramon is a teacher who has spent the last few years developing a comprehensive literacy program that includes the systematic, explicit development of decoding skills, yet manages to retain the literacy exploration, engagement, and joy of a more child-centered, holistic approach to instruction. Any changes in her classroom are usually precipitated by a combination of three factors: (1) Her ongoing assessment of her learners tells her change is in order; (2) she reads about a strategy or observes an activity that she feels would be beneficial in her class; (3) she has read research in a respected literacy journal such as *The Reading Teacher* that provides convincing evidence that a literacy practice she is considering is effective and should be tried. As an example of her responsiveness to research, Mrs. Ramon explains to us that she studiously avoids the following practices that experts say make learning to read more difficult for children (Flippo, 1997):

1. emphasizing only phonics instruction
2. drilling children endlessly on isolated letters or sound
3. making sure that children perform correctly or not at all
4. focusing on the one "best" answer
5. making perfect oral reading the most important literacy goal
6. focusing on skills at the expense of comprehension
7. using workbooks with every reading lesson
8. always grouping according to ability
9. following the basal without making adjustments
10. expecting children to spell all the words they read perfectly

Another reason Mrs. Ramon is so successful undoubtedly has much to do with the positive classroom climate she has strived to achieve. Four environmental factors immediately stand out when one enters her classroom. Let's examine them.

Print Saturation

The factory-like school building in this urban neighborhood is in desperate need of repair, but the visitor entering Mrs. Ramon's first grade classroom is struck at once by how enticing it is—in sharp contrast to the grim environment outside. Both bulletin boards in the room are colorfully designed with the written work and art of the children, and lively mobiles extending from the ceiling attest, in bold print, to the attributes of each learner in the class. Glancing around the room, the visitor observes a wide variety of print, including labels on the art and crafts work, labels on each item in the room, charts, several word walls, written questions about objects the children have brought in, a diversity of commercially produced books, and even more books written and published by the children. Visitors are struck, also, by how children are conversing about the tasks at hand at frequent intervals throughout the day. It seems that all day long the children are immersed in reading, writing, listening, and speaking, offering all children an abundance of opportunity to fill their personal linguistic data pools (Cambourne and Turbill, 1991).

Demonstrations

Showing children the intricacies of literacy is a tenet of balanced instruction and is far more potent than merely telling them about it (Weaver, 1998). There are many opportunities in Mrs. Ramon's classroom for demonstrations of how language and print work. When the teacher writes a label in front of the children to accompany their latest craft work, she sounds out the word for them, asking them to volunteer sounds they know, and offering explanations about new sounds and sound combinations. When she writes a short story summary in front of the children, thinking aloud as she decides what to say and how to spell the words, she demonstrates how drafts are written, how to deal with unknown spellings, how to scour the environment for words, and how reading, writing, and spelling are interrelated. When she rereads her writing, she shows the children how to edit and proofread and why it is sometimes necessary to rewrite. When Mrs. Ramon conducts a mediated reading lesson, she demonstrates how written language is read, what punctuation marks are for, what to do when they don't know a word, in which direction to begin, what sounds the various symbols make, and so forth. Finally, by reading daily to children, Mrs. Ramon shows that she thinks reading is enjoyable and worth setting aside time for. By selecting informational books, as well as story books, she introduces children to different purposes for reading.

High Expectations

Teachers who allow children to make decisions about their own learning are usually more successful than those who make all the decisions autocratically (Miramontes et al., 1997). Mrs. Ramon expects all of her students to learn and to take responsibility for many decisions about their own learning. To enable her students to meet her high expectations, Mrs. Ramon gives the children plenty of opportunities to take risks and experiment without fear of failure. She encourages them to be confident and to use the decoding strategies they know to take calculated guesses at unknown words when reading. She often allows them to choose their own writing topics and books to read during free reading time. She expects them to formulate hypotheses about written language through trial and error and make many mistakes as they experiment with invented spelling. Though she expects children to be conscientious about checking the spelling of words they have been taught, Mrs. Ramon does *not* presume that children's writing should always be perfect—especially in their initial drafts.

Teacher Feedback

Successfully accomplished teacher–student interactions are likely the key to literacy learning of children from diverse backgrounds (Au, 1993). Mrs. Ramon interacts with all her children about their reading and writing in such a way that her feedback is both supportive and instructive to her learners; she also insists that children respond to each other's work in this positive and respectful way. Moreover, this teacher is always careful not to communicate that some tasks are achievable by certain children but not others. To that end, Mrs. Ramon uses a flexible grouping system so that children do not feel stigmatized by lingering in low ability groups. At various times throughout the day, she may have children arranged into skill groups, interest groups, reading buddies, peer editing groups, cooperative groups, and jigsaw groups (see Chapter 10).

Mrs. Ramon's interactions with her students may take the form of a whole class lesson, a minilesson, a small group activity, or a one-to-one conference. Whatever form the interaction takes, the response is immediate and always emanates from Mrs. Ramon's careful observation of her students.

ORGANIZING THE CLASSROOM ENVIRONMENT

The quality of the classroom environment has received considerable attention in recent years as teachers have become increasingly aware of the need to *invite* children to learn in an organized fashion (Morrow and Rand, 1991; Neuman and Roskos, 1993; Rhodes and Shanklin, 1993). The physical arrangement of the classroom is also crucial because children must have plenty of room and a range of appropriate materials to be able to experiment with literacy, independently and in small groups (Fisher, 1998). Thus, one of the most immediate concerns of beginning and experienced teachers before their learners ever arrive in September is how to arrange the classroom space so that it is conducive to effective and enjoyable learning. As teachers plan layouts and schedules for their classrooms, they often begin very simply and cautiously. Later, as the need arises, they tend to subdivide the classroom into functional work areas for accomplishing specific literacy tasks and make more detailed instructional plans.

Room Arrangement

Mrs. Ramon, the first-grade teacher we have been visiting, has several useful areas in her classroom. The largest is a whole-class learning and sharing area.

Mrs. Ramon has just brought in a slightly threadbare, but brightly colored carpet for children to sit on when they use this area; this new feature has created quite a stir during shared reading time. Other areas in this teacher's classroom are quiet writing and publishing areas, a silent reading area with an overstuffed couch and beanbag chairs, reading conference areas in both corners, appealing display areas for books and artwork, and ample storage areas. Mrs. Ramon sees to it that areas for storing books, magazines, and other reading materials are attractive and well lit. Each area in the classroom is clearly labeled with neatly printed signs. Mrs. Ramon has learned, through experience, that neatness is important, because these very labels become models for children's written products and provide them with an opportunity for environmental reading.

Mrs. Ramon spends several weeks at the end of each summer considering how best to rearrange her classroom. A major objective of the physical design in her classroom has always been to create the optimal physical surroundings for learning from the environment and from each other. Each year she makes physical adjustments in her classroom as she reflects on a grouping arrangement that didn't work well, or as she decides to borrow a learning center idea from another teacher. For Mrs. Ramon, the flow of traffic seemed to be a problem last year. Therefore, classroom furnishings in her room this year are expressly designed to facilitate easy movement between classroom areas, to provide access to necessary materials, a clear view of the writing boards, and to set aside specific areas for demonstrations and small group work (see Figure 12.1 for this room layout).

Literacy Materials

If teachers make wise choices in the selection of literacy materials, literacy instruction can be made easier (Salinger, 1993). Over the eleven years that she has been teaching, Mrs. Ramon has amassed a rich variety of materials, supplies, and books that have been carefully organized and stored so that they are readily accessible to her students. *Manipulative,* or *hands-on, materials* are a standard feature in her classroom, as in most primary classrooms, but in this classroom literacy materials are viewed with equal respect because this teacher is aware that manipulating the tools of literacy production—pencils, paper, books, etc.—is a valuable part of children's early sound-to-symbol learning. While most furniture, such as tables and desks, is standard in primary classrooms, teachers can sometimes requisition other items they feel would enhance their literacy programs. The materials shown in Figure 12.2 are what Mrs. Ramon considers the "bare essentials" for an emergent literacy classroom.

FIGURE 12.1   *Mrs. Ramon's classroom.*

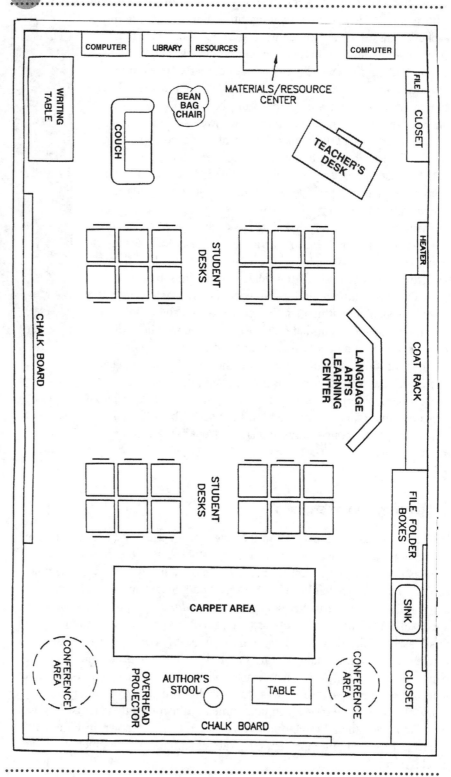

FIGURE 12.2   *Essentials for an emergent literacy classroom.*

FURNITURE

Teacher's desk and chair and a table
at which to work privately with the children

Desks or tables and chairs for each child

PRINTED MATERIAL

Trade books at different levels
Wordless books and picture story books
Multicultural and multiethnic trade books
Phonemic awareness materials
Connected texts at different levels
Predictable and patterned texts
Student-authored books

Song books
Magazines
Other printed material (e.g., catalogues,
   brochures, menus)
Spelling programs
Diagnostic tools

ENVIRONMENTAL PRINT/DISPLAY SPACE

Calendar
Teacher and student produced charts
Commercially produced charts
Signs and labels designating areas of the classroom
Notices to students and parents

Samples of children's work
Artwork with dictation or written comments
Letter charts with graphic reference material
Rules, class helper assignments, fire drill
   information, etc.

WRITING SUPPLIES

Many kinds of paper
Old envelopes and stationery
Many kinds of writing utensils
Alphabet stamps
Letter stencils
Staples, tape, and glue for bookmaking

Computer (optional)
Primary typewriter (optional)
Manipulative letters and letter stencils
Chalk and mini-chalkboards
Pocket charts and sentence strips

STORAGE SPACES

Storage space for supplies accessible to children
Storage space just for teacher
Book storage spaces
- bookcases
- revolving book racks for paperbacks
- crates

Cubbies for children's belongings
Storage space for children's work
- crates for file folders and
  learning center materials
- teacher file cabinet
- homework cubbies

OTHER SUPPLIES

Objects to observe and write about
Materials for experimentation, observation,
   and writing
Art supplies
Puppets
Flannel board

Globes, maps, atlases
Science and math equipment
Easels to hold chart paper, big books
Bulletin boards to display children's work
Tape recorders
Educational games and software

DEVISING AN INSTRUCTIONAL PLAN

Perhaps the most critical decision in setting up the classroom is wisely using the limited amount of time available (Allington, 1991). Each year Mrs. Ramon admits that she feels more and more pressured to cover the vast amount of material and topics she believes are vital for her learners. Thus, each year she, like most teachers, must make many adjustments in her instructional schedule and make weighty decisions about what information to discard and what to add to an already overcrowded curriculum.

When making these decisions, Mrs. Ramon keeps in mind the four components of an emergent literacy curriculum she believes to be critical to her students' success in learning about print; each provides support for her learners' continued growth in reading, writing, listening, and speaking. Mrs. Ramon will not negotiate about compromising any of the following four components:

1. Mediated literacy experiences and other supportive reading groups
2. Language experience approach stories and expository pieces
3. Extensive writing and composing experiences
4. A variety of opportunities for oral discussions, language play, drama, puppetry, and other oral and receptive language activities

With these essentials firmly in her mind, Mrs. Ramon has set up a schedule of daily instructional activities. Though unplanned events often interfere with this plan (fire drills, assemblies, absences, guest speakers, parties), an observer in the room would expect to see a day similar to the one on which we visit in mid-October (see the box below). Some of the strategies and tools discussed previously are boldfaced.

A day in Mrs. Ramon's classroom

Mrs. Ramon's class is self-contained and heterogeneously grouped. The instructional day begins at 8:30 and ends at 3:00. No specific time was assigned during our visit for pull-out or special programs such as art, music, physical education, or recess.

8:30–8:40 As we enter the room, we notice the children going about their daily business of communicating with one another and writing notes to each other and to the teacher, which they put in each other's mailboxes designed expressly for this purpose. They also eagerly **read aloud** to us the **morning message** that Mrs.

Ramon had written before they arrived. This message tells them about some enjoyable activity they can look forward to during the day or asks them a thought question. This morning's message asks, "Are you more like the sun or the rain?" which children immediately begin discussing among themselves. While these activities are going on, Mrs. Ramon usually takes a few moments to do a **running record** and **story retelling** with individual children using a daily rotation.

8:40–9:00 The whole class now congregates on the carpet to discuss the oversized calendar.

(continued)

Using this prop, they discuss the weather, mark in a symbol for rain, and chant the month, the day of the week, and the date. They pledge allegiance to the flag and sing a favorite song of the children's choosing. This day the choice is "Hooray for the World!" by Red Grammer. Every child seems to know the words but Mrs. Ramon has them written on the overhead projector and points to each as it is sung to reinforce the connection between written and spoken language. As the teacher takes attendance, she features the beginning sound of the day—/fr/—and applies it to every child's first name, **"the name game."** For example, *Nancy* becomes *Francy, Jennifer* becomes *Frennifer* and so forth. This lively language game is followed by a brief session of **interactive writing.**

9:00–9:05   Before their **shared reading lesson,** Mrs. Ramon does a brief review of the **phonics** components introduced yesterday, two different ways to represent /j/ (*j,* and *dge*). The teacher holds up the **word cards** for *jam, badge, jump, ledge, fudge,* and *jar.* She asks for volunteers to say each word. When a child says the word correctly, that child puts the word in the **pocket chart** and then helps Mrs. Ramon to sound out **(segment)** the word on the board. Finally, the teacher reads the nursery rhyme "Jack be nimble Jack be quick," asking them to chant it with her, raising a quiet hand every time they hear a word with a /j/.

Tomorrow Mrs. Ramon will have some children do a closed **word sort,** asking partners to sort a series of pictures representing words containing either *j* or *dge*. Other children will look in magazines for pictures containing these two sound representations. After much discussion of the words that have been found and how they fit in the children's chosen pattern, children will then be invited to put their discoveries on the **word wall** under the appropriate column.

9:05–9:50   For the **shared reading lesson,** children in Mrs. Ramon's room move into three different groups, though these groups are flexible and change frequently, depending upon the activity. Today the teacher is ready to do the first rereading of the **big book** *My Friends* by Taro Gomi, from the first-grade **basal reader** (Macmillan/McGraw-Hill). Four children who need extra reinforcement will be tracking the text as they listen to *My Friends* on tape; several other children need no further work with this story and are provided with a more challenging trade book that comes with the basal series, called *Grandfather Bear Is Hungry,* a Russian folk tale retold by Margaret Read MacDonald. These four children will **dyad read,** taking turns reading or summarizing a page of text. The remaining fourteen children participate in a **shared rereading** of the text in which Mrs. Ramon demonstrates left to right orientation as she reads and points out punctuation marks at the end of sentences. Since this group is preparing to learn the *ap* rime, Mrs. Ramon stops at the page that says, "I learned to nap from my friend the crocodile." She frames the word *nap* with a **word mask,** calling the children's attention to it. They orally stretch out the word and say it several times together. She asks a variety of **comprehension questions** during this rereading, asking how the girl feels about learning to walk from a cat, what they think the girl likes to do best, and so forth.

After finishing the rereading of this book, the children are asked to act out different action words in the book, such as jumping like a dog, marching like a rooster, and napping like a crocodile. This activity not only lends enjoyment and appreciation to the story but adds new words to the vocabulary of the English language learners in the class.

Tomorrow children will be given a small **decodable text** containing many of the same phonic elements such as the *ap* rime to read

(continued)

independently and then **partner read.** Such a successful experience with the already introduced phonic elements will help to reinforce these sounds in a real reading context, providing valuable practice with easily decoded text.

9:50–9:55 The above lesson ends with a five minute (usually less) **phonics lesson** on *ap.* The teacher models sounding out several words with the same rime: *nap, map, cap, rap,* and *tap,* stretching out the sounds so the children can easily identify them. After doing this several times, individual children are encouraged to try it.

Tomorrow Mrs. Ramon plans to pass out individual chalkboards and the children will write the letters as they stretch them out, holding them up as they finish, so she can immediately assess how individuals are doing.

10:00–10:35 **Writer's workshop** is a natural extension of the reading lessons. After children procure their **writing folders** from their cubbies, Mrs. Ramon takes five minutes at the beginning of this session to do a minilesson on the use of capital letters at the beginning of sentences, as this is an area she has observed to be a widespread concern with almost every child. She conducts this **minilesson** with the entire class, although such a lesson is often conducted for only the small group who has shown a particular need for it.

Mrs. Ramon then puts a writing prompt on the board: "A friend is _____." This sentence stem is not an assignment but only a writing option for those who are searching for a topic. After a very brief discussion about this topic, the children begin the writing process. Some children begin **drafting;** others are illustrating previously written pieces. Some children are sharing their ideas with a partner; others are offering feedback. **Peer editing conferences** and **teacher/student conferences** are occurring at tables set aside for this purpose. Mrs. Ramon,

when she is not conferencing with individual children about their work, walks around helping others to sound out words, observing, and taking **anecdotal notes** on their progress.

What amazes the observer in this classroom is how engaged the children are and how well they know the boundaries of the activities in which they may participate during writer's workshop. They know they are free to schedule their own time as long as they show progress toward their own goals.

10:35–11:35 Math instruction and practice activities. There is language happening even in this content-area subject, as Mrs. Ramon has a child do an addition problem on the blackboard and then queries the other youngsters, "What is another way to think about that?" Four children respond by telling the others their differing ways to think about and solve the math problem. Mrs. Ramon shares with us that later in the year children will keep **learning logs** that summarize, in words, the concept that has been introduced, such as "Tell what you do when you add two numbers."

11:35–12:15 Lunch.

12:15–12:35 After lunch Mrs. Ramon always looks forward to **reading aloud** to her students. For this activity, she selects quality **children's literature** from a variety of genres, cultures, and styles, balancing expository and narrative text. Today the teacher shares the beautifully illustrated Caldecott medal winner, *Officer Buckle and Gloria* (Rathmann, 1996). Mrs. Ramon feels this is one of the most important times in the day. She is engaging children in a positive experience with literature, introducing new vocabulary, and often thinking aloud through many of her comprehension strategies as she reads. The children clearly enjoy this time

(continued)

too, and they are encouraged to draw as they listen, later sharing how their sketches tell about what is happening in the story.

12:35–1:35   Social studies, science, health or other content-area and instructional activities. Much speaking, listening, reading, and writing are naturally integrated into these content areas. Today, following on the theme of friendship in the morning's story, Mrs. Ramon leads a multicultural social studies lesson, teaching the children, with the help of her linguistically diverse learners, to say "my friend" in the four different languages represented in the classroom. Children chant these words in the different tongues and then work on a poster showing themselves and a friend involved in an activity that portrays friendship. Tomorrow Mrs. Ramon will have the children create a **word web** on friendship, brainstorming ideas and, perhaps, using those ideas in their journals.

1:35–1:45   Drop everything and read (DEAR) time is a critical time in each day. Children quickly and quietly get trade books, magazines, or other reading material from their desks or from the classroom library and begin reading silently. As this is a school-wide program, everyone in the school—from the principal to the janitor—stop what they are doing to read. Afterwards, the teacher often invites the children to talk about what they are reading.

1:45–2:15   Spelling and other literacy-related activities. These activities include **drama, word sorts,** word building activities, small- and large-group sharing of writing, learning center activities, or a combination of these experiences. This day, pairs of children give each other a **post-test** on their spelling words for the first fifteen minutes, and correct their own errors by consulting their primary dictionaries. Then many of the children are involved in a

reader's theatre production of *The Boy Who Cried Wolf,* a story the children had very much enjoyed and wish to act out. The children, having heard the story several times for the purpose of acting it out, have now created roles for everyone. Besides the boy, the wolf, the townspeople, the sheep, and the wiseman, they have added parents, siblings, and a talking bird who tells the shepherd what to do. Every child has a speaking part that the teacher helps them to write down so they have a rough "script" to memorize.

Other children choose to go to the table that has been turned into a **learning center,** with the theme "What is a friend?" This physically appealing, specialized setting provides a series of tasks integrating a content area, such as social studies, with the language arts of reading, writing, listening, and speaking. Through self-selected, individualized activities, the children seek answers to questions independently, such as "What does a friend do?" Each of the activities has been introduced by the teacher, yet the step by step instructions are also written on cards next to the individual activities. For example, one gives children the directions for making finger puppet friends. It asks them to create a dialogue with a partner to resolve a problem between two friends. Children later share their product with the larger group.

2:15–2:40   Children write in their **dialogue journals** while Mrs. Ramon goes around the room transcribing text for the few children who are still primarily drawing pictures. She encourages others to sound out the words they are attempting to spell. Mrs. Ramon always carries her clipboard to take **anecdotal notes** on their progress—in this case—of their understanding of the **alphabetic principle.** The children who finish early love to review previous entries and to revisit their teacher's responses. Mrs. Ramon

(continued)

gives written feedback in each child's journal at least once a week.

2:40–2:50 Mrs. Ramon again **reads aloud** to her students, often finishing a story from the earlier session. Since she completed the early afternoon story, she chooses to read a short expository piece from *Cricket* magazine containing new information about why dinosaurs disappeared from the Earth. She tries to offer a variety of read-aloud materials, both expository and narrative, including genres from science fiction to folk tales, to whet the appetite of these burgeoning readers and expose them to many types of material. To conclude, the teacher asks children to turn to a neighbor and tell one new thing they learned about dinosaurs from listening to the piece.

2:50–3:00 Mrs. Ramon calls these final few moments in the school day "the day in review." She asks volunteers to share with the class what they consider to be the highlights of the day. She gains much insight into their young minds and sees, from their perspectives, what worked and what didn't. The children get a final oral language opportunity as Mrs. Ramon observes their comments. Children then do clean up as necessary and receive their weekly **parent packets,** which contain material corresponding to what they have studied this day. The parents are asked to review the material with their children, sign, and send it back with them the following day. This communication with parents enhances the literacy growth of the students, lets parents know what is happening in the classroom, and allows parents to assist in a positive way. The parent packet taken home by most of Mrs. Ramon's children this day is described in Figure 12.3. Other children may have more or less advanced assignments according to their needs.

After the children have left, we notice that Mrs. Ramon immediately puts anecdotal notes

FIGURE 12.3 *An example of a first grade homework packet.*

Help your child to practice the vocabulary words included from *The Cat Has a Nap.* This can be done in any of the following ways that are the most enjoyable for you and your child:

- Ask the child the words and give them to him/her when they are said correctly.
- Have your child make sentences with the word cards.
- Have your child write a new story with the words.
- Ask your child to spell the word as you say it.
- Put the words on the table. Say a word and ask the child to identify it.

Then, please listen as your child reads from the book *The Cat Has a Nap.* Be sure your child's finger is under each word as it is read. Ask the child to read the story twice. Make sure the reading is a "treat," not a "treatment."

As always, please read daily to your child, preferably a book that your child has chosen. Please initial as completed.

Monday _____
Tuesday _____
Wednesday _____
Thursday _____

in her children's work **portfolios,** reflecting on how she might offer interventions for some who need them and considering how she might best provide more challenge to others. Then she approaches to debrief us on her day of teaching which, she intimates, has been physically and emotionally exhausting, as always. However, this remarkable teacher confesses, "I cannot imagine a profession that is more personally rewarding and more fun than turning children on to the joys of literacy."

SUMMARY

Throughout this book we have explored ways to teach reading, writing, listening, and speaking to early readers and writers. The approach in this text has been a balanced one, in which children receive the explicit, systematic instruction in phonics necessary to help them become automatic decoders. This phonics instruction, however, was presented as a means to an end, so children could quickly concentrate on more critical tasks—what reading can mean and how it can make them feel. To that end, many strategies were included for making text meaningful and using text as a springboard to substantive writing activities. Yet reading about specific strategies, seeing only individual pieces of the big picture, is not completely satisfactory. Particularly if one has never taught, it is important to see how a real teacher manages to orchestrate all of these elements into a total program for a heterogeneous garden of children with various strengths and needs. With this in mind, I decided to observe one of the finest teachers I have ever known and invited you, the reader, to see for yourself what such a program might look like.

Though Mrs. Ramon has a challenging first grade class with a wide range of learners, she will most likely succeed—as she does year after year—at teaching every child in her class not only to read and write, but the enjoyment of these activities. How does she manage to achieve such lofty goals? Besides creating a balanced program of skills-based and holistic methods of teaching literacy, Mrs. Ramon has set up her class in a caring way that is respectful of all the individuals who are in her charge. Her instructional plans emanate from a program of ongoing observation and assessment and are adjusted according to her children's changing needs. She has gathered a host of inviting literacy materials and arranged them in a classroom designed to facilitate the various activities that she plans each day. She has saturated the room with print, so that children are constantly encountering the idea that *print* and *talk* are integrally connected. Additionally, Mrs. Ramon sincerely expects each of her learners to read and write—and they rise to the occasion; her confidence bolsters them when they face a challenging instructional situation. Above all, this teacher's interaction with her learners is continually constructive and positive; she is the consummate cheerleader and encourages the children to offer similar support to one another.

Perhaps the most crucial personal ingredient that makes Mrs. Ramon—and so many teachers like her—successful is her love of and enthusiasm for all aspects of literacy, and learning in general. Outside the classroom, Mrs. Ramon is constantly keeping up with new developments in literacy through journals, conferences, and attending and participating in in-service presentations. In her classroom, this teacher often shares her personal writing with children, delightedly looks up words she does not know in front of her students, and has been known to shed a tear or two, unabashedly, while sharing *The Velveteen Rabbit* with her first-graders.

Balance in literacy is possible when a competent and caring teacher creates a comprehensive program of direct instruction, writing, and literature-rich experiences. Mrs. Ramon's classroom is a working example of the achievement of these goals.

QUESTIONS

for Journal Writing and Discussion

1. Reflect on a teacher you know who seems to be highly effective in teaching young children to read and write. In light of this chapter, what would you say makes this teacher impressive? What do you believe made Mrs. Ramon such an effective teacher of early literacy? What are their similarities? Differences?

2. Brainstorm a list of ways you will ensure that the children in your class not only *can* read but do read. Share and discuss this list with others in your class.

3. Discuss the provisions that must be made in a classroom so that linguistically and culturally diverse learners will succeed. How do you believe such provisions effect native English-speaking children in the class?

SUGGESTIONS

for Projects and Other Activities

1. Arrange to observe an early childhood classroom. Make notes about the environment, the classroom climate, and the literacy activities in which the children engage. Your observation summary should be as objective as possible. Compare your experience with those of others in your class, and include in your discussion your personal responses to the classroom you observed.

2. Interview an early childhood educator. Ask this teacher how decisions are made in her classroom about changing instruction. Which is the most potent factor for changing a classroom practice for this teacher: (1) what research says, (2) what other teachers say, or (3) what the teacher observes?

3. Make a sketch of an ideal classroom, arranging furniture, materials, and storage space in a way most suited to what you believe to be a balanced literacy environment. Compare your sketch with the diagram of a literacy classroom in this chapter. How is yours different? Why? Share your sketch with others in your class, discussing the benefits and drawbacks of each design.

CHILDREN'S LITERATURE REFERENCES

BOOKS FOR DEVELOPING PHONEMIC AWARENESS

The following books are suitable for use in reinforcing particular letter sounds, patterns, and letter combinations.

Adams, P., and Strop, J. (1986). *Spunky the monkey.* Cleveland, OH: Modern Curriculum Press.

Ahlberg, J., and Ahlberg, A. (1978). *Each peach pear plum.* New York: Scholastic.

Alborough, J. (1992). *Where's my teddy?* Cambridge, MA: Candlewick Press.

Alda, A. (1992). *Sheep, sheep, help me fall asleep.* New York: Bantam Doubleday.

Alda, A. (1994). *Pig, horse, cow, don't wake me now.* New York: Bantam Doubleday.

Bayer, J. (1984). *A my name is Alice.* New York: Dial Press.

Brown, M. W. (1983). *Four fur feet.* New York: Doubleday.

Brown, M. (1994). *Pickle things.* New York: Parents Magazine Press.

Carter, D. (1990). *More bugs in boxes.* New York: Simon and Schuster.

Cameron, P. (1961). *"I can't," said the ant.* New York: Coward McCann.

Carlstrom, N. W. (1986). *Jesse bear, what will you wear?* New York: Macmillan.

Degan, B. (1983). *Jamberry.* New York: Harper & Row.

deRegniers, B., Moore, E., and Carr, J. (1988). *Sing a song of popcorn.* New York: Scholastic.

Fox, M. (1993). *Time for bed.* San Diego, CA: Harcourt Brace Jovanovich.

Galdone, P. (1968). *Henny penny.* New York: Scholastic.

Galdone, P. (1973). *The three billy goats gruff.* New York: Seabury.

Geraghty, J. (1992). *Stop that noise!* New York: Crown.

Gordon, J. (1991). *Six sleepy sheep.* New York: Puffin Books.

Grossman, B. (1995). *My little sister ate one hare.* New York: Crown.

Guarino, D. (1989). *Is your mama a llama?* New York: Scholastic.

Hague, M. (1993). *Teddy bear, teddy bear: A classic action rhyme.* New York: Morrow Junior Books.

Hawkins, C., and Hawkins, J. (1986). *Tog the dog.* New York: G.P. Putnam's Sons. (See also other books in this series).

Hutchins, P. (1976). *Don't forget the bacon.* New York: Morrow.

Hymes, L., and Hymes, J. (1964). *Oodles of noodles.* New York: Young Scott Books.

Johnston, T. (1991). *Little bear sleeping.* New York: G.P. Putnam's Sons.

Jorgensen, G. (1988). *Crocodile beat.* New York: Scholastic.

Kushkin, K. (1990). *Roar and more.* New York: Harper Trophy.

Komaiko, L. (1987). *Annie bananie.* New York: Harper & Row.

Krauss, R. (1985). *I can fly.* New York: Golden Press.

Leedy, L. (1988). *Pingo the plaid panda.* New York: Holiday House.

Lewison, W. (1992) *Buzz said the bee.* New York: Scholastic.

Lindbergh, R. (1990). *The day the goose got loose.* New York: Dial press.

Marzollo, J. (1989). *The teddy bear book.* New York: Dial.

Marzollo, J. (1994). *Ten cats have hats.* New York: Scholastic.

Most, B. (1991). *A dinosaur named after me.* San Diego: Harcourt Brace Jovanovich.

Obligato, L. (1983). *Faint frogs feeling feverish and other terrifically tantalizing tongue twisters.* New York: Puffin.

Ochs, C. P. (1991). *Moose on the loose.* Minneapolis: Carolrhoda Books.

Oppenheim, J. (1989). *Not now! said the cow.* New York: Bantam Books.

Otto, C. (1991). *Dinosaur chase.* New York: Harper-Trophy.

Parry, C. (1991). *Zoomerang-a-boomerang: Poems to make your belly laugh.* New York: Puffin.

Patz, N. (1983). *Moses supposes his toeses are roses.* San Diego: Harcourt Brace Jovanovich.

Philpot, L., and Philpot, G. (1993). *Amazing Anthony ant.* New York: Random House.

Pomerantz, C. (1993). *If I had a paka.* New York: Mulberry.

Prelutsky, J. (1982). *The baby uggs are hatching.* New York: Mulberry.

Prelutsky, J. (1989). *Poems of A. Nonny Mouse.* New York: Knopf.

Provenson, A. (1977). *Old Mother Hubbard.* New York: Crown.

Raffi. (1987). *Down by the bay.* New York: Crown.

Serfozo, M. (1988). *Who said red?* New York: M. K. McElderry Books.

Seuss, Dr. (1957). *The cat in the hat.* New York: Random house.

Seuss, Dr. (1965). *Fox in Sox.* New York: Random House.

Seuss, Dr. (1963). *Hop on pop.* New York: Random House.

Seuss, Dr. (1974). *There's a wocket in my pocket.* New York: Random House.

Shaw, N. (1991). *Sheep in a shop.* Boston: Houghton Mifflin. (See also other books in this series).

Sowers, P. (1991). *The listening walk.* New York: Harper & Row.

Slobodkin, E. (1976). *Caps for sale.* New York: Scholastic.

Speed, T. (1995). *Two cool cows.* New York: Scholastic.

Van Allsburg, C. (1987). *The Z was zapped.* Boston: Houghton Mifflin.

VanLaan, N. (1990). *A mouse in my house.* New York: Knopf.

Wadsworth, O. A. (1985). *Over in the meadow.* New York: Penguin.

Wells, R. (1973). *Noisy Nora.* New York: Dial Press.

Winthrop, E. (1986). *Shoes.* New York: HarperTrophy.

Wood, A. (1992). *Silly Sally.* San Diego: Harcourt Brace Jovanovich.

Ziefert, H., and Brown, H. (1996). *What rhymes with eel?* New York: Penguin.

PREDICTABLE BOOKS

The following books are suitable for increasing the listening comprehension of young learners, as they contain rhymes, rhythm, and/or repetition. Children are therefore able to anticipate certain key words and phrases.

Brown, M. (1957). *Good night moon.* New York: Harper & Row.

Carle, E. (1969). *The very hungry caterpillar.* Cleveland: Collins–World.

Carlestrom, N. W. (1986). *Jesse Bear, what will you wear?* New York: Macmillan.

Eastman, P. D. (1960). *Are you my mother?* New York: Random House.

Fox, M. (1986). *Hattie and the fox.* New York: Bantam Doubleday Dell.

Galdone, P. (1975). *Henny Penny.* New York: Houghton Mifflin.

Joslyn, S. (1958). *What do you say, dear?* New York: Scholastic.

Keats, E. J. (1972). *Over in the meadow.* New York: Four Winds.

Kent, J. (1971). *The fat cat.* New York: Scholastic.

Martin, B., Jr. (1967). *Brown bear, brown bear, what do you see?* New York: Holt, Rinehart, and Winston. (See other books in this series.)

Mesler, J., and Cowley, J. (1980). *In a dark, dark wood.* New Zealand: Wright Group.

Slepian, J., and Seidler, A. (1967). *The hungry thing.* New York: Scholastic.

Seuling, B. (1976). *Teeny tiny woman.* New York: Greenwillow.

Tafuri, N. (1984). *Have you seen my duckling?* New York: Greenwillow.

WORDLESS BOOKS

These books have no words, as the name suggests, and are useful for encouraging language development as children tell the story that goes with the pictures, reinforcing an understanding of story structure. The books are also ideal for English language learners who can share the story in their own language.

Alexander, M. (1970). *Bobo's dream.* New York: Dial.

Aruego, J. (1971). *Look what I can do.* New York: Scribner's.

Carle, E. (1971). *Do you want to be my friend?* New York: Crowell.

Day, A. (1985). *Good dog, Carl.* La Jolla, CA: Green Tiger.

de Paola, T. (1978). *Pancakes for breakfast.* San Diego, CA: Harcourt Brace Jovanovich.

Hutchins, P. (1971). *Changes, changes.* New York: Macmillan.

Keats, E. J. (1974). *Kitten for a day.* New York: Watts.

Kent, J. (1974). *The egg book.* New York: Macmillan.

Martin, R. (1989). *Will's mammoth.* New York: Putnam.

Mayer, M. (1967). *A boy, a dog, and a frog.* New York: Dial.

Mayer, M. (1977). *Oops!* New York: Dial.

McCully, E. (1984). *Picnic.* New York: Harper & Row.

Ormerod, J. (1981). *Sunshine.* New York: Lothrop.

Simmons, E. (1970). *Family.* New York: McKay.

Turkle, B. (1991). *Deep in the forest.* New York: Dutton.

Wiesner, D. (1991). *Tuesday.* New York: Clarion.

ALPHABET BOOKS

The following books are useful in introducing the letters and corresponding sounds of the alphabet in an enjoyable and whimsical way.

Brent, I. (1993). *An alphabet of animals.* New York: Little, Brown.

Ehlert, I. (1989). *Eating the alphabet: Fruits and vegetables from A to Z.* New York: Harcourt Brace Jovanovich.

Emberly, E. (1978). *Ed Emberly's ABC.* New York: Little, Brown.

Hague, K. (1983). *Alphabears.* New York: Holt, Rinehart, and Winston.

Hoban, T. (1982). *A, B, See.* New York: Greenwillow.

Hoban, T. (1987). *26 letters and 99 cents.* New York: Greenwillow.

Isadora, R. (1983). *City seen from A to Z.* New York: Greenwillow.

Kellogg, S. (1987). *Aster aardvark's alphabet adventure.* New York: William Morrow.

Kitchen, B. (1984). *Animal alphabet.* New York: Dial.

Lobel, A. (1981). *On market street.* New York: Greenwillow.

MacDonald, S. (1986). *Alphabatics.* New York: Bradbury.

Martin, B., Jr., and Archaumbault, J. (1989). *Chicka, chicka, boom, boom.* New York: Simon & Schuster.

Patience, J. (1993). *An amazing alphabet.* New York: Random House.

Sendak, M. (1990). *Alligators all around: An alphabet.* New York: HarperTrophy.

Seuss, Dr. (1991). *Dr. Seuss's ABCs* (2nd ed.). New York: Random House.

Tallon, R. (1979). *Zoophabets.* New York: Scholastic.

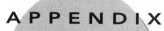
B TEACHER REFERENCES FOR EARLY LITERACY

RECOMMENDED BOOKS FOR TEACHERS

Adams, M. J. *Beginning to Read: Thinking and Learning about Print.* Cambridge, MA: MIT Press, 1990.

Allen, J., Shockley, B., and Michalove, B. *Engaging Children: Community and Chaos in the Lives of Young Literacy Learners.* Portsmouth, NH: Heinemann, 1993.

Areglado, N., and Dill, M. *Let's Write: A Practical Guide to Teaching Writing in the Early Grades.* New York: Scholastic, 1998.

Au, K. H., Carroll, J. H., and Scheu, J. A. *Balanced Literacy Instruction: A Teacher's Resource Book.* Norwood, MA: Christopher–Gordon, 1997.

Baltas, J., and Schafer, S. *Scholastic Guide to Balanced Reading.* New York: Scholastic, 1998.

Bartoli, J. *Unequal Opportunity: Learning to Read in the U.S.A.* New York: Teachers College Press, 1995.

Bean, W., and Bouffler, C. *Read, Write, Spell.* York, ME: Stenhouse, 1997.

Brooks, E. *Just-Right Books for Beginning Readers: Leveled Booklists and Strategies.* New York: Scholastic, 1998.

Cheek, E., Flippo, R., and Lindsey, J. *Reading for Success in Elementary Schools.* Madison, WI: Brown and Benchmark, 1997.

Collins, J. L. *Strategies for Struggling Writers.* New York: Guilford Publications, 1998.

Cramer, R. L. *The Spelling Connection: Integrating Reading, Writing, and Spelling Instruction.* New York: Guilford Publications, 1998.

Dill, M., and Areglado, N. *Let's Write: A Practical Guide to Teaching Writing in the Early Grades.* New York: Scholastic, 1998.

Dyson, A. H. *Social Worlds of Children: Learning to Read in an Urban Primary School.* New York: Teachers College Press, 1993.

Fisher, B. *Joyful Learning.* Portsmouth, NH: Heinemann, 1991.

Fraser, J., and Skolnick, D. *On Their Way: Celebrating Second-Graders as They Read and Write.* Portsmouth, NH: Heinemann, 1994.

Gentry, J. R., and Gillett, J. W. *Teaching Kids to Spell.* Portsmouth, NH: Heinemann, 1993.

Glazer, S. M. *Assessment Is Instruction: Reading, Writing, Spelling, and Phonics for ALL Learners.* Norwood, MA: Christopher–Gordon, 1998.

Good, T., and Brophy, J. *Looking in Classrooms* (6th ed.). New York: HarperCollins, 1994.

Goodman, Y. *How Children Construct Literacy.* Newark, DE: International Reading Association, 1990.

Goodman, Y. M., Watson, D. J., and Burke, C. L. *Reading Strategies: Focus on Comprehension.* Katonah, NY: Richard C. Owen, 1996.

Graves, D. *Building a Literate Classroom.* Portsmouth, NH: Heinemann, 1991.

Graves, D., Taylor, B., and van den Broek (eds.). *The First R: Every Child's Right to Read.* New York: Teachers College Press, 1996.

Graves, M. F., Juel, C., and Graves, B. B. *Teaching Reading in the 21st Century.* Needham Heights, MA: Allyn & Bacon, 1998.

Gregory, E. (ed.). *One Child, Many Worlds: Early Learning in Multicultural Communities.* New York: Teachers College Press, 1997.

Gunning, T. C. *Best Books for Beginning Readers.* Needham Heights, MA: Allyn & Bacon, 1998.

Harste, J., Woodward, V. A., and Burke, C. L. *Language Stories and Literature Lessons.* Portsmouth, NH: Heinemann, 1984.

Heath, S., and Mangiola, L. *Children of Promise: Literate Activity in Linguistically and Culturally Diverse Classrooms.* Washington, D.C.: National Association for the Education of Young Children, 1991.

Hiebert, E. H., and Raphael, T. E. *Early Literacy Instruction.* Fort Worth, TX: Harcourt Brace, 1998.

Hiebert, E. H., and Taylor, B. M. *Getting Reading Right from the Start: Effective Early Intervention.* Boston: Allyn & Bacon, 1994.

Hughes, M., and Searle, D. *The Violent E and other Tricky Sounds: Learning to Spell from Kindergarten through Grade 6.* York, ME: Stenhouse, 1997.

International Reading Association. *Literacy Development and Pre-First Grade.* Newark, DE: IRA, 1985.

McGee, L., and Richgels, D. *Literacy's Beginnings: Supporting Young Readers and Writers* (2nd ed.). Boston: Allyn & Bacon, 1996.

McIntyre, E., and Pressley, M. (eds.) *Balanced Instruction: Strategies and Skills in Whole Language.* Norwood, MA: Christopher–Gordon, 1996.

Moats, L. C. *Spelling: Development, Disability and Instruction.* Baltimore: York, 1995.

Mooney, M. E. *Reading To, With, and By Children.* Katonah, NY: Richard C. Owens, 1990.

Morrow, L. M. *The Literacy Center: Contexts for Reading and Writing.* York, ME: Stenhouse, 1997.

Morrow, L. M. *Literacy Development in the Early Years: Helping Children Read and Write* (2nd ed.). Boston: Allyn & Bacon, 1992.

Neuman, S. B., and Roskos, K. A. *Language and Literacy Learning in the Early Years: An Integrated Approach.* Fort Worth, TX: Harcourt Brace Jovanovich, 1993.

Osborn, J., and F. Lehr. (eds.) *Literacy for All: Issues in Teaching and Learning.* New York: Guilford Publications, 1998.

Ostrow, J. *A Room with a Different View: First through Third Graders Build Community and Create Curriculum.* York, ME: Stenhouse, 1995.

Paley, V. *Wally's Stories: Conversations in Kindergarten.* Cambridge, MA: Harvard University Press, 1981.

Preece, A., and Cowden, D. *Young Writers in the Making: Sharing the Process with Parents.* Portsmouth, NH: Heinemann, 1993.

Pressley, M. *Reading Instruction that Works: The Case for Balanced Teaching.* New York: Guilford Publications, 1998.

Schmidt, P. A. *Beginning in Retrospect: Writing and Reading a Teacher's Life.* New York: Teacher's College Press, 1997.

Smith, J. W. A., and Elley, W. B. *How Children Learn to Read.* Katonah, NY: Richard C. Owen, 1997.

Taylor, D. *From the Child's Point of View.* Portsmouth, NH: Heinemann, 1993.

Temple, C., Nathan, R., Temple, F., and Burris, N. *The Beginnings of Writing* (3rd ed.). Boston: Allyn & Bacon, 1993.

Templeton, S. *Children's Literacy: Contexts for Meaningful Learning.* Boston: Houghton Mifflin, 1995.

Tierney, R., Readence, J., and Dishner, E. *Reading Strategies and Practices: A Compendium* (4th ed.). Boston: Allyn & Bacon, 1995.

Vacca, J., Vacca, R., and Gove, M. *Reading and Learning to Read* (2nd ed.). New York: HarperCollins, 1991.

Wagstaff, J. *Phonics that Work! New Strategies for the Reading/Writing Classroom.* New York: Scholastic, 1998.

Wilde, S. (1992). *You Kan Red This!* Portsmouth, NH: Heinemann.

OTHER TEACHER RESOURCES

Auditory Discrimination in Depth. Lindamood, C., and Lindamood, P. Austin, TX: PRO–ED, 1969.

Basic Animated-Literacy English Handbook and Tapes. San Diego, CA: Los Amigos Research Associates. 619-286-3162.

Book Buddies: A Pioneering Program for Early Reading Intervention. Johnston, F. R., Invernizzi, M., and Juel, C. New York: Guilford Publications, 1998, 1-800-365-7006.

Celebrate Reading: Teacher's Guide, Grade 1, A-F. Glenview, IL: Scott Foresman, 1995.

DaisyQuest & Daisy's Castle. Erickson, E., Foster, K., Foster, D., and Torgeson, J. Austin, TX: PRO–ED. 512-451-3246.

Discovery Phonics: An Integrated Approach to Decoding Strategies. Columbus, OH: Modern Curriculum Press, 1990. 1-800-321-3106.

Early Success: An Intervention Program, Grades 1 & 2. Boston: Houghton Mifflin, 1995. 1-800-733-1047.

Glass Analysis for Decoding Only. Garden City, NY: Easier to Learn, Inc., 1970. 516-475-7693.

Leisy's Pan American ABCs: Latino Phonics. Culver City, CA. 310-836-6730.

Literature–Based Mini-Lessons to Teach Writing. Lunsford, S. New York: Scholastic, 1998. 1-800-724-6527.

More than Words: Activities for Phonological Awareness and Comprehension. Donnelly, K., et al. Tucson, AZ: Communication Skill Builders, 1992.

Mortimer Turns the Alphabet Loose: Early Childhood Alphabet Awareness Kit. Columbus, OH: Modern Curriculum Press. 1-800-321-3106.

Phonemic Awareness and Phonics Kit. Peru, IL: Open Court. 1-800-435-6850.

Phonological Awareness and Early Reading Program. Blachman, B. (under development).

The Phonological Awareness Kit. Robertson, C., and Salter, W. East Moline, IL: LinguiSystems. 1-800-776-4332.

Phonological Awareness Training for Reading. Torgeson, J., and Bryant, B. Austin, TX: PRO–ED. 1-512-451-3246.

Poetry Works! The First Verse Complete Set. Columbus, OH: Modern Curriculum Press. 1-800-321-3106.

Read-Along, Sing-Along Book of Animated Alphabet Songs. San Diego, CA: Los Amigos Research Associates. 619-286-3162.

Reader Rabbit's Interactive Reading Journey: Grades K–2. The Learning Company. 1-800-852-2255.

Ready Readers. Columbus, OH: Modern Curriculum Press. 1-800-321-3106.

Sorting Boxes with a Reading Curriculum Focus. Columbus, OH: Modern Curriculum Press. 1-800-321-3106.

Sound Foundations. Byrne, B., and Fielding–Barnesley, R. Melbourne, Australia: Peter Leyden Publishing. (02) 439-8755.

Sounds Abound. Catts, H., and Vartianen, T. East Moline, IL: LinguiSystems. 1-800-776-4332.

The Spanish-Animated Alphabet Handbook and Cassette. San Diego, CA: Los Amigos Research Associates. 619-286-3162.

The Spanish Read-Along, Sing-Along Book of Animated Alphabet Songs. San Diego, CA: Los Amigos Research Associates. 619-286-3162.

Touch Phonics: The Manipulative Multi-Sensory Phonics System. Newport Beach, CA: Touchphonics Reading Systems. 1-800-928-6824.

Waterford Early Reading Program. Provo, Utah: Waterford Institute. 1-800-669-4533.

Words Their Way: Word Study for Phonics, Vocabulary, and Spelling. Bear, D. R., Invernizzi, M., Templeton, S., and Johnston, F. Prentice–Hall. 1-800-223-1360.

Zoo Phonics. Groveland, CA: Zoo–Phonics. 1-800-622-8104.

RESOURCES FOR PARENTS

Family Literacy: Connections in Schools and Communities. Morrow, L. M. (ed.) Newark: DE: International Reading Association, 1995.

Fostering the Love of Reading: The Affective Domain in Reading Education. Castle, M., and Cramer, E. (eds.) Newark, DE: The International Reading Association, 1994.

Games for Learning: Ten Minutes a Day to Help your Child Do Well in School. Kaye, P. New York: Noonday Press, 1992.

Games for Reading: Playful Ways to Help Your Child Read. Kaye, P. New York: Pantheon, 1984.

Home: Where Reading and Writing Begin. Hill, M. Portsmouth, NH: Heinemann, 1989.

Jamie: A Literacy Story. Parker, D. York, ME: Stenhouse, 1997.

Laying the Foundations: A Parent-Child Literacy Training Kit. Push Literacy Action Now, 1332 G Street S.E., Washington, D.C. 20003.

Raising Readers: Helping your Child to Literacy. Bialostock, S. Winnipeg, Manitoba, Canada: Peguis, 1992.

The New Read-Aloud Handbook. Trelease, J. New York: Penguin, 1995.

Reading Begins at Home. Butler, D., and Clay, M. M. Portsmouth, NH: Heinemann, 1987.

Reading, Writing, and Rummy: More than 100 Card Games to Develop Language, Social Skills, Number Concepts, and Problem-Solving Strategies. Golick, M. Markham, Ontario, Canada: Pembroke Publishers, 1986.

Wacky Word Games. Golick, M. Markham, Ontario, Canada: Pembroke Publishers, 1995.

Writing Begins at Home. Butler, D., and Clay, M. M. Portsmouth, NH: Heinemann, 1988.

APPENDIX C

COMMERCIAL ASSESSMENT INSTRUMENTS

CRITERION-REFERENCED READING TESTS

Basic Inventory of Natural Language. San Bernadino, CA: CHECpoint Systems, 1979. (Grades K–12)

The Lollipop Test: A Diagnostic Screening Test of School Readiness. Atlanta, GA: Humanistics Limited, 1981. (First half of K to grade 1 entrants)

PRI Reading Systems. Monterey, CA: CTB/McGraw–Hill, 1980. (Grades K–9)

Reading Yardsticks. Chicago: Riverside Publishing Company, 1981. (Grades K–8)

Woodcock Reading Mastery Tests. Woodcock, R. W. Circle Pines, MN: American Guidance Services, 1986. (Grades K–12)

FORMAL READING TESTS

Biemiller Test of Reading Processes. Biemiller, A. Toronto, Ontario, Canada: Guidance Centre. (Grades 2–6)

California Achievement Test, Forms C and D. Monterey, CA: CTB/McGraw–Hill, 1978. (Grades K–12.9)

Gates–MacGinitie Reading Tests. MacGinitie, W. H. Chicago: Riverside Publishing, 1978. (Ages 6 1/2–17)

Iowa Test of Basic Skills: Primary Battery. Chicago: Riverside Publishing, 1985. (Grades K–3.2)

Metropolitan Achievement Test (7th ed.). San Antonio, TX: The Psychological Corporation, 1993. (Grades K–12.9)

Stanford Achievement Test (8th ed.). San Antonio, TX: The Psychological Corporation, 1992. (Grades 1.5–9.9)

Test of Reading Comprehension (TORC). Brown, V., Hammill, J., and Wiederholt, J. L. Austin, TX: PRO–ED, 1986.

FORMAL TESTS FOR EMERGENT READERS

Clymer Barrett Reading Test. Santa Barbara, CA: Chapman, Brook, & Kent, 1982. (Grades K and beginning 1)

Concepts about Print: Sand. Clay, M. M. Portsmouth, NH: Heinemann, 1972. (Pre–K to end of K)

Concepts about Print: Stone. Clay, M. M. Portsmouth, NH: Heinemann, 1979. (Pre–K to end of K)

CTBS Readiness Test. Monterey, CA: CTB/McGraw–Hill, 1977. (Grades K.0 to 1.3)

Metropolitan Readiness Test (5th ed.). Nurss, J. R., and McGauvran, M. E. San Antonio, TX: The Psychological Corporation, 1986. (First half of K to beginning Grade 1)

The Primary Language Record: Handbook for Teachers. Portsmouth, NH: Heinemann, 1994. (Pre–school to Grade 2)

Stanford Early School Achievement Test (SESAT). Madden, R., Gardner, E. F., and Collins, C. S. San Antonio, TX: The Psychological Corporation, 1982. (Grades K–1.9)

Test of Basic Experiences 2 (TOBE2). Moss, M. H. Monterey, CA: CTB/ McGraw–Hill, 1979. (Pre–K to end of Grade 1)

The Test of Early Reading Ability (TERA). Reid, D. K., Hresko, W. P., and Hammill, D. D. Austin, TX: PRO–ED, 1981. (Ages 3 to 7)

INFORMAL READING INVENTORIES

Analytical Reading Inventory (5th ed.). Woods, M. L., and Moe, A. J. Englewood Cliffs, NJ: Merrill/Prentice–Hall, 1995.

Bader Reading and Language Inventory. Bader, L. A. New York: Macmillan, 1983.

Basic Reading Inventory Pre-Primer–Grade Eight (5th ed.). Johns, J. L. Dubuque, IA: Kendall/Hunt, 1991.

Burns/Roe Informal Reading Inventory (3rd ed.). Roe, B. D. Boston: Houghton Mifflin, 1989.

Classroom Reading Inventory (7th ed.). Silvaroli, N. J. Madison, WI: Brown & Benchmark, 1994.

Diagnostic Reading Inventory (2nd ed.). Jacobs, H. D., and Searfoss, L. W. Dubuque, IA: Kendall/ Hunt, 1979.

Ekwall Reading Inventory (2nd ed.). Ekwall, E. Boston: Allyn & Bacon, 1985.

The Flynt–Cooter Reading Inventory for the Classroom (3rd ed.). Flynt, E. S., and Cooter, R. B., Jr. Columbus, OH: Merrill/Prentice Hall, 1998.

Reading Miscue Inventory: Alternative Procedures. Goodman, Y., Watson, D. J., and Burke, C. L. Katonah, NY: Richard C. Owens, 1987.

Reading Placement Inventory. Sucher, F., and Allred, R. A. Oklahoma City: The Economy Company, 1973.

Retrospective Miscue Analysis: Revaluing Readers and Reading. Goodman, Y. and Marek, A.M. Katonah, NY: Richard C. Owens, 1996.

PHONEMIC AWARENESS TESTS

Auditory Discrimination Test. Wepman, J. Los Angeles: Western Psychological Services, 1988.

Comprehensive Test of Reading Related Phonological Processes. Torgesen, J., and Wagner, W. Austin, TX: PRO–ED. 512-451-3246.

Lindamood Auditory Conceptualization Test. Lindamood, C., and Lindamood, P. Austin, TX: PRO–ED. 512-451-3246.

The Phonological Awareness Profile. Robertson, C., and Salter, W. East Moline, IL: LinguiSystems. 1-800-PRO-IDEA.

Scholastic Ready-to-Use Primary Reading Assessment Kit. Fiderer, A. New York: Scholastic, 1998. 1-800-724-6527.

Test of Awareness of Language Segments. Sawyer, D. J. Austin, TX: PRO–ED. 512-451-3246.

Test of Phonological Awareness. Torgesen, J., and Bryant, B. Austin, TX: PRO–ED. 512-451-3246.

INFORMAL CHECKLISTS AND ASSESSMENT DEVICES

HOW THE TOOLS IN THIS APPENDIX ARE ORGANIZED

KNOWLEDGE OF PRINT

Name _____   Date _____

INTEREST IN WRITING

_____ Very motivated (enjoys writing)

_____ Moderate (writes with prompting)

_____ Minimal (only writes if asked to do so)

AWARENESS OF DIRECTIONALITY

_____ Consistently writes from left to right and top to bottom.

_____ Sometimes writes from left to right and top to bottom

_____ No awareness of directionality evident

WORD REPRESENTATION

_____ Includes a vowel when representing a word

_____ Uses several letters to represent a word; not always a vowel

_____ Uses a phonetically correct initial consonant for words

_____ Can write own name

_____ Uses random shapes, letters, and numbers for writing

_____ Uses drawings alone to represent writing

CONCEPT ABOUT PRINT ASSESSMENT

Name _____ Date _____

BOOK ORIENTATION

_____ Can point to front of book

_____ Can point to back of book

_____ Can point to title

DIFFERENCE BETWEEN ILLUSTRATIONS AND PRINT

_____ Can point to illustrations

_____ Can point to print

_____ Can point to where text begins

DIRECTIONALITY OF PRINT

_____ Can show directionality of print on page

_____ Can point to beginning of text

_____ Can point to end of text

_____ Can show beginning and end of words on page (knows word boundaries)

PRINT TERMINOLOGY

_____ Can identify top and bottom of page

_____ Can point to a letter

_____ Can point to a word

_____ Can point to a specific word on request

_____ Can point to a specific letter on request

_____ Can point to a lower case letter

_____ Can point to an upper case letter

_____ Can identify different punctuation marks on request

INTEREST INVENTORY

Name _____ Age _____ Sex _____ Date _____

1. What do you like to do most when you have spare time?

   _____

2. What do you usually do after school?

   _____

   in the evenings?

   _____

   on Sundays?

   _____

   on Saturdays?

   _____

3. How old are your brothers and sisters? _____

   Do you get along with them? _____

   What do you like to do with them?

   _____

4. Do you take any special lessons?

   _____

5. Are your parents/grandparents from another country? _____

   Which one? _____   What language do they speak? _____

6. What kind of food do you like?

   _____

7. Have you ever been to a: *(circle all that apply)*

farm?	circus?	zoo?	museum?
amusement park?	concert?	picnic?	ball game?
swimming pool?	beach?	dairy?	firehouse?
airport?	library?		

8. Have you ever taken a trip by: *(circle all that apply)*

airplane?	train?	bus?	boat?

Where did you go?

_____

9. What types of work do you think you would like to do to earn money?

_____

10. What television programs do you like best?

_____

videos?

_____

computer programs?

_____

11. Do you ever listen to the news on TV? _____

12. What songs do you like?

_____

13. Do you have any pets? _____ What kind?

_____

What kind of pet would you like to have?

_____

14. Do you have books you read for pleasure at home?

_____

15. Do you like to have someone read aloud to you? _____

16. What is your favorite type of story? _____

17. Are there any books you would like to own?

_____

18. What book is your all-time favorite? *(only one title, please)*

_____

19. Do you enjoy shopping alone or with friends best? _____

20. Which video do you like best?

_____

21. Would you rather spend your relaxation time alone or with others?

_____

AN EARLY READER'S VIEW OF THE READING PROCESS

Name _____ Age _____ Sex _____ Date _____

1. Name someone you know who is a good reader. _____

   What makes him/her a good reader?

   _____

2. Do you think (person named in #1) ever comes to a word they don't know or an idea they don't understand when they are reading? _____

3. (If yes for #2) When they come to a word they don't know or an idea they don't understand, what do you think they do about it?

   _____

4. When *you* are reading and you come to a word you don't know, what do *you* do?

   _____

5. If you knew that someone was having trouble in reading, how would you help that person?

   _____

6. What do you think a teacher would do to help that person?

   _____

7. Who helped you to learn to read? _____

   How did they help you?

   _____

8. What would you like to be able to do better when you read?

   _____

9. Do you think that you are a good reader? Why or why not?

   _____

10. What do you like/dislike about reading?

    _____

    Additional notes or comments:

    _____

RESPONSE TO LITERATURE CHECKLIST

Name _____   Date _____

Responds to teacher's questions

            Never   *Sometimes*   *Frequently*   *Always*

Comments on or interprets text

            Never   *Sometimes*   *Frequently*   *Always*

Connects text to own life

            Never   *Sometimes*   *Frequently*   *Always*

Asks questions about text

            Never   *Sometimes*   *Frequently*   *Always*

Makes predictions

            Never   *Sometimes*   *Frequently*   *Always*

Shares own background information related to text

            Never   *Sometimes*   *Frequently*   *Always*

Strays from topic of text

            Never   *Sometimes*   *Frequently*   *Always*

PRIMARY READING
ATTITUDE SURVEY

Name _____ Date _____

How Do You Feel . . .

1. When you read?

2. About school?

3. About reading in your free time?

4. About going to the library?

5. About reading instead of watching TV?

6. About reading to your family?

7. About reading at your desk in school?

8. About how important reading is?

9. About reading at bedtime?

10. About writing your own stories?

11. About reading to try and learn something?

12. When someone else reads to you?

13. When you come to a new word in a story?

14. About reading in your favorite subject in school?

15. About your reading group in school?

16. About reading out loud?

17. About checking out books from the library?

18. About reading with your teacher?

19. About answering questions about what you read?

20. About taking reading tests?

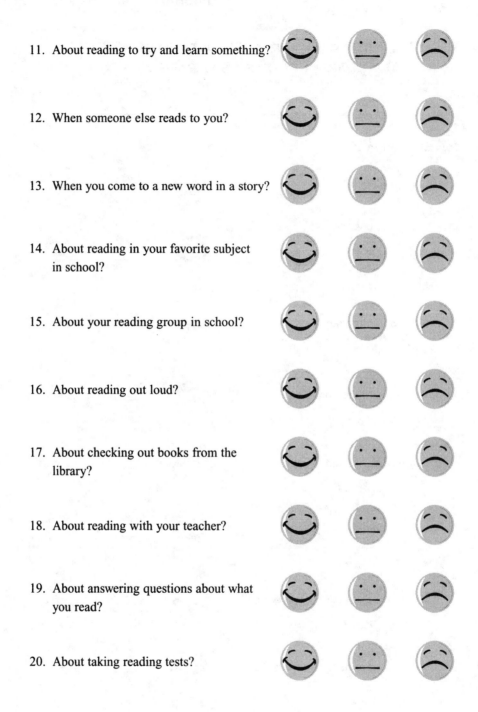

PRIMARY READING ATTITUDE SURVEY SCORING SHEET

Student Name _____

Teacher _____

Grade _____ Administration date _____

SCORING GUIDE

3 points 2 points 1 point

RECREATIONAL READING   ACADEMIC READING

1. _____   11. _____

2. _____   12. _____

3. _____   13. _____

4. _____   14. _____

5. _____   15. _____

6. _____   16. _____

7. _____   17. _____

8. _____   18. _____

9. _____   19. _____

10. _____   20. _____

Raw score _____   Raw score _____

Full scale raw score (Recreational + Academic) _____

Percentile ranks   Recreational _____

Academic _____

Full scale _____

QUICK PHONEMIC AWARENESS ASSESSMENT DEVICE

A high correlation exists between the ability to recognize spoken words as a sequence of individual sounds and reading achievement. Explicit instruction can increase the phonemic awareness of children. To assist in determining the level of phonemic awareness of each child in your class, the following assessment items may be utilized. Use as many samples as necessary to determine mastery.

Assessment 1   Isolation of beginning sounds. Ask the child what the first sound of selected words is.

"What is the first sound in *dog*?"

Assessment 2   Deletion of initial sound. Read a word and ask the child to say it without the first sound.

"Say the word *cat*. Say *cat* without the /k/."

Assessment 3   Segmentation of phonemes. Ask the child to verbally say the separate sounds of the word being read.

"What are the two sounds in the word *go*?"

Assessment 4   Blending of phonemes. Slowly read the individual sounds of a word and ask the child to tell what the word is.

"What word am I saying? /d/ /o/ /g/"

Assessment 5   Phoneme manipulation. Read a word and ask the child to replace the initial sound with another. Have the child say the new word.

"In the word *fan*, the first sound is a /f/. If you replace the /f/ with an /m/, how would you say the new word?"

ASSESSMENTS FOR
PHONOLOGICAL AWARENESS*

Directions for Use

Teachers: You will probably not need to complete these assessments for all of your students. Teacher observation and anecdotal records for each child in your class will determine which students need to acquire skills. Description of students to use assessment with:

- difficulty identifying sound elements
- difficulty recognizing when sounds rhyme
- unable to recognize familiar sight words
- nonreaders or emergent readers

For accurate results, follow the guidelines listed here. When completing assessments:

- Make sure children understand concepts being used, such as *beginning, end, first, last, same, sound,* and so on. Use terms they are familiar with.
- Always reinforce task to be completed by modeling or teaching, if necessary, during practice only. Continue until concept is clear, or it is apparent the student cannot perform the task. Record practice responses to refer to later.
- Require students to pronounce only sounds asked for, without adding extra sounds.
- A letter between two slash marks, for example /m/, represents the sound that letter stands for. Use during assessment to record student responses.
- A capital letter represents the name of the letter as a response. Record student response, but remind student to say the sounds, not the letter names.
- Put a check ✓ when student responds correctly, or record incorrect response. If an incorrect response is made before correct response, record error first, then put a check.
- When the student waits or hesitates more than 3 seconds, record with a <u>W</u>. Then, record the response, if any, and continue on to the next word.
- If no response is given, say "Try it" and record with a <u>T</u>. Then record the response, if any, and continue on to the next word.

A score of 4/5 or greater on each assessment task generally demonstrates adequate knowledge in this task. Lower scores reflect a need for some instruction in task. Teach identified tasks using Phonological Awareness Activity Guide at appropriate levels based on results.

*Developed by Katherine Beilby. Used with permission.

Name _____

Grade _____ Date _____

Phonological Awareness: Rhyme

Directions: Responses to rhymes must include more than the ending of the given word (e.g., jam, am is not acceptable). Nonsense words are an acceptable response. Record all responses on the line following each prompt given by teacher, including practice responses. Explain and model tasks during practice only.

   Practice: Say "Rhyming words sound the same at the end. I can rhyme with dad; mad, sad. Tell me a word that rhymes with; pin, (_____), fat, (_____), tie, (_____)"

Assessment:

1. sick _____   2. jam _____   3. dog _____   4. wet _____   5. cup _____

Score _____

Phonological Awareness: Matching Beginning Sound to Word

Directions: Require student to pronounce only the beginning consonant sound (not letter names). Reinforce correct responses during practice only.

   Practice: Say "I'm going to say a sound that you hear at the beginning of a word. I can say the first sound in mug; /m/; the first sound in rug; /r/. Listen closely and tell me the first sound in: man, (_____), sing, (_____), late, (_____)."

Assessment:

1. sun _____   2. not _____   3. like _____   4. five _____   5. mat _____

Score _____

Phonological Awareness: Blending Onset–Rimes

Directions: This task demonstrates how sounds can be put together to make words. Onset is the part of the word that precedes the vowel, while rime would include everything from the vowel on.

   Practice: Say "Now I will say the first sound and then the rest of the word to make a whole word. I can put these sounds together; /r/ un, run; /s/ et, set. Listen closely and tell me the word I have when I put these sounds together; /m/ op, (_____), /w/ eek, (_____), /s/ ome, (_____)."

Assessment:

1. /m/ ut _____   2. /f/ it _____   3. /n/ ap _____   4. /l/ et _____

5. /s/ ock _____

Score: _____

Comments:

Name _____

Grade _____ Date _____

Phonological Awareness: Segmenting Onset–Rimes

Directions: This task requires the student to take words apart by saying the first sound, and then the rest of the word. Reinforce tasks during practice only.

Practice: Say "I can say the sounds in a word; name, /n/ ame; let, /l/ et. Tell me the sounds in coat (_____), let, (_____), hip, (_____)."

Assessment:

1. lap _____   2. jet _____   3. fun _____   4. mom _____   5. sit _____

Score _____

Phonological Awareness: Blending Phonemes

Directions: This task requires the student to synthesize or blend each sound in a word. The teacher must pronounce the sounds in a word and have the students say the word quickly. Blending and segmenting tasks require very stretched pronunciation of words, without stopping between sounds.

Practice: Say "I'm going to say a word very slowly, and then I'll say it fast; /s/ /a/ /t/, sat. I'll say a word slowly. You say it fast. /h/ /i/ /de/ (_____), /b/ /i/ /g/ (_____)."

Assessment:

1. /f/ /a/ /t/ _____   2. /k/ /ee/ /p/ _____   3. /t/ /i/ /me/ _____

4. /p/ /e/ /t/ _____   5. /h/ /o/ /pe/ _____

Score _____

Phonological Awareness: Segmenting Phonemes

Directions: This task requires the student to analyze or segment each sound in a word. Segmenting is the opposite of blending. Each sound must be clearly articulated to receive full credit.

Practice: Say "I can say each sound in a word: came, /c/ /a/ /me/. Tell me each sound in the word sad (_____), deer, (_____)."

Assessment:

1. red _____   2. pig _____   3. home _____   4. bus _____   5. cake _____

Score: _____

Comments:

KNOWLEDGE OF SOUNDS AND LETTERS CHECKLIST

Have child: First: "Read letter names." Second: "Give letter sounds."

n □ f s □   n □ k s □   n □ i s □   n □ t s □   n □ c s □

n □ o s □   n □ x s □   n □ a s □   n □ g s □   n □ u s □

n □ z s □   n □ p s □   n □ j s □   n □ v s □   n □ q s □

n □ b s □   n □ r s □   n □ l s □   n □ m s □   n □ d s □

n □ n s □   n □ w s □   n □ s s □   n □ e s □   n □ y s □

n □ h s □   n □ ch s □   n □ th s □   n □ sh s □

Key: n □ name said correctly   s □ correct sound given

n ☑ name said incorrectly   s ☑ incorrect sound given

Note: If only long sound of a, e, i, o, u are given, ask for "another" sound. If not given ✓ □. (Also true of c and g.)

BEGINNING WRITER CHECKLIST

Name _____ Date _____

Key: 3 Almost always   2 Sometimes   1 Rarely

DRAWING

_____ Draws pictures most of the time

_____ Tells about pictures

_____ Draws pictures to accompany writing

COMPOSING/WRITING

_____ Generates story ideas orally

_____ Thinks of own ideas and writes them

_____ Uses models or themes in stories

_____ Uses patterns (scaffolds) for writing

WRITING FLUENCY

_____ Uses one or two word patterns

_____ Writes two to four lines

_____ Writes easy pattern books

_____ Writes two to four paragraphs

_____ Writes chapter books

USE OF WRITING PROCESS

_____ Prewrites (maps, webs, orally rehearses ideas)

_____ Reads writing to others

_____ Does multiple drafts

_____ Offers constructive feedback to others

_____ Makes change based on feedback

6-TRAIT ASSESSMENT FOR BEGINNING WRITERS*

1 EXPERIMENTING

IDEAS
— Uses scribbles for writing
— Dictates labels or a story
— Shapes that look like letters
— Line forms that imitate text
— Writes letters randomly

ORGANIZATION
— Attempts to write left to right
— Attempts to write top/down
— No sense of beginning and end yet
— Experiments with spacing

VOICE
— Communicates feeling with color, shape, line in drawing
— Work is similar to everyone else's
— Ambiguous response to task
— Awareness of audience not present

2 EMERGING

IDEAS
— Some recognizable words present
— Labels pictures
— Uses drawings that show detail
— Pictures are supported by some words

ORGANIZATION
— Consistently writes left to right
— Consistently uses top/down
— Experiments with beginnings
— Begins to group like words/pictures

VOICE
— Hints of voice present in words and phrases
— Looks different from most others
— Energy/mood is present
— Treatment of topic predictable
— Audience is fuzzy—could be anybody, anywhere

3 DEVELOPING

IDEAS
— Attempts a story or to make a point
— Illustration supports the writing
— Meaning of the general idea is recognizable/understandable
— Some ideas clear but some are still fuzzy

ORGANIZATION
— A title is present
— Limited transitions present
— Beginning but no ending except "The End"
— Attempts at sequencing

VOICE
— Expresses some predictable feelings
— Moments of individual sparkle, but then hides
— Repetition of familiar ideas reduces energy
— Awareness that the writing will be read by someone else
— Reader has limited connection to writer

4 CAPABLE

IDEAS
— Writing tells a story or makes a point
— Illustration (if present) enhances the writing
— Idea is generally on topic
— Details are present but not developed (lists)

ORGANIZATION
— An appropriate title is present
— Attempts transitions from sentence to sentence
— Beginning works well and attempts an ending
— Logical sequencing
— Key ideas begin to surface

VOICE
— Writing is individual and expressive
— Individual perspective becomes evident
— Personal treatment of a standard topic
— Writes to convey a story or idea to the reader
— Attempts nonstandard point of view

5 EXPERIENCED

IDEAS
— Presents a fresh/original idea
— Topic is narrowed and focused
— Develops one clear, main idea
— Uses interesting, important details for support
— Writer understands topic well

ORGANIZATION
— An original title is present
— Transitions connect main ideas
— The opening attracts
— An effective ending is tried
— Easy to follow
— Important ideas stand out

VOICE
— Uses text to elicit a variety of emotions
— Takes some risks to say more than what is expected
— Point of view is evident
— Writes with a clear sense of audience
— Cares deeply about the topic

*Source: Northwest Regional Educational Laboratory, 101 S.W. Main Street, Ste. 500, Portland, OR 97204. Used with permission.

WORD CHOICE
- Writes letters in strings
- Imitates word patterns
- Pictures stand for words and phrases
- Copies environmental print

SENTENCE FLUENCY
- Mimics letters and words across the page
- Words stand alone
- Patterns for sentences not in evidence
- Sentence sense not yet present

CONVENTIONS
- Writes letter strings (prephonetic: dmRxzz)
- Attempts to create standard letters
- Writes word strings
- Attempts spacing of words, letters, symbols or pictures
- Student interpretation needed to understand text/pictures

WORD CHOICE
- Recognizable words
- Environmental words used correctly
- Attempts at phrases
- Functional language

SENTENCE FLUENCY
- Strings words together into phrases
- Attempts simple sentences
- Short, repetitive sentence patterns
- Dialogue present but not understandable

CONVENTIONS
- Attempts semiphonetic spelling (MTR, UM, KD, etc.)
- Uses mixed upper and lowercase letters
- Uses spaces between letters and words
- Random punctuation
- Nonstandard grammar is common

WORD CHOICE
- General or ordinary words
- Attempts new words but they don't always fit
- Settles for the word or phrase that "will do"
- Big words used only to impress reader
- Relies on slang, clichés, or repetition

SENTENCE FLUENCY
- Uses simple sentences
- Sentences tend to begin the same
- Experiments with other sentence patterns
- Reader may have to reread to follow the meaning
- Dialogue present but needs interpretation

CONVENTIONS
- Uses phonetic spelling (MOSTR, HUMN, KLOSD, etc.) on personal words
- Spelling of high-frequency words still spotty
- Uses capitals at the beginning of sentences
- Usually uses end punctuation correctly (.!?)
- Experiments with other punctuation
- Long paper may be written as one paragraph
- Attempts standard grammar

WORD CHOICE
- Uses favorite words correctly
- Experiments with new and different words with some success
- Tries to choose words for specificity
- Attempts to use descriptive words to create images

SENTENCE FLUENCY
- Simple and compound sentences present and effective
- Attempts complex sentences
- Not all sentences begin the same
- Sections of writing have rhythm and flow

CONVENTIONS
- Transitional spelling on less frequent words (MONSTUR, HUMUN, CLOSSED, etc.)
- Spelling of high-frequency words usually correct
- Capitals at the beginning of sentences and variable use on proper nouns
- End punctuation is correct (.!?) and other punctuation is attempted (such as commas)
- Paragraphing variable but present
- Noun/pronoun agreement, verb tenses, subject/verb agreement

WORD CHOICE
- Everyday words used well
- Precise, accurate, fresh, original words
- Creates vivid images in a natural way
- Avoids repetition, clichés or vague language
- Attempts at figurative language

SENTENCE FLUENCY
- Consistently uses sentence variety
- Sentence structure is correct and creative
- Variety of sentence beginnings
- Natural rhythm, cadence and flow
- Sentences have texture which clarifies the important idea

CONVENTIONS
- High-frequency words are spelled correctly and very close on other words
- Capitals used for obvious proper nouns as well as sentence beginnings
- Basic punctuation is used correctly and/or creatively
- Indents consistently to show paragraphs
- Shows control over standard grammar

DEVELOPMENTAL SPELLING TEST
(THE "MONSTER TEST")

An easily administered 10-word checklist, such as the following developmental test devised by Gentry (Gentry, 1985; Cecil, 1990), makes it possible for teachers to assess young children's developmental phonemic awareness level.

WORDS	PRECOMMUNICATIVE SPELLINGS	SEMI-PHONETIC SPELLINGS	PHONETIC SPELLINGS	TRANSITIONAL SPELLINGS	CORRECT SPELLINGS
1. monster	random letters	mtr	mostr	monstur	monster
2. united	random letters	u	unitid	younighted	united
3. dress	random letters	jrs	jras	dres	dress
4. bottom	random letters	bt	bodm	bottum	bottom
5. hiked	random letters	h	hikt	hicked	hiked
6. human	random letters	um	humm	humin	human
7. eagle	random letters	el	egl	egul	eagle
8. closed	random letters	kd	klosd	clossed	closed
9. bumped	random letters	b	bopt	bumpt	bumped
10. type	random letters	tp	tip	tipe	type

From Gentry, J. Richard (1985). "You Can Analyze Developmental Spelling." *The Early Years* (9), 44–45.

BEGINNING SPELLER CHECKLIST

Name _____   Date _____

IDENTIFICATION OF WORDS IN CONTEXT

_____ Guesses at words

_____ Looks at pictures and then guesses

_____ Looks at beginning of word

_____ Tries to figure out first sound

_____ Uses strategies to sound out word

PICTURES & WORD SORTS

_____ Can sort pictures accurately

_____ Can explain why he sorted pictures that way

_____ Can sort words accurately

_____ Can explain why she sorted words that way

_____ Can sort pictures/words independently

_____ Can sort words quickly

SPELLING LISTS & TESTS

_____ Recognizes misspelled words

_____ Can find words with the same patterns as spelling list words

_____ Achieves 80% or better accuracy on spelling post-tests

SPELLING IN WRITING

_____ Shows appropriate concern about accuracy

_____ Invents spelling when needed

_____ Spells learned words correctly

_____ Writes with spaces between words

_____ "Chunks" syllables and sounds in words

_____ Segments (sounds out) words

Student Profile

Name _____

Reading	Letter names	Letter sounds	Decodes words	Reads words	Reads sentences	Reads fluently/comprehends

Writing	Writes letters	Copies writing from board	Writes words using phonics	Writes Sentences	Writes simple stories	Writes stories with structure

Speaking	No verbal response	Single word responses	Responds with phrases	Responds with sentences	Questions & answers	Gets in class discussions

Comments _____

_____

_____

_____

_____

_____

By Rita Lehmann and Janet Rodgers. Used with permission.

KID GRAPH

Directions: Color in the squares for the amount of minutes spent in recreational reading each day. Ask your parents to sign their name on the line below showing that they have checked the amount of time you have spent reading.

	Sun.	Mon.	Tue.	Wed.	Thur.	Fri.	Sat.
15 min.							
14 min.							
13 min.							
12 min.							
11 min.							
10 min.							
9 min.							
8 min.							
7 min.							
6 min.							
5 min.							
4 min.							
3 min.							
2 min.							
1 min.							

My child has read the actual amount
of time noted on the graph. _____

RIMES AND COMMON WORDS CONTAINING THEM

ack:	lack, back, Jack, stack, sack, pack, quack, tack
ail:	tail, pail, mail, quail, fail, wail, sail
ain:	pain, main, stain, gain, rain, vain
ake:	sake, take, bake, lake, wake, fake, rake, cake, make
ale:	pale, gale, dale, sale, bale, hale, male
ame:	name, game, same, tame, lame, came, dame, fame
an:	ran, pan, can, Nan, fan, tan, man, than
ank:	sank, thank, bank, tank, stank, dank, shrank
ap:	cap, map, lap, sap, gap, nap, zap, tap
ash:	dash, cash, stash, lash, mash, gash, trash, crash, flash
at:	cat, bat, Nat, mat, pat, sat, at, tat, rat, that, scat
ate:	gate, hate, late, sate, plate, slate, crate, fate
aw:	saw, paw, claw, law, jaw, straw, raw, flaw
ay:	day, play, stay, say, gray, ray, lay, gay, jay, way
eal:	seal, meal, steal, heal, deal
eat:	meat, beat, heat, cheat, feat, wheat
ell:	tell, smell, sell, well, swell, bell, fell, shell
est:	test, best, west, vest, jest, nest, pest, chest
ice:	nice, mice, rice, lice, ice, spice
ick:	pick, Nick, tick, lick, stick, thick, Dick, brick, sick
ide:	side, bride, tide, bide, pride, hide, ride

ite:	kite, bite, sprite
ight:	right, night, tight, flight, might, bright
ill:	bill, hill, kill, thrill, fill, shrill, drill, sill, pill, will, Jill, dill, Lill, mill, quill
in:	chin, fin, bin, win, sin, twin, din, grin, pin, tin
ine:	fine, mine, twine, wine, vine, nine, line
ing:	king, string, sing, thing, ring, wing, bring, swing
ink:	link, think, rink, mink, drink, wink, sink, blink, stink, kink
ig:	big, wig, twig, jig, pig
ip:	lip, skip, sip, flip, whip, dip, drip, trip, tip, hip, ship
ir:	sir, whir, stir, fir
ock:	rock, lock, sock, mock, knock, block, clock
oke:	poke, broke, stroke, Coke, joke, woke, choke
oil:	boil, toil, soil
ook:	book, look, took, hook, crook
op:	chop, mop, crop, top, stop, flop, plop, drop, hop, shop
ore:	sore, tore, more, core, bore, wore, snore, chore, shore, store
uck:	stuck, truck, buck, suck, pluck, struck, duck, luck
ug:	bug, plug, rug, dug, hug, drug
ump:	bump, clump, jump, dump, hump, lump, pump
unk:	junk, bunk, sunk, hunk, stunk, dunk

FRY'S LIST OF "INSTANT WORDS"

FIRST 100 WORDS
(APPROX. 1ST GRADE)

GROUP 1A	GROUP 1B	GROUP 1C	GROUP 1D
the	he	go	who
a	I	we	an
is	they	then	their
you	one	us	she
to	good	no	new
and	me	him	said
we	about	by	did
that	had	was	boy
in	if	come	three
not	some	get	down
for	up	or	work
at	her	two	put
with	do	man	were
it	when	little	before
on	so	has	just
can	my	them	long
will	very	how	here
are	all	like	other
of	would	our	old
this	any	what	take
your	been	know	cat
as	out	make	again
but	there	which	give
be	from	much	after
have	day	his	many

SECOND 100 WORDS
(APPROX. 2ND GRADE)

GROUP 2A	GROUP 2B	GROUP 2C	GROUP 2D
saw	big	may	fan
home	where	let	five
soon	am	use	read
stand	ball	these	over
box	morning	right	such
upon	live	present	way
first	four	tell	too
came	last	next	shall
girl	color	please	own
house	away	leave	most
find	red	hand	sure
because	friend	more	thing
made	pretty	why	only
could	eat	better	near
book	want	under	than
look	year	while	open
mother	want	should	kind
run	got	never	must
school	play	each	high
people	found	best	far
night	left	another	both
into	men	seem	end
say	bring	tree	also
think	wish	name	until
back	black	dear	call

THIRD 100 WORDS (APPROX. 3RD GRADE)

GROUP 3A	GROUP 3B	GROUP 3C	GROUP 3D
ask	hat	off	fire
small	car	sister	ten
yellow	write	happy	order
show	try	once	part
goes	myself	didn't	early
clean	longer	set	fat
buy	those	round	third
thank	hold	dress	same
sleep	full	tell	love
letter	carry	wash	hear
jump	eight	start	yesterday
help	sing	always	eyes
fly	warm	anything	door
don't	sit	around	clothes
fast	dog	close	through
cold	ride	walk	o'clock
today	hot	money	second
does	grow	turn	water
face	cut	might	town
green	seven	hard	took
every	woman	along	pair
brown	funny	bed	now
coat	yes	fine	keep
six	ate	sat	head
gave	stop	hope	food

PHONICS TERMS & ORTHOGRAPHY CHART

COMMON PHONICS TERMS

accent (primary)   The syllable in a word that receives the strongest and loudest emphasis.

analytic phonics   A whole-to-part phonics approach that emphasizes starting with whole words and identifying individual sounds as part of those words. Efforts are generally made to avoid pronouncing the sounds in isolation. Also known as *implicit phonics.*

auditory discrimination   The ability to hear similarities and differences between sounds as they appear in spoken words.

base word   A word to which prefixes and/or suffixes are added to create new but related words. The simplest member of a word family.

breve   An orthographic symbol, (˘), placed above vowel graphemes to indicate pronunciation.

circumflex   An orthographic symbol, (ˆ), placed above vowel graphemes to indicate pronunciation.

closed syllable   Any syllable with a consonant phoneme. *Examples:* come /m/; love /v/; ran /n/.

compound word   A word made up of two or more base words. *Example:* football.

consonants   Sounds represented by any letter of the English alphabet except *a, e, i, o,* and *u.* Consonants are *sounds* that are made by restricting the breath channel.

consonant blend   Sounds in a syllable represented by two or more letters that are blended together without losing their own identity. *Examples:* green /g/ /r/; swing /s/ /w/; clap /c/ /l/.

consonant cluster   Two or more consonant letters appearing together in a syllable which, when sounded, represent a blend. *Examples:* gr, cr, str.

decoding   The process of determining the pronunciation of an unknown word.

deductive instruction   Instructional procedure that centers on telling children about generalizations and having them apply those generalizations to specific words. A general-to-specific analysis.

digraph   Two letters that stand for a single phoneme or sound. *Examples:* shout /sh/; what /wh/; rang /ng/; meat /ea/. A digraph is a grapheme containing two letters and one sound.

dipthong   A single sound made up of a blend of two vowel sounds in immediate sequence and pronounced in one syllable. *Examples:* oil /oi/; toy /oy/.

grapheme   A letter or combination of letters that represents a phoneme. *Examples:* The phoneme /b/ in *bat* is represented by the grapheme (letter) b; the phoneme /f/ in *phone* is represented by the graphemes p and h.

macron   An orthographic symbol, (−), placed over a vowel to show that it is pronounced as a long sound.

onset   The consonant sound(s) of a syllable that come before the vowel sound. (See the definition of *rime* for examples of onsets.)

open syllable   Any syllable ending with a vowel phoneme. *Examples:* see /e/; may /a/; auto /o/.

phoneme   The smallest sound unit of a language that distinguishes one word from another. *Examples:* the phoneme /h/ distinguishes *hat* from *at;* the words *man* and *fan* are distinguished by their initial phonemes /m/ and /f/ respectively.

phoneme blending   The process of recognizing isolated speech sounds and the ability to pronounce the word for which they stand.

phoneme segmentation   The ability to isolate all the sounds within a word.

phonemic awareness   The ability to recognize spoken words as a sequence of individual sounds.

phonetics   The scientific study of human speech sounds.

phonics   A method in which basic phonetics, the study of human speech sounds, is used to teach beginning reading.

phonogram   A letter sequence comprised of a vowel grapheme and an ending consonant grapheme(s). *Examples: -it* in *bit, lit,* and *sit,* or *-ain* in *pain, gain,* and *rain.*

r-controlled vowel   When a vowel is followed by the letter *r,* it makes the vowel sound neither long nor short. *Example:* in the word *car,* the vowel sound becomes /a/; in the word *more* it becomes /ô/.

rime   The part of a syllable that includes the vowel sound as well as any consonant sound(s) that come after it. The graphic representation of a rime is referred to as a *phonogram. Example:* in the word *cat,* the onset is /c/ and the rime is /at/.

root   Often used as a synonym for *base word.*

schwa sound   An unstressed sound commonly occurring in unstressed syllables. It is represented by the symbol, /ə/, and closely resembles the short sound for *u. Examples: i* in *April; io* in *station; u* in *circus.*

silent letter   A name given to a letter that appears in a written word but is not heard in the spoken word. *Example: knight* has six written letters but only three are heard; *k, g,* and *h* are "silent."

slash marks   Slanting lines (/ /) enclosing a grapheme(s) indicate that the reference is to the sound and not to the letters.

syllable   A unit of pronunciation consisting of a vowel alone or a vowel with one or more consonants. There can be only one vowel phoneme (sound) in each syllable.

synthetic phonics   A part-to-whole phonics approach that emphasizes the learning of individual sounds, often in isolation, and combining them to form words. Also known as *explicit phonics.*

umlaut   An orthographic symbol, (··), placed above vowel graphemes to indicate pronunciation.

visual discrimination   The ability to visually perceive similarities and differences. In reading, this means to perceive similarities and differences in written letters and words.

vowels   Sounds represented by the graphemes (letters) *a, e, i, o, u,* and sometimes *y* and *w,* in the English alphabet. Vowels are sounds that are made without closing or restricting the breath channel.

An Introduction to English Orthography.

CONSONANTS

b	ball
d	dust
f	fast
h	hat
j	jar
k	kite
l	last
m	man
n	near
p	put
qu	quack
r	ran
t	tack
v	vase
w	wall
x	x-ray
z	zoo

VARIANT CONSONANTS

c, g	
	cot
	cent
	get
	giraffe

DIGRAPHS WITH h

ch	chin
	school
	charade
gh	ghost
ph	phone
sh	shine
th	thin
	then
wh	whale
	whom

DIGRAPHS WITH FIRST SILENT LETTER

ck	neck
gn	gnat
kn	know
wr	wren

DIGRAPH CLUSTER FOLLOWING A SHORT VOWEL

dge	ledge
tch	match

ADDITIONAL DIGRAPH

ng	song

BLENDS—INITIAL

r	green
l	clear
s	spine
	strap
tw	twine

BLENDS—FINAL

ld	held
lk	talk
nd	pond
nk	sink
nt	want

SPECIAL COMBINATION OF CONSONANT AND VOWEL

ci	crucial
si	pension
ti	nation

VOWELS

SINGLE—SHORT

a	ă	apple
e	ĕ	elephant
i	ĭ	itch
o	ŏ	octopus
u	ŭ	umbrella

SINGLE—LONG

a	ā	ape
e	ē	event
i	ī	ivy
o	ō	open
u and	ū	uniform
	o͞o	crude

SINGLE—THIRD SOUND

a	ä	father (fäther)
o	o͞o	move (mo͞ve)
u	o͝o	bush (bo͝osh)

SCHWA ə IN UNACCENTED SYLLABLES

a	əmong
e	blankət
i	Aprəl
o	bacən

DIGRAPHS/DIPHTHONGS WITH a

ai as	/ā/	pain
ay as	/ā/	play
au as	/aw/	caution
aw as	/aw/	straw

DIGRAPHS WITH e

ee as	/ē/	weed
ea as	/ē/	meat
	/ĕ/	dead
	/ā/	great
ie as	/ē/	belief
	/ī/	tie
ei as	/ē/	(after c) receive
	/ā/	rein
ey as	/ē/	monkey
	/ā/	prey

DIGRAPHS AND DIPHTHONGS WITH o

oa as	/ō/	bloat
oi as	/oy/	noise
oy as	/oy/	toy
oo as	/o͞o/	soon
	/o͝o/	took
ou as	/ow/	trout
	/ŭ/	young
	/ō/	soul
	/o͞o/	troupe
ow as	/ow/	owl
	/ō/	blow

REFERENCES

Adams, M. J. *Beginning to Read: Thinking and Learning about Print.* Cambridge, MA: MIT Press, 1990.

Adams, M. J. and Bruck, M. Resolving the great debate, *American Educator, 19(7)*, 10–20, 1995.

Adams, M. J. Why not phonics and whole language? In W. Ellis (ed.), *All Language and the Creation of Literacy.* Baltimore: The Orton Dyslexia Society, 1991.

Adams, M. J., Foorman, B. R., Lundberg, I., and Beeler, T. *Phonemic Awareness in Young Children.* Baltimore: Paul H. Brooks, 1998.

Adams, M. J., Treiman, R., and Pressley, M. Reading, writing and literacy. In I. Sigel and A. Renninger (eds.), *Handbook of Child Psychology, Vol. 4: Child Psychology in Practice*, New York: Wiley, 1996.

Alegria, J., Pignot, E., and Morais, J. Phonetic analysis of speech and memory codes in beginning readers. *Memory and Cognition, 10*, 451–456, 1982.

Allen, R. V. *Language Experiences in Communication.* Boston: Houghton Mifflin, 1976.

Allington, R. L. Children who find learning to read difficult: School responses to diversity. In E. H. Hiebert (ed.), *Literacy for a Diverse Society: Perspectives, Practices, and Policies.* New York: Teachers College Press, 1991.

Altwerger, B., Edelsky, C., and Flores, B. M. Whole language: What's new? *The Reading Teacher, 41(2)*, 144–154, 1987.

Anderson, R. C., Wilson, P. T., and Fielding, L. G. Growth in reading and how children spend their time outside of school. *Reading Research Quarterly, 23,* 285–303, 1988.

Anderson, R. C., Hilbert, E. H., Scott, J. A., and Wilkonson, I. A. G. *Becoming a Nation of Readers: The Report of The Commission on Reading.* Washington, D.C.: National Institute of Education, 1985.

Ashton–Warner, S. *Teacher.* New York: Simon & Schuster, 1965.

Atwell, N. Nancie Atwell talks about teachers and whole language. *Instructor, 102(4),* 48–49, 1992.

Au, K. H. *Literacy Instruction in Multicultural Settings.* Orlando, FL: Harcourt Brace, 1993.

Au, K. H. Paper presented at the Notre Dame Reading Conference, South Bend, IN, June 25, 1991, sponsored by Houghton Mifflin, Boston.

Au, K. H. Using the experience–text–relationship with minority children. *The Reading Teacher, 32,* 478–479, 1979.

Aulls, M. W., and Graves, M. F. *Quest: New Roads to Literacy.* New York: Scholastic, 1985.

Ausubel, D. P. Viewpoints from related disciplines: Human growth and development. *Teachers College Record, 60,* 245–254, 1959.

Baer, G. T. *Self-Paced Phonics: A Text for Education* (2nd ed.). Upper Saddle River, NJ: Merrill, 1999.

Baghban, M. *Our Daughter Learns to Read and Write: A Case Study from Birth to Three.* Newark, DE: International Reading Association, 1984.

Ball, E. W., and Blachman, B. A. Does phonemic awareness training in kindergarten make a difference in early word recognition and developmental spelling? *Reading Research Quarterly, 26 (1)*, 49–66, 1991.

Balmuth, M. *The Root of Phonics: A Historical Perspective.* McGraw Hill, 1982.

Barclay, K., and Coffman, T. I know an old lady: Linking literacy and lyrics. *Teaching K-8, 6,* 28–29, 1990.

Barone, D. The written responses of young children: Beyond comprehension to story understanding. *The New Advocate, 44,* 536–541, 1990.

Barrantine, S. J. Engaging with reading through interactive read-alouds. *The Reading Teacher, 50(1),* 36–43, 1996.

Baumann, J. F., and Kameenui, E. J. Research on vocabulary instruction: Ode to Voltaire. In J. Flood, J. M. Jensen, D. Lapp, and J. R. Squire (eds.), *Handbook on Teaching the English Language Arts*, pp. 604–632. New York: Macmillan, 1991.

Bear, D. R. Learning to fasten the seat belt of my union seat without looking around: The synchrony of literacy development. *Theory into Practice, 30(3),* 149–157, 1991.

Bear, D. R., Invernizzi, M., Templeton, S., and Johnston, F. *Words Their Way: Word Study for Phonics, Vocabulary, And Spelling Instruction.* Upper Saddle River, NJ: Merrill, 1996.

Beck, I. Developing comprehension: The impact of the directed reading lesson. In R. C. Anderson, J. Osborn, and R. J. Tierney (eds.), *Learning to Read in American Schools: Basal Readers and Content Texts.* Hillsdale, NJ: Lawrence Erlbaum, 1984.

Beck, I. L., and Juel, C. The role of decoding in learning to read. *American Educator, 3,* Summer, 1995.

Beck, I. L., and McKeown, M. Conditions of vocabulary acquisition. In R. Barr, M. Kamil, P. Rosenthal, and P. D. Pearson (eds.), *Handbook of Reading Research, 2,* 789–814, 1991.

Bergeron, B. What does the term "whole language" mean? Constructing a definition from the literature. *Journal of Reading Behavior, 22,* 301–329, 1990.

Bialostok, S. Offering the olive branch: The rhetoric of insincerity. *Language Arts, 74(8),* 618–627, 1997.

Bissex, G. L. *Gnys at Wrk: A Child Learns to Read and Write.* Cambridge, MA: Harvard University Press, 1980.

Blachman, B. A. Getting ready to read: Learning how print maps to speech. In J. F. Kavanagh (ed.), *The Language Continuum: From Infancy to Literacy.* Timonium, MD: York Press, 1991.

Blachowicz, C. E. Vocabulary instruction: What goes on in the classroom? *The Reading Teacher, 2,* 132–137, 1987.

Blachowicz, C. E., and Lee, J. J. Vocabulary development in the whole literacy classroom. *The Reading Teacher, 45,* 188–195, 1991.

Blevins, W. *Phonics from A to Z: A Practical Guide.* Jefferson City, MO: Scholastic, 1998.

Bolton, F., and Snowball, D. *Teaching Spelling: A Practical Resource.* Portsmouth, NH: Heinemann, 1993.

Bond, G., and Dykstra, R. The cooperative research program in first-grade reading instruction. *Reading Research Quarterly, 2,* 5–142, 1967.

Bridge, C., Winograd, P. N., and Haley, D. Using predictable materials vs. preprimers to teach beginning sight words. *The Reading Teacher, 36(9),* 884-891, 1983.

Buckley, M. H. When teachers decide to integrate the language arts. *Language Arts, 63,* 369–377, 1986.

Butler, A., and Turbil, J. *Towards a Reading and Writing Classroom.* Portsmouth, NH: Heinemann, 1986.

Byrne, B., and Fielding–Barnsley, R. Phonemic awareness and letter knowledge in the child's acquisition of the alphabetic principle. *Journal of Educational Psychology, 81,* 313–321, 1989.

California Department of Education. *Language Arts: Reading, Writing, Listening, and Speaking Standards.* Sacramento, CA: California Department of Education, 1998.

California Department of Education. *Teaching Reading: A Balanced Comprehensive Approach to Teaching Reading in Prekindergarten Through Grade Three.* Sacramento, CA: California Department of Education, 1996.

California Reading Association. *Building Literacy: Making Every Child a Reader.* Sacramento: The California Reading Association, 1996.

Calkins, L. M. *The Art of Teaching Writing.* Portsmouth, NH: Heinemann, 1994.

Cambourne, B., and Turbill, J. *Coping with Chaos.* Portsmouth, NH: Heinemann, 1991.

Cambourne, B., and Turbill, J. Assessment in whole language classrooms: Theory into practice. *Elementary School Journal, 90,* 337–349, 1990.

Carbo, M. An evaluation of Jeanne Chall's response to "debunking the great phonics myth." *Phi Delta Kappan, 71(4),* 152–158, 1988.

Carbo, M. Debunking the great phonics myth. *Phi Delta Kappan, 70(8),* 226–240, 1988.

Cardoso–Martins, C. Sensitivity to rhymes, syllables, and phonemes in literacy acquisition in Portuguese. *Reading Research Quarterly, 30*, 808–828, 1995.

Carr, E., and Wixon, K. K. Guidelines for evaluating vocabulary instruction. *Journal of Reading, 29*, 588–595, 1986.

Cecil, N. L. *The Art of Inquiry: Questioning Strategies for K–6 Classrooms.* Manitoba: Peguis, 1995.

Cecil, N. L. *For the Love of Language: Poetry for All Learners.* Winnipeg, Manitoba: Peguis Publishers, 1994.

Cecil, N. L. *Freedom Fighters: Affective Teaching of the Language Arts.* Salem, WI: Sheffield, 1994.

Cecil, N. L. Instilling a love of words in children. In E. H. Cramer and M. Castle (eds.), *Fostering the Love of Reading: The Affective Domain in Reading Education.* Newark, DE: International Reading Association, 1994.

Cecil, N. L. *Teaching to the Heart: An Affective Approach to Reading Instruction.* Salem WI: Sheffield Publishers, 1994.

Cecil, N. L., and Lauritzen, P. *Literacy and the Arts in the Integrated Classroom: Alternative Ways of Knowing.* White Plains, NY: Longman, 1994.

Chall, J. *Learning to Read: The Great Debate.* 3rd ed. New York: McGraw Hill, 1995.

Chall, J. *Learning to Read: The Great Debate.* New York: McGraw Hill, 1967.

Chall, J. Learning to read: The great debate 20 years later—response to "debunking the great phonics myth." *Phi Delta Kappan, 70 (7)*, 521–525, 1989.

Cheek, E. H., Flippo, R. F., and Lindsey, J. D. *Reading for Success in Elementary School.* Madison, WI: Brown & Benchmark, 1997.

Clay, M. M. *An Observation Survey.* Portsmouth, NH: Heinemann Educational Books, 1993.

Clay, M. M. *Becoming Literate: The Construction of Inner Control.* Portsmouth, NH: Heinemann, 1991.

Clay, M. M. What is and what might be in evaluation. *Language Arts, 67(3)*, 288–298, 1990.

Clay, M. M. *The Early Detection of Reading Difficulties* (3rd ed.). Auckland, New Zealand: Heinemann, 1985.

Clay, M. M. *Stones. The Concepts About Print Test.* Auckland, New Zealand: Heinemann, 1979.

Clay, M. M. *Reading: The Patterning of Complex Behavior.* Portsmouth, NH: Heinemann Educational Books, 1972.

Clymer, T. The utility of phonic generalizations in the primary grades. *The Reading Teacher, 16*, 252–258, 1963.

Cole, A. D. Beginner-oriented texts in literature-based classrooms: The segue for a few struggling readers. *The Reading Teacher, 51,* 488–500, 1998.

Cooper, J. D. *Literacy: Helping Children Construct Meaning.* Boston: Houghton Mifflin, 1997.

Cossu, G., Shankweiler, D., Liberman, I. Y., Tola, G., and Katz, L. Awareness of phonological segments and reading ability in Italian children. *Applied Psycholinguistics, 9*, 1–16, 1988.

Cousin, P. T., Weekly, T., and Gerard, J. The functional uses of language and literacy by students with severe language and learning problems. *Language Arts, 70,* 548–556, 1993.

Cudd, E. The paragraph frame: A bridge from narrative to expository text. In N. L. Cecil (ed.), *Literacy in the '90s: Readings in the Language Arts.* Dubuque, IA: Kendall/Hunt, 1990.

Cunningham, A. E. Explicit versus implicit instruction in phonological awareness. *Journal of Experimental Child Psychology, 50*, 429–444, 1990.

Cunningham, P. M. *Phonics They Use: Words for Reading and Writing* (2nd ed.). New York: Harper–Collins, 1995.

Cunningham, P. M. What kind of phonics instruction will we have? In C. K. Kinzer and D. J. Leu (eds.) *Literacy Research, Theory, and Practice: Views from Many Perspectives.* Forty-First Yearbook of the National Reading Conference, 17–31. Chicago: National Reading Conference, 1992.

Cunningham, P. M. *What kind of phonics instruction will we have?* Presentation to the National Reading Conference, Palm Springs, December, 1991.

Cunningham, P. M., and Allington, R. L. *Classrooms that Work: They Can All Read and Write.* White Plains, NY: Longman, 1998.

Cunningham, P. M., and Cunningham, D. P. *Making More Words.* Carthage, IL: Good Apple, 1997.

Cunningham, P. M., and Cunningham, D. P. *More Making Words.* Carthage, IL: Good Apple, 1997.

Dechant, E. V. *Improving the Teaching of Reading* (3rd ed.) Englewood Cliffs, NJ: Prentice Hall, 1982.

DeGroff, L. Is there a place for computers in the whole language classroom? *The Reading Teacher, 43,* 568–572, 1990.

deManrique, A. M. B., and Gramigna, S. La segmentacion fonologica y silabica en ninos de pre-escolar y primer grado [The phonological segmentation of syllables of children in preschool and first grade]. *Lectura y Vida, 5*, 4–13, 1984.

Diamond, L., and Mandel, S. *Building a Powerful Reading Program: From Research to Practice.* Sacramento, CA: The California State University Institute for Education Reform, 1996.

Downing, J., and Thomson, D. Sex role stereotypes in learning how to read. *Research in the teaching of English, 11*, 149–155, 1977.

Duffelmeyer, F. A., and Banwart, B. H. Word maps for adjectives and verbs. *The Reading Teacher, 46*, 351–353, 1993.

Duffy, G., Roehler, L., and Hermann, B. Modeling mental processes helps poor readers become strategic readers. *The Reading Teacher, 41*, 762–767, 1988.

Durkin, D. Dolores Durkin speaks on instruction. *The Reading Teacher, 43*, 472–476, 1990.

Durkin, D. What classroom observations reveal about reading comprehension instruction. *Reading Research Quarterly, 14*, 481–533, 1979.

Durkin, D. *Children Who Read Early.* New York: Teachers College Press, 1966.

Eeds, M. and Wells, D. Grand conversations: An exploration of meaning construction in literature study groups. *Research in the Teaching of English, 23*, 4–29, 1989.

Ehri, L., and Robbins, C. Beginners need some decoding skills to read words by analogy. *Reading Research Quarterly, 27*, 13–29, 1992.

Eldredge, J. L. *Teaching decoding in holistic classrooms.* Englewood Cliffs, NJ: Merrill/Prentice Hall, 1995.

Elkonin, D. B. U.S.S.R. In J. Downing (ed.), *Comparative Reading.* New York: Macmillan, 1973.

Elley, W. B. Vocabulary acquisition from listening to stories. *Reading Research Quarterly, 24(2)*, 175–187, 1989.

Englert, C. S., and Hiebert, E. H. Children's developing awareness of text structures in expository materials. *Journal of Educational Psychology, 76*, 65–74, 1984.

Farnan, N., Lapp, D., and Flood, J. Changing perspectives in writing instruction. *The Reading Teacher, 35*, 550–556, 1992.

Fielding, L. G., and Pearson, P. D. Reading comprehension: What works. *Educational Leadership, 2*, 62–68, 1994.

Finn, P. J. *Helping Children Learn to Read.* White Plains, NY: Longman, 1990.

Fischer, P. E. *The Sounds and Spelling Patterns of English: Phonics for Teachers and Parents.* Morrill, ME: Oxton House Publishers, 1993.

Fisher, B. *Bobbi Fisher Classroom Close-ups: Organization and Management.* Level K–2 (video). White Plains, NY: Longman, 1998.

Fitzpatrick, J. *Phonemic Awareness: Playing with Sounds to Strengthen Beginning Reading Skills.* Cypress, CA: Creative Teaching Press, 1997.

Flesch, R. *Why Johnny Can't Read.* Cutchogue, NY: Buccaneer Books, 1955, reprinted 1993.

Fletcher, J., Shaywitz, S., Shankweiler, D., Katz, L., Liberman, I., Stuebing, K., Francis, D., Fowler, A., and Shaywitz, B. Cognitive profiles of reading disability: Comparisons of discrepancy and low achievement definitions. *Journal of Educational Psychology, 86(1)*, 6–23, 1994.

Flippo, R. F. Sensationalism, politics, and literacy: What's going on? *Phi Delta Kappan, 41*, 301–304, 1997.

Foorman, B., Francis, D., Beeler, T., Winikates, D., and Fletcher, J. Early interventions for children with reading problems: Study designs and preliminary findings. *Learning Disabilities: A Multi-disciplinary Journal* (in press).

Forseth, C. A., and Avery, C. *And with a Light Touch: Learning about Reading, Writing, and Teaching with First Graders.* Portsmouth, NH: Heinemann, 1993.

Fountas, I. C., and Pinnell, G. S. *Guided Reading: Good First Teaching for All Children.* Portsmouth, NH: Heinemann, 1996.

Freppon, P. A. Children's concepts of the nature and purpose of reading in different instructional settings. *Journal of Reading Behavior, 23(2)*, 139–163, 1991.

Freppon, P. A., and Dahl, K. L. Learning about phonics in a whole language classroom. *Language Arts, 68*, 190–197, 1991.

Fresch, M. J., and Wheaton, A. Sort, search, and discover: Spelling in the child-centered classroom. *The Reading Teacher, 51*, 20–31, 1997.

Fry, E. *Elementary Reading Instruction.* New York: McGraw–Hill, 1977.

Gambrell, L. B., and Almasi, J. F. (eds.). *Lively Discussions! Fostering Engaged Reading.* Newark, DE: International Reading Association, 1996.

Gaskins, I. W., Ehri, L. C., Cress, C., O'Hara, C., and Donnelly, K. Procedures for word learning: Making discoveries about words. *The Reading Teacher, 50(4)*, 312–327, 1997.

Gentry, J. R. Learning to spell developmentally. *The Reading Teacher, 34,* 378–381, 1981.

Gentry, J. R., and Gillet, J. W. *Teaching Kids to Spell.* Portsmouth, NH: Heinemann, 1993.

Gill, C. H., and Scharer, P. L. Why do they get it on Monday and misspell it on Friday?: Teachers inquiring about their students as spellers. *Language Arts, 73,* 1996.

Glazer, S. M. Do I have to give up phonics to be a whole language teacher? *Reading Today, 12(4),* 37–43, 1995.

Goldenberg, C. Instructional conversations: Promoting comprehension through discussion. *The Reading Teacher, 46(4),* 316–326, 1993.

Goodman, K. S. Putting theory and research in the context of history. *Language Arts, 74(8),* 595–599, 1997.

Goodman, K. S. *What's Whole in Whole Language* (2nd ed.). Portsmouth, NH: Heinemann, 1990.

Goodman, K. S. "A linguistic study of cues and miscues in reading." *Elementary English,* 42, 639–643, 1965.

Graves, D. H., and Hansen, J. The author's chair. *Language Arts, 60,* 176–183, 1983.

Graves, M. F. Vocabulary learning and instruction. *Review of Research in Education, 13,* 91–128, 1986.

Graves, M. F., Watts, S., and Graves, B. *Essentials of Classroom Teaching: Elementary Reading.* Boston: Allyn & Bacon, 1994.

Griffith, P. L., and Olson, M. W. Phonemic awareness helps beginning readers break the code. *The Reading Teacher, 15(7),* 516–523, 1992.

Grossen, B. *30 Years of Research: What We Now Know about How Children Learn to Read.* New York: The Center for the Future of Teaching and Learning, 1997.

Guillaume, A. M. Learning with text in the primary grades. *The Reading Teacher, 51,* 476–486, 1998.

Hall, M. A., *Teaching Reading as a Language Experience* (3rd ed.). Columbus, OH: Merrill, 1981.

Hansen, J. *When Writers Read* (2nd ed.). Portsmouth, NH: Heinemann, 1991.

Harlin, R. P. *Effects of whole language on low SES children.* Paper presented at the National Reading Conference, Austin, TX, December, 1990.

Harris, A. J., and Sipay, E. R. *How to Increase Reading Ability* (9th ed.). New York: Longman, 1990.

Heilman, A. W. *Phonics in Proper Perspective* (8th ed.). Columbus, OH: Merrill, 1997.

Heimlich, J. E., and Pittelman, S. D. *Semantic Mapping: Classroom Applications.* Newark, DE: International Reading Association, 1986.

Henderson, E. H. *Teaching Spelling* (3rd ed.). Boston: Houghton Mifflin, 1995.

Hennings, D. G. *Beyond the Read Aloud: Learning to Read through Listening to and Reflecting on Literature.* Bloomington, IN: Phi Delta Kappan Educational Foundation, 1992.

Hills, T. W. Reaching potentials through appropriate assessment. In S. Bredekamp and T. Rosegrant (eds.), *Reaching Potentials: Appropriate Curriculum and Assessment of Young Children* (Vol. 1). Washington, D.C: National Association for the Education of Young Children, 1992.

Hohn, W., and Ehri, L. Do alphabet letters help pre-readers acquire phonemic segmentation skill? *Journal of Educational Psychology, 78,* 752–762, 1984.

Holdaway, D. The structure of natural language as a basis for literacy instruction. In M. L. Sampson (ed.), *The Pursuit of Literacy: Early Reading and Writing.* Dubuque, IA: Kendall/Hunt, 1986.

Holdaway, D. *The Foundation of Literacy.* Sydney; Portsmouth, NH: Ashton Scholastic, distributed by Heinemann, 1979.

Hong, M., and Stafford, P. *Spelling Strategies that Work: Quick Lessons that Help Students Become Effective Writers.* Jefferson City, NJ: Scholastic, 1998.

Honig, B. *How Should We Teach Our Children to Read: The Role of Skills in a Comprehensive Reading Program, a Balanced Approach.* San Francisco: Far West Lab, 1996.

Hoskisson, K., and Tompkins, G. E. *Language Arts: Content and Teaching Strategies* (4th ed.). Columbus, OH: Merrill, 1997.

Hyde, A. A., and Bizar, M. *Thinking in Context: Teaching Cognitive Processes across the Elementary Curriculum.* White Plains, NY: Longman, 1989.

Invernizzi, M., Abouzeid, M., and Gill, J. T. Using students' invented spellings as a guide for spelling instruction that emphasizes word study. *Elementary School Journal, 95,* 155–167, 1994.

IRA Board. IRA Board issues position statement on phonemic awareness. *Reading Today, 26,* June/July, 1998.

Jacobs, J. Why Juan and Jenny can't R–E–A–D. *The San Jose Mercury,* August 17, 1995.

Jacobs, V., Baldwin, E. L., and Chall, J. *The Reading Crisis: Why Poor Children Fall Behind*. Cambridge, MA: Harvard University Press, 1990.

Jalongo, M. R. *Young Children and Picture Books: Literacy from Infancy to Six*. Washington, D.C.: National Association for the Education of Young Children, 1988.

Johnson, D. D. Sex differences in reading across cultures. *Reading Research Quarterly, 9(1)*, 67–86, 1973.

Johnson, D. D., and Baumann, J. F. Word identification. In P. D. Pearson (ed.), *Handbook of Reading Research*, New York: Longman, 1984.

Johnson, D. D., and Pearson, P. D. *Teaching Reading Vocabulary* (2nd ed.). New York: Holt, Rinehart, and Winston, 1984.

Juel, C. *Learning to Read and Write in One Elementary School*. New York: Springer–Verlag, 1994.

Juel, C. Beginning reading. In R. Barr, M. Kamil, P. Mosenthal, and P. D. Pearson (eds.), *Handbook of Reading Research, 2*, 759–788, 1991.

Juel, C. Learning to read and write: A longitudinal study of 54 children from first through fourth grades. *Journal of Educational Psychology, 80,* 437–447, 1988.

Lee, D. M., and Allen, R. V. *Learning to Read through Language Experience.* (2nd ed.). New York: Meredith, 1963.

Levine, A. The great debate revisited. *Atlantic Monthly 27,* 38–44, 1994.

Liberman, I., Shankweiler, D., Fischer, F. and Carter, B. Explicit syllable and phoneme segmentation in the young child. *Journal of Experimental Child Psychology, 18*, 201–212, 1974.

Lundberg, I., Olofsson, A., and Wall, S. Reading and spelling skills in the first school years predicted from phonetic awareness skills in kindergarten. *Scandinavian Journal of Psychology, 21*, 159–173, 1980.

Manning, M., and Manning, G. Reading: Word or meaning centered. *Teaching PreK-8, 25(2)*, 98–99, 1993.

Manning, M., and Manning, G. They say, you say. *Teaching K-8 , 37(6)*, 50–54, 1993.

Mathews, M. M. *Teaching to Read: Historically Considered*. Chicago: University of Chicago Press, 1966.

McAfee, O., and Leong, D. *Assessing and Guiding Young Children's Development and Learning*. Boston: Allyn & Bacon, 1994.

McCracken, M. J., and McCracken, R. A. *Spelling through Phonics*. Manitoba, Canada: Peguis, 1996.

McCracken, R. A., and McCracken, M. J. *Stories, Songs, and Poetry to Teach Reading and Writing: Literacy through Language*. Chicago: American Library Association, 1986.

McIntyre, E., and Freppon, P. A. A comparison of children's development of alphabetic knowledge in a skill-based and whole language classroom. *Research in the Teaching of English, 28*, 391–417, 1994.

McKeown, M. G. The acquisition of word meaning from context by children of high and low ability. *Reading Research Quarterly, 20*, 482–496, 1985.

Meloth, M. Enhancing literacy through cooperative learning. In E. Hiebert (ed.), *Literacy for a Diverse Society: Perspectives, Practices, and Policies*. New York: Teachers College Press, 1991.

Mills, H., O'Keefe, T., and Stephens, D. *Looking Closely: Exploring the Role of Phonics in One Whole Language Classroom*. Urbana, IL: National Council of Teachers of English, 1991.

Miramontes, O. B., Nadeau, A., and Commins, N. L. *Restructuring Schools for Linguistic Diversity: Linking Decision Making to Effective Programs*. New York: Teachers College Press, 1997.

Moats, L. C. *Spelling: Development, Disabilities, and Instruction*. Timonium, MD: York Press, 1995.

Moats, L. C. The missing foundation in teacher education. *American Educator, 19,* 43–51, 1995.

Moore, M. A. Electronic dialoguing: An avenue to literacy. *The Reading Teacher, 45,* 280–286, 1991.

Morphett, M. V., and Washburn, C. When should children begin to read? *Elementary School Journal, 31,* 496–503, 1931.

Morrow, L. M. Using story retelling to develop comprehension. In K. D. Muth (ed.), *Children's Comprehension of Text: Research into Practice*. Newark, DE: International Reading Association, 1989.

Morrow, L. M., and Rand, M. K. Promoting literacy during play by designing early childhood classroom environments. *The Reading Teacher, 44,* 396–402, 1991.

Nagy, W. E. *Teaching Vocabulary to Improve Reading Comprehension*. Clearinghouse on Reading and Communication Skills and the National Council of Teachers of English and the International Reading Association. Urbana, IL: ERIC, 1988.

Nagy, W. E., and Herman, P. Incidental vs. instructional approaches to increasing reading vocabulary. *Educational Perspectives, 23,* 16–21, 1985.

Nagy, W. E., Herman, P., and Anderson, R. Learning words from context. *Reading Research Quarterly, 19,* 304–330, 1985.

Neuman, S. B., and Roskos, K. *Language and Literacy Learning in the Early Years: An Integrated Approach.* New York: Harcourt Brace, 1993.

Noyce, R. M., and Christie, J. F. *Integrating Reading and Writing Instruction in Grades K–8.* Boston: Allyn & Bacon, 1989.

Ogle, D. K-W-L: A teaching model that develops active reading of expository text. *The Reading Teacher, 39,* 564–570, 1986.

Ollila, L. O., and Mayfield, M. (eds.), *Emerging Literacy.* Needham Heights, MA: Allyn & Bacon, 1992.

Palinscar, A. S., Brown, A. L., and Martin, S. M. Peer interaction in reading comprehension instruction. *Educational Psychologist, 22,* 231–253, 1987.

Parker, D. Politics and pedagogy: The bookends of California's literacy crisis. *Clips: A Journal of the California Literature Project, 2(3),* 4–9, 1995.

Pearson, P. D. Teaching and learning reading: A research perspective. *Language Arts, 70,* 502–511, 1993.

Pearson, P. D. Changing the face of reading comprehension instruction. *The Reading Teacher, 38(8),* 724–738, 1985.

Pearson, P. D., and Camperell, K. Comprehension of text structures. In R. B. Ruddell, M. R. Ruddell, and H. Singer (eds.), *Theoretical Models and Processes of Reading.* Newark, DE: International Reading Association, 1994.

Peetoom, A. *Shared Reading: Safe Risks with Whole Books.* Richmond Hill, Ontario, Canada: TAB Publications, 1986.

Peha, S. *All's Well That Spells Well: A Few Thoughts on the Teaching of Spelling.* Unpublished manuscript, 1996.

Peha, S. How the writing happens: An introduction to writing process. Unpublished manuscript, 1996.

Peha, S. Where the writing happens: Welcome to writer's workshop. Unpublished manuscript, 1996.

Peregoy, S. F., and Boyle, O. F. *Reading, Writing, and Teaching in ESL: A Resource Book for Teachers K–12.* White Plains, NY: Longman, 1996.

Pflaum, S. W. *The Development of Language and Literacy in Young Children.* Columbus, OH: Merrill, 1986.

Pflaum, S. W., Walberg, H. J., Karegianes, M. L., and Rusher, S. P. Reading instruction: A qualitative analysis. *Educational Researcher, 9,* 12–18, 1980.

Porter, C., and Cleland, J. *The Portfolio as a Learning Strategy.* Portsmouth, NH: Heinemann, 1995.

Ransom, K. A. IRA leaders comment on position statement. *Reading Today, 14(5),* April/May, 1997.

Raphael, T. E. Question-answering strategies for children. *The Reading Teacher, 36,* 186–190, 1984.

Read, C. *Children's Creative Spelling.* London: Routledge and Kegan Paul, 1986.

Reutzel, D. R. *Fingerpoint Reading and Beyond: Learning about Print Strategies (LAPS).* Reading Horizons, 1995.

Reutzel, D. R. Breaking the letter a week tradition: Conveying the alphabetic principle to young children. *Childhood Education, 69 (1),* 20–23, 1992.

Reutzel, D. R. and Cooter, R. B. *Teaching Children to Read: From Basals to Books* (2nd ed.). Englewood Cliffs, NJ: Prentice-Hall, 1996.

Rhodes, L. K., and Nathensen–Mejia, S. Anecdotal records: A powerful tool for ongoing literacy assessment. *The Reading Teacher, 45,* 502–511, 1992.

Rhodes, L. K., and Shanklin, N. *Windows into Literacy: Assessing Learners K-8.* Portsmouth, NH: Heinemann, 1993.

Richgels, D. J. Invented spelling ability and printed word learning in kindergarten. *Reading Research Quarterly, 30,* 96–109, 1995.

Rinsky, L. A. *Teaching Word Recognition Skills.* Scottsdale, AZ: Gorsuch Scarisbrick, 1993.

Roberts, T. Skills of analysis and synthesis in the early stages of reading. *British Journal of Educational Psychology, 45,* 3–9, 1975.

Rosenshine, B., Meister, C., and Chapman, S. Reciprocal teaching: A review of the research. *Review of Educational Research, 64,* 479–530, 1996.

Routman, R. *Invitations: Changing as Teachers and Learners K–12* (2nd ed.). Portsmouth, NH: Heinemann, 1995.

Routman, R., and Butler, A. *Why Talk about Phonics?* Urbana, IL: National Council of Teachers of English, 1995.

Rupley, W. H., and Blair, T. R. *Teaching Reading: Diagnosis, Direct Instruction, and Practice.* Columbus, OH: Merrill, 1988.

Salinger, T. *Models of Literacy Instruction.* New York: Macmillan, 1993.

Salvia, J., and Yesseldyke, J. E. *Assessment* (7th ed.). Boston: Houghton Mifflin, 1998.

Samuels, J. S., and Farstrup, A. E.(eds.). *What Research Has to Say about Reading Instruction.* Newark, DE: International Reading Association, 1992.

Schlagel, R., and Schlagel, J. The integrated character of spelling: Teaching strategies for multiple purposes. *Language Arts, 69*, 418–424, 1992.

Schwartz, R., and Raphael, T. Concept of definition: A key to improving students' vocabulary. *The Reading Teacher, 39*, 198–205.

Shaywitz, S., Escobar, M., Shaywitz, B., Fletcher, J., and Makuch, R. Evidence that dyslexia may represent the lower tail of a normal distribution of reading disability. *New England Journal of Medicine, 326(3)*, 145–150, 1992.

Shefelbine, J. Finding the right balance. *Clip: A Journal of the California Literature Project, 3(1)*, 23–24, 1997.

Shefelbine, J. Learning and using phonics in beginning reading. *Scholastic Literacy Paper, 10*, New York: Scholastic, 1995.

Simpson, J. *The Three Billy Goats Gruff.* illustrated by C. Russell. Auburn, ME: Ladybird Books, 1993.

Slepian, J. and Seidler, A. *The Hungry Thing.* New York: Scholastic, 1985.

Smith, F. Learning to read: The never-ending debate. *Phi Delta Kappan, 73(4)*, 432–441, 1992.

Smith, F. On the psycholinguistic method of teaching reading. *Elementary School Journal, 71(4)*, 10–14, 1971.

Smith, N. B. *American Reading Instruction.* Newark, DE: International Reading Association, 1986.

Snider, V. E. A primer on phonemic awareness: What it is, why it's important, and how to teach it. *School Psychology Review, 24(3)*, 443–455, 1995.

Spache, G., and Spache, E. *Reading in the Elementary School* (4th ed.). Boston: Allyn & Bacon, 1977.

Spiegel, D. L. Blending whole language and systematic direct instruction. *The Reading Teacher, 46,* 38–48, 1992.

Spiegel, D. L. Reinforcement in phonics materials. *The Reading Teacher, 43(4)*, 328–330, 1995.

Spiegel, D. L., and Fitzgerald, J. Improving reading comprehension through instruction about story parts. *The Reading Teacher, 39,* 676–682, 1986.

Spiro, R. J., Bruce, B. C., and Brewer, W. F. (eds.). *Theoretical Issues in Reading Comprehension.* Hillsdale, NJ: Erlbaum, 1980.

Stahl, S. A. and Fairbanks, M. M. The effects of vocabulary instruction: A model-based meta-analysis. *Review of Educational Research, 56,* 72–110. 1986.

Stahl, S. A. Differential word knowledge and reading comprehension. *Journal of Reading Behavior, 15,* 33–50, 1983.

Stahl, S. A. Saying the "P" word: Nine guidelines for exemplary phonics instruction. *The Reading Teacher, 45(8)*, 618–624, 1992.

Stahl, S. A., and Kapinus, B. Possible sentences: Predicting word meanings to teach content area vocabulary. *The Reading Teacher, 45*, 36–43, 1991.

Stanovich, K. Matthew effect in reading: Some consequences of individual differences in the acquisition of literacy. *Reading Research Quarterly, 21(4)*, 360–407, 1986.

Stanovich, K. E. Speculation on the causes and consequences of individual differences in early reading acquisition. In P. Gough, L Ehri, and R. Treiman (eds.), *Reading Acquisition.* Hillsdale, NJ: Erlbaum, 1992.

Stanovich, K. E. and Siegel, L. S. The phenotypic performance profile of reading-disabled children: A regression-based test of the phonological-core variable-difference model. *Journal of Educational Psychology, 86(1)*, 24–53, 1994.

Stanovich, K., and Stanovich, P. How research might inform the debate about early reading acquisition. *Journal of Research in Reading, 18(2)*, 87–105, 1995.

Stauffer, R. G. *The Language Experience Approach to the Teaching of Reading* (2nd ed.). New York: Harper & Row, 1980.

Stauffer, R. G. *Teaching Reading as a Thinking Process.* New York: Harper & Row, 1969.

Steptoe, J. *Mufaro's Beautiful Daughters: An African Tale.* New York: Lothrop, Lee & Shepard, 1987.

Sulzby, E. Assessment of writing and children's language while writing. In W. H. Teale and E. Sulzby (eds.), *Emergent Literacy: Writing and Reading.* Norwood, NJ: Ablex Publishing, 1990.

Sweeney, J., and Peterson, S. *350 Fabulous Writing Prompts: Thought-Provoking Springboards for Creative, Expository, and Journal Writing.* New York: Scholastic, 1996.

Tangel, D., and Blachman, B. A. Effect of phoneme awareness instruction on kindergarten children's invented spelling. *Journal of Reading Behavior, 24*, 233–261, 1992.

Tangel, D., and Blachman, B. A. Effect of phoneme awareness on the invented spelling of first-grade children: A one year follow-up. *Journal of Reading Behavior, 27*, 153–185, 1995.

Teale, W. H. and Sulzby, E. *Emergent Literacy.* Norwood, NJ: Ablex, 1986.

Tierney, R. J., Readence, J. E., and Dishner, E. K. *Reading Strategies and Practices: A Compendium* (3rd ed.). Boston: Allyn & Bacon, 1990.

Tompkins, G. E. *Best Teaching Practices* (video). Boston: Allyn & Bacon, 1997.

Tompkins, G. E. *Literacy for the 21st Century: A Balanced Approach.* Upper Saddle River, NJ: Merrill/Prentice Hall, 1997.

Torrey, J. W. Reading that comes naturally. In G. Waller and G. E. MacKinnon (eds.), *Reading Research: Advance in Theory and Practice, 1,* 115–144. New York: Academic Press, 1979.

Trachtenburg, P. Using children's literature to enhance phonics instruction. *The Reading Teacher, 43,* 648–654, 1990.

Trelease, J. *The New Read Aloud Handbook* (4th ed.). New York: Penguin, 1995.

Valencia, S. A portfolio approach to classroom reading assessment: The whys, whats, and hows. *The Reading Teacher, 43,* 338–340, 1990.

Vellutino, F. R. and Scanlon, D. Phonological coding, phonological awareness, and reading ability: Evidence from a longitudinal and experimental study. *Merrill–Palmer Quarterly, 33*, 321–363, 1987.

Vellutino, F. R. Introduction to three studies on reading acquisition: Convergent findings on theoretical foundations of code-oriented versus whole-language approaches to reading instruction. *Journal of Educational Psychology , 83(4)*, 437–443, 1991.

Vogt, M. E,. *Whatever happened to comprehension? A review of the literature.* Paper presented at the Teacher Education Symposium, Long Beach, CA, January, 1997.

Wagner, R. K. and Torgesen, J. K. The nature of phonological processing and its causal role in the acquisition of reading skills. *Psychological Bulletin, 101*, 192–212, 1987.

Wagner, R. K., Torgesen, J. K., and Rashotte, C. A. Development of reading-related phonological processing abilities: New evidence of bidirectional causality from a latent variable longitudinal study. *Developmental Psychology, 30*, 73–87, 1994.

Walmsley, S. A., and Adams, E. L. Realities of whole language. *Language Arts, 70(4)*, 272–280, 1993.

Watson, D. Reader-selected miscues. In D. Watson (ed.), *Ideas and Insights: Language Arts in the Elementary School.* Urbana, IL: National Council of Teachers of English, 1987.

Weaver, C. *A Balanced Approach to Reading: Becoming Successfully and Joyfully Literate* (videotape & facilitator's guide). Bothell, WA: The Wright Group, 1998.

Wilde, S. *You Ken Red This! Spelling and Punctuation for Whole Language Classrooms.* Portsmouth, NH: Heinemann, 1992.

Williams, J. P. The case for explicit phonics instruction. In J. Osborn, P. Wilson, and R. C. Anderson (eds.), *Reading Education: Foundations for a Literate America*, Lexington, MA: Lexington Books, 206–13, 1985.

Wink, J. Jonathan: Linking critical pedagogy and literacy. *Clip: A Journal of the California Literature Project, 2(4)*, 27–30, 1996

Wiseman, D. L. *Learning to Read with Literature.* Boston: Allyn & Bacon, 1992.

Yopp, H. K. Read-aloud books for developing phonemic awareness: An annotated bibliography. *The Reading Teacher, 48(6)*, 538–543, 1995.

Yopp, H. K. Developing phonemic awareness in young children. *The Reading Teacher, 45*, 696–703, 1992.

Young, E. *Lon Po Po: A Red Riding Hood Story from China.* New York: Putnam, 1990.

Zutell, J. The directed spelling teaching activity (DSTA): Providing an effective balance in word study instruction. *The Reading Teacher, 50*, 98–108, 1996.

GLOSSARY

achievement test   A formalized test that measures the extent to which a person has assimilated a body of information or possesses a certain skill after instruction has taken place.

alliteration   A pattern in which all words begin with the same sound.

alphabetic principle   The principle that there is a one-to-one correspondence between phonemes (or sounds) and graphemes (or letters), such that each letter consistently represents one sound.

analog   A strategy of comparing patterns in words to ones already known.

anecdotal notes   Written observations taken by the teacher—usually on a clipboard—of literacy-related behaviors in an authentic literacy context.

antonyms   A pair of words that have opposite meanings.

assessment   Procedure of evaluating by observing children's growth in the normal course of classroom activities, projects, and units of study.

automaticity   The stage of reading at which learners are considered independent, fluent readers.

basal reader series   A coordinated, graded set of textbooks, teacher's guides, and supplementary materials from which to teach reading.

big books   An enlarged version of a book used by the teacher for mediated reading instruction so that students can track the print and attention can be focused on particular phonemic elements.

camouflage   A vocabulary-enriching activity in which learners must try to disguise a chosen word by creating an oral story using several words above their normal speaking vocabulary. The other students must try to guess the hidden word.

closed sort   Word sorts that classify words into predetermined categories.

cloze procedure   An instructional technique in which certain words are deleted from a passage by the teacher, with blanks left in their places for students to fill in by using the context of the sentence or paragraph.

comprehension   The interpretation of print on a page into a meaningful message that is dependent upon the reader's decoding abilities, prior knowledge, cultural and social background, and monitoring strategies.

concepts about print   Concepts about the way print works, including directionality, spacing, identification of words and letters, connection between written and spoken language, and understanding the function of punctuation.

constructivist model of learning   A learning theory suggesting that children are active learners who organize and relate new information to their prior knowledge.

context-relationship procedure   A strategy utilized to help students integrate new words into their meaning vocabularies.

contextual clues   The syntactic and semantic information in the surrounding words, phrases, sentences, and paragraphs in a text.

controlled vocabulary   A system of introducing only a certain number of grade-level appropriate words before the reading of each basal story, with periodic review.

conventional spelling stage The final stage of spelling development, in which the child has mastered the basic principles of English orthography and most words are spelled correctly.

correct spelling stage *See* conventional spelling stage.

criterion-referenced test A test for which scores are interpreted by comparing the test taker's score to a specified performance level rather than to the scores of other students.

critical reading Reading to evaluate the material.

cueing systems The four language systems that readers rely upon for cues as they seek meaning from text: graphophonic (based on letter–sound relationships); syntactic (based on grammar or structure); semantic (based on meaning); and pragmatic.

curriculum-based assessment Assessment that ties evaluation directly to the literacy curriculum to identify instructional needs.

decodable text Beginner-oriented books that contain the same letters or word patterns currently being studied, or those previously taught.

decoding The translation of written words into verbal speech for oral reading or mental speech for silent reading.

developmental spelling stages Stage-like progressions that children advance through when learning to spell, characterized by increasingly complex understandings about the organizational patterns of words, including precommunicative, prephonetic, phonetic, transitional, and conventional spelling stages.

diagnostic tests Age-related, norm-referenced assessment of specific skills and behaviors children have acquired compared to other children of the same chronological age.

dialogue journals Journals that provide a means of two-way written communication between learners and their teachers, in which learners share their thoughts with teachers, including personal comments and descriptions of life experiences, and the teachers, in turn, write reactions to the learners' messages.

direct instruction Teacher control of the learning environment through structured, systematic lessons, goal setting, choice of activities, and feedback.

directionality of print The concept that, in English, writing goes from left to right and from top to bottom. Directionality of print varies among languages.

dramatic play Simulating real experiences with no set plot or goal.

DRTA (the Directed Reading Thinking Activity) A time-honored format for guiding students as they read selections, usually from basal reading programs.

dyad reading A paired reading activity in which students alternately read aloud or listen and summarize what their partner has read.

echo reading A strategy where a lead reader reads aloud a section of text and others follow immediately after it, or echo the leader's reading.

ELL (English language learner) A person who is in the process of acquiring English as a second language.

emergent literacy A developing awareness of the interrelatedness of oral and written language that occurs from birth to beginning reading.

encoding Transferring oral language into written language.

environmental print Print that is encountered outside of books and that is a pervasive part of everyday living.

ESL (English as a second language) A program for teaching English language skills to those whose native language is not English.

experience-text relationship A lesson format for narrative text that helps students to develop prior knowledge and relate it to what they read.

experiential background The fund of total experiences that aid a reader in finding meaning in printed symbols.

expository frame A basic structure for expository text designed to help students organize their thoughts for writing or responding to text.

expository text A text written in a precise, factual writing style.

expressive writing Personal writing that expresses emotion such as diaries or letters.

fluency The reading level at which words are identified automatically.

formal assessment Commercially designed and produced tests given on single occasions.

formal (standardized) test A testing instrument for which readability and validity can be verified; the results of these tests are based on right or wrong answers and individual scores are interpreted against national norms.

frustration level A level of reading difficulty at which a reader is unable to cope; when reading is on the frustration level, the reader recognizes approximately 90% or fewer of the words encountered and comprehends 50% or fewer.

grade-level equivalent score A conversion of a score on a test into one that tells how a child compares with others in the same grade; e.g., a grade equivalent score of 4.5 on a reading test would suggest that the child is reading as well as children in the normative sample who are in the fifth month of fourth grade.

graded word list A list of words at successive reading levels.

grand conversation A response to text strategy whereby students share personal connections to the text, make predictions, ask questions, and show individual appreciation.

grapheme A written symbol that represents a phoneme.

graphophonic cues Cues based upon sound or visual similarities.

group profile A listing of scores on a specific reading or writing skill that allows the teacher to view the strengths and weaknesses of the whole class for purposes of reteaching and reporting to parents and others.

guided reading procedure A teacher-mediated instructional method designed to help readers improve skills, comprehension, recall, and appreciation of text.

high-frequency words Words common in reading material that are often difficult to learn because they cannot be easily decoded.

holistic approach A whole-to-parts approach where meaning is considered to be more critical than the underlying skills of reading.

independent level A level of reading difficulty low enough that the reader can progress without noticeable obstructions; the reader can recognize approximately 98% of the words and comprehend at least 90% of what is read.

individual dictation A strategy in which the student dictates a message while the teacher writes it down, sounding out the words in front of the child.

informal assessment Nonstandardized measurement in which a teacher seeks to learn about what a student is able to do in a certain area of literacy, interprets the results, and uses those results to plan instruction.

informal reading inventory An informal assessment instrument designed to help the teacher determine a child's independent, instructional, frustration, and reading capacity levels.

instructional level A level of difficulty low enough that the reader can be instructed by the teacher during the process; in order for the material to be at this level, the reader should be able to read approximately 95% of the words in a passage and comprehend at least 75%.

interactive electronic books Computerized programs that allow learners to read books on a computer while responding to questions about the text exploring various aspects or sidelines of the text, and often even adapting the text.

interactive writing A mediated writing experience used to assist emergent readers in learning to read and write. With help from the teacher, children dictate sentences and the teacher verbally stretches each word so children can distinguish sounds and letters. Children use chart paper to write the letter while repeating the sound.

interest and attitude inventory An informal assessment device that allows teachers to discover how their students feel about reading and about themselves as readers.

interest inventory A list of questions used to assess a person's preferences in a particular area.

intervention The corrective instructional program the teacher devises as a result of assessment.

invented spellings Unconventional spellings, or approximations, resulting from an emergent writer's initial attempts to associate sounds with letters; also called temporary spellings.

jigsaw grouping A collaborative learning technique in which individuals become experts on one portion of text and share their expertise with a small group, called their home group. Each member of the home group becomes an expert on a different part of the text and shares their new knowledge with the group so that each group member will get a sense of the whole text.

journals   Journals are kept by children in the same way artists keep sketch books. Children write in them regularly to record life events of their choosing or, for very beginning writers, to complete sentence stems offered by the teacher. At the beginning reader stage, journals are often accompanied by illustrations and are rarely corrected.

language arts   The global term for reading, writing, listening, and speaking.

Language Experience Approach   An approach in which reading and the other language arts are interrelated and the experiences of children are used as the basis for the material that is written and then used for reading.

learning center   A location within the classroom in which children are presented with instructional materials, specific directions, clearly defined objectives, and/or provisions for self-evaluation.

learning logs   Journals students use to summarize a day's lesson and to react to what they have learned.

letter name stage   *See* phonetic stage.

literacy   The competence to carry out the complex reading and writing tasks in a functionally useful way necessary to the world of work and life outside the school.

literal comprehension   Understanding those ideas that are directly stated.

literary sociogram   A diagram used to help students understand the complexity of the relationships among characters in a story or chapter.

long vowels   Vowels that represent the sounds in words that are heard in letter names, such as the /a/ in ape, /e/ in feet, /i/ in ice, /o/ in road, and /u/ in mule.

look-say method   An early meaning-based method of reading instruction requiring children to use the context alone to figure out words they did not know.

masking device   A sliding frame used to help children focus on a particular word or part of a word.

Matthew effect   The phenomenon that suggests that skilled decoders get better at reading while poor decoders tend to fall further behind.

meaning vocabulary   That body of words whose meanings one understands and can use.

mediated reading   Large or small group instruction in which the teacher guides the children in selected reading skills.

metacognition   A person's awareness of his or her own thinking and the conscious efforts to monitor this awareness.

metacognitive strategies   Techniques for monitoring one's own thinking.

minilesson   A short lesson on reading procedures, concepts, strategies, or skills taught based upon teacher observation of the need for it.

miscue   An unexpected reading response (deviation from text).

miscue analysis   A procedure that lets the teacher gather important instructional information by providing a framework for observing students' oral reading and their ability to construct meaning.

morning message   Children observe as the teacher writes a meaningful morning message addressed to all the children on the board about a specific event that is planned for the day, or an interesting question. It is used as an instructional tool for discussing skills children are learning, such as conventions of writing or phonic elements.

morpheme   The smallest meaning-bearing linguistic unit in a language.

motivation   The incentive to do something; a stimulus to act.

multicultural   Classrooms are multicultural settings when children from a variety of cultures learn together daily making it necessary to know how children's perceptions, knowledge, and demeanor are shaped by their experiences at home and in their own community.

narrative text   Text that contains the structural features of a story.

nonstage theory   A theory that suggests that unskilled and skilled readers use the same strategies to figure out unknown words.

norm-referenced test   A test designed to yield results interpretable in terms of the average results of a sample population.

normative group   A large number of students chosen to represent the kinds of students for whom an assessment device is designed.

norms Statistics or data that summarize the test performance of specified groups, such as test takers of various ages or grades.

one-to-one correspondence An awareness that letters or combinations of letters correspond directly with certain sounds in the English language.

open sort A type of picture or word sort in which the categories for sorting are left up to the child.

onset All the sounds of a word that come before the first vowel.

oral synthesis Hearing sounds in sequence and blending them together to make a word; sounding out.

orthographic knowledge Understanding of the writing system of a language, specifically the correct sequence of letters, characters, or symbols.

parent packets Folders containing early reading and writing reinforcement activities that can be completed at home with a child's parents or caretakers.

percentile Raw scores are converted to percentiles so that comparisons can be made. Percentiles range from 1 to 99 with 1 being the lowest and 99 being the highest.

phoneme The smallest unit of sound in a language.

phonemic awareness The ability to attend to sounds in the context of a word independent of the meaning of the word.

phoneme blending Blending individual sounds to form a word.

phoneme counting Counting the number of sounds in a word.

phoneme deletion Omitting the beginning, middle, or ending sounds of a word.

phoneme isolation Identifying the beginning, middle, and/or ending sounds in a word.

phonemic segmentation The process of separating sounds within a word.

phoneme substitution Substituting beginning, middle, or ending sounds of a word.

phonetic stage The third stage of spelling development, in which consonants and vowels are used for each spoken syllable.

phonics The association of speech sounds with printed symbols.

phonics generalizations Rules that help to clarify English spelling patterns.

phonology The study of the sound system of language.

picture sort A precursor to the word sort activity in which children categorize pictures according to their common sounds.

picture walk An instructional strategy in which the teacher guides the children through the text by looking at and discussing the pictures before reading the story.

play centers Areas of the classroom containing inviting props and set aside for spontaneous dramatic play.

polysemantic A word having multiple meanings, such as the word *fast*.

portfolio Portfolios serve as places to collect evidence of a child's literacy development. They may include artifacts collected by the child, the teacher, or both.

predictable books Books that use repetition, rhythmic language patterns, and familiar patterns; sometimes called pattern books.

precommunicative stage The initial stage of spelling development, in which the child scribbles random letters with little concept of which letter makes which sound.

predictive questions Questions designed to activate students' prior knowledge before they read in order to focus their attention on key ideas as they read.

prefixes Meaningful chunks attached to the beginnings of words, such as re + play = replay.

preliterate stage *See* prephonetic stage.

prephonetic stage The second stage of spelling development, in which the child becomes aware of the alphabetic principle.

primary language The first language a child learns to speak, or their home language.

process-oriented assessment Assessment that relies on the teacher's observation of the child's actual reading and writing abilities.

QARs (question–answer relationships) A strategy in which students become aware of their own comprehension processes, particularly the importance of the knowledge they bring to text and their role as active seekers rather than passive receivers of information through reading.

r-controlled vowels   Vowels that occur in a syllable preceding an *r* and the vowel sound is modified, such as the /r/ in car.

readability   An objective measure of the difficulty of written material.

reader's theatre   A form of drama in which participants read aloud from scripts adapted from stories and convey ideas and emotions through vocal expression.

reading   The construction of meaning from coded messages through symbol decoding, vocabulary awareness, comprehension, and reflection.

reading buddies   A social reading activity in which students read and reread books with a partner who may help them with unfamiliar words and encourage them to continue reading.

reading capacity level   The highest level of material children understand when the passage is read to them.

reading interest inventory   An informal assessment device used to determine a child's interests so that the teacher can match appropriate reading material to them.

reading process   The steps a reader goes through to construct meaning from what the author has written.

reading product   Some form of communication that results from the reading process.

reading rate   Speed of reading, often reported in words per minute.

reading readiness   The level of preparedness for formal reading instruction.

reader's theatre   An oral interpretation strategy in which children are helped to see that reading is an active process of constructing meaning. Unlike a play, there is no costuming, movement, stage sets, or memorizing of lines.

reciprocal teaching   A technique to develop comprehension and metacognition in which the teacher and students take turns predicting, generating questions, summarizing, and clarifying ideas in a passage.

recreational reading   An independent reading activity for motivating voluntary reading interest and appreciation rather than instruction.

repeated readings   Students reread a selection for a different purpose and think again about what they have read. Rereading helps improve a young reader's speed, accuracy, expression, comprehension, and linguistic growth.

retelling   Teachers analyze children's retellings of text to gauge their level of comprehension and use of language. In examining the retellings, teachers look for the number of events recalled, how the child interprets the message, and how children use details or make inferences to substantiate ideas.

rime   The first vowel in a word and all the sounds that follow.

root word   A word to which prefixes and/or suffixes are added to create new, but related, words.

rubber-banding   The process in which the teacher stretches out all the sounds in a word so learners can pay attention to each phoneme or sound.

running records   A procedure for analyzing students' oral reading and noting their strengths and weaknesses when using various reading strategies.

scaffolding   A support mechanism by which children are able to accomplish more difficult tasks than they could without assistance.

schema   A pre-existing knowledge structure developed about a thing, place, or an idea; a framework of expectations based upon previous knowledge.

semantic cues   Meaning clues.

semantic gradient   An vocabulary-enriching activity that allows children to discuss the many shades of meaning of words, beginning with a word and ending with its opposite.

semantic map   A graphic representation of the relationship among words and phrases in written material.

sentence stems   The first two or three words of a sentence followed by blank spaces offered to students to support initial attempts at writing.

sentence strips   Rectangular pieces of tag board or construction paper upon which are written individual sentences from a story students have read.

shared reading   A mediated technique whereby the teacher reads aloud while students follow along using individual copies of the book, a class chart, or a big book.

short vowels   Vowels that represent the sound of /a/ in apple, /e/ in end, the /i/ in igloo, the /o/ in octopus, and the /u/ in bus.

sight vocabulary   Words that are recognized by the reader immediately, without having to resort to decoding.

signal words   Those transitional words that signify sequence, such as *first, next,* and *finally.*

silent period The initial stage in second language acquisition when a learner is increasing receptive vocabulary but not able to express ideas orally.

skills-based approach A parts-to-whole approach to reading instruction in which all the reading skills are taught sequentially.

skills-based assessment Assessment focusing on the use of tests to measure reading and spelling skills as well as the subskills of these areas.

sound boxes Place holders for sounds used by children during phonemic awareness exercises.

spelling conscience A desire to spell correctly as evidenced by a student's proofreading material or using resources to find out how to spell unknown words.

spelling consciousness The ability to recognize that a word that has been written down is spelled correctly or incorrectly.

SSR See sustained silent reading.

stage theory A theory that suggests that children go through three stages in acquiring literacy: the "selective cue stage," the "spelling-sound stage," and the "automatic stage."

stanine A way of reporting test scores that distributes them into nine groups, with 1 being the lowest and 9 the highest.

story frame A basic outline for a story designed to help students organize their ideas about what they have read.

story grammar A set of rules that define story structures.

structured listening activity An activity in which students listen to a story accompanied by visuals that support the action in the story, and then retell the story with the help of the visuals.

suffixes Meaningful chunks attached to the ends of words, such as play + ing = playing.

sustained silent reading (SSR) A program for setting aside a certain period of time daily for self-selected, silent reading. During SSR time, each child chooses material to read for a designated period of time, typically 10–15 minutes for beginning readers. Everyone, including the teacher, reads without interruption.

syllable juncture stage *See* conventional spelling stage.

syllables The units of pronunciation that include a vowel sound.

synonyms Groups of words that have the same, or very similar, meanings.

syntactic cues Clues derived from the word order, or grammar, of the sentence.

talk-to-yourself chart A chart to help children self-assess their ability to read and spell new words.

teachable moments The spontaneous, indirect teaching that occurs when teachers respond to students' questions or when students otherwise demonstrate the need to know something.

think aloud A strategy in which the teacher models aloud for students the thinking processes used when reading or writing.

think, pair, and share A cooperative learning strategy in which children listen to a question, think of a response, pair to discuss with a partner, and then share their collaboration with the whole class.

tracking Indicating understanding of the one-to-one correspondence of spoken and written words by finger-pointing.

trade books Any books that can be purchased by the general public in book stores, through mail order houses, or at book fairs.

transactional model A perspective of early reading instruction from cognitive psychology and psycholinguistic learning that views children as bringing a rich prior knowledge background to literacy learning.

transitional stage The fourth stage of spelling development, in which the child is able to approximate the spelling of various English words.

transmission model A perspective of early reading instruction from behavioral psychology that views children as empty vessels into which knowledge is poured.

validity The degree to which a test measures what it purports to measure

Venn diagram A set of overlapping circles used to graphically illustrate the similarities and differences of two concepts, ideas, stories, or other items.

vicarious experiences Indirect experiences, not involving the senses.

vocabulary   The knowledge and use of words.

within word stage   *See* transitional stage.

word attack   The process used to decode words.

word bank   A collection of sight words that have been mastered, usually recorded on index cards.

word building   An activity in which children arrange letter cards to spell words, practicing phonics and spelling concepts.

word hunt   An activity in which children search for words that correspond to a certain pattern that has been identified by them or by the teacher.

word map   A visual illustration of a word showing its meaning by offering examples, explaining what it is, and what it is not.

word play   A child's manipulation of sounds and words for purposes of language exploration, practice, and pleasure.

word sort   An activity in which students sort a collection of words into two or more categories.

word wall   A chart or bulletin board on which are placed, alphabetically, important vocabulary to be referred to during word study activities.

wordless books   Picture story books without words.

writing process   The process by which a piece of writing is completed for publication, involving prewriting, drafting, revising, editing, and publishing.

writing prompts   Motivational ideas or structures that are offered by the teacher to inspire students to write.

AUTHOR INDEX

Subject Index